PARANORMAL TEMP AGENCY

BOOKS 1-3 SPECIAL COLLECTION

MOLLY FITZ

Editor: Jennifer Lopez, Mistress with the Red Pen
Cover: TM Franklin

PO Box 873543
Wasilla, AK 99687

WITCH FOR HIRE

My name is Tawny Bigford. I'm 35, single, and I love hot showers. Seriously, all I wanted was a hot shower to start my day off right, but when I went to confront my landlady about the broken plumbing, I wound up talking to her corpse instead.

Now everyone thinks I'm to blame for her murder—not the best way to make an impression on the new neighbors, let me tell you. But how can I prove I'm innocent when I know practically nothing about the woman I supposedly killed?

Especially not the fact that she was the official Beech Grove Town Witch. Her former boss—a snarky black cat named Mr. Fluffikins—says I have to fill her vacated role until the real killer can be caught and brought to justice.

So, whether I like it or not, I've just been recruited to the Paranormal Temp Agency. Now I need to solve my landlady's murder, figure out how to wield my newly granted powers, and maybe even find a way to fit in around here.

Yup. All in a day's work for this novice witch.

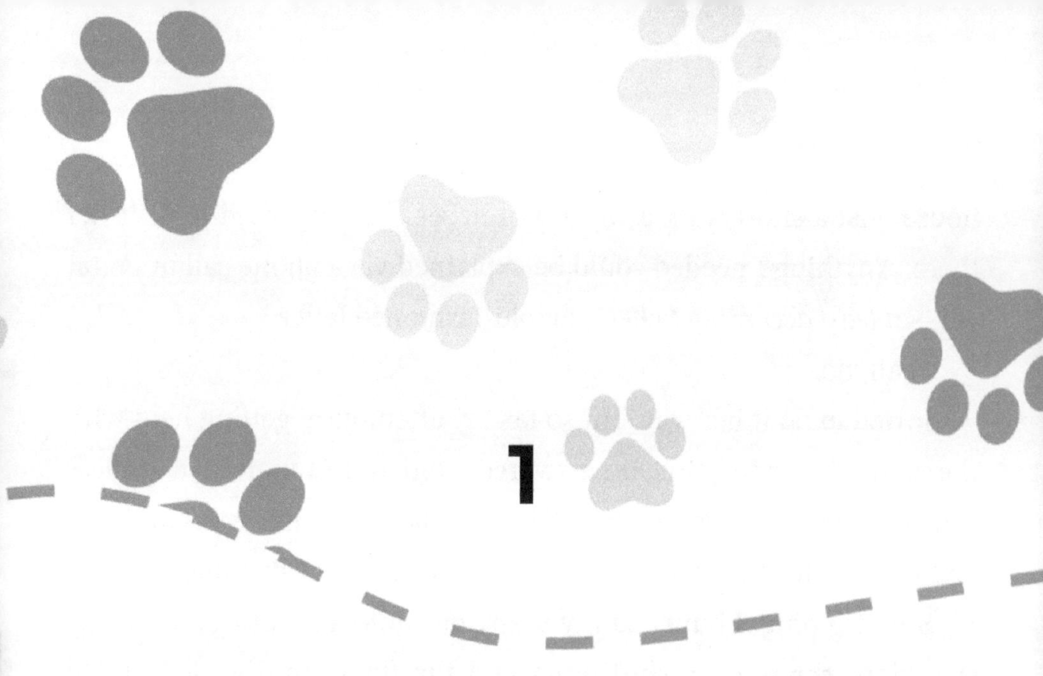

1

"Aaaaaaaaaah!" A scream tore from my chest as I leaped away from the frigid stream gushing out of the old showerhead.

Normally I loved starting my mornings with a slow and steamy rinse while I let all of my thoughts boing around my brain and eventually meld themselves into some kind of plan for the day. Ever since moving to Beech Grove a couple weeks back, however, I was lucky to get a good five minutes of warmth before the water heater suddenly gave up the ghost and a punishing spray of liquid ice ruined my good mood.

"That's it!" I shouted as I twisted the faucet off. My landlady would be hearing from me today, whether she liked it or not.

For her part, old Mrs. Haberdash had given me very careful instructions when I signed up to rent the small guest home at the back edge of her hilltop property. Even though she lived in the main house, just a short walk away, I was never ever supposed to visit her there. Anything I needed could be explained via a phone call or better yet—*at least according to her*—an old-fashioned letter.

Yeah, no.

I tried to do it her way, but so far my attempts at getting help with the plumbing had gone unanswered, and unfortunately, a useless shower made for a useless me. I'd tried playing by her rules and still had nothing to show for it. Now it was a time to play by mine.

Still dripping, I bunched my soapy hair into a bun to get it off my shoulders, threw on a shift dress and flip-flops, and headed out to finally confront my apathetic landlady.

I guess now would be a good time to introduce myself.

The name's Tawny, Tawny Bigford. Tawny is short for *Tanya,* a name I've hated ever since Tanya Mills stuck a chewed-up wad of bubble gum in my hair during our second grade spelling test. So now I'm Tawny.

I'm 35, love my showers—as you already know—and am wonderfully, happily, unapologetically single.

Sure, I had a husband once. George was his name. But several years into our marriage, he decided he made a much better pair with some PTA mom named Patricia.

A PTA mom!

As the story goes, they'd bumped into each other outside of the local middle school one afternoon, and it was love at first sight. Why George was there in the first place, I'll never understand. It's not like we had kids of our own or any other reason for him to find himself at exactly the wrong place and wrong time.

But it happened and changed all of our lives in the process.

Honestly, I'd have rather he slipped off with his younger, prettier secretary. At least then I could bemoan the cliche.

But he and Patricia, who is two years his senior, are disgustingly happy together. Most days I just pretend that neither of them exists.

Okay, so I may sound *a little* bitter. And I may live by myself in a rented guest house, but—disappointing showers not withstanding—I absolutely love my life. Basically I write two books per year, ship them off to my publisher for a paycheck, and then do whatever I want with the rest of my time.

Yes, I could write more to make more, but why? I'm perfectly happy to live frugally because that means living freely. And as such, I have more hobbies than any one person should probably ever have.

But I digress...

This wasn't the time to discuss my hobbies, it was the time to confront Mrs. Haberdash and to demand a steady supply of hot water that lasted more than five minutes per day. It was, after all, a simple and basic necessity.

On her doorstep now, I sucked in a deep breath to calm my rage, raised my hand, and knocked gently.

Just kidding, I pounded on that door with every bit of ire I had in me.

When no one answered, I started to shout. "I know you're in there! And I need to talk!"

Still nothing, so I tried the doorknob and was surprised to find it unlocked, given how much I knew the woman valued her privacy.

I pushed it open and charged in, ready to give old Mrs. Haberdash a piece of my mind.

Unfortunately, while all this righteous storming was going on, I hadn't kept an eye on my feet. I hadn't thought I needed to, but something big and heavy was lying on the ground just beyond the threshold and I slammed right into it, lost my balance, and thudded to the ground in an awkward tangle of limbs.

Not just my own, but Mrs. Haberdash's, too. *Uh-oh.* My stomach churned with an aching certainty.

"M-M-Mrs. Haberdash?" I asked, my voice quavering with fright as I turned my face toward the old woman sprawled across the entryway floor.

Her mouth remained firmly closed, her eyes glued open, her body even colder than the shower I'd just escaped.

Yup, she was dead, and—thanks to my unfortunate stumble—I'd just gotten my DNA all over her corpse.

No, no, no! I attempted a scream but came up short.

And here I thought a cold shower was the absolute worst way to start the day. Oh, when would I ever learn to leave well enough alone?

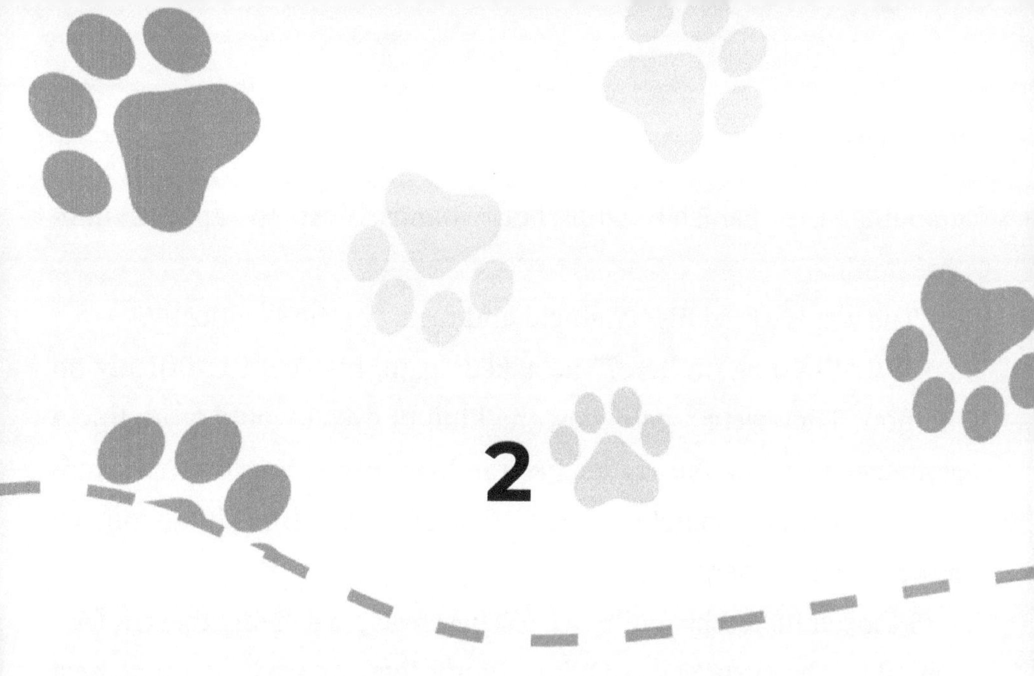

2

I scrambled away from Mrs. Haberdash's prone body in an awkward crab walk that sent an uncomfortable twinge tearing through my underworked arm muscles—because even though I had a lot of hobbies, none of them related to fitness.

"That's okay about the plumbing," I sputtered, despite knowing Mrs. Haberdash could neither hear me nor do anything about it now. "I'll just... Yeah. So bye for now."

I used the banister at the base of her grand staircase to pull myself to my feet, but before I could fully regain my composure, another horrible thing happened.

Law enforcement arrived.

"What's going on in here?" A tall man with thick salt-and-pepper hair and a light beard glanced from Mrs. Haberdash to me and back again, then picked up the radio attached to his belt and—

"Stop!" I cried, unsure of what to do with my hands. I ended up grabbing the banister with both hands, just to appear non-threatening.

The cop lowered his handheld and regarded me skeptically.

"What's going on here?" he asked again, his eyes fixed firmly on me now. They were a pale gray, the kind of eyes I would write into a character to show the reader he was handsome. And he was handsome, but unfortunately, I had a few more pressing things on my mind at the moment.

I looked incredibly guilty here. There was no denying that. In fact, I wouldn't be surprised if Officer Pretty Eyes pressed me up against the wall and started reading me my rights at that very moment. *Brain, stop freaking out!*

I needed to stop thinking about what could happen here and just focus on remaining calm and collected while I explained exactly why it was I'd wound up alone with a dead body.

"Well... I..." I fumbled for my words, sighed, and began again. "I mean... Mrs. Haberdash is dead, so..."

Oh, c'mon, Tawny! If you can't use your writing superpowers to explain away something you didn't even do, what's the point of even having them?

I simpered at him uncomfortably, waiting for the guy to either arrest me or to tell me to be on my way. It didn't seem like there was much chance for an in-between here. I mean, *I* would have arrested me.

"Yes, dead. I can see that," he said, glancing toward her body demonstratively before snapping his gaze back to mine.

A jolt shot through me, but whether it was excitement, fear, or something else entirely, I couldn't quite tell.

"Why did you kill her?" he pressed, his eyes boring into mine as if trying to see straight into my thoughts.

"I didn't!" I stomped my foot for good measure. Maybe my body could say what my words could not. "This morning in the shower..."

He raised one suggestive eyebrow that sent flames straight into my cheeks. Why did he have to be so good looking? That made this whole situation so much worse. I'd always been great at writing banter, but not so great at actually doing it in real life. Besides, it's not like flirting could get me out of this one.

"No, not that. I mean, yes, the hot water," I back-pedaled again and then panicked when he reached back toward his belt. "Wait! I didn't kill her! How could you even think that?"

He crossed his arms and stared down the bridge of his nose at little old me. "How could I think that? Easy. I've never seen you a day in my life, not until you suddenly showed up at a murder scene."

I gasped in horror. "Murder? No, she wasn't murdered. I mean, at least not by me. And, hey, why do you automatically assume foul play? You've been here all of five seconds and have hardly even glanced at her. Don't you have to do like an investigation or something first?"

Ugh. Me and my big mouth!

First I couldn't defend my innocence, and then I accused him of not doing his job properly. I may have written one or two police characters in my books, but that wasn't quite enough to make me an expert here.

He groaned and shook his head. “Yes, and I will investigate, just as soon as I’m done questioning the suspect.”

I backed up until my shoulders were pressed flat against the wall. “Look, Deputy Quick Draw, Mrs. Haberdash is my landlady. I was just coming to lodge a complaint. A small one. Nothing to kill anyone over.” I inserted a nervous laugh here as one does when a topic is quite literally *dead* serious.

“She was like this when I got here,” I added as an afterthought.

“Looks like she’s been here for a while,” he said with a sniff.

“I don’t know anything about any of this. I just wanted some hot water for my morning shower. That’s all.”

Gathering every last vestige of strength, I pushed off from the wall and carefully navigated around poor Mrs. Haberdash in a last-ditch effort to get the heck out of there.

The cop’s light eyes roamed over me, and the slightest smile quirked on his lips.

“Hang on,” he said, stopping me in my tracks as a heavy veil of horror dropped over me once again. “You’re going to have to come with me.”

Noooooooo!

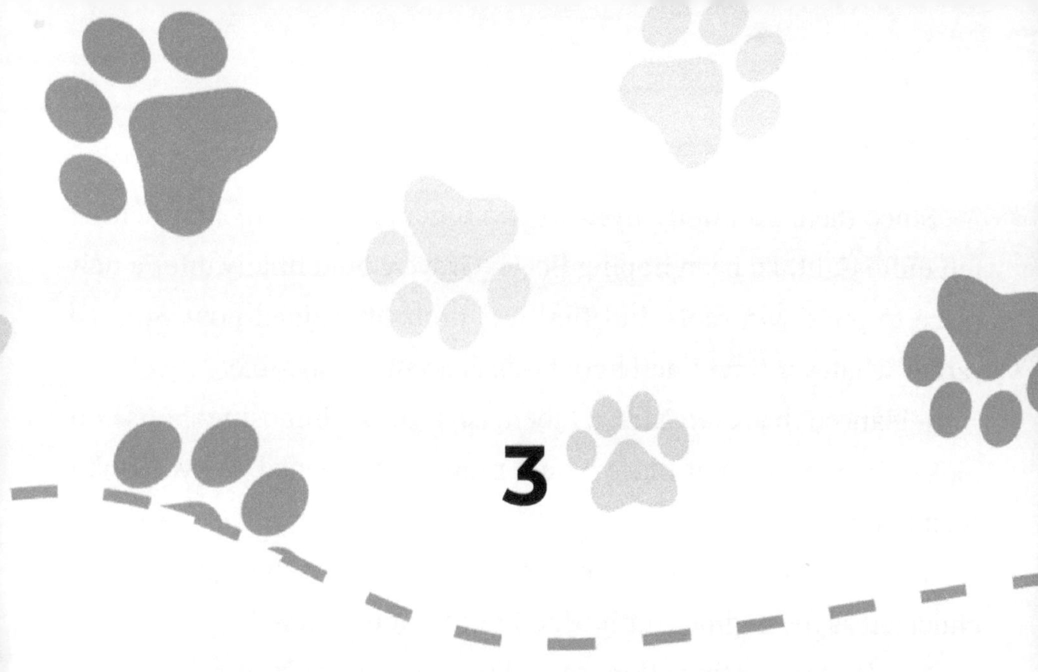

3

Officer Quick Draw left me no time to argue. When I hesitated to follow him toward his squad car, he unhooked a pair of handcuffs from his belt loop and dangled them before me. "Would you prefer we give these babies a workout instead?"

Motivation had arrived. And just like that, I was power walking across my dead landlady's dead lawn and yanking open the passenger side door to throw myself inside.

The officer gave me a strange look, but I shrugged it off. "If I'm not under arrest, then I'm not riding in the back. I've lived in enough small towns to know how fast and far rumors can fly." Things couldn't get much worse at this point, so I had to fight for whatever small dignities I could retain. I'd already been driven out of my former hometown by the embarrassment of my ex-husband's indiscretion.

Since then, I'd briefly lived in two other small towns, but neither felt quite right. I'd been hoping Beech Grove would finally offer a new place to put down roots, but that was probably ruined now. Still, I'd rather whatever time I had here be as pleasant as possible.

I glanced back at Mrs. Haberdash's dark, imposing house. It looked like the kind of place where murders happened. Why hadn't I seen that before?

The cop slammed his door, jabbed his key into the ignition, and chuckled as the engine rumbled to life. "So you're new."

I nodded in confirmation. "And I'm guessing you're not."

"Born and raised right here in Beech Grove," he admitted with a faint blush. "It's all I've ever known. What I don't know is your name. You still haven't told me that little piece of info." He smiled to himself as he maneuvered the squad car with me in it. It would have been easy to like him under other circumstances, but now he would forever be the guy who took me in for murder.

I offered a sarcastic laugh to hide my discomfort. "It's kind of hard to introduce oneself when one's companion is hurling murder accusations around like they were *Mardi Gras* beads."

"Oneself, eh? *Smart.* You a new professor at the academy, then?" We'd already pulled out of the driveway and were rumbling down the torn-up back road. He did glance at me briefly as if making some kind of assessment.

"What academy?" We were at least an hour away from any kind of big city. Seemed a weird place for something as fancy as an academy.

He frowned but didn't clarify. "How about we try starting over here? Hi. I'm Parker Barnes. It's nice to meet you."

I kept my eyes fixed firmly ahead and nodded.

"And you are?" Parker prompted after several silent moments passed.

"Tawny," I answered even though I really didn't want to.

"There. Now that wasn't so hard, was it?"

I shook my head and let out a beleaguered sigh. "I'd really rather not make chit-chat with some guy who thinks I killed my landlady. Let's just get the questioning over with and go on our separate ways. Okay?"

"Touché, madame. Lucky for you, we're already there."

The car jerked to a stop, shocking me with how short this journey had been.

I widened my eyes at the sight of the sprawling brick building before us. It wasn't just a single building, but a whole complex—and it definitely wasn't a police station. I didn't remember ever passing it before on my walks through town, either. Though it obviously wasn't far from where I lived, judging from the short time between climbing into this cruiser and reaching our destination.

"I thought you were taking me to the station?" I said, crossing my arms across my chest in open defiance.

"This is the station, at least for our purposes today. C'mon. We've lost too much time already."

I turned to stare at him. He didn't look like your garden variety murderer-rapist-all-around-psycho, but that didn't mean he wasn't. I refused to follow him blindly just because he wore a uniform. Uniforms could be faked, after all.

"Everything only *just* happened. How have we lost time?" I

demanded, sitting firm. “And, no, I know better than to go into a strange building with a strange man. I’m staying right here.” Not that camping out in his strange car was any better, but still, a girl had to stand up for herself—otherwise who would?

“Okay, but if anyone asks, you’re the one who chose to do this the hard way,” Parker answered with yet another frown before exiting the car.

I watched as he marched around the car, came to my side, and then flung the door open. “Out,” he said firmly.

I opened my mouth to argue but let out a scream instead. My hands were moving to unbuckle the seatbelt, my feet to pull me from the car. I had told neither of them to do those things. “Hey,” I cried in a pathetic protest. “Stop it.”

“Follow me,” Parker said, obvious enjoyment now dancing in his light eyes.

My legs answered as if they belonged to him instead of me. The no-good traitors.

And into the unmarked office in the non-police building I went, thanks to my frighteningly bossy companion and inexplicably disobedient limbs.

Yup, this day just kept on getting worse and worse.

And that definitely didn’t bode well for whatever happened next.

4

We entered a chilly office space that sat dark and dim despite how brightly the late morning sun shone outside. Okay, so I might have slept in a little that day, but I was between books so it didn't really matter.

"Your instincts were bang on," Parker said to someone I couldn't see. "Haberdash is dead. And I found this one at the scene."

"Well, that doesn't bode well for the rest of the day," a smooth voice responded from somewhere deeper inside. Each of his words rolled directly into the next without taking any small breaks for breath. I'd almost describe it as serpentine, although that description wasn't exactly right, either.

More than a little intrigued, I whipped my head from side to side but still couldn't locate the speaker. "Who's there? What do you want with me?"

The disembodied voice chuckled, and I thought I caught a glimpse of movement at the edge of the room, but just as quickly as I spotted it, the dark form had slunk back into the even darker shadows.

"Well, that certainly isn't good. Take her to the conference room," the voice instructed in that same overly polished manner. "I'll summon the others."

Parker placed a hand at the small of my back, and I wriggled away from him. "Don't touch me," I snapped.

"Sorry," he said, seeming genuinely apologetic. He cleared his throat before speaking again. "Follow me. Um, please."

My legs snapped into action, despite my mind screaming for them to stop, turn around, and run as fast as I could out the door.

I was a lifeless marionette in his hands, little Pinocchio before the fairy godmother brought him to life.

We walked down one hall, turned, and then walked to the end of another that opened into a large meeting room with a glass ceiling. I'd have been impressed if I weren't already equal parts agitated and terrified.

"What do you want with me?" I demanded, searching Parker's eyes, hoping that with the right expression I could convince him to let me go before any serious damage was done.

"Have a seat," he said with what seemed like a sad shake of his head. I wasn't buying that. If he was so sad about this, then he wouldn't have kidnapped me in the first place.

My hands moved to grip the nearest chair and pull it back.

"You don't have to," Parker said suddenly, and my hands fell limply to my sides. "Unless you want to."

"I'd rather stand," I managed through gritted teeth. "Actually I'd rather go."

I started toward the door.

"No!" he cried, and I froze in place. "I'm sorry. I know you must have a million questions, and you'll get answers for all of them. Well, most at least. We just have to wait for—"

The door flew open and four people marched in, glancing briefly in my direction as they assembled themselves around the table. Most were much older than me or Parker. At least one of them looked like he was mere days away from celebrating his one-hundredth birthday. A long white beard hung limply against his chest, making him look a bit like Merlin in a business suit. Why would a one-hundred-year-old man need a business suit, and why would he be wearing it now? These were but a few of the many questions flying through my mind as I studied the new arrivals.

I had just peeked under the table to check out the footwear of a particularly well-dressed woman who appeared to be in her late fifties or early sixties when a black cat trotted through the doorway and leaped up onto the table in one graceful, confident pounce.

"Now that we're all here," the voice I'd heard in the outer room began.

Of course, I didn't hear what he said next, because an internal scream took over my brain as I realized that same smooth voice was coming from the cat. *The cat!*

And it's not just that the cat was talking—he seemed to be in charge, too.

He placed one paw directly in front of the other and sauntered across the table, his glowing yellow eyes fixed right on me. "Well?"

"Well, wh-what?" I stuttered. I also struggled and strained, but nothing I tried released my legs back into my control.

"Are you the one who killed her?" The words danced out from the cat's mouth, and I realized now why it sounded so strange. He didn't need his tongue to form the sounds. That removed a lot of the wet breathiness out of speech.

"No answer," he said thoughtfully. "Does that mean you plead guilty?"

"No!" I shouted. "Now let me go!"

The cat turned to Parker and waited.

The once-confident police officer appeared frazzled in the company of the demanding feline. "She was there when I arrived. I thought we could—"

"Make use of her until we find out who really did it. Provided it's not actually she who committed the deed, of course. Brilliant idea, Barnes." The black cat strolled back to the head of the table, and the people seated on either side murmured their agreement.

I still had no idea what was going on, but at least now I knew they didn't plan to kill me. "Excuse me," I piped up. "Make use of me how?"

"Oh, you'll see soon enough," the cat promised with a rather unfriendly chuckle.

With that, Parker rose from his seat and strode toward me with one hand extended as he shot me an uneasy smile.

The others rose from their chairs, too, and formed a line behind him, waiting for their turn to greet me themselves, apparently.

When I hesitantly returned Parker's handshake, he said, "Welcome to the Paranormal Temp Agency. You're hired!"

What? How could I be hired when I hadn't even applied for a job?

Also, there was the small fact that I was most definitely not a paranormal person. I was normal with a capital *N*, and I didn't like what was happening here one bit.

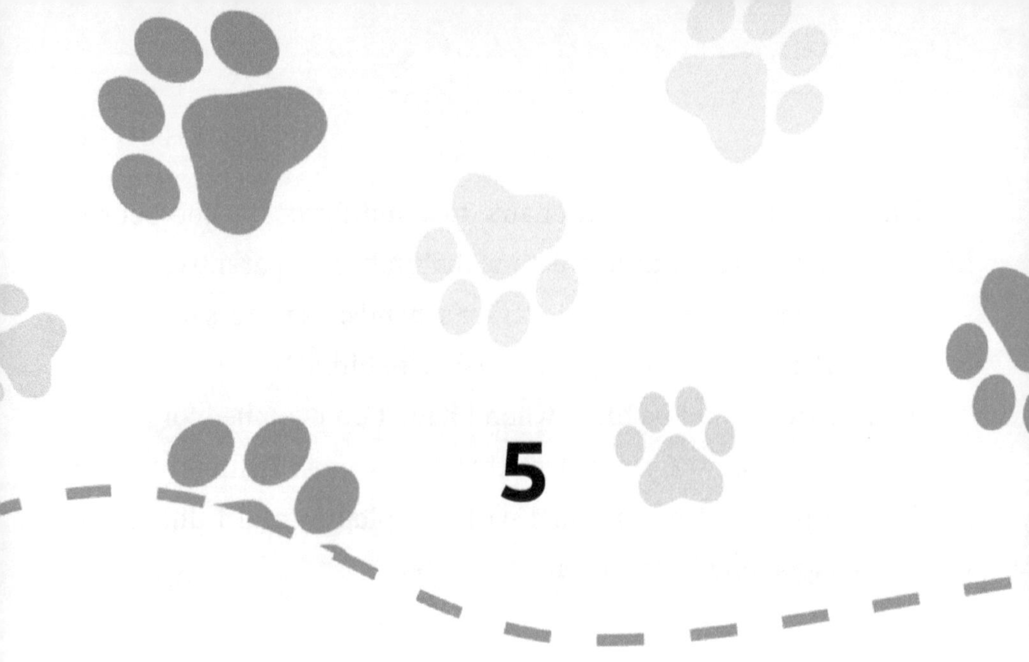

5

I'd just discovered a murder, been kidnapped, and then offered a job by a talking cat. How much weirder could this day get?

I shook my head vehemently. "Sorry, I already have a job."

"It's not up for debate," the cat hissed back at me. "Get her up to speed and fast, Barnes. My patience here is wearing thin."

"Okay. Okay. Where to begin?" Officer Parker Barnes wondered aloud while I was left to wonder if he really was a police officer or if it had all been a ruse from the start.

"This time, you probably want to be sitting down," he said, pulling out a chair for me.

I crossed my arms over my chest and stood firm. "I managed to survive the talking cat without passing out. I think I can handle whatever you're going to say next."

"Suit yourself." He chuckled, but I thought I saw a flicker of respect cross his face. "Lila Haberdash was Beech Grove's Town

Witch, and now that she's dead the position is open. In the meanwhile, it's yours."

"Uh-huh, uh-huh." I nodded my head adamantly. "There's just one problem with that."

"You're not a witch?" Parker asked with one eyebrow quirked.

"I'm not a witch!" I shouted in confirmation, wringing my hands as I did. "So, thanks but no thanks. I'll just be on my way."

"Enough with this game already," the cat snapped. "If you can't handle her, I'll just have to take over. Come here!"

I raced to his side against my own volition. I was really getting sick of all this mind control stuff.

The cat lifted his nose high in the air, leaving me with a perfect view of the small white patch at the top of his chest. Normally, I liked cats. Not enough to own one, mind you, but I liked them well enough when they were other people's pets. This one, however, had recently risen to the top of my list of people—um, creatures—I didn't much care for.

"You've been hired on to the Paranormal Temp Agency," he told me with a twitch of his nose and a flick of his tail. "It's not a job you're allowed to turn down."

"I think I know what I'm allow—"

"Stop arguing and listen. You *will* fill Lila's old post as Town Witch until we're able to uncover her actual killer to take on the role permanently. Nonc of this is up for debate."

"Why does finding the killer matter? Can't you just put up a job advertisement on Spooks R Us or something?"

"Cute," he said with a scowl. "You're filling in for Lila, whether you like it or not. Help us find the murderer, and you'll be off the hook sooner. End of story."

Parker cleared his throat, then explained the part that still confused me most. "Magic passes to the nearest host when its original owner passes. So whoever killed Lila likely absorbed her magic—a magic which is grounded in Beech Grove and is meant for its designated witch."

I stood still, considering this. Parker's explanation made sense, but it also begged so many new questions. Mainly, what would have happened if no one else had been around? What if Mrs. Haberdash had died of natural causes and then her magic had found its way over to me, the sole resident of the guest house on the edge of her property?

I still didn't like that I was expected to help clean up this mess when it had nothing to do with me. I felt sad for Mrs. Haberdash, of course. Even though she wasn't a great landlady, she hadn't deserved to be murdered. But I also didn't deserve to be put in harm's way, especially if the person who'd offed Haberdash decided to come for me next.

Maybe I still had a quick and easy way out of this, though. I raised my hand and pointed at the cat.

"Come to me," I said, trying to push power into the simple command, the way I'd seen both the cop and the cat do.

Boss cat rolled his eyes. "Should I take this feeble attempt at magic as your confession of guilt?"

"No," I mumbled as embarrassment burned at my cheeks.

"Even if you do have magic, which at this point I sincerely doubt, you still aren't strong enough to command me. No one is. That's why I'm the boss, and you're the temp. Got it?"

"Whatever," I answered drolly. "So I don't have magic. That should be the end of this conversation, then. How can I fill in as the Town Witch without having any magic? Clearly, you've got the wrong woman here."

"You'll be granted everything you need to perform your duties, including some temporary magic."

I bit back an argument. There was a lot wrong with this scenario, but also... *I'd just been offered magic!* How could I possibly say no to that?

"Fine," I stated with a shrug instead. "Then I guess I accept. Can I please have my magic now?"

"Tonight at orientation. Eleven o'clock sharp."

"Sorry, I sleep at night."

"Not anymore you don't." The cat turned away from me with an irritated flick of his tail and faced the rest of his board. "Disperse."

Everyone left except for Parker and me.

"Sorry to drag you into all this," he said. "But take it from someone who knows, don't mess with Mr. Fluffikins so much. Your life will be much easier if you show him some respect."

I burst out laughing, but Parker only looked afraid.

Seriously though, what could a little black cat named Mr. Fluffikins even really do to me?

Unfortunately, I'd find out later that night.

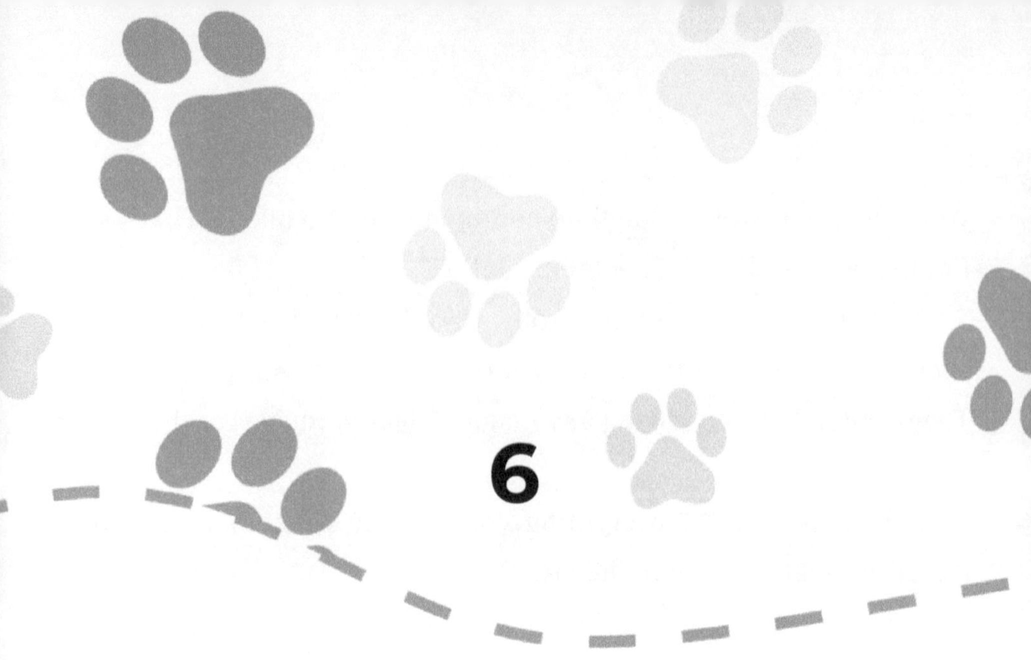

6

After Parker dropped me off back home, I finally finished the shower I'd started what felt like a lifetime ago. Yes, it was still uncomfortably cold, but that discomfort helped me work some of the shock out of my bones. Actually, it was just what I needed.

As I toweled off, I made a mental catalog of the things I knew:

My landlady was a witch.

She'd been murdered.

Her killer was still out there.

Now I was expected to fill her emptied shoes.

That night I'd be given temporary magic.

And my boss was a talking cat.

I wrote fiction for a living—telling stories was my literal job—and still I couldn't have come up with something quite this crazy, even if I'd tried.

In fact, if it had been up to me, I'd have chosen a much more worthy heroine to take my place, and instead of a jerky cat, I'd probably have written Parker into the authoritative role. It would make for an interesting office romance premise. Opposites attract, enemies to lovers... Yeah, it checked all the boxes for the makings of a good book.

Still, I guess that's why people liked to say that life was stranger than fiction.

First that harlot of a PTA mom, and now this. What a riveting life I led.

Fully dried off now, I slipped into my favorite pair of jeans and an old T-shirt, then pulled on my running shoes. Did I ever run? No, don't be silly. But it made me feel like I could if I had to, wearing shoes meant for that purpose.

Then again, if things went south with my training tonight, I might actually have to put the poor sneakers to use for the first time in their miserable lives. I shuddered. *Best not to think about that.*

Suited up in my inconspicuous casual wear, I headed outside and crept down the worn path to my former landlady's main residence.

Imagine my surprise when I found I wasn't the only one who'd had that idea.

A young woman wearing a black maxi dress with a floral printed cardigan, scuffed up combat boots, and a big floppy sunhat stood in front of the house staring up at a second-floor window. She was so immersed in her inspection that she didn't seem to notice me approaching.

I hesitated. Would it be better if I turned back and pretended this whole thing had never happened?

It was too late for that, I supposed. I was a part of this now, whether I liked it or not.

And so, I raised my hand in greeting and shouted, "Hello there!"

The other woman startled so badly, she somehow managed to dislodge her hat, which the wind immediately swept up in a sudden playful gust.

We both ran after it, but a high up tree branch claimed it before either of us even had a chance.

The stranger bit her lip and turned toward me. "That was my favorite hat."

"That was my favorite landlady," I said, deciding just to jump into it as I motioned toward the now vacant house. "Did you know her well?"

"Not really," the woman said with one last lingering glance toward her lost hat. Now that her face was fully exposed, I could tell she was even younger than I'd originally guessed. I wouldn't be surprised if she'd only just finished high school in the last year or two.

"I'm Tawny," I offered with a warm smile. "And you are?"

"Nobody important," she mumbled with another glance toward her lost sun hat. Her long black tresses blew in the breeze, giving her an almost ghastly appearance. "I really should be on my way."

"Wait," I cried, not entirely sure how I meant to follow that up. But I couldn't just let her get away. What if she was the murderer? I owed it to my former landlady to find out.

"What are you doing here?" I demanded when she turned back to me with a resigned sigh. "Did you know Mrs. Haberdash was murdered?"

Her eyes bore into mine, direct and determined but also giving nothing away. I suddenly became very aware that I had confronted someone who could be lethally dangerous. *Was* this the killer? Did she have the magic that belonged to the town?

When she didn't answer, I took a guess. "You did. Didn't you? Know she was killed, I mean. But do you know why someone would want her dead?"

"It was a mistake coming here," she spat, then turned on her heel and strode off so quickly I didn't have a prayer of catching her despite having donned my running shoes.

"Wait," I called after her again, but that nameless girl didn't acknowledge me and didn't turn back.

Well, shoot.

I'd had the suspect right here but hadn't been able to get anything useful out of her. If she'd been a friend or family member, she'd have said something, right? Her sudden departure screamed of a guilty conscience—but could she be guilty of murder?

Whatever the case, I had a feeling this strange visitor would turn up again sooner rather than later. Hopefully, though, it wouldn't be with murderous intent, especially now that she knew I suspected her.

Gah!

What was wrong with me? I hadn't merely tiptoed around danger, I'd dived headfirst in after it.

7

I spent the rest of that day trying and failing to write some pages to make my agent happy. Of course I had way too much on my mind to focus, which meant my agent would just have to get used to being unhappy with me for a while.

Parker turned up outside my cottage at fifteen minutes to eleven that night. Apparently he was my official keeper when it came to all things Paranormal Temp Agency.

And even though I didn't feel I needed a constant chaperone, I was grateful that at least it was him. I mean, he had less sass than the cat. And he wasn't so bad on the eyes, either.

The old me would have leaned into that attraction a little, flirted whenever the moment felt right. But this was the new me, a woman who I was quite frankly still getting to know.

Ever since I stumbled over Mrs. Haberdash's dead body and

straight into this brave new world full of strange magic, I'd been changed. Sure, it had happened just this morning, but both of these once-in-a-lifetime occurrences together made for a monumental shift in what I knew about myself and the greater world around me.

I strode out to Parker's car, wearing a confidence I didn't quite feel. I also wore a flowy black floor-length skirt with a tight black leather bustier, old boots which were mostly hidden beneath the skirt, and my favorite statement piece of jewelry—a shiny black metal necklace with a series of interesting shapes that kind of looked like an eagle if you squinted a bit.

Apparently I'd also shown up with more cleavage than my escort had anticipated. He turned beet red under that beard of his the moment his eyes locked onto said cleavage.

"You didn't have to get dressed up for this," he muttered, clenching his hands even tighter around the steering wheel.

"Is that your way of saying I look nice?" I teased. Okay, maybe the old me was still in there a little bit.

Parker coughed. "Sure. Let's go with *nice.* Um, did you have a good day?"

"I don't think there's much recovering from a murder accusation and the discovery of magic, so let's just call today *interesting* instead."

"We know you probably didn't kill her if that helps," he offered with an apologetic shrug.

Oh, good. They knew I *probably* wasn't guilty, which meant I wasn't fully in the clear yet. It also meant... "So I guess you didn't catch the real killer yet," I said with a sigh.

"No, but we have some leads." Parker's expression remained firm, serious.

Me, on the other hand, I preferred to lighten the mood a bit—especially when I was already feeling scared out of my mind. "So, what are you? Are you actually a cop, or was all that pomp and circumstance this morning simply for my benefit?"

I expected him to loosen up some at my playful banter, but no dice. He adjusted himself in his seat, sitting taller, commanding even more of a presence. His jaw clenched, and his shoulders tightened. Was he afraid of me, or just not good with people in general?

"I am an officer of the law, yes," he said, his voice deeper than usual. "I'm also the paranormal liaison to the force."

"So you're a double cop?" I asked, scrunching up my nose playfully.

Finally a smile spread across his face. "Something like that, yes."

"And the cat's your boss. What about all the other people who were there this morning?" If anyone was going to give me information, it would be Parker, so I decided to press him for all I could on the drive over. It would be easier to influence him privately without the watchful eyes of Mr. Fluffikins.

He glanced at me for a moment and the car jerked toward the curb. Maybe expecting him to multi-task behind the wheel wasn't the best idea I'd had that day.

Parker returned his attention to the road. "You mean, the other liaisons. Right?"

"If that's who was sitting around that conference room table, then yeah." I thought back to the woman with the fantastic outfit and the ancient guy with the Merlin beard and business suit. The other two had made less of an impression on me, but whoever they were, they were important enough to be at that meeting, which meant I shouldn't simply forget they existed.

Parker nodded and readjusted his hands on the wheel. "Yes, we're all liaisons. I'm the liaison to the police force. Each of them keep an eye on other key influencing bodies around the region."

I bit my lip to keep from frowning. I was beginning to feel stupid, considering how little I knew, and I hated nothing more than feeling stupid. "That's pretty vague. Are you saying you speak up for the paranormal interests with the police?"

The car jerked as Parker suddenly hit the brake—whether accidentally or on purpose, I couldn't quite tell. He eased off before we came to a full stop. Luckily, no one had been driving behind us, or we'd both have a serious case of whiplash right now.

Parker's voice turned pitchy and panicked. "No, no. Gosh, no. Non-magic people don't know anything about us, so there's definitely no speaking up about anything. We watch to protect us from them. Not the other way around."

The fact that he was so nervous had to mean I was hitting on all the good questions, right? I decided to keep going, even though I was more than a little concerned for my safety with such a reactive driver behind the wheel. "Uh, hello. I'm non-magic, but you wasted no time in showing your hand to me."

"You showed up at the murder scene for one of our most important magical locals, so yeah. We had no choice but to bring you in. Besides, you'll have some magic in you before the night is through."

A shiver of excitement passed through me. I was about to get magic. That almost made the whole being a murder suspect thing worthwhile.

Almost.

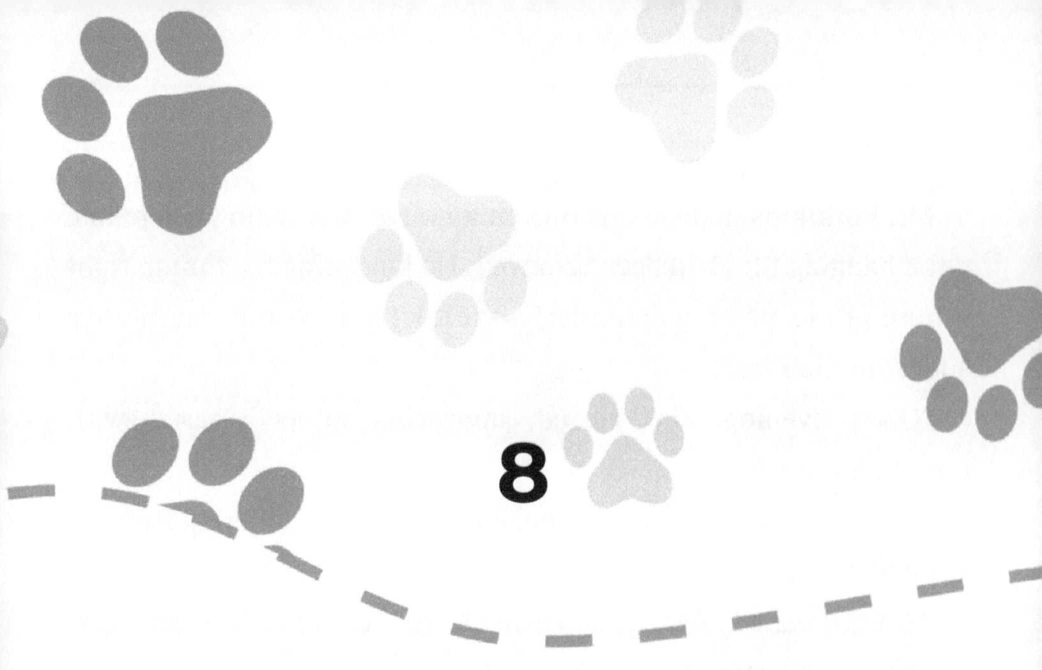

8

The drive over was short and bumpy, thanks to Parker's erratic behavior behind the wheel. This time I was actually happy to see the dark office complex, because it meant we had made it to our location without the epic car crash I'd half-anticipated.

Inside Paranormal HQ, Parker guided me in the opposite direction we'd gone that morning. A series of long halls delivered us to a large, echoing space where all the furniture had been cleared away and the carpeting ripped out.

"You're definitely not getting the security deposit back on this place," I mumbled, remembering the time I'd forfeited one of my own, thanks to an ill-fated attempt at candle making. Incidentally, that was not a hobby I'd decided to keep.

I turned toward Parker to see how my joke had gone over, but before I could meet his eyes, we were joined by a new arrival.

Mr. Fluffikins hopped down from a hole in the ceiling where one of the hanging tiles had been removed. He landed with a thump right in front of me, proving definitively—at least to me—that cats always landed on their feet.

"Good evening," he purred, appearing rather pleased with himself, if not with me.

"Thanks for bringing her to me, Barnes," he said, offering Parker a curt nod. "That will be all. Dismissed."

"Wait," I called after his departing form, but either he didn't hear me or he didn't care.

I glanced back toward the black cat with growing discomfort. Something told me he wouldn't be gentle in making my big introduction to magic.

"Human," he said, flicking the tip of his tail rhythmically as he regarded me. "It is time to—"

"My name's Tawny," I informed him.

His eyes widened as if my speaking my name had somehow been an insult. "That's not important. What's important is that—"

"Actually, my name is kind of important, and I'll thank you to use it." If I didn't put some rules in place now, I doubted I'd be able to introduce them later. And if I was going to be around long enough to do this Town Witch thing right, then I definitely needed to at least push for him to use my actual name.

Mr. Fluffikins rose to all four feet and paced a circle around me. "That's a rather tall demand from someone who still hasn't been cleared of murder."

"Actually it's a fairly simple request. You're asking me to learn magic and temporarily fill in for a witch. All I'm asking is that you treat me with a little respect."

The cat stopped, cocked his head to the side, and watched me with swirling golden eyes.

We both remained silent, unwilling to budge. As far as I was concerned, I had more leverage here. He may have magic, but he also needed me—and it had to be me for some reason, even though I had no idea why.

After what felt like a small eternity, the cat finally laughed. Not just a small chuckle, but a side-splitting display of amusement.

"You won't go easy on me, I see. I hope you know I'll extend you that same courtesy. So *Tawny* it is, but keep in mind, your future demands will be met with far more resistance."

"Thank you," I said between clenched teeth. Even though he'd finally given in, I still felt on edge. Why couldn't Parker have stayed with us? It would have been so much easier, having a friendly face along for the ride, even if he, too, was still largely a stranger. But I'd take the handsome cop over the scary magic cat any day of the week.

"So what now?" I asked when Mr. Fluffikins didn't make any effort to explain himself.

"Well, now," he said, while studying the unsheathed claws on one of his front paws. "Now I grant you temporary access to magic."

"Magic," I repeated, relishing the power of the word on my tongue.

The black cat nodded and schlinked those claws back into his paw. "It won't be a perfect match for Lila's, but it will be a fair replica and should allow you to temporarily fill her post. That is, unless you actually did kill her and have already absorbed her magical legacy."

"I didn't—" I was promptly cut off by a strong gust of wind that tore through the room and knocked me off my feet.

Ouchy ouch ouch. Everything hurt. My head, my chest, and especially my butt.

"What was that?" I screamed. He wanted me—needed me—to help him, right? So why was he attacking me all of a sudden?

Mr. Fluffikins opened his mouth, but instead of answering my very reasonable question, he unleashed a pulsing plume of fire.

It whipped out fast and determined, flying toward me much faster than I could ever hope to move even if I wasn't already knocked flat on my rear.

Then in a split instant, the flame disappeared, right before crashing into my face and turning me into a melted ball of wax.

"You're crazy!" I shouted, but fear made my words sound jumbled and drunken. "Let me out of here!"

Fluffikins laughed as he took slow deliberate steps in my direction. I took a deep breath and braced myself for whatever came next. We both knew I didn't have a snowball's chance in Miami of coming out the victor here.

But, oh, what a way to die!

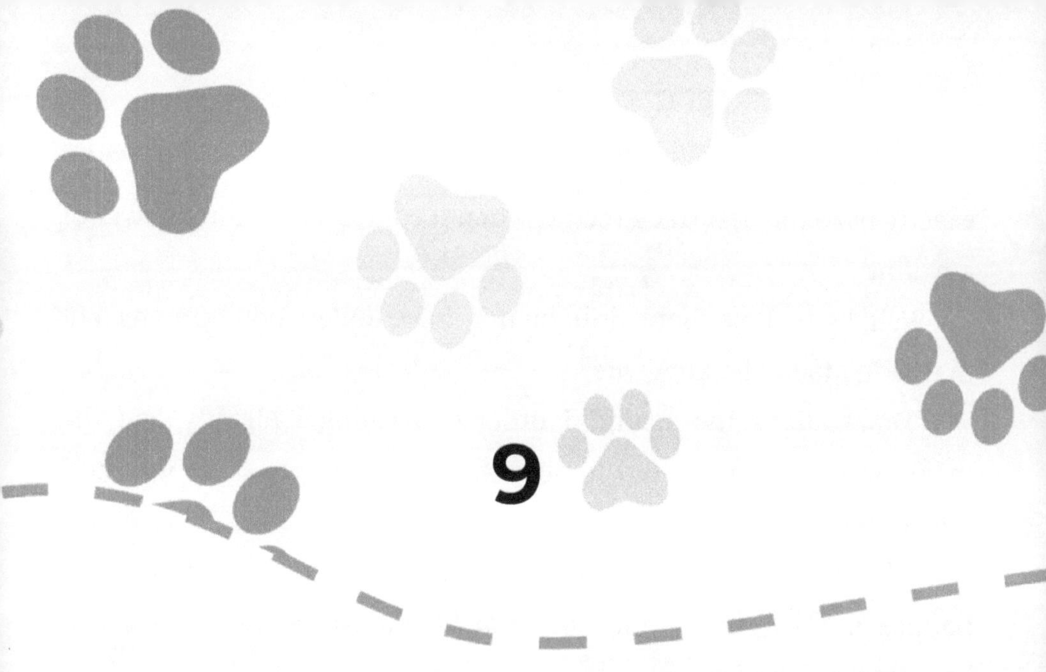

9

"Relax," Fluffikins drawled as he stepped closer and closer.

Instantly my muscles loosened, and a calming thrum reverberated through my core.

The magical cat watched me for a moment.

When he decided I had well and truly followed his order, he continued with his horrifying presentation. "I had to make sure you didn't already have magic that you were attempting to hide. I can tell you don't have much practice, which means you wouldn't have been able to prevent yourself from unleashing your defenses at the sudden arrival of an external threat."

"You're crazy," I spat again. My body was calm, but my mind still reeled. "I don't have any magic, and I definitely don't appreciate you trying to turn me into roast Tawny!"

A smile stretched from one of his whiskered cheeks to the other. "Trusting a human with magic is no small thing. Your kind doesn't exactly have the best track record when it comes to wielding power of any kind."

Well, he had me there. Still, he may have understood humans, but that didn't mean he knew *me.*

"Don't attack me again," I ordered, wishing I already had the magic so I could force him to obey my command the same way he'd forced me to be calm.

"I hadn't planned on it. Now wait there." He crouched into a low pounce and then leaped into the same hole in the ceiling from which he'd emerged earlier.

Fluffikins was an unnaturally gifted jumper, that was for sure. *Oh, right. Magic, duh.*

When he returned, he had a simple silver brooch clutched in his mouth. It looked like a cross between a butterfly and a bow and appeared to be made of gleaming silver. He dropped it at my feet. "Your choice of attire isn't exactly suitable," he said in that off-putting almost serpentine way of his.

I glowered at Fluffikins. He may be the boss here, but that didn't give him the right to control every aspect of my life. His latest barb stung, especially since I'd put so much effort into looking nice.

"No more insults," I growled.

But he didn't back down. Instead he buckled down. "It's just you have so much skin exposed. This is your magical badge." He placed a paw on the silver brooch. "It needs to be placed close to your heart to have the best effect."

I glanced down at my expansive cleavage and grimaced. "Oh, I see. *Hmmmm.*"

"Could you maybe just...?" His words fell away and, well, if you've never seen a black cat blush, I promise it's a sight to behold. Fluffikins coughed, which turned into a hack, which soon resulted in a slimy hairball being spat up right by my feet. Charming.

I grabbed the gleaming brooch, trying my best to not look at the mess that sat dangerously close. "How's this?" I asked after popping it at the very top of my bustier so it jutted slightly above the neckline.

"Well, let's put it to the tests." Fluffikins regained his composure, winked, then threw another gust of wind my way.

This time I raised both hands in front of me, and the wind immediately died down without so much as ruffling a single hair on my head. Shocked, I studied my hands in search of the magic which had just come out of them. They still looked—and felt—exactly the same.

I didn't have much time to think about it, though, because next came the fire. Instinctively, I thrust my hands forward and pushed out a stream of water that collided with Fluffikins's flames, causing both to blink out of existence.

The cat wore a smug expression now. "See. You can't help but defend yourself."

"But how? I definitely didn't do any of that on purpose." I continue to study my hands carefully as if they'd suddenly reveal all the secrets of the universe. Unfortunately, I still felt just as confused as ever—and possibly more.

"Wielding magic is as easy and natural as breathing air for those who have it. Yes, you must practice to strengthen it, but our natural aptitudes are innate within us."

"But I don't naturally have magic. I shouldn't have been able to do the things I just did," I argued. I didn't write fantasy, but I'd read enough of it to know that magic required lots of practice and self-control. This thing with Fluffikins tonight was turning out to be the exact opposite.

He shrugged as if none of this meant anything to him. "Everyone has the potential. Few just ever realize it's there."

"So every single person in the whole entire world has magic?" I marveled at this. How could such a big thing be kept a secret? Was it because of people like Parker and Fluffikins and all the other paranormal liaisons around the world? Was I part of that now? *Wow.*

"When it comes to adult humans, it's less than a fraction of a percent," Fluffikins informed me with a contented grin. "Most are too caught up with the other aspects of their busy lives."

"You said adults," I pointed out as I finally pulled myself to my feet. "Does that mean—?"

"Yes, many children can still access their innate magic, but as they grow older, the adults in their lives convince them it isn't real, and eventually most will lose that spark."

"That's actually really sad," I choked out.

"We already have more than enough messes to clean up from the few humans who keep their magic. Why do you think there are so many stray cats around? It's our job to keep an eye on you and fix things before the other humans realize they're broken."

"So stray cats are...?"

"Field agents, yes. If you ever have any extra money laying around, try to donate to your local shelters. We've lost too many good agents to..." He shuddered. "Never mind."

"I'll do what I can," I promised, wondering whether it would be okay to pet him or if such a gesture would be more condescending than comforting. "So what now?"

"Now, you head home and get some rest. I'll come for you in the morning to get you started on your Town Witch duties."

I wanted to thank him, to apologize for the friends he'd lost in the field, but before I could say anything, he raised his voice and bellowed, "Barnes!"

Parker appeared almost immediately, grabbed me by the arm, and led me away. Well, it looked like I'd have to wait for tomorrow to get any more answers.

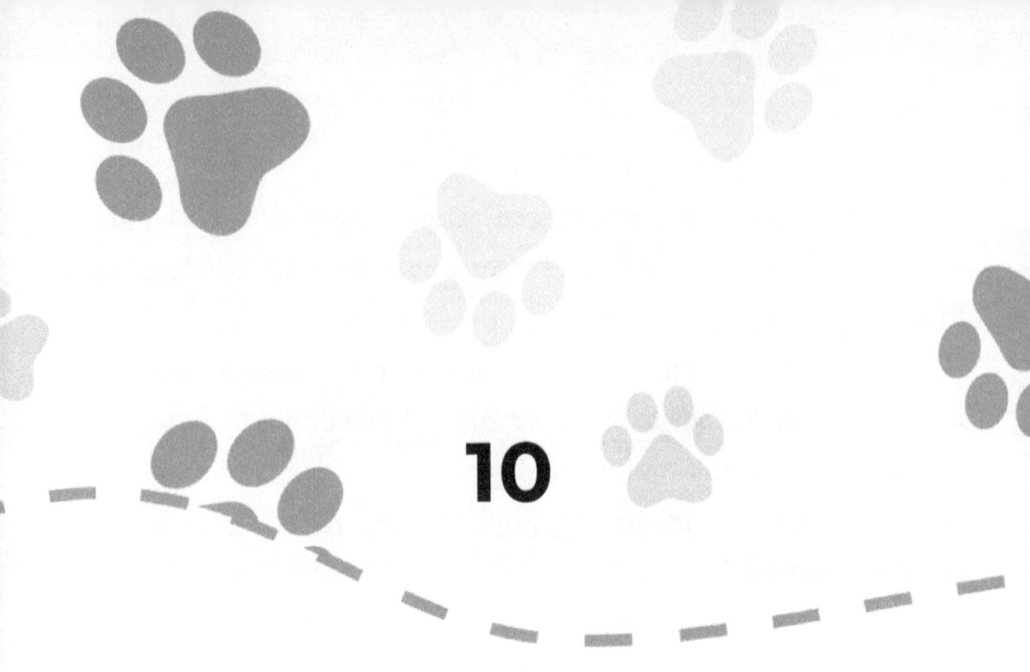

10

I knew I should try to get some sleep, but I was way too excited to make such a thing possible. I still had so many new questions spinning about my brain, and they needed answers.

Of course, Parker had remained relatively tight-lipped on the drive back home, which left me to my own internal musings.

One thought in particular dominated my mind from the get-go: "OH MY GOSH, I HAVE MAGIC NOW! WHEEEEEE!"

Eager to put my new powers to the test once I was home, I tromped outside and stood in the yard, hoping for some violent winds I could silence... But the night remained calm, still, and highly uncooperative. I briefly considered setting up a campfire to douse with whatever decided to fly forth from my hands. Then again, who said my abilities were limited to soothing the elements? Both Parker and Fluffikins had worked some form of mind control on me, and even though I didn't have anyone to influence with me now, I bet I could do almost anything I set my mind to.

Let's see...

Fluffikins had pulled the magic out of me easily without either of us having to think much about it, but now that I was left to my own devices I didn't really know where to start.

I studied the brooch affixed to my top as if it would flash the answer in big bold letters. Nope, no such luck.

I still didn't even know what my new job as a Town Witch temp entailed. What would my responsibilities be? What kind of magic would I be able to perform? Fluffikins had offered precious little by way of explanation.

Luckily, as an author by trade, I was already well accustomed to indulging my imagination. True, I mostly wrote contemporary romance set in the real world—you know, the world that up until today I'd assumed had no magic. Usually when I wrote my books, I dreamed up cute ways for the heroines to meet their heroes or huge romantic gestures for the heroes to use to win back the heroines after messing things up royally. And while I was really good at doing both those things, neither helped in exploring my newly granted paranormal abilities.

Maybe if I wanted to cast a love spell or something... Wait, was that a thing I could actually do now? My breath hitched as I realized just how endless the possibilities might be.

This, of course, made me wonder how much of the common lore surrounding witches was based on reality and how much was simply the work of overactive imaginations like mine.

I ran through the ways I'd seen witches portrayed in the popular media.

Black cat familiar? *Check.*

Green and ugly? *Heck no.* I mean, at least not green and probably not ugly, either.

Fancy spell book? *Not yet.*

A flying broom? *Wait a sec...*

Would I really be able to fly? And if so, would I need a broom?

Yes, flying, was definitely going on the to-do list.

I was half-tempted to try it now by jumping off my roof and letting those survival instincts kick in like they had with Fluffikins, but that didn't seem like the smartest stunt to pull when I had no one around to magic up some healing or call an ambulance in case it all went wrong.

Flying would definitely have to wait...

But what else could witches do?

Hmmm. Maybe I could shape shift. I mean, why not?

Determined to find something I could do on my own, I headed to the one tiny bathroom in my rental cottage, placed both hands on the counter, and stared at myself in the mirror.

Let's see. Let's see. What could I shift into?

My eyes locked on the shower curtain with its bright pink flamingo print, the one item infused with any personality in this functional but not exactly appealing room.

A flamingo, okay. I pictured the bird in my mind, cataloging everything I knew about them from their flamboyantly colored feathers right down to their preference for standing on just one foot at a time.

Squeezing my eyes shut, I held the image in my mind and pictured myself becoming that image.

Just. Think. Pink.

It was a perfectly logical method, and I gave the visualization thing all I had... But still nothing happened.

Darn it!

I opened my eyes again, ready to tell off my reflection for her refusal to follow instructions. Instead, I let out a sharp gasp.

I hadn't turned into a flamingo, but my hair *had changed* into a bright bubblegum pink that matched the color of the birds on the shower curtain perfectly.

Pink hair. I'd done that with magic—my magic!—and it didn't look half bad, considering.

Granted, I still didn't know how I'd managed to change just my hair when I'd meant to change my whole body, but I was thrilled I had done something. Even if it was just a small something.

I revisited my earlier list.

Green? *No.*

Ugly? *Not with this cool new hairdo.*

Yes, I'd harnessed my new powers and done something magical. Not a bad start at all for this novice witch. Whatever this Town Witch thing entailed, I could do it.

And who knew? Maybe I could tackle flying tomorrow.

Famous last words.

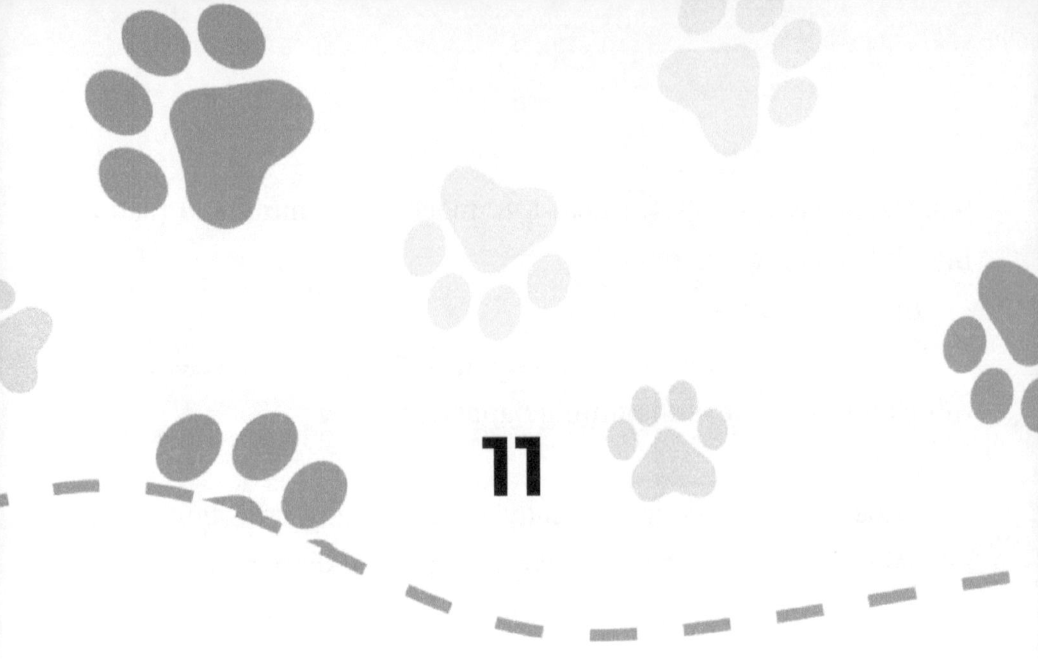

11

The next morning, a horrible screeching sound wrested me from an already fitful sleep. I bolted upright, pushing my back against the antique headboard and sending a certain black cat tumbling from the bed.

"What are you doing here?" I cried, clutching the comforter to my chest.

Mr. Fluffikins hopped back onto the foot of my bed and eyed me wearily. "I already told you we'd be picking up with your training this morning."

"But it's still dark outside." I knew I was whining like a child who'd just been woken up for the first day of school after an especially satisfying Christmas break, but I didn't care. I was too angry to worry about how I was coming across to the very person—*er,* cat—who had gotten me so angry to begin with. "Plus you said nothing about breaking into my house. That is not okay."

He squinted his eyes and growled, then straightened back up, proud and tall, showing off that little white patch on his chest. "I didn't break in. I simply used magic to gain entry," he explained in a languid drawl. "And it's six in the morning, a perfectly good time to wake up and share some breakfast with your new mentor."

I stared at Mr. Fluffikins, mouth agape. Not only had he shown up inside my bedroom at this unseemly hour, but now he expected me to make breakfast, too? Well, I hope he liked cold cereal, because that's all he was getting.

"Wait for me downstairs," I commanded, but Fluffikins did not budge. "I mean it. I'm not wearing any pants and need some time to make myself decent."

"You didn't seem too concerned about appearing decent last night," he bit out.

Oh, no. I was not about to be slut-shamed by a talking cat. "Get out of here!" I screamed and threw my pillow at him.

At least this time he listened. "The others will be here soon, so please do make haste," he informed me on his way out.

"Oh, I'll make something, all right," I muttered under my breath as I hurried to pull on the first pants I found.

When I emerged from my room, I was wearing pajama bottoms and a tank top. I refused to make myself any less comfortable when Fluffikins would likely disapprove of whatever I wore anyway.

He sat waiting at my kitchen table—or rather, on it. He'd been joined by a stern-looking woman I recognized from the boardroom yesterday, although she hadn't spoken much then and didn't make very much of an impression now.

"Tawny," Fluffikins rasped. "This is Greta. She'll be helping with your orientation today."

"Hi, Greta," I said as I passed them both and made my way to the fridge. I didn't keep much food on hand, but I had an entire shelf full of my favorite cold brew coffees. I grabbed one, twisted off the cap, and took a long, life-giving gulp. Definitely the best part of my morning, especially since my shower was still on the fritz.

When I lowered the glass bottle, I found both of my uninvited guests staring openly at me.

"Greta is our school liaison for the region," the cat said. "She looks after our interests as far as public education is concerned, much like how Barnes watches the police force."

I nodded. "Got it."

Hmmm, why did Greta get to go by her first name while Fluffikins always called Parker by his last?

Instead of answering my unspoken question, my new boss said, "As I'm sure you've already determined for yourself, she's the perfect person to begin your magical education."

Greta drummed her fingers on the tabletop and offered me a smile. "Shall we begin?"

"First, breakfast," Fluffikins corrected, then actually had the audacity to lick his chops. "I'm afraid I didn't have time to grab any for myself before coming here."

You could have come later, I thought. *Much later.*

"Breakfast, fine. What do magical cats like to eat?"

Fluffikins and Greta exchanged an amused glance.

"All cats are magical," she told me with a chuckle. "It's only people that aren't."

I ignored the implication that I should have already known the ins and outs of their strange secret world and got right back to the point. "So, what? You want some canned tuna or something?"

"Hey! That stereotype is offensive," the black cat hissed. "I'd much more prefer a fine cut of steak."

"I don't have any steak." And even if I did, I wouldn't be up to preparing it for a bossy cat first thing in the morning, especially since I only ever bought enough for one—me. "I don't even think I have tuna, come to mention it. How about a bowl of milk?"

He sighed and laid down on his side, shedding his fine black hairs all over my formerly clean kitchen table. "I suppose it will have to do, although I'll have you know, I'm lactose intolerant. Then again, I do deserve a bit of a treat with—" he looked me up and down "—all the stress I've been under lately. Next time, however, I expect you to be better prepared."

Apparently Fluffikins had never heard the whole thing about beggars and how they can't also be choosers. He was super lucky this was a job I couldn't quit and that the magic was enough of a draw to get me to swallow my pride and pour the last of my skim milk into a bowl for him.

I took my morning cereal dry.

What a way to start the day!

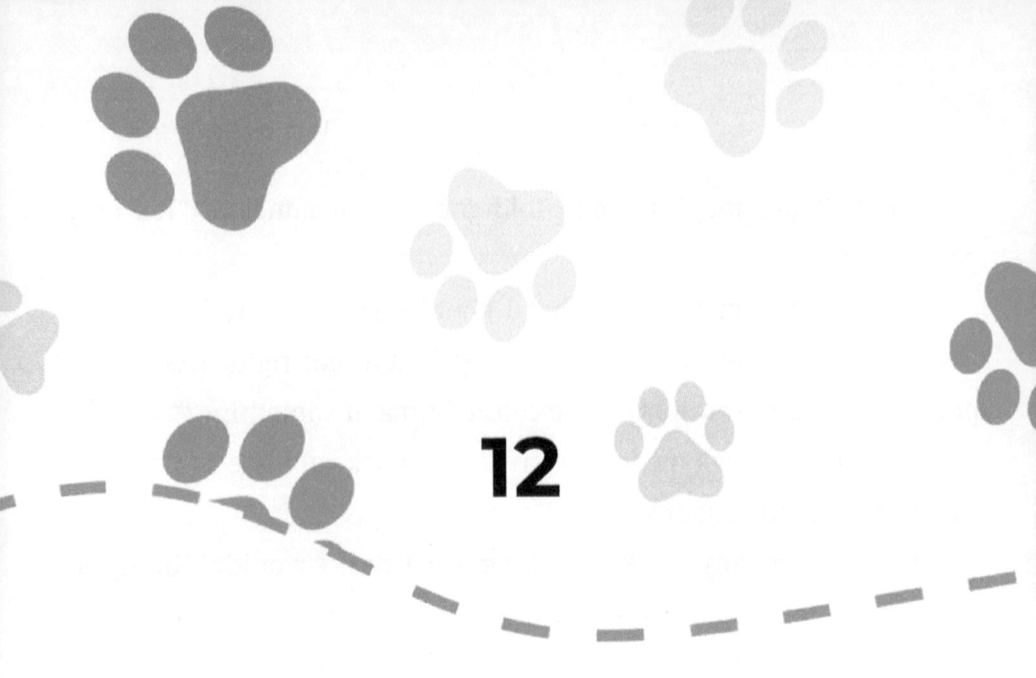

12

After a very quick yet somehow also very uncomfortable breakfast, Fluffikins excused himself, leaving me and Greta to ourselves.

"So you want to learn how to be a Town Witch?" she asked, quirking an eyebrow made of such light hair that it almost looked translucent. Something was off about Greta, but I couldn't figure out what.

Realizing I had started to stare, I forced my gaze toward the floor. "Not that I want to, per se, more like I've been instructed to."

She laughed at this, and it sounded like the tinkling of bells. "Ah, the good old PTA. Nobody applies and yet everyone gets a job."

My stomach churned at the acronym. I'd been burned by the PTA before, and even though these three letters represented an entirely different organization this time, a fresh wave of outrage still washed over me.

Greta studied me in such a way that made me wonder if her powers came with the ability to read minds. I was just about to ask when she cleared her throat and said, "Let's start at the beginning. Shall we? Do you know what a Town Witch does?"

I shook my head. "All I know is that the magic is tied to the town, and that Lila Haberdash had the job until somebody snuck into her house and killed her."

Greta cringed. Her pale skin turned pink, making her whitish-blonde hair even more pronounced. "Yes, both those things are true."

"Wait. Has it officially been ruled a murder now?" I'd been so caught up in the magic stuff that I'd done a poor job following up on the investigative side of the situation.

"Oh, yes, but we knew that right away," she answered with a flippant wave. "Magic inevitably comes to an abrupt and violent end. *Always.*"

My stomach catapulted at that, threatening to spew the delicious coffee I'd only just entrusted to it. "How?"

Greta cocked her head to the side. "How what? How did she die? Magic, obviously."

"Oh." Well, that was clear as mud. I still didn't know an awful lot about magic, but if Fluffikins was looking for evidence that I hadn't done the deed, then the means should definitely be proof enough of my innocence.

"Try not to worry about it, dear," Greta said with a pinched expression as she grabbed my hand and gave it a squeeze. "Lila lived a good life while she still had it. For now, it's your turn to take up the Beech Grove Witch mantle, and soon it will be someone else's."

"The killer's, you mean?"

She sighed and let go of my hand. "That's often how these things work, yes."

I had at least a million questions but sensed her patience with me was already wearing thin. "Okay, so what do I need to know in order to do this job?"

And to not get killed, while I'm at it.

Greta gave me the first genuine grin I'd seen since meeting her. It brightened her whole face, which, when combined with her pale blond hair, gave her an almost angelic appearance.

"Let me escort you to your new office, and I'll explain some things along the way." She crossed my living room like she owned the place and held the door open so I could exit in front of her.

Even before we stepped foot off the porch, I knew we were headed to Mrs. Haberdash's main residence. My new office was the crime scene. *Wonderful.*

"The Town Witch," Greta explained as she fell into step beside me with a smooth, even stride, "acts as a conduit for the magic that occurs naturally within the land this town was built upon. So she has her own magic but can also pull from the stores of magic that belong to the town."

I bobbed my head as if this all made perfect sense. In theory, it did. But in practice? Well, that was another matter entirely.

"Why would she need to use the land's magic?" I asked.

"To protect the town and all its residents. As you can probably guess, it's a very important job." She quickened her pace, and I had to jog to keep up. Was this to prevent me from asking any more questions? Because it only gave me more—like why would she need to be evasive with me?

Instead I asked, "So if this is such an important job, why would you choose to entrust it to me? I didn't even know magic existed until less than twenty-four hours ago."

"Oh, it wasn't my choice, dear." She snorted in a rather unladylike way that clashed with the grace with which she carried herself. "It wasn't anyone's choice. You simply happened to be at the right place at the right time."

"Or the wrong one," I couldn't help muttering aloud.

She stopped and turned back to study me again, as if searching for something she'd tried and failed to find before.

"You won't have to do much," Greta reasoned after a couple uncomfortable moments of silence. "In fact, you won't be able to."

"Because the killer already got away with all of the town's magic," I filled in.

"Yes, but he or she will be back. And soon."

Finally I caught up with her and asked, "Why's that?"

She let out a shaky breath. "Because if the magic is kept away from its source for too long, it will die—and its vessel will die right along with it."

I shivered in the cool morning air. Well, at least the stakes weren't high or anything...

13

Greta and I finished our trek to Mrs. Haberdash's main house without saying anything else. Suddenly the desire to understand this new world of magic paled in comparison to the knowledge that the killer would be returning to the scene of the crime and I'd be right there waiting.

The house sat dark and empty, as if a part of it had died along with its owner.

"I'm glad it's just us this time," I said, remembering the strange run-in I'd had with the young woman yesterday. I glanced toward the tall aged tree where her floppy sunhat had gotten stuck and was surprised to find it gone.

The girl had most definitely left without it, which meant she'd also come back. Probably in the dead of night.

"What do you mean? Who else were you expecting to find?" Greta asked, watching me closely. Always watching.

"Oh, I just meant Parker," I said, preferring to keep at least some of my cards close to the chest.

Greta shook her head. "He's already got more than enough to handle in his role as liaison to the force. Notice how there isn't any crime scene tape around? Lila was one of ours. Getting the normie police involved would only slow down the inevitable."

"The return of the killer, you mean?"

Greta's expression blanked. "What? Oh, yes. Of course, that's what I meant."

Uh-huh. I was starting to realize I couldn't even trust Greta as far as I could throw her, which wasn't far at all, given my disdain for regular exercise. Still, she was who I had right now. I'd learn whatever I could from her and then check back with Parker—or, heck, even Fluffikins—for confirmation later.

Greta smiled over at me, but I could tell it wasn't genuine. "There's no time like the present. Let's get down to business." She swept her hand in an upward flourish and the front door creaked open.

The first thing I noticed was that Mrs. Haberdash's body had been cleared away. The grand entryway sat empty, but something in the air shimmered almost like a mirage. It was as if the house itself were waiting for something. Was that something me?

I stepped inside and felt its energy envelop me like a warm bath. Granted, I much preferred hot showers, but this new sensation relaxed me all the same. In fact, it almost felt as if I were floating. That was silly, of course, given that I was standing firmly on the hardwood floor. Nothing looked different. It's just that *I felt* different.

Greta walked a slow circle around me, muttering to herself. Her whispered words were too quiet for me to make out, not until she stopped in front of me and grabbed onto both of my wrists, holding them at the pulse points. "It's calling to you. Isn't it?"

I nodded. What was the point in arguing?

"Then the first part was much easier than we expected it to be. The town has already accepted you as a host for its magic."

"But this is supposed to be temporary," I argued, unable to tear my eyes away from her intent, blistering gaze.

"That was the initial plan, yes, but we have to listen to what the land wants, too."

"Which is me?" I squeaked.

"It most certainly seems that way."

"But its magic is with Mrs. Haberdash's murderer," I pointed out without blinking, afraid to look away. I didn't like where this was headed. It was even worse than the mind control Fluffikins and Parker had both exerted over me. I could avoid a single person, but what if the land itself decided it wanted to influence me? My only hope would be to move away from town—which, sure, I didn't have roots down or anything, but it would still take time to make a run for it.

"For now. There are ways to change that, of course."

"You don't mean—"

"That you kill the killer and claim the magic for yourself?" she asked with a smirk.

I gulped hard and nodded. Did she honestly expect me to take a life as part of a stupid temp job? Magic was cool and all, but not cool enough to make me change the core of my beliefs. Murder was wrong. That should have been a given here.

Greta crossed her arms over her chest and shifted her weight from one side to the other. "Of course that's what I mean."

"I'm not killing anybody," I argued fruitlessly. For all I knew, Greta or any of the others could force me to do it with their mind control magic.

"We'll see," my supposed mentor told me with a light laugh.

My stomach dropped to the floor right beside where Mrs. Haberdash's body had lain sprawled less than twenty-four hours ago.

I liked the idea of magic, but in practice, it was proving to be way too much for me to handle. I wasn't a witch, but I was even less of a murderer.

Whether or not the intended victim was guilty of a terrible crime, it definitely wasn't my job to mete out justice.

But just how easily could I quit the Paranormal Temp Agency and resume my normal life as if nothing had ever happened?

I was beginning to feel this situation had escalated to *do or die.*

What would happen if I refused both those options?

14

Greta showed me around the house, which frankly appeared to be falling apart at the seams. She walked me through each room, describing the items in it and what purpose each held. It was boring with a capital *B*.

Seriously, how was any of this meant to contribute to my magical training? We were already working on a tight schedule here, and instead of teaching me spells or potions, my assigned mentor spent the last ten minutes describing how Mrs. Haberdash had bespelled her socks to make them three degrees warmer than room temperature. Not even the magic she'd used to accomplish the task, mind you —just the fact she'd done it at all.

How was any of this supposed to help me catch a killer? Every single time I tried to ask a more relevant question, Greta brushed me off by changing the topic. At this rate, I might learn to tailor my pants with magic by the time the day was through, but I'd never learn anything cooler like how to fly or… I don't know, evade a death blow, maybe.

The only thing that managed to keep my attention at all was the bedroom closet. Greta drifted in and began flipping through the previous tenant's wardrobe, explaining the type of Town Witch duties each selection could be worn for.

Ugh. Why did I need to know any of this?

My mind wandered yet again, turning Greta's nasally voice into a buzzing drone as I glanced around the room in search of something more interesting to ponder over. That's when the fantastic black hat sitting on the top shelf of that closet caught my eye.

Of course, I had no qualms about interrupting Greta, seeing as I hadn't really been listening anyway. "What's that?" I asked, motioning toward the black velvet hat that had been embellished with a purple satin sash.

Greta's eyes lit when they landed upon it. "Oh, good find. This is the most important item in a Town Witch's entire wardrobe and possibly the single most important item she owns. I can't believe the murderer would have left this here."

Instead of waiting for her to explain further, I grabbed the hat off the shelf and unfurled the top, finding it ended in a perfect delightful point.

A burst of energy shot straight into my chest, lighting me from the inside. The hat was speaking to me in the only way it could—through its magic. Without so much as a second thought, I plopped it right on top of my newly pinkened hair. And the exact moment that witch's hat hit my head, a vivid picture filled my mind. I saw Mrs. Haberdash going about her business, checking the mail (proof she'd received my letters!), heading to the kitchen to make tea, and then...

She dropped the kettle to the floor with a crash that sent hot water flying everywhere. I couldn't just see and hear it, I felt the burn, too. I glanced down but only saw my own feet beneath me.

"It's time then?" Mrs. Haberdash asked with a gasp while my vision had been pulled away.

I closed my eyes to snap my attention back to the scene unfolding in my mind, but all I saw was the spilled water on the floor.

A heavy weight settled on my chest, turning breathing into a struggle. The sound of echoing footsteps approached, but I couldn't see who was there with her—with me.

A rush of wind blew over me and an icy chill wrapped itself around me. The scene snapped out of focus and...

"What are you doing?" Greta cried, holding the hat clutched firmly in one manicured hand as she stared at me in horror.

"The hat," I murmured, still trying to make sense of what had just happened. "I think it wanted to show me what happened to Mrs. Haberdash."

"I told Fluffikins this was a bad idea," she spat as she shoved the hat back into the closet. After she slammed the doors shut, she formed a *C* with her thumb and index finger and moved them in a swift pendulum motion.

"We have to find out what happened. Mrs. Haberdash deserves justice." I ran toward the closet and pulled hard at it, but the doors wouldn't budge.

"That's not your job," Greta snapped.

"But I'm the new Town Witch for—"

"You're a temp!" she exploded, leaving me behind as she charged out of the room. "And I refuse to train someone with so little regard for..."

I chased her from the room, down the hall, and to the top of the stairs. Greta now stood stock-still, not moving or speaking, hardly even breathing.

"What's happening?" I asked in a desperate whisper. "Why aren't you—?"

But then my legs locked in place, frozen. In fact, the only part of me I could still move was my eyes. I directed my gaze to the base of the stairs, and that's when I saw her.

The same young woman I'd met the day before stood at the ground level with both arms raised.

"You again," she said with a cold smile. "You should have stayed out of this while you had the chance."

She was definitely right about that.

I wanted to look to Greta for guidance, but I could barely make her out in my peripheral vision. I hoped she had a plan, because I sure didn't.

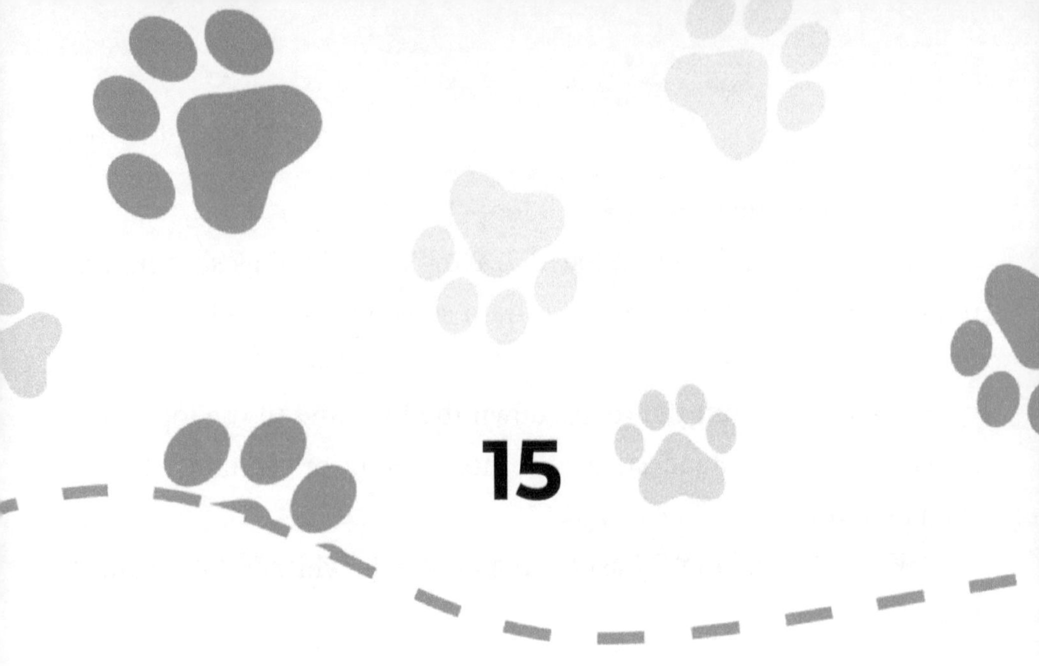

15

I twisted and wriggled, but still I couldn't escape the young witch's magical grip. I was straining hard enough to break out into a sweat, but my limbs didn't so much as twitch from all that effort. She had me in a powerful hold, and I didn't have the slightest hope of defending myself if this encounter turned violent.

"Melony Haberdash," Greta growled between clenched teeth, remaining perfectly still as she stared the other woman down. "I should have guessed it would be you."

Melony's cruel stare softened, but her grip held tight. "Just so you know, I had nothing to do with my great aunt's murder. Why would I kill her when I was next in line to inherit her position?"

She paused briefly, then her eyes snapped to me with a burning new intensity. "I found this one stalking around the property yesterday, and now she's here again today. Doesn't seem like such a coincidence. Does it?"

Greta's voice came out choked. "No, you've got it wrong. She's just the temp."

"Ha! Seems to me like you're playing right into her hand. First she steals the magic and then she gets free training from the board by playing innocent. That's pretty brilliant, actually. Maybe I should be taking notes."

Greta continued to struggle beside me. A flash of movement below her hip suggested she'd regained control of her fingers but still couldn't move her full hand yet. "She's a normie, I swear to you. At first I had my suspicions, too, but she honestly knows nothing. She just almost killed herself by replaying the murder."

My heart practically stopped at this new revelation. *I'd almost died?* Just by putting on that witch's hat? *Yikes.* That meant Greta had saved me from my foible. At first I'd thought she'd cut the encounter short because she didn't want me to discover that she was the killer, but now it seemed like she'd chosen to protect me. Is that why she was wasting time rather than giving me any real training?

Whatever her reasons for keeping me naive, I sure could use some magical ability right now.

All I had were the instincts Fluffikins had highlighted last night, but Melony had set a trap that caught us off guard. Neither Greta nor I had a chance to react before falling under her spell.

That left the one thing I'd always had, even before I knew about magic. *My words.*

It was time to speak up for myself. If I could convince Melony I wasn't a threat, maybe she would let me go.

"I didn't kill Mrs. Haberdash," I shouted at her through tears.

"I've never killed anyone. I shouldn't even be here. This is clearly business that I have no part of. I never asked to be made a witch. I just write books!"

Melony studied me, sizing me up the same way Greta had earlier. She must have found what she was looking for because a few seconds later the magical vise snapped open and I fell to the ground.

"Where's my aunt's hat?" the young witch asked me as I picked myself up.

I turned back toward the room we'd just exited. "I'll go get it for—"

"No!" Greta screamed, but it was too late. Melony was already charging up the stairs and into her late aunt's bedroom.

"What have you done?" Greta muttered, still bound tightly by Melony's magic.

"But she said she didn't..." My words fell away. Why had I believed her when she clearly had the most to gain from Mrs. Haberdash's untimely demise?

"She's not the killer," Greta admitted as she turned her head very slightly to look toward me. Little by little, the spell was thawing, but would Greta be free in enough time to stop Melony from getting away?

She grunted from the strain of trying to break the spell, then added, "I could tell she was speaking the truth with us just now, but—"

"Yes!" Melony cried from the other room, causing Greta to stop mid-sentence. "I've got you now."

"Hey! What did you see? Do you know who did it?" I asked as she rushed back down the stairs, cradling the old hat against her chest, without so much as a second glance toward me and Greta. Maybe I should have continued to play dumb, but if she'd spoken truthfully before, perhaps she would do so now. My gift of verbal persuasion was the only option I had, since I didn't know how to summon my new magic on command.

But Melony ignored us both, flinging open the front door and charging outside. As soon as the door slammed behind her, the hold on Greta released completely.

She fell to the floor, weak and heaving.

"What happened?" I asked as I helped her back onto her feet.

Greta's eyes appeared vacant as she explained, "She used the hat to call up the murder scene just like you did, but as a more experienced witch she knows how to manipulate the memories so they don't pose a threat to her."

"She saw the murderer," I said with a sharp inhale.

Greta nodded meekly. "Yes. And she's on her way to kill him to assume the town magic."

I'd done this. I'd found the hat and then I'd guided Melony straight to it. I still didn't know who'd killed Mrs. Haberdash, but it would be my fault when that person met their untimely end. And it would be my fault when the crazed teenager was filled with some of the strongest magic in the region, which I doubted she'd use to make things better for its residents.

Gulp.

16

Two choices. That's what I had at this point.

I could buckle down to help Greta, Parker, Fluffikins, and crew find—and save—the murderer. But once we saved him or her, did they want me to do the killing for them?

I was still so confused about what was expected of me here. Magic was weird, and yet the rules that governed it were weirder still. It also seemed like they shifted according to who I was talking to at the moment. If Greta wanted me to stay on permanently, what did Fluffikins think? Or Parker? Did they expect me to kill for them? If I remained steadfast in my refusal, would they force me to comply?

This brought me to option number two. I could get the heck out of here and pretend this whole thing had never happened.

"Okay, so good luck with everything!" I shouted to Greta before I sprinted down the stairs just as fast as my feet would carry me.

What? I hadn't survived thirty-five years on this earth by having no sense of self-preservation. All the other players here had magic. *Real magic!*

Yeah, they'd given me a temporary dose, but I definitely didn't know enough to protect myself. Besides, Melony was already on her way to off the killer and assume her aunt's stolen magic. They didn't need me as a temp anymore, and they definitely didn't need me as a contract killer. Way too much could go wrong there, and I refused to jeopardize my entire life and future.

Now if I didn't help them, which I wasn't going to, my life would still be pretty up in the air. No matter what happened, I'd be living in the backyard of a murderer—Melony.

That would be bad. *Hmmm.*

I ran through my options a couple more times while racing back to the guest cottage I called home. Despite everything, at least my running shoes were finally living up to their name.

By the time I reached the front door, I'd made up my mind all over again. It was time to check the real estate listings online and move myself as far from this crazy place as I could. Honestly, the sooner the better. I'd just fire up my laptop and…

And nothing, at least not yet.

It seemed I had a guest.

"I heard trouble is brewing," Mr. Fluffikins announced from his perch on the back of my sofa, one paw crossed daintily over the other.

I eyed him suspiciously. "Yeah, it just started like five minutes ago. How did you get here so fast? Did you teleport or something?"

He hung his head and laughed. "Of course not. *I flew.*"

"Oh, yes, because that makes more sense."

The black cat remained seated, watching me closely.

I sighed, knowing if I didn't say something soon, he'd start making all sorts of demands. I still didn't want this stupid temp job, and I wasn't exactly up to playing the kindly hostess, either.

"Why are you here?" I said with a scowl. "You don't need me anymore."

Fluffikins stood and stretched, arching his back high like a cat on Halloween or a seriously talented yogi, or both. "Actually, we need you more than ever. Come with me."

"I'm sorry, this is all a little much for me. I'd really rather not die today. Or any day, really. But especially not today. Thanks."

"Then it's imperative you stay under my protection, and I can't look after you if you're running away. Now can I?"

Crud. He had a point.

I rolled my shoulders, but the nervous tension remained. "Why am I a part of this? Why do you need me at all?"

"You might want to be sitting for this," Fluffikins said slowly, almost compassionately.

I sunk down onto the sofa, and Fluffikins came over to situate himself on my lap.

"Now pet me," he ordered, locking me in his glowing golden gaze. I knew petting an animal was supposed to be good for your blood pressure, but I needed a lot more than that to calm me down.

So I refused. "I'm good, thanks."

"Pet me!" he commanded in a way that brooked no argument.

He didn't force me with his powers, but I still complied, finding it easier to get through whatever he wanted so I could carry on with my normal life—boring but happy, just what I needed.

The moment my fingers made contact with his silky black hair, a new vision flooded my brain. It was like what I'd experienced with the hat, but even more vivid, possibly because it was being projected by a living being instead of an inanimate object.

Fluffikins purred softly but otherwise didn't interrupt as I explored his memories.

With a hitched breath, I yanked my hand back, cutting the vision short. I'd already seen more than enough. Much to my surprise, Fluffikins had revealed an answer I didn't expect but also couldn't contest after having witnessed it so clearly.

"You did it," I choked out, sliding him off my lap and hopping back to my feet. "You ordered the hit on Mrs. Haberdash."

But why was he telling me now? And why hadn't he told me before? Was this some kind of Bond villain moment where he revealed the beauty of his plan before offing the victim?

And where did I actually fit into all of this?

Was it just dumb luck, or was something greater at play here?

I didn't want to know, but I needed to find out.

Knowledge was power, and it might have been the only thing that could save me now.

17

I pointed a shaky finger at Fluffikins, who was still seated on the sofa in front of me. "You killed my landlady. She was your... your colleague, if not your friend. Why should I listen to anything you have to say? And why should I help you?"

"I didn't kill her," the cat said in that strange breathless way of his, not so much as lifting a paw as he regarded me calmly.

I, however, continued to shout. "But you hired the killer. That makes you just as good as."

He stood and stretched. "I don't have time to debate this with you, Tawny, so I'll cut straight to the point. Do you want more people to die or not?"

Honestly, I just wanted this to all go away, but despite all the magic involved in this horrible situation, that didn't seem to be an option. "I still don't know why I'm a part of this. Can't you just go away and leave me alone?"

"We never meant to involve anyone outside of the board," he admitted with a sad shake of his head. "But when you stumbled upon Lila's body, we had no choice but to bring you in."

"You knew I didn't kill her. This whole time, you knew!" I sputtered. "And since you're the one who ordered the hit, I'm willing to bet you know who the real killer is, too. So, why make me a temp? Why give me magic at all?"

"We took you in for your protection. The rest of it was a ruse, to misdirect anyone who showed up to sniff around Lila's murder with the hopes of gaining her magic. And, look, that's precisely what happened. You would have been a target, no matter what, having shown up yesterday morning."

"You made me a target!" This was the one point I just couldn't get past. Even though I'd accidentally walked onto the scene, there had to be countless other ways to keep me safe. Giving me magic seemed mighty extreme, especially since they hadn't done much to teach me to use it. What was the whole point?

"You were already a target," Fluffikins shouted back, losing his calm for the first time since the conversation had started. "Playing into it bought us all time, but now that time has run out. We can't stand here arguing. We need to act while we still have time!"

"I don't understand. If Melony isn't coming for you or for me, then who is she after?"

"She's going after the actual killer, the person who absorbed the town magic. She wants it for herself by any means possible. We need to get to him before Melony does."

"To who?" I demanded, stomping my foot. The more Fluffikins

explained, the less I understood. “Who are we rushing off to save now?”

“The person who killed Lila Haberdash. Barnes.”

My mind kind of exploded then. Fluffikins had ordered Parker to kill Mrs. Haberdash? I really wanted to know the why, but I also believed Fluffikins when he said our time was running out.

I still had to ask. “Parker killed her? Why? Why would he do that?” My voice trembled as I tested these words aloud.

“Because it’s what Lila wanted,” he admitted. His chest heaved with the weight of this revelation, making the little white patch bob within the mass of black fur.

I raised an eyebrow at him. I believed what he was telling me, but that didn’t mean I understood. A part of me doubted I’d ever fully understand, no matter how many questions I asked. “She wanted someone to murder her?”

“Yes, and she trusted us to get it done right.” He hopped off the couch and landed by my feet.

“None of this makes any sense!”

Fluffikins stared up at me with bright golden eyes that seemed to see right through me. “Can you please just trust me on this? We’ve lost too much time already. Do you want to save Barnes or not?”

I’d seen the look in Melony’s eyes as she first questioned Greta and me and then charged out of the house with that enchanted hat. She was out for blood. *Parker’s blood.*

And I also knew deep in my gut that Parker was an okay guy. He’d been kind to me and seemed earnest in wanting to help me. Even if he’d been the one to get me mixed up in this whole magical business

—which I still did not appreciate, by the way—it didn't mean he deserved to die for it.

"But how can I help? I'm just a human," I mumbled, feeling so useless in that moment.

Fluffikins's eyes twinkled. "Ah, but you have magic now. What do you say? Join the good guys?"

Well, what choice did I have now? The stakes felt much higher now that someone I knew and liked was in jeopardy. I sighed and nodded. "If you're sure you need me and that you'll keep me safe, then I'm in."

"Great. We've already wasted more time than I'd prefer, but luckily Melony is a low level witch. She'll have needed to travel by the traditional means, so we still have time to beat her to our destination. Follow me." The cat ran to the door and let himself outside.

I followed after, wondering if I was crazy for agreeing to help with what little information I'd been given.

"Now grab my tail," Fluffikins shouted into the still morning sky.

I crouched down, closed my eyes, and clenched that tail like my life depended on it. The soft fluffy appendage turned hard in my grip and then it started to grow. When I opened my eyes again, I was no longer holding onto a tail but rather a broomstick, and I was no longer standing in my front yard.

I was flying.

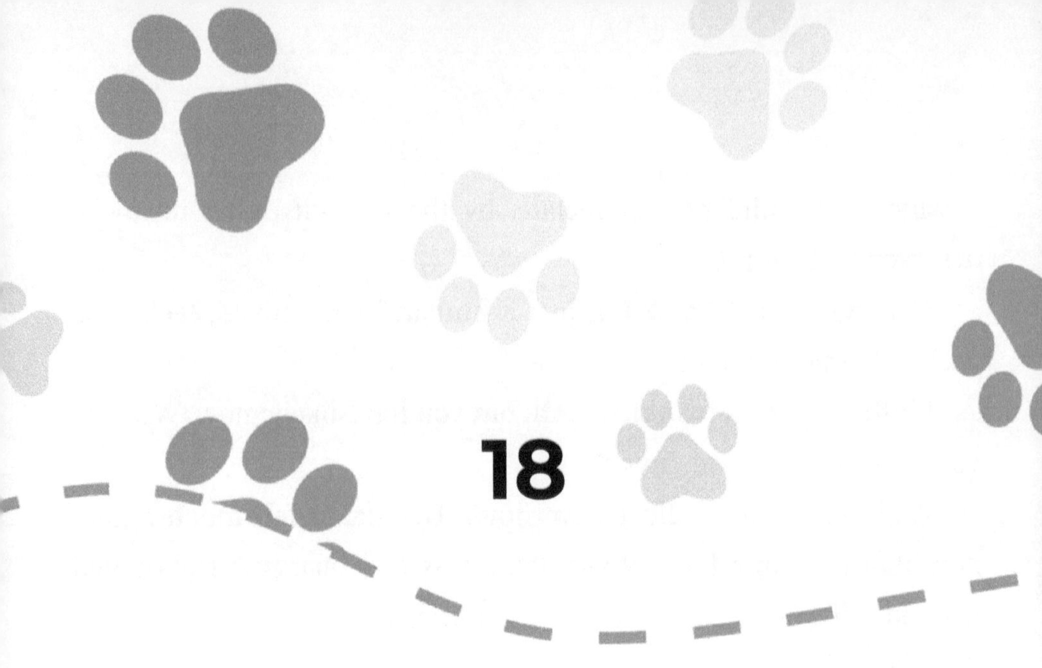

18

The speeding wind whipped the bottoms of my pajama pants against my ankles—or rather it was the speeding me on top of the broom that I'd somehow managed to conjure from my talking feline escort's tail.

Fluffikins flew effortlessly at my side. He looked as if he were suspended mid-leap as he zipped through the air like a bullet.

So there we were, racing against time to save a killer from being killed, because apparently he'd killed for the right reasons while his would-be killer wanted to kill him for the wrong reasons.

Yeah, I was confused, too.

I was also more than a little upset that I'd ended up wearing my frumpy PJs for this momentous encounter. I didn't have much time to worry about either of these things, though, because Fluffikins and I arrived at our destination a couple short minutes after we'd departed.

I recognized the office complex from my visits the day before. This seemed like a good place to start, but would Parker even be there? He'd told me he had a regular policeman's job, too, which meant he probably didn't spend all day waiting around Paranormal HQ just in case the boss cat needed him.

Heck, for all I knew, Melony might have found him already.

Mr. Fluffikins muttered something under his breath, and the glass-topped conference room opened up like a blossoming flower. Pink glittering magic swirled about us as the building sucked us in like a Venus flytrap.

My broom disappeared and I lurched toward the floor. But then the pink stuff caught me and guided me gently into one of the many executive chairs that lined the table. This felt similar to the sensation I'd experienced in Mrs. Haberdash's house, like I was floating in a bath of perfectly temperate water. The pink pulsed gently, calming and comforting me, providing a featherlight massage.

Fluffikins landed in front of me in a perfectly graceful and well executed maneuver that was all his own. The pink magic parted to allow him passage rather than coaxing him forward like it had done for me.

"I hereby call an emergency board meeting," he said, his words echoing around the room. "All liaisons are required."

The pink magic gathered into a ball and bounced up through the open roof into the sky above.

"Wh-what's going on? Where's P-Parker?" I sputtered. I felt the absence of the atmospheric magic acutely despite having only been under its effects for a few seconds.

Fluffikins paced the length of the table anxiously. "He's on his way, along with the others. I rarely call an emergency meeting, but when I do, they have no choice but to travel here immediately."

"What's all this pink glittery stuff?" I asked, watching as it twisted and danced just above the open ceiling. "I didn't see it when I was here yesterday."

"You didn't have magic when you were in the board room yesterday. It was here, but you couldn't yet see it. It's always here," he answered distractedly as he continued to cross the table back and forth.

"What is it?" I wanted to know, but more than that I needed to keep him talking, to protect me from my own thoughts and worries.

"It's but a small piece of the earth's most concentrated and most powerful magic, taken right from its very core. Each of our agencies around the globe has been granted a part to keep us connected to the whole. It works to stabilize the balance within each region and prevent any one center from gaining too much power." He spoke so smoothly and eloquently that I wondered if he was quoting something or someone verbatim.

"How does it do that?"

Pace, pace, pace.

I was growing more frightened by the minute, especially since Fluffikins appeared rattled, too.

He took a few more loops of the table and then plopped himself down across from me. "By sparking non-magical humans' so-called intuition and influencing them to act in a way that is good for humanity as a whole, even if they believe they are acting on selfish desires."

"Huh. I've got to admit, this is all a bit out there. I was just coming around to this whole Town Witch thing, and now you expect me to wrap my head around a living strain of magic that balances all of humanity?"

He shrugged. "You asked. I merely answered."

"Why am I here?"

"Because the magic chose you. There was a reason you discovered Lila's body, that you bumped into Barnes, even that you were there when Melony showed up to reclaim the hat."

"I'm nobody special."

He nodded. "My inclination would be to agree with you, but the magic is always right."

I folded my arms across my chest. "If the magic is so high and mighty, then how come terrible things still happen every day? People are murdered, as we well know. Kids are taken from their parents, wars kill millions. Why doesn't the magic stop any of that from happening?"

"Balance encompasses both dark and light, good and bad. It's difficult to understand for the uninitiated. Still, it has chosen you as someone who will play a significant role in what is to come."

"Now there are prophecies?" I gasped as goosebumps rose to my arms.

The cat's eyes flashed, but he quickly looked away, focusing his gaze just over my left shoulder. "No, no. I have no idea what happens next, but whatever it is, you'll be an important player."

I bit my lip as I thought about this. Part of me wanted to yell at Fluffikins for dragging me deep into this agency mess without explaining any of it in a way I could actually understand, but another very big part of me understood that I'd have never agreed to get mixed up in things here if he'd led with any of the craziness that had come to light over the last few minutes.

"What if I'm not enough?" I asked instead. This wasn't just my greatest worry now. It was my greatest fear in life. I hadn't been enough for my ex-husband. My rate of producing books was quickly not becoming enough for my literary agent. With all those failures to my name, could I be enough for something that mattered this much?

Fluffikins fixed his eyes on me, unblinking. "Oh, but Tawny. You already are."

19

Not even two minutes after Fluffikins's summons, the other members of the board began descending upon the room to join us at the table.

First came Greta. "I put the best wards on the house that I could to bolster the ones already there. Lila's spells are fading fast now that she's no longer in residence," she informed us before she'd even landed in her spot.

Next came the old guy in the suit. "You've removed me from a very important procession, I'll have you know."

"It will wait," his cat boss snarled. "What we have now affects the entire region across all departments."

The old guy blinked hard and his mouth hung slightly agape. "All?"

Fluffikins nodded solemnly as two more liaisons fell from the sky and took their rightful seats. "Now let's begin."

"Wait? Where's Parker?" I choked out as I searched the sky for his familiar form. "Why isn't he here yet?"

"If he is able, then he will come," Greta said from the seat beside me, reaching under the table to squeeze my hand.

If? But hadn't Fluffikins said attendance was required? Did Greta mean he might already be dead or incapacitated?

I clung tight to her hand, needing whatever small comfort I could find there.

"Beginning now." Fluffikins began to pace up and down the table once again. This time like a general. "First let me say, I'm sorry to have acted without the full board's knowledge, especially now that I see my quick action did not have a positive effect on the outcome."

He paused, but nobody spoke to fill the silence. We all waited.

"Lila Haberdash was compromised," the cat revealed. "And so she requested that I organize her death so that we could control the passage of the town's magic to its next host."

Gasps rose up around the room. Only Greta beside me did not react. She already knew, I realized then. She knew everything, all of it. And she clearly disagreed, at least with my involvement in the fallout. Not because she didn't like me, but because she wanted to protect me. My first impression of her had been completely wrong.

"How was she compromised?" the old guy asked.

Fluffikins stopped and raised a paw to his forehead as if in pain. "Lila's grandniece, Melony Haberdash, manipulated her grandfather into revealing the family's magical legacy, including how power was passed from one heir to the next."

"So she was going to kill Mrs. Haberdash," I supplied.

"Yes, Lila certainly thought so. Magic isn't meant to be revealed until the preparations for a transfer are nearly complete, precisely to prevent this kind of thing from happening. But Lila's brother, Melony's grandfather, always resented that the magic had skipped him as the first born and gone to his sister. My guess is Melony didn't have to press too hard to gain the information she sought."

"I warned you," the old guy said with a sad shake of his head. "Lila was a great asset to this town, but she didn't come from good stock. That brother of hers never recovered from losing out on the position, even though he wasn't even suited to it in the first place. Now he's sending his heirs two generations down to cause trouble? We should have taken him out years ago when he first started causing trouble."

"Lila never wanted harm to come to her family. I think a small part of her always hoped they could reconcile," Greta answered. "It was only right to respect her wishes."

"Lila was one of the good ones," Fluffikins agreed. "Unfortunately, her family took advantage of her kind heart."

"What's Melony going to do now? And how do we know she's acting alone? If her grandfather started this, couldn't he still be in on it?" I asked aloud. On the inside I still yearned for Parker. What if Melony had already gotten to him? What if I never saw him again?

"We don't know what the plan is, only that it needs to be stopped," Greta explained softly, still holding tight to my hand.

"Well, where is she? Can't we lock her up in a magical prison and throw away the key? We've got to do something!"

"It's not that simple," the cat argued.

"Magic always comes to a violent end," Greta said, echoing the same warning she'd given me earlier.

"Then why would you put Parker at risk like this? If you knew Melony was coming for Lila, shouldn't you have all known that she would come for him when she realized what had happened?" A mass of rage began to form in my gut. They'd knowingly endangered Parker. It wasn't right.

Fluffikins sighed. "We didn't have as much time as we'd hoped. Ultimately, Barnes volunteered to pick up the mantle because he didn't want to risk Greta in his place."

She squeezed my hand under the table. "He said the worst thing that could happen would be to compromise our schools. If we want a better world, then we need to guard the future like the treasure it is."

No wonder I liked the guy. He was handsome, brave, and loved kids. If I wasn't such a pessimist about love, I may have succumbed to the crush that was threatening to overtake my heart. Instead I swallowed down all the many things I was feeling in that moment and asked the one thing that mattered most. "How do we stop Melony?"

I decided then and there that I would help in whatever way I could. Whether it was to protect Parker or to avenge him, I was fully in.

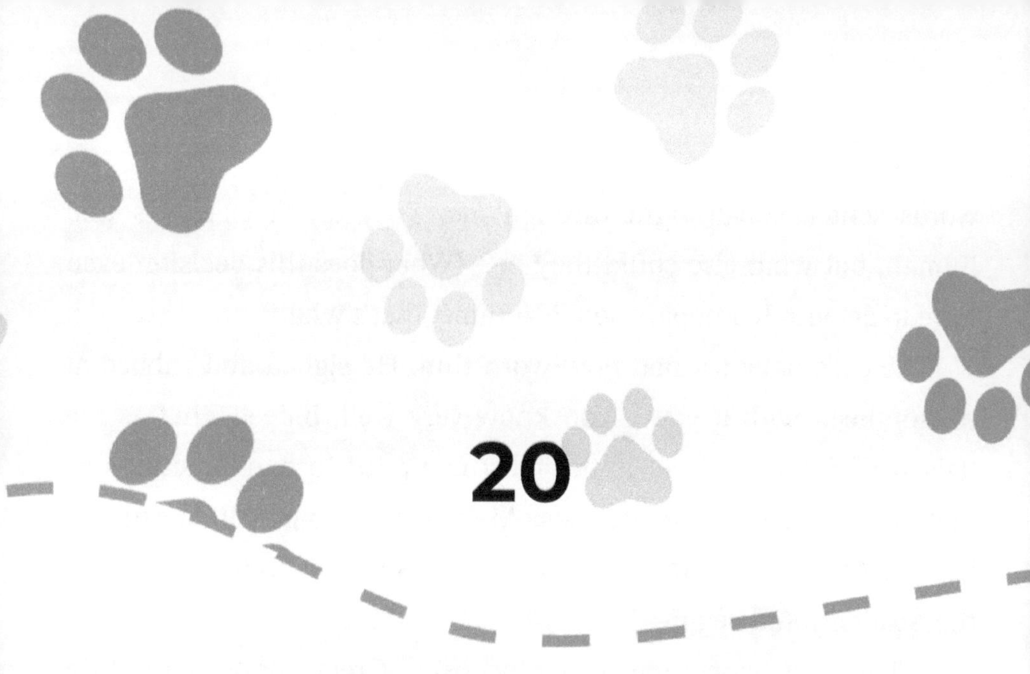

20

Despite the urgency of my question and the fact that it was a pretty great one to ask, Fluffikins failed to acknowledge it.

Perhaps he would have, but one of the liaisons immediately hopped to her feet and placed a hand on each of her ample hips. “Why wasn't the entire board informed? I personally would have loved to hear about all this before it all hit the fan.”

“Apologies, Connie,” the cat drawled. Was he actually sucking up to her when he was the one in charge? “Lila preferred that as few people as possible know about the plan to preemptively end her life. As you know, it's the ultimate sacrifice and highest duty for a Town Witch to die protecting her town. She knew what needed to be done, and she didn't want anyone trying to change her mind.”

“But *she* knew.” Connie pointed at Greta accusingly. Her growled words sent a shiver right through me. They didn't exactly sound human, but what else could they be? "What does this decision even have to do with her department? Nothing, that's what!"

The cat's patience had now worn thin. He sighed and rubbed at his forehead with a paw. "You know very well, indeed, that as the liaison of Schools, Greta is the most equipped to handle situations that impact the future. Besides, Melony is young, still a student herself. At least once this summer is over, she is expected to head to the Academy and begin—"

"That's not happening now, obviously," Greta interjected with a sullen expression.

"And Parker was informed," Fluffikins continued as he directed an unhappy glare at Connie, "because the impending crime fell directly into his role as liaison to the Force."

"Still, Commerce would have liked to be notified," Connie pouted, refusing to back down.

"Agriculture, too," the plain-looking middle-aged man beside her chimed in. Excluding me and Parker, he appeared to be the youngest in the group by at least two decades.

Everyone's eyes sought out the centenarian in the business suit.

"Nah," he said with a wave of his hand. "Cemetery is good. We prefer not to handle them until they need us to."

"Cemeteries?" I whispered to Greta.

"Yes, it's one of the five essential regional departments."

Now having heard a few new departments mentioned in rapid succession, I started a mental checklist. The PTA board had Police,

Schools, Commerce, Agriculture, and Cemeteries—then there was the Town Witch and Fluffikins, of course. Whatever he did.

I decided to come right out and ask him. "Everybody here has a job, even me, although I'm just a temp. What's your role, Mr. Fluffikins?" I used the Mr. assuming he'd be more likely to answer my question if I showed him some respect in asking it.

"Why, I'm the Diplomat, of course. It is me who is in charge of this region as a whole." Well, I guessed that made sense. Little by little, I was starting to get it, but...

"I just have one question, though. Actually two. Wait, it's three."

He rolled his paw to signal for me to go ahead.

"Okay, so first, where's Parker? Also, how do we stop Melony? And if you have time, please explain why this place is called the Paranormal Temp Agency. It seems like nobody here is a temp except for me."

"Parker will be here as soon as he can if he can, and once we have him here, Melony will no doubt come to us. It's the best-case scenario since we have the global magic source to protect us."

I glanced up toward the ceiling where the glittering atmospheric magic had settled in like a heavy pink fog.

Fluffikins continued, "You're our only temp currently, but make no mistake, we have quite the revolving door of helpers."

"If that's the case, why not hire more people to your board on a full-time basis? Is it because you don't want to pay benefits?"

Across the table Connie chuckled, making her over-sized bosom bounce. I couldn't tell if she liked me or not, but I could definitely tell she wasn't a fan of Fluffikins.

The cat rolled his eyes before fixing them back on me. "The magical balance is in constant flux, and thus our needs change. A majority of magic users keep their abilities discreet and go about to live a mostly normal human life."

"So it's only you guys who are supercharged?"

"We're the strongest," Greta said, "because we're able to use our abilities regularly. Practice makes perfect, after all." Now she finally sounded like a teacher. As I got to know everyone better, it was easier to understand how they fit into their roles.

"Okay, so let me see if I'm understanding this correctly," I said. "Most people don't have magic, and most of the people who *do* have magic don't really use it."

"Yes, other than instinctively as you saw during our orientation last night," the cat supplied.

Had that startling display of elemental wrath really only happened last night? Wow. It took me a second to process that before moving on.

"The liaisons are the strongest magic users because they use their powers regularly," I surmised.

"Yes, that's right," Greta encouraged.

"Okay, so then why are we all so afraid of this Melony chick? She's only—what?—eighteen?" I shuddered at the realization that I could practically be her mother. Thank goodness, I wasn't.

Everyone watched and waited for me to push forward with my train of thought, and so I did.

"She's not a liaison, which means she is not a regular magic practitioner. We know she has some, because of the confrontation Greta and I had with her, but—can someone please explain this next part—why is a room full of the region's most powerful magic folk hiding from a little girl?"

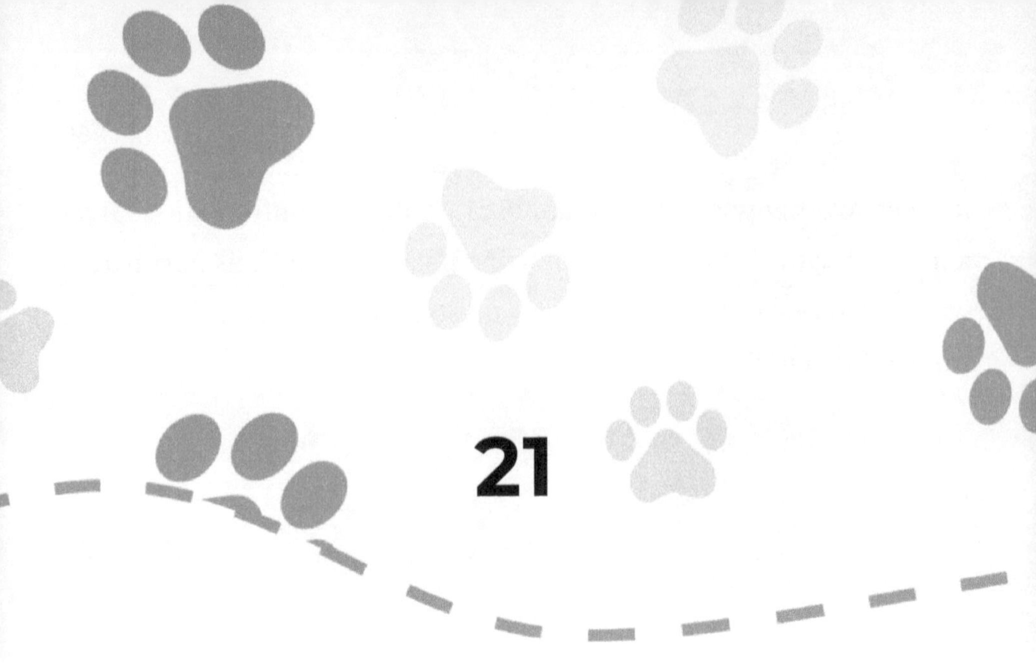

21

Nobody spoke until at last Fluffikins took a deep breath and said, "That's not a bad question. We could easily overpower Melony, but just because we can doesn't mean we should."

I threw my hands up in the air—something I was doing a lot of lately, quite frankly. "Seriously, guys? One second you present yourselves as these noble defenders of the balance, and the next you talk yourselves out of easily solving a very simple problem. You do realize it's only going to turn into a much bigger problem, right? I mean, what happened to that whole noble balance spiel you just gave me like three minutes ago?"

Greta placed both hands flat on the table in front of her. The whitish eyebrows framing bright blue eyes gave her an almost lupine appearance. "I understand there's much about our world you can't yet grasp, but there are nuances, which however small and seemingly inconsistent are important to uphold, especially for those in positions of power."

"So you're not dealing with Melony because—*what?*—it would look bad? Greta, you're the one who told me magic always comes to a violent end. Melony's the instigator here, so why aren't you taking action?" Whether or not I'd ended up with the PTA by some stupid fluke, I was here now and I would make my opinions known. Namely that their attempt at an explanation made little to no sense.

When Greta shook her head, one of her tight blonde curls fell out of place. "It's not our place to end a life."

"Are you kidding me?" I exploded. I couldn't help it. "You're the one who ended Mrs. Haberdash's!"

"At her request, yes. She made a sacrifice to protect this town, but also to protect her next of kin." Greta looked tired but not any less steadfast in her explanation. Even though their supposed logic wasn't making much sense to me, it clearly held up with her.

I softened my voice. Greta wasn't the enemy here. Flawed thinking aside, nobody in this room presented a threat to me or this town. Melony on the other hand... "Why would she want to save somebody who wanted to kill her? And what exactly do you plan to do when Melony shows up with the goal of offing Parker? And for the last time *where's Parker?* Because he certainly isn't here, and it seems plain old stupid to sit around waiting for whatever happens next when we can get out there and control the future!"

Fluffikins tsked. "Spoken like a true normie. Have you been listening to anything Greta or I have tried to explain?"

I turned all my frustration on the small black cat. "Yes, I'm listening, but all I hear is words and excuses. You have the power to end this, but instead you're sitting here helpless. You're not helpless, and you should be out there helping Parker!"

Fluffikins flexed his paws and the claws shot out menacingly. "I've never been so—"

"*Whoa, whoa, whoa.* Calm down." Parker's familiar voice floated down from above as he drifted toward his seat. "I'm right here."

The pink magic in the air shimmered briefly, then whooshed back to the ceiling. Now that everyone was accounted for, the glass ceiling closed in on itself, shutting out the larger world.

Greta placed a hand on my side and leaned toward me like she wanted to say something to me in private, but I didn't care to find out what that was.

Parker was here! He was okay!

I leaped out of my chair and ran over to hug him. It didn't matter that I hardly knew him—he was alive and quite possibly a hero. The fact that he'd been in uncertain danger made me realize just how much I instinctively liked him, right from the beginning.

He stood to meet me and winced as I wrapped both arms around him, but then settled into the embrace.

"Are you okay?" I whispered, pulling back to look into his eyes.

The sharp gray appeared dulled, but his smile appeared genuine. "I'm okay," he confirmed with a relieved sigh.

Fresh cuts and scrapes covered his face, neck, and arms, but none of them appeared too serious. What had held him back? Had he gone ahead and acted while the rest of the board sat here twiddling their thumbs?

I wouldn't put that past him.

Parker was one of them, but he was also different.

More human somehow.

Maybe it was because as a policeman, he was accustomed to seeing things in black and white—right or wrong. And what Melony wanted to do was wrong. Clearly, he saw that.

But despite these convictions, would he act against the boss cat's wishes? Had he already? I knew I was assuming a lot, but a part of me just knew Parker was one of the good guys. Maybe the best guy.

"I was so worried," I murmured, tightening my hold. I wanted him to be that hero, but even more than that I just wanted him to be safe and here with me. That crush I'd tried to prevent from taking hold had definitely wrapped its vise grip around my heart. *Stupid feelings.*

"Where were you?" Fluffikins demanded, stalking over to us. "Why the delay?"

Parker let me go. For a moment, he hung his head as if too tired to answer. But then he picked himself back up and said, "Melony came to see me."

Melony.

22

I put a hand on Parker's shoulder.

He flinched before glancing away. The smile that followed came a couple seconds too late to be natural.

Ugh. I was really worried about him now. Had something terrible already happened? Was he merely putting on a strong front for me and the others?

"What do you mean she came to see you?" I pressed, willing—*begging*—him to tell me the truth. "Are you sure you're okay?"

He pressed his lips in a straight line, then pulled out the chair in front of him and took a seat. "I'm here. Aren't I?"

"What happened?" I asked, refusing to leave his side even though it seemed I'd been dismissed.

"Enough, Tawny. Take your seat," Fluffikins commanded as he paced back to the head of the table, then plopped onto his rear. "Now. Give us the full report, Barnes."

I kept my eyes glued on Parker as I trudged back to my seat beside Greta.

Everyone waited with bated breath.

Parker folded his hands in front of him and sighed. "She caught up with me while I was on my way into the station. There were too many normies around, so I led her to an empty lot on the outskirts of town. I expected her to jump straight into an assault once we were both out of our cars, but instead she wanted to talk. Said the Town Witch job was hers, that it was bad enough her great aunt Lila had stolen it right out from under her grandfather, that she wasn't going to let the wrong person have the job for even a second longer."

"But you're here now, and you say you're okay," I said, dumbfounded. "So, what happened?"

"Tawny, silence!" Fluffikins bellowed and followed it up with a low, threatening growl. "I realize you have a lot of questions, but you are not the one who's in charge here."

Parker frowned. "She told me to surrender, but I refused. That was when she attacked. I tried not to hurt her, but she came at me so fast, I couldn't avoid…" His voice cracked, and he stopped speaking.

"We promised Lila she would remain unharmed," Greta interjected, popping to her feet so fast, her chair fell back behind her.

Parker ran his hands through his hair and let out a choked sob. "I know. I'm so sorry. It's the magic. With Lila's plus my own, it's too much. I couldn't control it."

"This is very worrying, indeed," Fluffikins said with a flick of his sleek black tail.

"I would have gotten here sooner, but I didn't want to lead Melony right to our HQ. That is, if she even managed to survive," Parker offered meekly. "I didn't know what else to do. I'm sorry if I've complicated matters for the board."

"So what happens now?" I asked when no one else moved to speak. "The threat is gone, right? So everything goes back to normal?"

"But at what cost?" Greta bit out, wrapping her arms around herself as she swayed on her feet. "You've defied Lila's last wish. Melony was the only remaining heir to the Haberdash legacy. Other than her grandfather, of course."

What was going on here? None of these explanations were making things any clearer, so I asked a question even though Fluffikins had ordered me to stay silent. "So Melony would have become the Town Witch eventually, anyway? If that's the case, why would she kill her aunt? Just to make it happen a little sooner?"

"She wasn't ready," Greta said, reaching down to rub my shoulder but I ripped it away. "Melony still has a lot of growing up to do first, and Lila had already become so ill. She wouldn't have been able to fight off an attack if it had come."

"But Parker has the powers now. Whether or not Melony is okay, the Haberdash legacy is dead."

"That doesn't mean the people need to be," Greta countered.

Connie, the well-dressed head of Commerce, spoke up next. "By appointing someone outside of her family, Lila knowingly destroyed her own line."

Greta's bright blue eyes flashed red. It startled me so much, I kept my mouth clamped shut as the others fought. "What choice did she have? People are more important than power."

"The girl could have grown into the role," the middle-aged guy who headed up Agriculture said.

"Or it could have destroyed her," Greta shot back, eyes still aflame.

"Enough!" Fluffikins shouted, and the fire in Greta's eyes disappeared. She took her seat beside me, and I moved to the opposite edge of mine, still completely unsettled.

"What now?" she asked calmly, sweetly—but I no longer took her good nature for granted. "Beech Grove needs its Town Witch."

All eyes turned to me. "I can't..." I sputtered.

"The magic we gave you was only temporary," the cat pointed out. "To become the official Town Witch, you'd need to kill your predecessor."

Parker's eyes found mine, and he stared at me as if seeing me for the first time.

"But Parker..." I mumbled.

"Yes, we're in a bad spot," Fluffikins admitted. "One person can't fill two roles indefinitely. It leaves the region too vulnerable."

"Then what are we going to do?" I cried, feeling beyond helpless. Rather than being resolved, things were only going to get worse. Would that mean more lives lost? I hated this.

"We'll have to find a new liaison to the Force, but the process takes a while, unfortunately," Fluffikins said. "Usually we are better prepared for transitions, but Lila requested that we act fast and figure out the other details once the immediate threat had been mitigated."

"Can I help? You don't need me as a temp witch, anymore. Right?

I can do the double cop thing." As scared as I was to be a part of this, it would be even worse to turn my back on them now.

"But you're not an officer," Parker said with a deadpan expression as he clenched his jaw.

"Can't you wave your magic wand and change the records?" I asked Greta since she was closest to me.

It was Fluffikins who answered for all of them. "We'd be even more vulnerable to have someone who hasn't been properly trained in either magic or policing in such a vital role."

"Then what? There must be something we can do!" I was on the verge of tears now. I hated that it made me look weak, but I was weak. Then again, if the strong ones weren't willing or able to fix the situation, doing so fell to me.

Parker stood suddenly, commanding everyone's attention. "Actually, I believe there is something. If you'll just hear me out..."

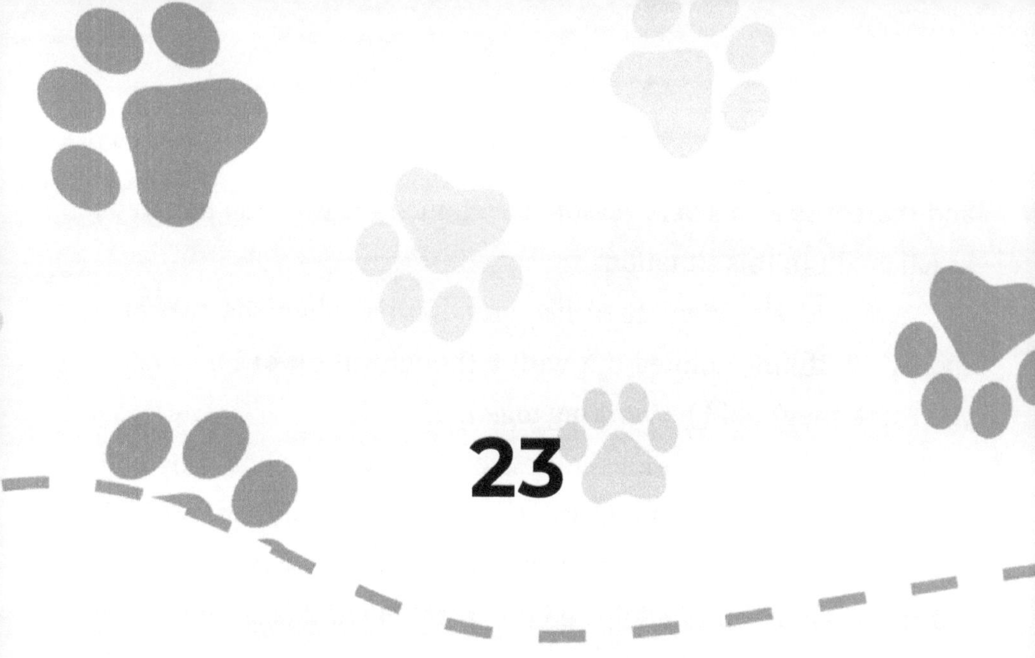

23

Parker barely spoke above a whisper. "I think there's a chance Melony could still be alive—badly injured and perhaps permanently wounded, but alive and well enough to call for reinforcements."

A memory swam to the front of my mind. While certainly menacing in our confrontation, Melony had also appeared frightened and desperate. If she'd wanted to hurt me or Greta, she could have easily done so while we were frozen in place.

But she hadn't.

She'd simply taken what she came for—*the old hat*—and left. She'd also asked Parker to surrender before mounting an attack, but what if he'd misread the situation? What if she hadn't meant to hurt him, either? What if we'd all gotten it wrong?

I bit my lip to keep from speaking out. Melony was already injured and possibly dead. It may be too late for anyone to help her, and there was also a very reasonable chance I was giving her way too much credit in this situation.

"You said she mentioned her grandfather when the two of you spoke," Fluffikins pointed out with a thoughtful tilt of his head. "Do you think they could be working together?"

My head spun with all the possibilities. Melony could be evil or she could be a scared kid, trying to impress the only family she had left. I certainly hadn't expected Parker to be Mrs. Haberdash's murderer—nor had I anticipated the fact that she'd been the architect of her own demise.

"Anything's possible, I suppose," Parker said in response to the boss cat, although his words felt as if they were specifically intended for me. Did he also suspect there was something more hidden just beneath the surface?

He cleared his throat and continued, "Even if she didn't survive, there's a chance he will still come looking for her… and then for revenge."

Fluffikins resumed his pacing. I realized he did this whenever his thoughts moved faster than his words could. "Which puts us in a doubly vulnerable spot," he hissed, though it held no anger. "We're down a board member and may have to square off against a bonded enemy."

This new information cut my internal line of questioning short.

"What does that mean?" I asked, glancing from Parker to Fluffikins. "A bonded enemy?"

It was Greta who answered. "A grandfather and daughter—or any two blood relations, really—working toward the same purpose could amplify their magic through their family bond. It's like multiplying their powers rather than simply adding them together. So instead of 10 and 10 making 20, it makes 100. It's why some magic folk choose to have large families. They are practically unstoppable with so many bonds amplifying their powers."

"Most would use that bond only to protect themselves, but the Haberdashes..." Parker shook his head. "They've never been keen on following the rules."

"We have to find and stop them," I cried, my hesitation receding in light of this new information. "How can I help?"

"You can't," Fluffikins said with a deep frown that pulled his whiskers toward his chest. "But the rest of us can ward the town as a protective measure just in case Melony's grandfather hasn't joined her yet. Do you still remember the power points?" he asked the rest of the board.

They all nodded solemnly. I took it they weren't talking about a computer program.

"I want to help, too," I insisted. "I still have magic. It may not be much, but maybe it will be enough to make a difference in whatever happens next."

"No, Tawny," Greta said in a cool, disconnected voice as she turned toward me. The fire had returned to her eyes, but it was only a dull flicker. I wouldn't have noticed it at all if she hadn't already been sitting so close.

She put a hand on my shoulder and pressed her forehead to mine. "It's very noble that you want to help, but this isn't your battle to fight. We've been protecting the magical interests in this region for years. Sometimes that includes stopping dangerous transfers of power. We're all trained for this..."

She grabbed both of my hands and pulled me to my feet with her.

I took a deep breath and waited.

Greta's eyes flashed, then returned to their normal blue color.

"We're all trained for this," she repeated. "But you're not."

With that last sentiment, she raised her other hand to my chest and ripped the magic brooch from my shirt.

My knees buckled, but I didn't fall despite feeling as if all the strength had been zapped from my muscles.

The pink glittery magic snapped out of sight as whatever power I'd briefly held within me fizzled and died. The silver brooch that held my borrowed magic glowed in Greta's hand. Taunting me. Practically daring me to take it back.

But I saw what power did. It turned answers into questions, loved ones into enemies, and safety into danger. Terrible things happened each and every day, and the board allowed them to happen as part of maintaining some kind of sacred balance.

But why did we need a balance at all? If I had magic, I'd use it to make a better world, not uphold a flawed and broken one.

Magic or not, I could still help.

Maybe because of my lack, I could help more. I could offer a human perspective.

"I'm not going anywhere," I said, standing firm.

But Greta shouted and gave me a mighty shove. "Go! Return to your life and stop interfering with ours."

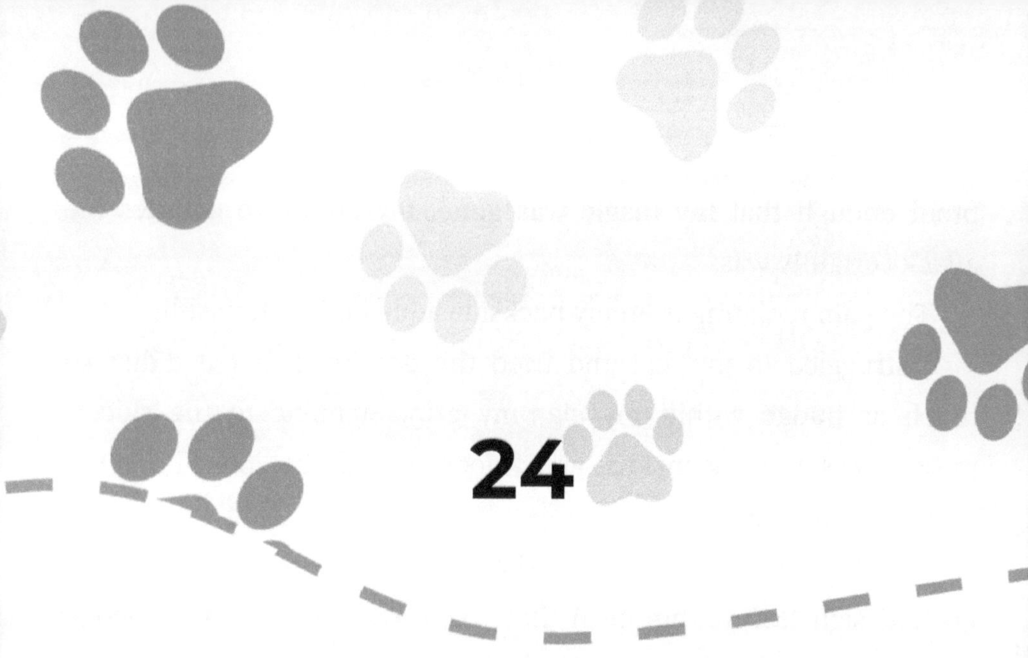

24

Of course, I now had a million questions flying through my brain, but before I could ask a single one, Greta shoved me again. And hard.

I struggled to see past her, hoping someone else would step in or speak up.

Parker studiously avoided my gaze.

Meanwhile Mr. Fluffikins summoned a blast of air so strong, it pushed me out into the empty hallway and slammed the conference room door behind me.

I landed on my rear with a heavy thump, just like I had last night when the bossy black cat had tested my magic by launching a sneak attack.

He'd said that if I'd had powers, I wouldn't be able to stop the impulse to protect myself. If Greta ripping off my brooch hadn't been proof enough that my magic was gone, my failure to counter the attack certainly was.

The pain radiating from my backside added injury to insult.

I struggled to my feet and tried the doorknob, but it didn't so much as budge within my clammy grip. Stepping to the side, I pressed myself up against the glass-block column that looked into the room. "Let me in!"

I could hardly see more than shapes and movement past the 80s-tastic design feature, but even that was taken away when someone conjured a dark barrier to block my view

I stopped and listened.

Silence.

Had they also put up a sound barrier? Or had they all exited through that glass ceiling already?

Parker had mentioned power points, something about protecting the town from outside attacks. My guess was that wherever these points were, it wasn't inside the dingy office complex.

They were on the move—or at least they would be soon. I was out of options here, so I ran outside, wondering if I had any chance of following on foot. Provided I was even able to spot them in the first place. I doubted both possibilities, given that my morning's journey on the magic broom had taken me well above civilian speed limits.

They needed my help. I knew that deep within my bones, even if they didn't. One way or another, I would find a way to—what was it Fluffikins had said?—to tip the balance.

Think, Tawny, think!

I knew Melony was either dead or in danger.

That her grandfather may also be involved, and if he was, that would be way worse than facing her by herself.

As the current holder of the town magic, Parker was at risk, too.

The board had discussed venturing to the power points to protect the town... And that's where my definite knowledge ended. Everything I knew about power points had more to do with making slide presentations than warding off dark magic. I had no car, and Greta had taken my magic away, both of which left me stranded in this mostly abandoned modern office complex.

So what now?

In the absence of a plan, I chose to head home. After all, there was only one place I thought might have the answers I needed, and that was Mrs. Haberdash's house. I went there now, not because I was giving up, but because I knew that eventually the board and their foes would make their way back to where it all began.

And when they did, they would need me.

The house knew that, even if they didn't.

Why else would its magic have embraced me right away?

I found it especially strange that Greta had been the one to force me away. She'd seen the way the house opened up to me. She knew I was a part of this better than any of the rest of them did.

But they'd all been so quick to accept me into their group and even quicker to kick me to the curb. Why?

I slogged along the sidewalk, wishing I'd worn my running shoes so I could move a little faster to match the urgency of the situation.

I'd hardly made it around the block when a blast of burning light knocked me off balance and pushed me onto my poor sore bum once again.

Holding one hand over my eyes as a shield, I strained to see into the light. Was this a new enemy?

No, it was just Greta.

Okay, not *just Greta.*

It was Greta with enormous white wings stretched wide on each side. "Grab my hand," she ordered, and I knew better than to argue.

As soon as our fingers made contact, she launched back into the sky, pulling me along with her. "What's happening?" I managed to ask between frightened gasps for air.

"He's lying," she said with a quick glance my way. The flames had returned to her gaze, and she looked both beautiful and terrifying.

"What? Who's lying? And wait, are you a… an…?"

"Yes, I'm an angel, and Parker was lying."

Whoa. There was a lot to process there. I wanted to respond with something intelligent, but instead I just said, "Um, are you sure?" like some kind of mortal idiot… which I guess I was, considering the company.

"Almost everything he said was a lie, but I don't know why."

"So does that mean…?"

"Yes, Melony is fine. They never had a confrontation."

Finally I found some helpful words. "Then why didn't you stop everyone from going to ward the town?"

"Because something's not right. I didn't want to alert Parker to the fact I was on to him."

"How did you know he wasn't being honest?"

She pointed to herself and smiled. *"Angel."*

"Right."

"We need to act fast before he realizes that I haven't joined the others. Do you still want to help?"

She probably should have asked that before she catapulted me into the sky, but whatever. I was in this to win it, even though I had no idea how victory might look or what it would ultimately entail.

"Yes. I'll help. What do you need me to do?"

She flashed me a magnanimous smile that sent a shiver right through me. "You, my dear, are going to serve as our bait."

Wonderful.

25

"Where are we going?" I shouted into the wind as the angel and I picked up speed. "And how will I be used as bait?"

"We're going to the place where this whole thing started," Greta said as we zipped toward our location.

Not even a minute later, we clunked down right in front of Mrs. Haberdash's house, the place I'd been headed on my own, anyway.

"What's the plan?" I asked as Greta made her wings disappear with a quick flick of both wrists.

"Haven't really got much of one." She reached into her pocket and pulled out my brooch. Even though I hadn't been granted magic long enough to know what I was doing with it, I immediately felt relieved. If nothing else, my instinctual abilities could protect me—at least for a little while. I hated how much I wanted it, even though I was already beginning to suspect that magic did terrible things to a person's mind. Even knowing it could corrupt me, I wanted it. *Desperately.*

"It's a decoy," Greta explained, dashing my hopes just as quickly as she'd lifted them. Oh, well. It was definitely for the best. "Wear it. Pretend you're searching for something specific."

I thought about this for a moment. I also thought about how unfortunate it was that my pajama pants had no pockets. I shoved the decoy into my bra to keep it safe, then asked, "What should I be looking for?"

"Doesn't matter. Just tear around the house and generally make a nuisance of yourself. If one of the Haberdash heirs is around, they'll come find you." She stepped forward and I studied the back of her simple pastel pantsuit. There was no sign of the enormous wings that had delivered us to this location mere seconds ago. No tears from where they'd emerged through the fabric. No hint that she was anything other than an ordinary human being.

"What will you do?" I asked skeptically.

She glanced toward the horizon and frowned, which was not exactly comforting. "I'll be watching from nearby, just as soon as I come back from informing Mr. Fluffikins of my observations."

Horror flooded my chest. "So I'll be alone in there?"

"Not for long, but I need to warn the others so they can be on the lookout. I know it's a lot to ask, but I promise to keep you safe. That's why I had to push you away. I couldn't let Parker know that I suspect him." She turned and stared off into the distance.

"You suspect Parker now? Of what?" Parker was the easiest for me to relate to on the board. I truly liked him, but I'd been wrong about people before.

Greta, for instance, had rubbed me wrong many times since I met her earlier that morning, but she also seemed the most genuinely concerned with what happened to me—and to Melony. Despite her warnings that magic always came to a violent end, it seemed she still yearned for a peaceful resolution here.

She worried her lip and brought her gaze back to meet mine. "I don't know, but it's not like him to lie. Back in the boardroom, didn't you notice that he seemed a bit, well… off?"

Actually I had, but I thought it was just because of the trauma of potentially killing someone. I chose not to acknowledge that. I wanted to trust Greta, but I was still so confused about this brave new world of magic and danger. I mean, she was probably one of the good guys—being an angel and all—but how could I know for sure?

I suspected I wouldn't know anything for sure until it actually came to pass. Which meant my goal here was to find the truth and use it to guide my actions.

Oh, also to not die.

That was definitely important.

"You said you'd keep me safe. How can you guarantee that if you're not here?" I mumbled nervously.

Greta scanned the horizon again and shifted her weight from foot to foot before speaking. "Step forward," she instructed.

I did, and she grabbed my hand by the wrist, then placed it over my heart.

The blinding light shone again.

I blinked hard as I watched it pass from Greta's chest into my hand, up my arm, and then eventually into my chest, where the light faded and disappeared.

"You have my armor of light. It will be enough to keep you safe for the time I am gone," she said with a pained expression. Did it hurt her to lose this magic, the way losing mine had weakened me momentarily?

"What? I can't accept this. What about you?" I couldn't let her sacrifice herself like this. There had to be another way…

"I," she said with a wistful grin as she let out her wings again, "will just have to do my best not to die."

Before I could argue, she launched into the sky, leaving me to set my part of the non-plan into motion. And so I took a deep breath, rolled my shoulders like some kind of boxer prepping to go into the ring, and jogged up the porch steps to the empty house.

No, I didn't have any magical offenses, but I could still help somehow.

Greta believed in me enough to trust me with her very life, and I refused to let her down.

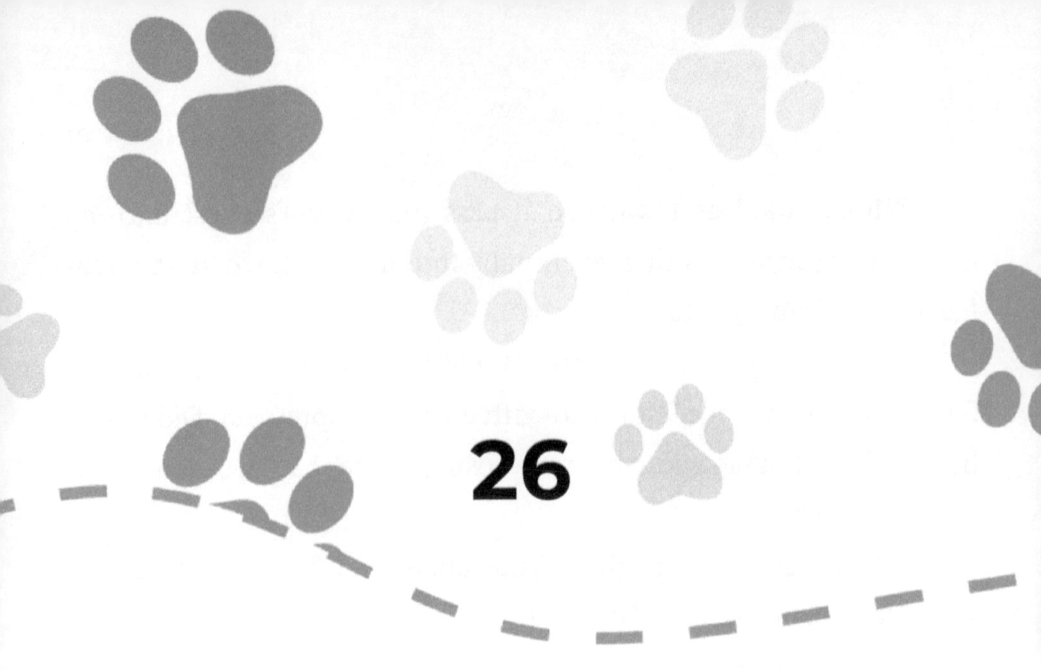

26

Greta had readily admitted she didn't really have a plan for us to follow. Neither of us knew for sure what was going on with Parker—or Melony for that matter.

Trouble was brewing, and we'd just have to deal with the resulting chaos as it came.

I couldn't offer much beyond my willingness to help, but that still might be enough to bait the bad guys... Um, whoever they turned out to be.

I thought about this more as I made my way upstairs to the late Mrs. Haberdash's bedroom. Greta had instructed me to pretend I was searching for something, and my performance would be far more convincing if I actually was trying to find something.

Melony had come for the old witch's hat earlier. Might there be additional magical accessories just waiting to be discovered?

I thought of the decoy brooch nestled in my bra, and decided, yes.

An accessory seemed a far better bet than trying to find some kind of revealing paper or book. Much more my style, too.

Maybe I'd get lucky and uncover something that could actually help. And if I didn't, that was also fine.

After all, I wasn't expected to actually find anything, just to create a distraction.

Greta hadn't given me much to go on—I suspected that was because she didn't know much herself—but she had revealed that Parker was lying to us. Could that mean Melony had already gotten to him and that he was now under her control? I remembered how helpless I felt when Parker and Fluffikins each took their turn manipulating my movements and emotions.

But how could Melony have overpowered someone like Parker? He was a much more experienced magic user, and he even had the town magic to bolster said powers even further. Not to mention, he had at least sixty pounds of muscle on her.

Granted, Melony had managed to hold both me and Greta when we had our confrontation earlier that morning, but maybe that was simply because she'd taken us by surprise.

Hmm. Now that I actually had more than a few fleeting seconds to think things over, I realized just how much wasn't adding up here.

Melony had surprised Greta and me at the house earlier that day. And when she left us, I ran to my house and found Fluffikins waiting. He conjured a broom and flew me back to the PTA complex with him. He'd also said Melony wasn't able to travel by magical means.

If that was the case, how could Melony have had the time to find Parker and follow him to the edge of town, have a talk, and then have a confrontation within that space of time before Parker joined us at the conference room table?

Yes, he was the last to arrive, but still we were only talking a span of maybe ten minutes here. For the first time since moving to this little town, I wished I'd brought a car with me. The town was considered tiny because of its population, but it still boasted a fair amount of land.

I punched my address into the maps app. Mrs. Haberdash's property—including my guest house—was centrally located, which made it easy to walk into town when I needed to. That had been a big selling point for me, actually.

Now that I was studying the map, I noticed we were dead center in the square-shaped area of the city's boundaries. I used my index finger to tap the city border and added it as a destination point. My app informed me that the quickest route by car would take about twelve minutes.

I didn't have exact timestamps for the events of this morning, but the accepted timeline seemed off.

Parker had either gotten confused or was purposefully lying to the board. Greta had already confirmed that.

But he'd also proudly told me he was a local, born and raised in Beech Grove. In fact, it was one of the first things he said to me—well, after accusing me of being a murderer, that is. I doubted he'd have made an error in calculating the time given his familiarity with the town, and I also doubted he'd tell a lie he knew could be easily disproved.

So why hadn't the others noticed this inconsistency?

Or had they but chosen not to acknowledge it?

I was missing something big here, and I doubted I was the only one.

See, this was exactly the kind of thing that happened from making decisions too fast! Yet another reason it was so important for me to start my days with a slow, contemplative shower. Thanks to Fluffikins, I hadn't even gotten a quick and cold shower that morning.

I'd only had a single serving of coffee, too.

And it wasn't even eight o'clock yet. *Yawn.*

I rummaged through the late Mrs. Haberdash's jewelry box and lifted a large emerald ring to inspect it more closely.

"Drop that," someone ordered from the doorway in a gruff voice. Despite the added vitriol, I instantly recognized the speaker.

I turned to face Parker, holding the ring tight. "Make me," I challenged through clenched teeth. I was taking a big chance here and prayed my instincts were bang on.

He paused for a moment, but that was enough to confirm my suspicions.

"You're not Parker," I said, slipping the ring onto my finger and placing a hand on each hip in open defiance.

27

Parker unleashed a fiery blast and sent it careening right at me. Yeah, this definitely wasn't the same guy I'd met the day before.

I tried to dodge, but the surge of magic shot out so fast I didn't have a chance. The flames crashed straight into me, but I hardly felt a thing. Only warmth, acknowledgment. The light in my chest glowed as the borrowed angel armor absorbed the full impact.

"They know," Parker growled, and for a moment he looked too stunned to take any further action.

But that moment quickly passed and he hurled himself onto me, trapping my smaller body beneath his large, muscly one.

"Let me go!" I flailed against him.

"Tell me where the others are," he demanded, but still he couldn't force me to do it against my will. This wasn't Parker. He didn't have the same powers.

"No," I told him with another grunt. "I won't tell you anything until you explain who you are and what you want."

If I could get and keep him talking until Greta returned, then everything would be okay. I was definitely doing my job as bait. Now I just had to hope my fisherman would come to the rescue before the armor took one too many hits and I got gobbled up whole.

"Who are you? Why are you even a part of this?" fake Parker demanded rather than offering any answers of his own.

"I'm Tawny," I said blithely. The goal was to keep him talking, so if he wanted to hear about me, I was more than ready to offer up some info. "I'm just a temp."

"They took your magic and kicked you out. Why are you in this house? What are you looking for?"

I absolutely was not going to tell him that I was only here to distract him, so instead I reached for my writer skills and concocted a story—a bit of pure and simple fiction to save the day.

"I live in the guest house out back. When they took my magic and kicked me out, I figured I'd been stiffed. I needed the money, though, that's why I even took the lousy job in the first place. Figured with everyone's attention focused elsewhere I could creep in here and find something to hock. Make sure I got some kind of payment for all my efforts."

"You made a bad choice," he hissed above me. "Because, see, now that you're here, I can't just let you go."

"Then let me help you," I suggested, giving up the struggle. The safest way to avoid getting hurt was to make him think I was on his side.

But it was to no avail. “I don’t need help from a normie. This will be easier without you here to get in the way.” He sent another surge of flames into my body, but I felt nothing this time. Just how long could this angel armor hold out? I really, really didn’t want to find out.

“What’s protecting you?” my attacker asked, further proof that he was not the Parker Barnes I knew and had even begun to care about a little.

“I don’t know,” I lied. I would have shrugged, but I still couldn’t move beneath him. “Magical residue, maybe? As you said, I’m nothing but a normie. Please just let me go.”

Another roar of ineffectual flames crashed against me.

“Use me as bait,” I suggested in a squeaky voice. Panic had begun to set in. Would Greta make it back in time, or would the next blast be the one to break through my armor?

“What?” he asked, his hand lifted to conjure another blow, then paused.

“Don’t just kill me. Use me as a bargaining piece for whatever it is you want.” If I could be the bait for the good guys, then I could be the bait for the bad guys, too. Only Greta had the full picture. I had to trust that she would be back soon and make sure I escaped this scuffle alive. I mean, if you couldn’t trust an angel, then who could you trust?

He pondered this for a few moments, and when at last he spoke again, it wasn’t to me. “There you are. Now get in here, and help me tie her up,” he said, pressing me harder into the ground. My face now lay flat against the heavy pile carpet in Mrs. Haberdash’s bedroom.

The echoing footsteps paused just outside the doorway.

"Well? Were you able to incapacitate any of them?" fake Parker pressed.

"No, unfortunately. They went to the power points as you anticipated, but they were unable to complete the ritual," a husky feminine voice answered.

I couldn't see much from my unfortunate position, but it was enough to recognize the pair of feet that joined us, dressed in thick black combat boots and a long flowy skirt.

Melony had arrived.

"Why not?" the man holding me down asked with a growl.

"One of their members suspected something and came to alert the others. I was just about to converge on the cat when it happened."

"What did she say? Come out with it already!" My attacker shoved me into the floor with all his might, but the angel armor held strong.

Melony drew closer but remained a couple steps back. "I couldn't hear, but the two of them took off together."

"They're going to warn the others. That means we don't have much time," the man said. "We have to finish this now. We might never get the chance again."

I swallowed hard.

Whatever came next, I knew it wouldn't be good.

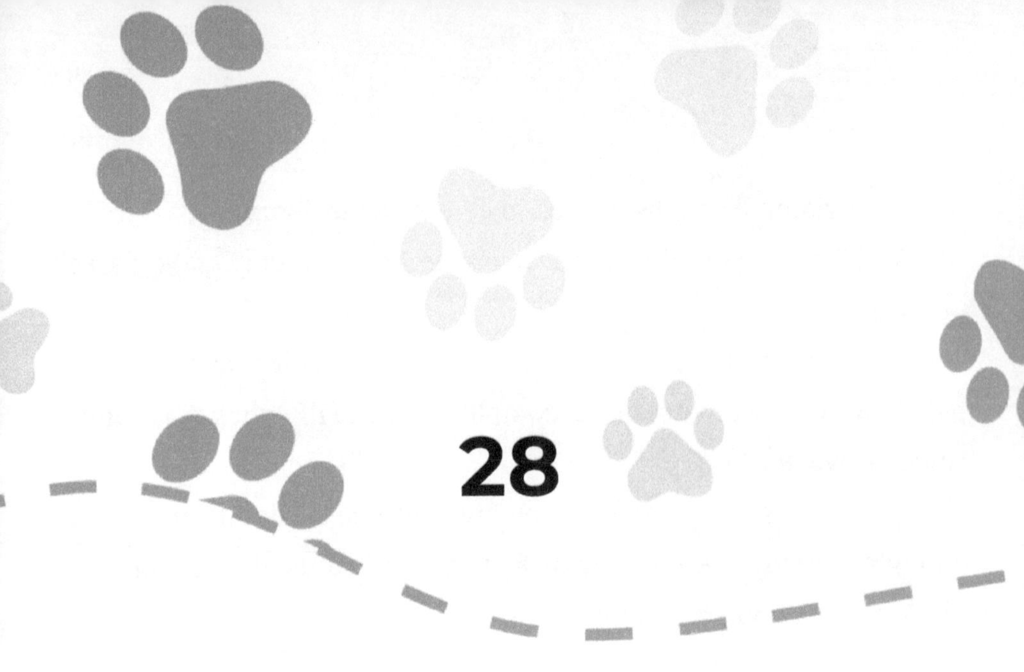

28

"Why are you doing this?" I shouted, but my words got lost in the thick pile of the carpet. "What do you want?" I tried again, forcing the question from the side of my mouth.

"You think we wanted my stupid aunt's town magic? *Please,*" Melony spat as she bound my wrists behind my back. "We've got much bigger fish to fry."

Well, at least she was keeping with the established metaphor, even if she hadn't exactly been let in on the whole thing.

"Melony, hush," the fake Parker scolded from where he was tying my ankles together.

She pulled back for a second before applying herself with even more vigor. "Sorry, Grandpa."

Oh, no. The family bond. This was exactly what Greta and the others had wanted to avoid.

Panic wrapped around my chest even tighter than my bonds. "Where's Parker? What did you do to him?" I mumbled again.

"He's dead," the Parker clone said with a laugh. "And soon you will be, too."

Oh, no. Were we really too late?

If they'd been able to kill Parker with his double dose of magic, then I didn't stand a chance. I was just one normal magic-less person up against two very magical people with an amplified family bond. I couldn't even get my hands or feet free to try to fight my way out of this or to make a run for it.

Would the other members of the board be able to defeat this villainous pair, or was the town of Beech Grove now doomed—and the entire region of Peach Plains right along with it?

A crash sounded from downstairs. Had my help finally arrived?

"Stay here," the fake Parker—Melony's grandfather—said. "I'll go investigate."

"Why are you doing this?" I asked the girl when the two of us were alone. "Is your life really so bad?"

"I don't have to answer that." She crossed her arms over her chest but remained standing sentinel over me.

"Is this even something you want? Seems to me like your grandpa is the one calling all the shots. What makes you think he's going to share any of the magic he gains with you?" If I found the right words, perhaps I could sway Melony to my side. She'd had the chance to defeat me and Greta earlier, but she'd chosen not to. There had to be good in there somewhere.

She glowered at me. "Hush up. You don't know anything.

Grandpa promised that if I help him with his plan, he'll make sure I take up my rightful place as Town Witch."

"If you say so," I responded casually.

She dug a heel into my back, but the armor of light held up, keeping me from feeling any of the pain. Okay, so maybe she was capable of inflicting some pain—but murder?

Everyone believed she'd come to town in order to kill her aunt, but what if they were wrong? What if Melony was after something else?

As we waited alone in that room, I turned Melony's last statement over and over in my mind. Her grandfather had said he'd make sure she became Town Witch.

As in future tense... As in it hadn't happened yet...

Which meant Melony *didn't* already have the town magic. Her grandfather wouldn't have killed Parker himself if he'd promised the magic to Melony. I still didn't know what they were after, but it was clearly something much bigger than the Beech Grove town magic.

They weren't after Parker. Perhaps they'd never been.

Chances were he was still alive.

Bigger fish to fry, Melony had said before her grandfather cut her off. Could I trick her into revealing more?

"What are you going to do with me?" I asked, turning slightly so it was easier to speak.

Melony's eyes met mine, and she flinched.

Perhaps she would have offered an answer, but I never got the chance to find out.

A strained cry rose from downstairs, silencing both of us.

Melony crept toward the door, and I remained on the floor, unable to do more than wriggle in place.

The next thing I heard was fake Parker shouting, "You're not going anywhere. Now march."

Melony ran out of the room to help, and I was able to move myself into a position that afforded me a better view of the doorway.

A minute later, the two of them strode in, pushing a burned and bloody Greta into the room before them. Without her angel armor to protect her, she'd been badly wounded by grandpa Haberdash's magical blows. She was barely conscious as they pushed her into the floor and tied her up as well.

She'd come to save me but had ended up in the line of fire herself.

Parker was missing, and the two of us had been captured. That left Fluffikins, Connie from Commerce, the old guy, and the slightly younger one who headed up Agriculture.

Would they be enough to stop Melony and her grandfather before they got their hands on whatever they were after?

Think, Tawny. Think!

If I couldn't unravel their plan, maybe I could still put a few chinks into it.

I didn't know how the family bond worked, but maybe I could still find a way to sever it.

Maybe I could still save the day.

No magic required.

29

"Where are the others?" Grandpa Haberdash kicked and barked at Greta, but his latest blow had rendered her unconscious and unable to answer. I hated seeing him use Parker's likeness to hurt us. No matter what happened after today, I knew I'd never be able to shake the image from my mind.

"They're coming. I just know it," Melony said, then worried her lip as she waited for her grandfather's acknowledgment.

He cracked his knuckles and scowled, not even looking at Melony as he said, "Stay put, and make sure these two don't cause any trouble. And do not under any circumstances leave this house. Do you hear me?"

Melony bobbed her head enthusiastically. "Yes, Grandpa."

And with that, her grandfather charged out of the room and down the long staircase. I listened but couldn't hear the door downstairs open or shut. My guess was that he had remained inside, lying in wait and ready to ambush whoever arrived next.

"So..." I wiggled onto my side so I could see Melony as I spoke. Perhaps her face would reveal something her words would not. I was fighting for my life here and had to use everything I had at my disposal. "Since we're both stuck here, want to tell me your master plan? I'm sure it's super smart."

She crossed her arms and looked away. "No."

Hmmm. If I couldn't appeal to her vanity, perhaps I could poke at her insecurities. I tried to shrug, but that didn't quite work considering my bonds. "I understand. I mean, we're both useless anyway. Might as well let the tough guys fight it out and tell us about it later."

Melony scoffed. "You may be useless, normie, but I'm not."

"Hey, why are you calling me a *normie?*" I tried to look hurt as I asked this. Vanity and insecurity hadn't worked, so what about humanity?

She rolled her eyes. "Because you don't have any magic, duh."

"Don't I, though? I'm the Town Witch."

She studied me for a moment, then shook her head. "No, the guy who killed my great aunt is."

"Maybe he's the official Town Witch, but as a temp for the PTA, I have an exact replica of the magic right here." I struggled against my bonds, then sighed.

She glanced back to me, uncertain. "Right where?"

"Well, I was instructed to keep the magic vessel close to my heart so that it would work best."

Melony took a step closer. "Where is it? Give it to me."

"I put it in my bra," I said with a grunt.

"That's gross."

"Well, do you want it or not?" I asked casually, trying to convey that it didn't matter to me if she accepted my help. A plan had started to form in my mind, though, and if I could get Melony to do her part, then Greta and I just might have a chance here. "I bet you'd be even more powerful than your grandpa if you had this extra jolt of magic. He wouldn't leave you on daycare duty then."

"Give it to me," she said again. Her eyes didn't light on fire the way Greta's had, but I recognized a spark of greed.

I grunted and struggled against my bonds again. I had to make the show good. "I can't," I moaned, then flipped onto my back. The motion would have really hurt my tied-up wrists, but the angel armor was still protecting me from pain, thank goodness. I pressed out my chest as far as I could. "Come get it yourself. I can't exactly get it for you."

"Eeew, no." She sniffed in disgust and took a giant step back.

We both fell silent for the next couple minutes.

Neither of us moved until the sudden sound of a door banging open caused us both to jump in our skins.

"Last chance," I mumbled, trying hard to hide my desperation. "Take my magic and go be part of the action. I mean, if you're not there with him, how can you be sure your grandfather will even cut you in once he gets what he wants?"

Melony bit her lip again, then hurried over to my side. "I'll untie you for just a second, and just one hand. Give me the magic vessel, don't do anything funny, and I'll make sure you live. It's not like Grandpa and I have a use for you, anyway."

"Deal." I flashed her a relieved smile. Not because she was offering me a way out, but because she'd fallen so perfectly into my trap.

I gave myself a quick mental pep talk as Melony struggled to untie just one hand. Downstairs, I heard Fluffikins shout, "Who are you, and what have you done with Parker?"

A series of crashes and slams followed as Melony used a fresh length of rope to tie my left wrist to the bonds that held my ankles before she finally got to work on freeing my right hand.

I was patient with her, like a good hostage.

"Okay, give it to me," she said when at last my hand was fully freed. I reached into my bra and found the decoy brooch Greta had entrusted to me. *Huh.* Who knew this thing would actually come in handy?

Melony accepted it greedily, wiping it off on the hem of her shirt before pulling it to her face for a closer inspection. She was too distracted by both the brooch and the action downstairs to immediately retie me, just as I had counted on.

While she studied the empty magic vessel, I brought my free hand back to my chest and pressed it against my heart, summoning the light within. It started small like a pinprick but then grew into a magnificent fruit-sized orb.

By the time Melony realized what I was doing, I had already thrust my hand toward Greta's unconscious body and allowed the light to flow out of me and into her.

The angel's eyes snapped open, full of white heat. I watched in awe as her wounds closed up and she regained full vitality.

Now that I no longer had her armor, I gasped as a sudden wave of pain crashed over me. The wrist that was still held captive behind my back had been twisted at an unnatural angle when I flipped myself onto my back. And when Melony had fastened it to my feet, that only made the break worse.

Yup, it was definitely broken.

Greta shouted beside me and ripped through the ropes that had held her.

"Go!" I urged in a hoarse whisper. "Take Melony out of here. Out of the... house."

I didn't see what happened next, because I passed out from the pain.

30

My head felt foggy. I heard hushed voices speaking around me but couldn't make out any of the words.

Ugh. How long had I been out? What day was it?

I'd had the craziest dream filled with talking cats, evil grandpas, and some kind of flaming angel. Well, that was one for the sleep journal. My therapist would love hearing about the story my nocturnal brain had concocted this time.

I brought my hands up to wipe the winkies from the corners of my eyes, then opened them.

A sleek black cat with a cute white patch on his chest stared down at me with glowing golden eyes. Huh, that was weird. When had I adopted a cat? I'd only lived in this town for a couple weeks, tops. I hadn't even unpacked all my boxes yet, but I'd gone out and adopted a pet?

Someone placed a warm hand on my forehead. Who was here

with me? I was in my own room, not a hospital. Yet these people seemed to know me.

Fear sent my heart galloping full speed ahead as I turned and found a pale-haired woman wearing a simple pantsuit and a giant smile. "Oh, Tawny. I'm so glad you're okay."

I closed my eyes, took a deep breath, then opened them again. This time I spotted an incredibly handsome man with a salt-and-pepper beard and nicely toned arms standing behind the lady. His light gray eyes appeared curious—and also familiar somehow.

"May I have a moment with her?" he asked the others, who agreed and swiftly departed. Even the cat left. Wow, they really had him trained!

The handsome stranger sank down onto his knees and gripped my hand between his. "How do you feel?" he asked, concern reflecting in his pale eyes.

"Okay," I answered cautiously. It didn't seem like he wanted to hurt me, but what was he doing in my house while I slept? That was definitely kind of creepy. "Confused."

He glanced back toward the door. It was still shut.

"What do you remember?" he pressed, turning my hand over in his as if he couldn't quite believe it was real.

I tried so hard, but nothing came to mind. Just the weird dream and long, pleasant sleep. I knew my answer would disappoint him, but I also had no idea what to say in order to make him happy. Instead, I simply asked, "About what?"

He licked his lips and tried again. "What's my name?"

"I don't know. Is it Steve? You look like a Steve." I smiled to soften the blow in case I got it wrong. Even though this man was a stranger to me, *he* clearly knew *me.*

The man hung his head and chuckled. When he looked back at me, I thought I caught the glimmer of a tear that refused to fall.

"Forgetting is the protocol," he said, making me even more confused than before. "I mean, it's the *usual* procedure." He shrugged.

I furrowed my brow but said nothing. What could I say? *Hey, crazy guy. I have no idea what you're talking about. Get out of my bedroom!*

He continued on, undeterred. "But, Tawny, there is nothing usual about you."

"Who are you?" I asked. My throat felt dry. My head foggy. None of this was making any sense.

He waved his hand in a semi-circle, then flicked his index finger straight up, watching me the whole time.

"Who am I?" he prompted again. "Think, Tawny. You know this."

And suddenly the fog lifted, revealing images from the past day and a half. Fluffikins sharing his memories with me as he purred on my lap, Greta propelling me through the air with strong and steady wings, that old guy in the suit whose beard reached down to his belt buckle, but more than anything... the man standing right before me.

I couldn't stop the enormous smile that blossomed on my face. "You're Parker."

"And what do you last remember happening?"

A frightening vision filled my mind. We'd almost been defeated. A horrible pain. I passed out.

"Melony and her grandfather," I said, trying to slow the swirl of images as I spoke. "They were in Mrs. Haberdash's house. Said they had bigger fish to fry. That you were dead. Greta gave me her armor of light, but then I gave it back. Did she get Melony out of the house?" That had been the last thing I'd said before losing consciousness—to get Melony out of there—based on a sneaking suspicion I had that somehow the house amplified their family bond that much further. But had I been correct?

Parker raised my hand to his lips and gave it a lingering kiss. "Yes, you were right about everything. The moment Greta vaulted through the window with Melony in her grasp, the connection broke and the others were able to overpower her grandfather."

"But why?" I knew Melony's grandfather had urged her not to leave the house, but I still didn't understand the full extent of it.

"Simple," Parker said with a crooked grin. "Lila Haberdash lived her entire life in that house. Her parents lived there before her, and their parents before them. Over time, the house has absorbed generations of family magic—so much so that it became a part of them."

"And it amplified their bond," I said, finally understanding.

He nodded and looked as if he wanted to say something else, but I still had more questions that needed to get out of me.

"What were they after? Why did they need that extra power if Mrs. Haberdash was already dead?"

"They were never after her. At least the grandfather wasn't." He took a deep breath and squeezed my hand before letting it go. "They wanted the board."

"Who? Fluffikins?"

"Yes. And Connie. And Greta. And Buckley. And—"

"All of you." I exhaled slowly, taking this new information in. If Melony and her grandfather had been successful, they could have destroyed the magical balance completely. Could have done whatever they wanted with all that power, no matter how horrible.

Parker nodded, confirming my suspicions. "We are the strongest in the region. If they were able to assume all our power for themselves, they'd be unstoppable. They thought with Lila out of the way, they could use the house to help accomplish that."

"But they failed."

"They failed. Thank goodness for that." Parker looked so tired now. Was that because he'd been worried about me? How long had I been out? How badly had he been hurt?

"Where were you?" I asked gently.

Luckily, he didn't seem to take offense. "Incapacitated," he stated simply.

"Oh." I decided not to press further. Instead I switched back to the previous topic, "So their whole plan hinged on everyone coming to the house?"

"Since it was a major source of their power, yes. But they were also counting on us coming one by one, so we'd be easier to defeat. That's why Melony's grandfather took my form, so he could sway our actions. He dropped just enough hints to raise suspicions, then sent us to the power points in order to divide us."

This all made sense, but it didn't complete the puzzle. Not yet. "But they didn't kill me or Greta when they had the chance. Why?" This more than anything, I needed to know.

Parker shrugged and pressed his lips together in a tight line. "I don't think Melony ever quite understood the full extent of her grandfather's plan. I don't think we do, either."

"What happened to him?"

"Fluffikins dropped him off in the farthest possible region from here. New Zealand, I think."

"But he'll be back." This wasn't a question, because I already knew for sure it would happen.

"Yes. This time we'll be expecting him, though."

"What happens now?"

"The board will find a new Liaison to the Force, and I'll work at filling Lila's very big shoes as Town Witch. You go back to living your normie life. Hopefully, though, you'll be up for frequent visits from your new landlord and friend?"

"I'd like that," I said, feeling like an old-timey movie heroine. Now would have been the perfect time for Parker to sweep me off my feet —or rather my bed—and give me that sweet and perfect first kiss.

Instead, he leaned forward and hugged me tight, then whispered in my ear, "This will be our little secret. Okay?"

"My lips are sealed. Well, on one condition," I whispered back.

"Anything," he promised. He also wouldn't stop smiling.

"Would you please fix my hot water heater before you go? I could really use a nice long shower."

PSYCHIC FOR HIRE

After my last assignment almost killed me, I thought I was done with the Paranormal Temp Agency. Turns out we were just getting started...

The board of paranormal liaisons is down a member, leaving Beech Grove vulnerable to outside magical influence. Worse still, the stray cats who work as our field agents are disappearing from the streets—and they're not winding up in shelters.

Now my boss, a black cat named Mr. Fluffikins, has ordered me to go undercover as a phony psychic and find out what's happening to the missing feline agents.

Last week I didn't even know magic existed; this week it's up to me to help save it.

Yup, all in a day's work for this part-time psychic.

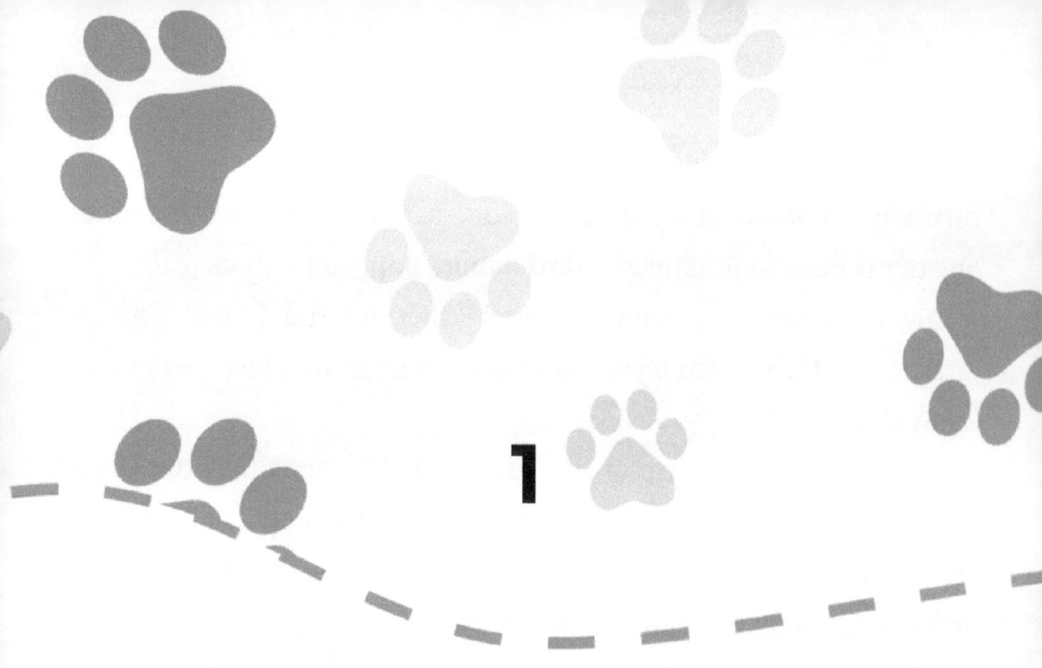

1

My name's Tawny Bigford. I'm a 35-year-old part-time romance author, and I just found out that magic is real.

You see, it all started one morning when I stumbled upon my new landlady's dead body. From there I was whisked away by a dashing cop who wasn't exactly there to investigate her murder. He delivered me to the PTA—no, not the one you're thinking—the Paranormal Temp Agency.

They're the special governing body that protects magical interests in our fair Peach Plains region of Georgia and are one of many such boards set up all across the globe.

Once they determined I was not at fault for my landlady's death, they ordered me to act as her temporary replacement. Not as a landlady, but as the official Beech Grove Town Witch. Oh, boy!

From there it was all talking cats, flying brooms, and one twisty turn after another. Every time someone actually bothered to answer one of my questions, at least a dozen more popped up in its place.

By the time we caught the real killer on the loose, I had a terrible headache from trying to keep it all straight. Here's what I do know...

The board is made up of five paranormal liaisons plus the Town Witch and the assigned Diplomat in charge. Our local Diplomat is a little black cat who loves following rules almost as much as he loves making demands; his name is Mr. Fluffikins.

Then we have sweet, matronly Greta as the liaison to Schools. I recently found out she's an angel—um, wow!

Parker Barnes is that same cop who initially brought me into this crazy supernatural ring. He's also the reason I remember everything that happened even though the others attempted to wipe my memory. Beyond that, his role is a bit more complicated. I'm still trying to figure it out for myself.

Lastly, we have Connie in charge of Commerce, Buckley as head of Agriculture, and some old dude in a suit who serves as the emissary for Cemeteries. Yeah, I still don't know his name...

I was recently the temporary Town Witch, but now that they have someone more permanent to fill the role, I should be out of a job. The board works with temps for a reason. They're easier to control, and the fewer people who know the full truth about what they do, the better. They'd rather tell lots of people part truths than let anyone too deep into their circle and risk exposure. I guess that's why I find them so confusing.

Even though I'm a little sad to have lost the magic they granted me—I only had it for less than twenty-four hours, mind you—I'm more than ready to get back to my normal life.

The boss cat, however, seems to have other ideas...

Uh-oh.

It's been three days since the madcap magical adventure that changed my world and everything I knew about it. Three days since yet another cold shower led to a murder mystery that turned into a magical conspiracy that almost cost me my life.

Three days.

That's longer than the entire adventure lasted. I don't even think a full twenty-four hours passed between me stumbling over Mrs. Haberdash's corpse and the PTA board catching the bad guys and put a stop to their dastardly plan.

In fact, I know it wasn't.

So how can such a short span of time change literally everything?

For one thing, I have a new landlord now. And while my previous landlady Mrs. Haberdash studiously avoided me, Parker Barnes finds at least half a dozen excuses to stop by every single day.

Yes, that Parker.

It's kind of hard to push magic out of my mind when the same guy who introduced me to it in the first place is always hanging around my doorstep.

And it definitely doesn't help that I have a big fat crush on him. Ever since my ex-husband found a new wife—while we were still married, I might add—I've sworn off love for a life of complete personal freedom.

So while Parker's swoony gray eyes may make my heart gallop, they also make my stomach churn. That's why I've imposed three new rules.

Three days. Three rules.

They are no more magic, no more men, and no more madcap adventures.

That was it. Should've been easy enough to follow. Especially since the rest of the board assumes I have no recollection of what happened.

But then…

Crash!

I jumped out of bed and ran down the hall as fast as my feet would carry me. Too late I realized that I probably should have found some kind of weapon to take with me.

It was hardly six in the morning. Who could have possibly…?

A spark of light flooded the living room even though I hadn't flipped the switch.

"Good morning, Tawny," Mr. Fluffikins said from where he was seated right beside a broken vase that had once held an arrangement of fake flowers. I didn't have the money to constantly buy fresh, and I hated watching something so pretty and vibrant wilt and die, so it had always been fake for me.

I glanced from the mess to the cat who had no doubt created it and back again, then threw my hands in the air and headed back down the hall toward my bedroom.

"Tawny, wait!" he cried after me. "I know you remember!"

I mumbled my three rules to myself. Fluffikins's appearance threatened to break at least two of said rules, and that was not okay.

"Go away," I mumbled and continued to drag myself back toward bed.

"I won't," he insisted, trailing after me now. "Not until you at least hear me out."

"I'm not making you breakfast." The last time he appeared at my place before sunrise, that's what he had demanded. It was a safe bet that's what he wanted now.

"I already ate," he countered. "And you clearly haven't forgotten anything despite the fact I very clearly remember wiping your memory."

This stopped me dead in my tracks. I shuddered and then asked, "What do you want then?"

"The PTA has a new assignment for you," he said, and then my knees gave out beneath me.

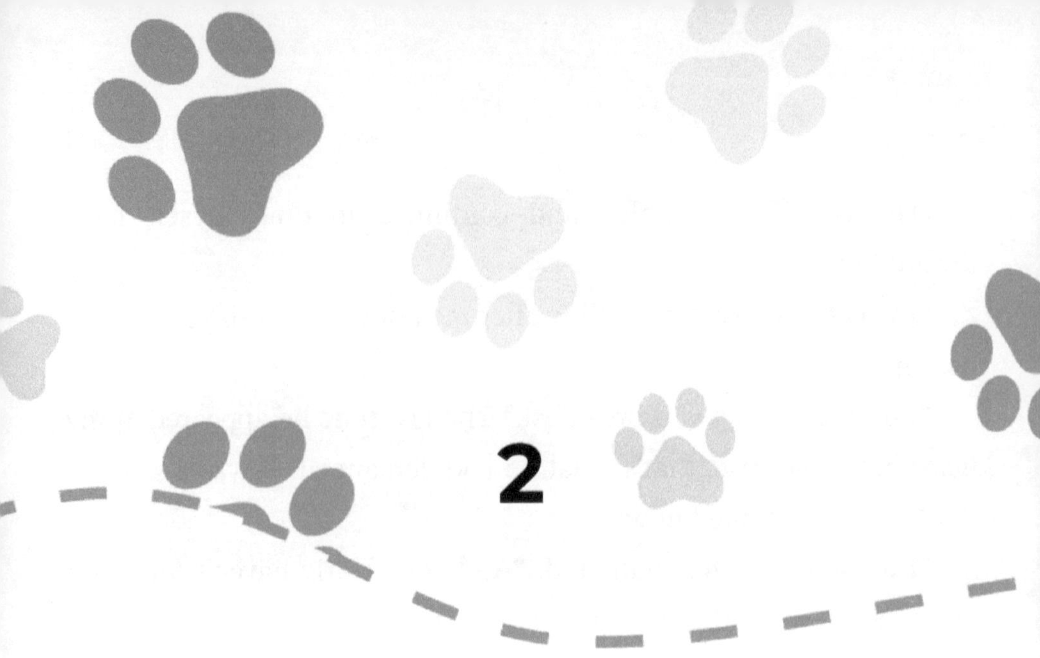

2

I awoke a short while later. A very big part of me hoped this false start to my day was nothing more than a bad dream, but no.

My former boss, Mr. Fluffikins, sat curled up on my chest, and he was staring at me intently. "Are you done with the theatrics now?"

"Get off me," I spat, brushing him off so I could sit up and clutch my pounding head.

"A little more respect for your employer, please," he rasped.

My employer, ha! I'd never applied to work for the Paranormal Temp Agency nor did I want to. I was quite happy in my role of part-time romance writer, full-time free to do whatever I wanted.

That was, until Fluffikins and crew turned up and made everything topsy-turvy.

The black cat continued to sit close by, glaring at me.

A cloud of little black hairs blew into my face and made me

sneeze. I didn't bother to cover my mouth, hoping the disgusting spray would finally rid me of my unwanted feline visitor.

He groaned and trotted down the hall. "I'll wait for you at the kitchen table. Come when you're ready, and perhaps bring a bit of steak or shrimp?"

Of course. Simple cream wasn't good enough for this nuisance. It was only pricey cuts of meat that could appease him. But why did I even care enough to remember? I didn't want him in my space, and I didn't want to be in his, either.

So I lay there splayed across the old threadbare carpet in my tiny cottage rental for quite some time, hoping if I delayed long enough that Fluffikins would see himself out.

Unfortunately, it was not my lucky day.

"What are you doing here?" I moaned as I shuffled into the kitchen.

Fluffikins sighed as if I were the one showing up uninvited in his home. "I already told you, the board has a new assignment for you."

I grabbed a banana from the fruit bowl on top of my fridge and stared daggers at the little black cat while I unpeeled. "I don't accept."

He rolled his oversized golden eyes at me. "The matter's already been decided."

That was when I choked on a piece of banana, wheezing and coughing as it slid down my throat. "Decided? Without me? Not again."

"That's why I'm the boss, and you're just a temp."

"What if I don't want to be a temp?"

"Too late," he revealed with a flick of his tail.

"You know, you could try flattery on occasion," I pointed out, leaning back against the fridge and closing my eyes. It was still way too early for any of this. I needed at least another week to recover from the last time this little black cat had turned my world upside down. Yet here he was again, and if there was a way to get him to take "no" for an answer, I hadn't quite figured that out yet.

"I don't need to tiptoe around your delicate human feelings." His voice grew deeper and more off-putting. Fluffikins had this creepy way of slurring all his words into a single nonstop sound. It completely destroyed any cuteness his whiskers and fuzzy face lent him and took him straight into the realm of night-time horrors. "What I need is your help recovering our missing field agents."

I opened my mouth to tell him off again but stopped when I realized what he'd just said. "Field agents have gone missing?"

He hung his head. "Yes, some of our finest."

Previously, Mr. Fluffikins revealed that what most humans consider to be stray cats are actually agents working in the field to help maintain the magical balance and alert the various regional paranormal boards to any possible signs of upset.

"Do you need me to go check the local shelters to see if they're there?" I offered. As much as I didn't want to set a precedent of him being able to call on me at any time and for any reason, I did have a heart. If actual lives were at stake here, then…

"Don't be silly," he hissed, whipping his eyes back up to mine. "That's the first place we looked, but no such luck. What's more, agents continue to disappear from the street."

I pulled out a chair and took a seat. "What's happening to them?"

"No idea, and I don't really have time to pluck another normie human from the streets and train her in our ways. Since Barnes made sure you didn't forget your time with us, we might as well put you to use."

"So glad to hear I'm your first choice." I swallowed back any further retort.

"Since this is a diplomatic issue, naturally you will be working directly for me." He did not look pleased about this, and neither was I.

"Naturally," I repeated, working hard to keep my expression neutral.

Mr. Fluffikins narrowed his eyes and glowered at me, an obvious intimidation tactic. Still, it totally worked.

"Fine, but only because lives are possibly on the line," I ground out in full admission of defeat.

"Lives are always at stake when magic is involved. Didn't you learn anything the last time around?"

"I guess not," I said around a giant mouthful of banana mush. "So when do we start?"

"Right now," he said, jumping off my kitchen table and making a break toward the door.

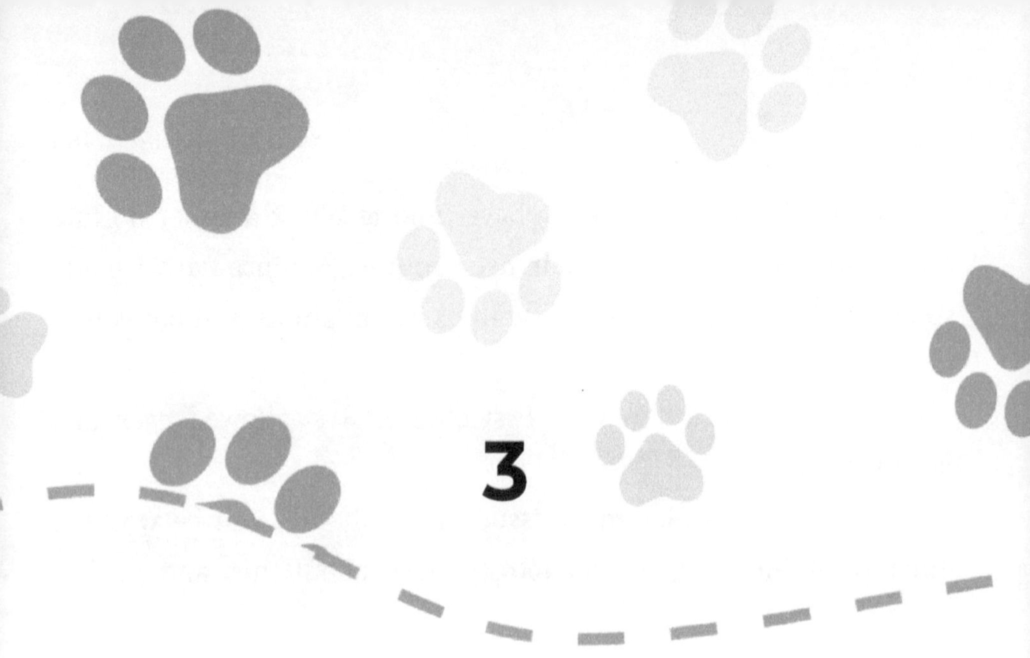

3

Instead of giving chase as Fluffikins darted toward my door, I stayed glued to my seat and let out an enormous yawn. The last time I'd gotten a proper night's sleep was during the short magical coma I'd been put in following my last big assignment from the boss cat. Ever since then, it had been terrifying flashbacks or long nights spent lying awake and questioning how I'd ever missed something as big as the existence of magic—let alone for 35 years.

Needless to say, I was pretty darned tired. Especially when taking the early hour into consideration.

Still, if lives were on the line, I guessed I could put in one more assignment for the job I'd never asked for and definitely didn't want.

"Let me take a quick shower to wake myself up some and then I'm all yours," I said with an agreeable smile. As soon as I said these words, I knew they would not be well received.

Sure enough, Fluffikins curled his upper lip at me and shook his head. "What part of *we start now* do you not understand? It's the *now*, isn't it?"

I glowered at him. Could I just ignore his wishes and head to the shower, anyway? No, he'd probably follow me in there, and the last thing I needed was an obnoxious feline staring at my naked body and making snide remarks. "Why are you so mean?" I bit out.

"Why are you so lazy?" he shot back.

I scoffed, but my tired brain was unable to come up with the perfect snarky comeback. Instead, I threw my hands in the air and marched toward the door.

The black cat followed me outside into the dawning sunlight, appearing quite pleased with himself.

I raised a hand to shield my eyes. "Now what?"

"Hold me," the cat said almost sweetly, but I was nobody's fool—and especially not his.

"Eww, no."

"Do you want to fly or not?"

"I can't fly, Mr. Fussy Britches. You took my magic." I could feel him staring at me with those unnervingly intelligent eyes, but I continued to glance toward the horizon.

"First off, that magic was never yours," he corrected in that serpentine way of his. "It belongs to the Paranormal Temp Agency. Secondly, pick me up and hold me tight to your chest."

"But—" I began to argue, but that quickly turned into a loud, sonorous, "OUCH!"

Fluffikins growled and sunk his claws into my pajama pants, then proceeded to climb me like a scratching post.

Instinctively, I grabbed for him and pried him and his sharp claws from my side. As soon as I did, a burst of pink magic shot forth from his little cat body and propelled us up into the sky above my guest cottage.

Ahh, who could forget the sparkly pink magic that held more power than all of the board members put together? In fact, I'd been actively trying to and hadn't been able to yet.

I clutched Mr. Fluffikins's slinky body for dear life as we flew faster and faster toward our destination. I'd definitely enjoyed flying more the first time around, when I was seated on a broom and seemed to have at least some control of the process.

At a loss, I squeezed my eyes shut and focused all my energy on squeezing that crazy cat to my chest. I didn't open them again until I felt my bottom fall into a padded office chair.

"That's enough! Let me go!" Fluffikins cried, hissing and snarling as he struggled against my death grip.

I let go as instructed, and he jumped onto the table, then took to vigorously grooming himself—soiled by my touch, apparently. The sparkling pink magic that grounded this place rose toward the glass ceiling of the large conference room and pulled the panels shut, closing me and Fluffikins inside.

"I thought there wasn't any time to shower," I mumbled in irritation. Even if I was just a temp, I didn't appreciate the double standard at play here. After all, I hadn't asked for any of this. Yet again, all I'd wanted was a nice, hot shower to start my day.

"I can't just leave your sweaty palm stink on my fur," he explained as he groomed, making his voice muffled and even more difficult to understand than usual. "Besides I'm the boss, ergo, the rules are different."

"Uh-huh." I crossed my arms over my chest and stayed like that for at least five minutes as the cat saw to his impromptu ministrations. Part of me was tempted to walk right out of there and find my way home, but I knew the PTA wouldn't let me go that easily.

"Excuse me, I thought we were in a rush here?" I whined, kicking back against the legs of my chair.

"Almost... done..." he informed me between long, dramatic licks.

I groaned and laid my head on the table. Maybe I could grab some quick shut eye? After all, who knew how long Fluffikins would spend grooming himself once he started? Didn't cats groom themselves like twenty hours per day—or was that sleep? Well, whatever normal cats did, Fluffikins wasn't among them. Even though he claimed all cats had magic, I doubted all of them could talk to humans the way he did.

Another five minutes passed before he finally finished and fixed a pair of impatient, unblinking eyes on me. "Well, what are you waiting for? Let's go!"

I raised my head just in time to see him running away, as if I had been the cause for the delay.

I was starting to suspect he kept temps around just so he had someone to yell at when things didn't go to expectation.

Which meant I was in for an absolutely fabulous day.

4

"Wait," I called after the quickly departing cat. Why did it seem like he was always beckoning me to follow him, anyway?

"Where's everyone else?" I asked after him now.

Mr. Fluffikins didn't stop, just yelled back to me as he continued to trot down the dark office building halls, giving me no choice but to jog and catch up. "There is nobody else. You can't expect us to call the full board in whenever you visit."

"But I didn't... Oh, just forget it." No matter how angry he made me, there was no point in arguing with him. Fluffikins would always pull rank, and I'd inevitably end up more upset than I started. Still, it would have been nice to have Greta or Parker or literally anyone else to serve as a buffer between me and the ornery feline.

I was still holding out hope for the sudden appearance of an ally when Fluffikins led me into a cavernous warehouse-like space that I instantly recognized as the spot he'd hurled gusting winds and fireballs at me a few days back during our last "training." Anxiety spiked at the unpleasant memory, causing me to stop just short of the entryway.

"What are you doing?" he growled from across the space. "Get in here, and get in here now!"

I gulped down my fear with the shoddy reasoning that Mr. Fluffikins needed my help and thus wouldn't hurt me. *Probably.* Although the last time I was under his protection, I'd almost been murdered by a disinherited magic user and his gothy granddaughter. But who was keeping track?

I marched right up to him, my breaths coming quick and shallow—but still coming, all the same. The sooner I did what he wanted, the sooner he'd leave me alone. Hopefully, this time for good.

When at last I reached Fluffikins, he leaped up into an opening in the ceiling, scampered overhead for a bit, and then descended back to the floor in an unnerving mix of natural grace and unnatural magical showmanship. He spat a shiny silver item at my feet.

"My magic," I cried. "Do I really get it back?"

This ornate piece of jewelry looked like a cross between a butterfly and a bow. The last time it had been bestowed to me by Fluffikins and the PTA, it had magic that mimicked that of the Town Witch, the role I was expected to play while they sussed out the murderer of the town's former witch in charge.

I hadn't had it for long or really even done much with it, but I craved it all the same.

The strength of the sudden desire that overtook me was frightening.

No more magic. That was one of my three rules. Yet as I stooped down to collect the brooch, anticipation surged through my veins.

"You really think we'd give you that much power again? You practically got us all killed… what? A week ago?" Leave it to a cat—especially this cat—to put me back in my place.

"Half a week ago," I corrected despite myself, then shook my head and raised my voice. "That doesn't matter, though. If this doesn't have my magic, then what does it have?"

He placed a paw on my foot, and I had only a thin ankle sock to protect me from the claws. "That magic was never yours. Remember, you're a temp."

"How could I forget," I mumbled under my breath at the same time craving this job and loathing it.

"Any questions?"

"I still have no idea what I'm doing here or why you chose me."

He tilted his head to the side and studied me. "That's not really a question now. Is it?"

"Um."

"Very well, then. Pin the asset to your shirt and follow me."

"Wait," I called again. It seemed I was always asking him to wait, but now that my mind had caught up a little bit, I did have something to ask. "Last time I couldn't see the magic until you gave me my powers. This time I could see it right away. Why?"

He chuckled under his breath. "Observant. That will do you well for today's mission."

I smiled and nodded. Then waited. Then asked, "Well, aren't you going to answer?"

"I'm the Diplomat, so it's up to me to decide who can see it and when."

"So it wasn't the brooch before? Just you."

"I'm far more impressive than a tiny piece of jewelry," he scoffed. "How do you think the magic got in there in the first place?"

"Oh," I mumbled, at a loss for words.

"Oh," he mimicked and rolled his eyes. "Now pin the asset to your shirt and follow me."

This time, I did as instructed, then trailed after him as we returned to the board room.

"Shut the door," he told me, once we were inside. He'd already jumped up onto the long table and started stalking back and forth. "Lower the screen."

"What screen?" I asked, searching the walls and ceiling but seeing nothing beyond the room, bare furniture, and swirling pink magic.

"Not you," he said coldly.

The pink magical essence that connected Fluffikins's board to the others around the world swirled to reveal a large projector screen. An image came into focus of Fluffikins standing on the table with the screen behind him.

"What the...?" I started, but then let my words fall away.

"The magic of technology," he revealed with a satisfied smirk.

That's when it hit me. He hadn't given me a single drop of magic, just a fancy piece of surveillance equipment.

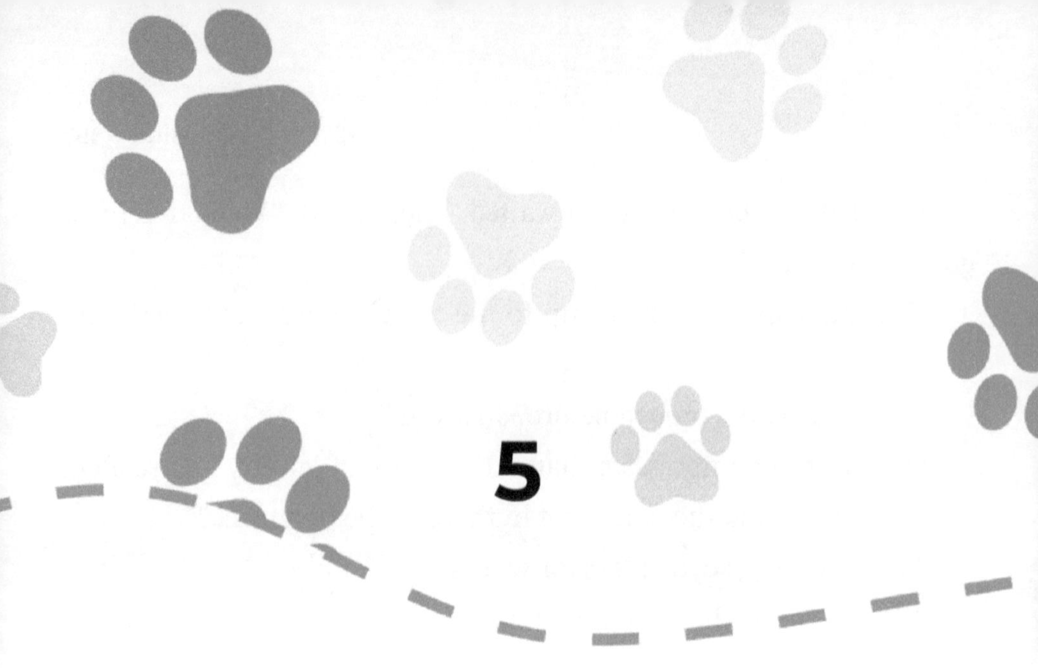

5

I clenched my jaw in irritation. "So you don't actually need my help. You just need someone to wear the cam for you."

"Exactly." The cat bobbed his head enthusiastically. "We need someone unremarkable that other magical folk won't notice. That's where you come in."

"Gee, thanks." He'd insulted me many times before, and he would insult me many times again. I couldn't base my entire self-worth on what one stupid cat thought, even if he was the one in charge.

He marched down the table and stopped in front of me, whiskers twitching contemplatively. "Although what were you thinking with that hair color? It's not quite as forgettable as the rest of you."

I reached up and touched my bubblegum pink hair. It was the one piece of evidence that I'd ever had any magical abilities at all. I'd tried to turn myself into a flamingo—long story—and instead wound up with this unique and vibrant new hairdo. It had really grown on me, too.

"I'm not changing my hair," I said between gritted teeth. Okay, maybe I was still a little sensitive, but no one liked to be insulted. Right?

"I'm not saying *you* change it." Mr. Fluffikins spun in a tight circle and then pointed his paw at me dramatically. "I'll do it for you!"

I shot up from my chair in protest. "You can't do that. Magic or not, I have rights!"

Fluffikins's mouth fell open and his eyes widened as he glanced down at his pointer paw.

"What?" I demanded, almost afraid to learn what had unsettled the normally blasé feline.

He didn't answer, but he did look from me to his paw several times as he murmured to himself under his breath. I thought I heard the words, "not possible" somewhere in there but couldn't be too sure.

Still, I needed to know what was going on here, so I ripped the brooch from my chest and pointed it at my face. A flash of a second later, my image filled the projector screen, bubblegum pink hair and all.

"Oh," I said, watching myself talk on screen. "You tried to change my hair, but you couldn't. Does that mean I'm stronger than you?" I couldn't help but laugh at this unexpected turn of events.

Mr. Fluffikins hissed. "It was just a joke. I was never going to change your stupid hair."

We both knew that was a lie. But I still didn't understand how my accidental trick performed with very temporary magic could withstand the bureau-cat's attempt to undo it. He was the strongest magical creature in the entire region, unless...

"Okay, enough gawking," he spat, turning tail and marching toward the back of the table. "It's time for your makeover."

"No. You're not changing my hair," I reminded him with a scowl. His inability to change it just now was most likely a fluke. In the greater scheme of things, I had far more important things to focus on. Like getting through this assignment with both my sanity and my sense of self intact.

"The hair can stay, but the rest of you needs an upgrade." He hopped off the table and trotted over. "Now stand."

I clambered to my feet. Part of me was offended, but the other part was too intrigued to resist. What might a magical makeover entail?

"I may be out of my element here," the cat admitted as he walked circles around me. "Summon Connie," he enunciated these two words better than I'd ever heard him say anything before. He actually paused after each syllable.

As soon as he'd given the command, the screen disappeared from the center of the room and that same sparkling pink magic shot through the roof like a golden retriever giving chase to a ball.

"Should just be a few moments," Fluffikins informed me, jumping up and plopping his butt down on the table, then licking a paw and dragging it over his forehead.

"Connie's Commerce, right?" I asked, remaining standing as my best to remember who everyone was. I hadn't gotten to know anyone the last time around, other than Parker, Greta, and my present company. Fluffikins was in charge of the board, but it also comprised six other important magical figures for the community. In addition to the chairman, there was the Town Witch and liaisons to the force, schools, cemeteries, agriculture, and commerce.

While I hadn't gotten to know Connie very well during our previous adventure, I remembered she'd been very well-dressed and a bit brusque in her speech. She certainly wasn't afraid to contradict Fluffikins or anyone else, either.

And a few minutes later, she floated down to join us in the board room. Despite the early hour, she looked as if she'd just spent the past couple hours in the salon. She had on a full face of makeup and wore her hair perfectly coiffed. Despite her larger size, she moved with effortless grace. So entranced was I that I almost couldn't look away.

"What is it?" she snapped in the cat's direction.

"I'm sending Tawny here out to investigate the disappearing field agents. She needs to look the part." He seemed unbothered by her rudeness, even though he always gave me heck whenever I made a snide remark.

"Hmmm." Connie bit her lip as she studied me. A small droplet of blood blossomed from the resulting pressure, and her tongue shot out to lick it off.

I took a giant step back in fright.

"What? You never see a vampire before?" she asked, then bared her fangs completely, much to my surprise and horror.

I took another step back until my back pushed into the wall and let out a low, guttural whine. Was this really how I would die?

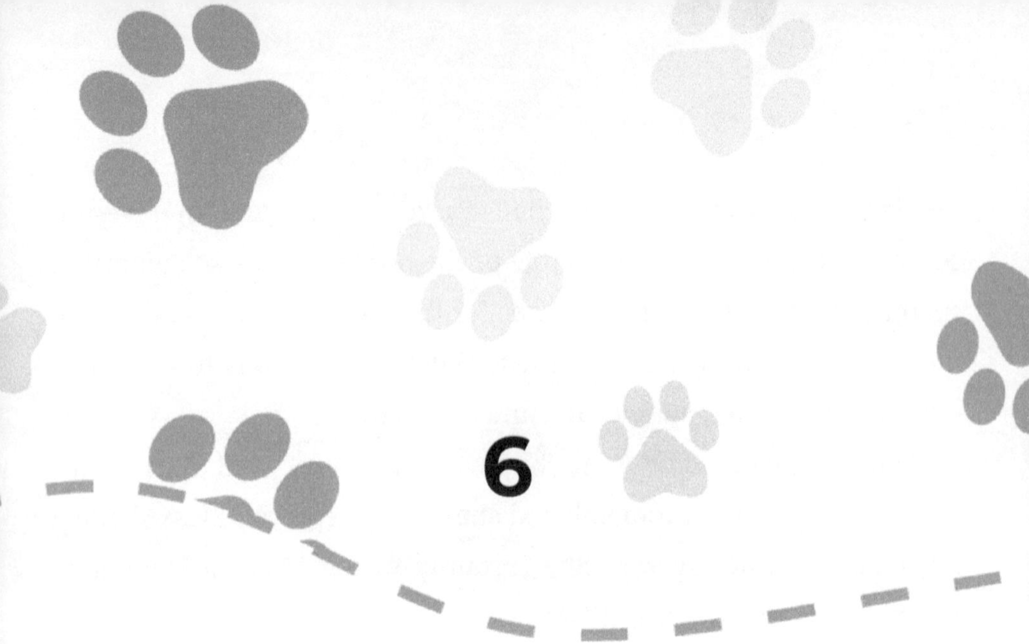

6

"So talking cats, witches, and angels are all A-OK, but you draw the line at vamps, huh?" Connie's words were playful, but her expression clearly conveyed irritation. Perhaps even a hint of hostility.

"I..." What was I supposed to say? *No, no, no. You're just fine. Please accept my blood by way of apology?* Because that was not going to happen.

"Sorry," I squeaked.

Connie shook her head with a frown. "Sorry isn't good enough." She stepped closer, eyes focused on the wild pulse beating within my neck.

Mere inches separated us now. Backed into the wall, I had no means of escape. I gulped hard, willing myself not to stress vomit all over Connie's designer heels.

"Please don't eat me," I whined pathetically, clenching my eyes closed and holding my breath.

Connie and Fluffikins both burst out laughing at my obvious terror.

"Please don't eat me, you big scary vampire!" the cat cried out in a nasally voice that was apparently meant to sound like mine.

I opened my eyes again. Now that I was no longer quite as afraid, I was livid.

"Normies," Connie said with a sigh, a slight smile playing at the edges of her lips. Her blood red lips.

"I… I don't appreciate you making fun of me," I sputtered, trying to appear calmer and more collected than I actually felt. "It's not my fault I've never met a vampire in real life before."

"Actually," Fluffikins pointed out with a bemused expression. "You probably have. Just didn't realize it at the time."

My mouth fell open in shock.

"Let me guess," Connie interjected, throwing a hand on her hip and staring at me just as intently as before. It was then I realized that she never blinked. "You've read all the old classics like Dracula, Twilight, Interview with a Vampire?"

"I mean, yeah. I'm an author. I like to read." As much as I wanted to appear fine with this latest revelation, my instincts were still screaming at me to run for cover.

"Um, are we calling Twilight a classic now?" I added to lighten the air between us.

Nobody laughed at my joke.

Connie's nose twitched as if she were going to sneeze, and then she said, "Normies get so much wrong, and by the time they finally get something right, it's completely outdated."

"Oh... kay," I said, because it seemed she expected me to say something.

"Vampires don't drink blood. Not anymore," she continued. This is the point I realized that her chest didn't rise and fall with the normal breaths of everyday life. Probably because she wasn't alive. She was a freaking vampire.

I furrowed my brow and stared at her, partially in disbelief and partly in continued horror. "Then why did you just...?"

She cracked a grin for the first time. "To mess with you. Obviously."

"Do you drink deer blood like the Cullens?" The better I understood the intimidating creature standing before me, the less I would fear her. At least, that's what I hoped.

"No, dear. I'm dead. I don't have to eat or drink anything at all."

"So you're more like a zombie?"

She waved a finely manicured hand at me dismissively. "No, no. I also don't eat brains."

Fluffikins hopped up on the table and cleared his throat. "Allow me to intervene. Otherwise this could take all day."

We both turned toward the boss cat, awaiting an explanation.

"Vampires drain the life-force from humans to survive," he revealed.

A shiver ran through me. "Yeah, blood."

Connie shook her head. "It used to be, but not anymore."

"Then what—?"

"Money," they both said at once.

I thought about this for a moment but couldn't reconcile what they were saying now with the stories I'd always heard about vampires growing up.

"In your 'modern' world..." Connie made air quotes here. "Money is immortality. If you have enough, you can practically buy your way out of death."

"No, that's not right. Rich people die all the time," I argued, refusing to believe what she was telling me. She was right. It seemed I drew the line at vampires.

"Just the normies. Magicks can live forever, if we want to," Fluffikins supplied. "It's part of the reason everyone says cats have nine lives."

"No, that's not right, either. Mrs. Haberdash died just last week," I mumbled, referring to my former landlady, whose death had begun my whole association with the Paranormal Temp Agency.

"She didn't want to become a vampire," Fluffikins clarified for everyone. "I did present her with that option before cementing our plan."

"Prejudiced old hag," Connie said, then added another colorful curse to top it off.

"If being a vampire is so great, then why wouldn't she go that route?" I wondered aloud.

"Too many questions," Fluffikins said with an agitated flick of his tail. "Connie's role at the PTA is not what we should be focusing on here. You need a makeover."

"There are certain things you must agree to live without," Connie whispered, her eyes fixed directly on me. "You gain immortality, but for some the price is too great."

"What's the—?"

"Enough," Fluffikins growled. "Just give her the look and get out of here."

"I don't like you." Connie glowered at the cat.

He turned his nose up and scoffed. "I never asked or expected you to like me, but you have a job to do, so do it already."

Well, at least it wasn't just me that Mr. Fluffikins treated like crud. Still, I had so many more questions I wanted to ask Connie. Hopefully, I would get the chance later...

7

Having now been unceremoniously dismissed from the board room, Connie led me to a private office I hadn't stepped foot in before.

"Is this yours?" I asked, glancing around the dark, windowless space. Rather than a typical desk and chair setup, it sported two elegant and expensive-looking club chairs separated by a marble-top end table and flanked by a deep purple shag rug.

She scoffed. "More or less, I guess. It's more for staging than anything else, and usually that falls to me because Fluffikins is a bit of a sexist and old Greta couldn't style her way out of a cardboard box."

I looked at her askance. "Staging?"

It was a perfectly logical question to ask, but Connie came across incredibly impatient. "Makeup, scene-setting, glamour. It's always me Fluffikins calls on when any beautification is required."

“Why don’t you like him?” I risked asking. As much as the black cat bothered me, at least he was predictable. I had to stay on my toes around the Commerce Liaison. Whether or not she would actually try to drink my blood, everything about her flashed DANGER in big neon letters.

“It’s not that I don’t like him. It’s that I can’t.”

I rolled my eyes at her. Darn me and my wry reflexes. “Oh, okay. That clears things up.”

She turned away from me and walked up to the wall standing opposite of the seating area. “You already know too much as it is. They should have wiped your mind and left it at that. And Fluffikins definitely shouldn’t have brought you in for a second assignment when you did such a crap job with the first.”

I frowned. “Oh, I see. You don’t like me much, either.”

“I really don’t,” she agreed as she pushed aside a panel to reveal an enormous hidden closet.

I gasped at the gorgeous luxury wardrobe hidden within the junky office building. It stretched back farther than my eyes could see. It had definitely been expanded by magic. But what use did the board have for this enormous costuming department?

Connie breathed deep as she continued inside. “Wait there,” she barked. Meanwhile, I wondered why she’d chosen to inhale so dramatically when she clearly didn’t need to breathe at all. What was she trying to communicate here?

“I still don’t understand why I need a makeover,” I called, craning my neck to try to spot her among the multi-colored garments.

“You needed one anyway, with or without this assignment. You’re not supposed to wear your pajamas outside of the bedroom, dear." Even from this distance her derision came across loud and clear.

I crossed my arms to hide my ratty T-shirt and silently fumed. This ornery old vampire made Fluffikins seem like Ms. Congeniality by comparison.

"How's the search for the new Liaison to the Force going?" I called a few moments later in an awkward attempt to make conversation.

"Not so great," she called back without the slightest hint of passion.

"Yeah, it will be hard to replace Parker," I agreed. Secretly, I preferred him in the role of Town Witch, because it meant we got to be neighbors. I definitely felt safe with him on the property, and I enjoyed watching him through my window as he tidied up the garden between our residences.

"That incompetent hack?" Connie asked, then laughed cruelly. I was starting to suspect she didn't much care for anyone.

From there on out, I stopped trying to engage her and instead waited quietly for her to return.

When she did, she held a stack of dark silken garments in her arms—mostly black with some deep purples thrown in for contrast.

I cracked a smile and attempted a joke. "Is it a paranormal thing, or do we all wear black to honor our black cat overlord?"

Connie snorted. "I wear what I want. You'll wear this." She pushed the clothes at me, then stepped out of the closet and slid the panel closed to give me a bit of privacy.

At first I thought the outfit she picked was far too large for my frame, but then I realized that the shirt, skirt, and cardigan were all big and billowy by design. I looked like the grandmother of the bride at a goth wedding. *Fabulous.*

Not seeing how to open the panel wall, I knocked, and Connie slid it open for me.

She pursed her lips and nodded slightly, then motioned toward a side table. "There are your accessories," she said of the giant mound of necklaces, bangles, and jewelry that appeared to be made of coins.

I gulped. "All of it?"

"Yes, hopefully it will be enough." She said this with a straight face.

"I thought the whole purpose was for me to be, you know, incognito," I argued as I picked up an oversized ring and slid it onto one of my fingers.

"And to do that you're going undercover." She lowered herself into the nearest chair. Neither her steps nor her seating herself made even the slightest sound. Even if she didn't want my blood, Connie Commerce was still very clearly an apex predator.

Suddenly, it became very important to me to keep her talking. That way at least I would know where she was at all times. "What am I going undercover as? Shahrazad?"

"A street psychic, actually."

My ears perked up. "What?"

"You'll set up a table downtown with your crystal ball and other props, and you'll watch. Or rather, Fluffikins will watch through you."

"You realize this is going to be incredibly embarrassing for me, right?"

"Aw, you still have dignity. *Cute.*" Something told me she didn't actually find it that cute, but whatever.

I pushed a metallic headband over my forehead and layered several necklaces together. After adding bracelets that ran halfway to my elbows on each side, I spun in a little circle to show off my new look. "Ta da!"

Connie grimaced. "What's that? Don't do that."

And I sighed. "Can I go back to the boss cat now?" I couldn't believe I was actually excited to be back in his presence.

"One last thing," Connie said, then snapped her fingers.

"Do I want to know what you just did?" I asked hesitantly.

"Nope. Now off you go!"

Before I could say anything more, she pushed me out the door and slammed it behind me. It seemed I'd be returning to Fluffikins on my own.

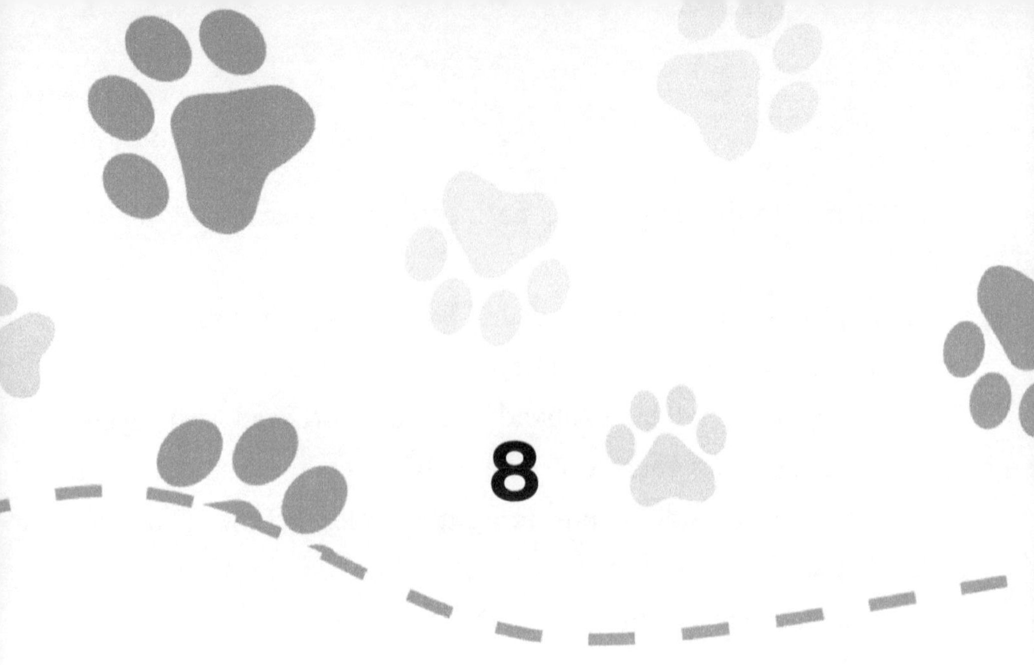

8

"Took you long enough," Fluffikins complained the second I appeared in my glorious new garb. "Let's go."

I expected him to fly us to our next destination, but instead the lanky black cat led me outside to the parking lot where a beat-up old truck idled in the closest available space.

Parker waved from the driver's seat. His salt-and-pepper hair had recently been trimmed, showing off his gorgeous gray eyes better than ever. I couldn't help but smile.

"You humans are so obvious," Fluffikins moaned just before I opened the passenger side door. "Your mating pheromones smell worse than my litter box."

Parker, who'd apparently heard every word, laughed into the back of his hand.

Meanwhile I stood there rooted in place and absolutely mortified.

I asked myself for the hundredth time that day why I'd submitted myself to such embarrassment. It wasn't on Parker's behalf. I could see him any day now that we were neighbors. So why did I let this little cat order me around?

Unbothered by my change in mood, Fluffikins jumped into the truck and took a seat at Parker's side, flicking his tail impatiently the way a human might tap her foot.

"Come on in," Parker coaxed. "I won't bite," he added, then chomped his teeth together flirtatiously. Okay, so now they were working together to make me miserable. *Wonderful.*

I let out a deep breath and then slid in, taking care not to make eye contact with either of my companions. "Why aren't we flying?" I asked as Parker backed out of the parking space.

"We can't exactly land in the middle of downtown without drawing some unwanted normie attention," Parker explained, pulling out of the complex now.

"Okay. That makes sense," I agreed.

Fluffikins placed a paw on my leg and waited for me to make eye contact. "Since you know so much about vampires from your books, do you know something of psychics as well?"

I couldn't tell if he meant to be sarcastic or not. I also had no idea how to answer that question. It's not like I'd be channeling people's dead loved ones or anything. As far as I knew, the plan called for me to fake my way through to a breakthrough in the case. Mostly I was a pawn—a strangely dressed pawn with an overblown backstory—but a pawn, nonetheless.

"Vampires, huh? I guess that means Connie helped with this little makeover. You look nice by the way, Tawny."

My heart fluttered in my chest. I loved the positive attention from Parker, but at the same time I wished I'd never met him. If we hadn't met, then he'd have let my memory stay wiped so I could move past all this magic stuff. Or perhaps I never would have gotten involved with the PTA at all. After all, he was the one who'd dragged me in against my will.

Fluffikins started to cough and hack. "Gag me on a hairball. There are those pheromones again."

Parker was quick to come to my defense. "Go easy on her. This is all very new to her."

"The PTA could have been done with her altogether, if not for your interference," the cat snapped back. "Since when do you care about our temp's feelings? Going soft in your middle age?"

Parker shook his head, drawing my attention away from the road. When he caught my gaze, he offered a reassuring smile. "Don't worry about him. This should be a much easier assignment than last time. You just have to hang out, tell a few fortunes, and keep an eye out for any trouble."

I twisted my hands in my lap. "Two out of three are easy. The one problem being that I don't know how to tell the future."

"That makes you no different than 99.9% of working psychics out there, then. You think actual magicks waste their time on norms?"

"Oh, wow. Thanks for that," I mumbled, shifting my gaze toward the side window.

"I didn't mean you. You're different."

"Pheromones," the cat mewled in agitation.

"Oh, c'mon, Mr. Fluffikins," Parker ground out. "Do you expect us not to talk to each other at all?"

"In my presence, no." I glanced over at the little cat and saw him sitting with his head held high and his expression unflinching.

"Then next time call someone else to drive the truck," Parker shot back.

"You know I would do it myself if I could."

"Yeah, but you can't, thanks to those clumsy paws of yours."

There was a story here, and any other time I would have pursued it until the bitter end. Today I just wanted to learn how to do my assignment so I could finish it to the demanding cat's satisfaction and go back home to my boring, predictable normie life. Who cares if the PTA looked down on me and my mostly simple life? I loved it exactly as it was... before they'd decided to mess that all up.

"Tawny," Parker said gently. "You'll be fine. Just say general things and watch how the customer responds. Pick up clues from their dress, talk, what have you. Believe me, it'll be enough."

"Sounds like you've done this before," I pointed out, unable to stop the smile that bloomed on my face. I really needed to stop crushing on him—for my own sanity and future safety.

He laughed and shrugged his shoulders. "Maybe once or twice as a party trick."

"You normies are so easy to impress," the cat added with a note of derision.

"And you magicks make everything needlessly difficult," I spat.

"There's no reason that I needed to dress up like this in order to run some simple surveillance."

"Actually, there is," Parker said, surprising me.

"What do you mean?"

"You'll see," he said with a smile I took as a warning for what was to come.

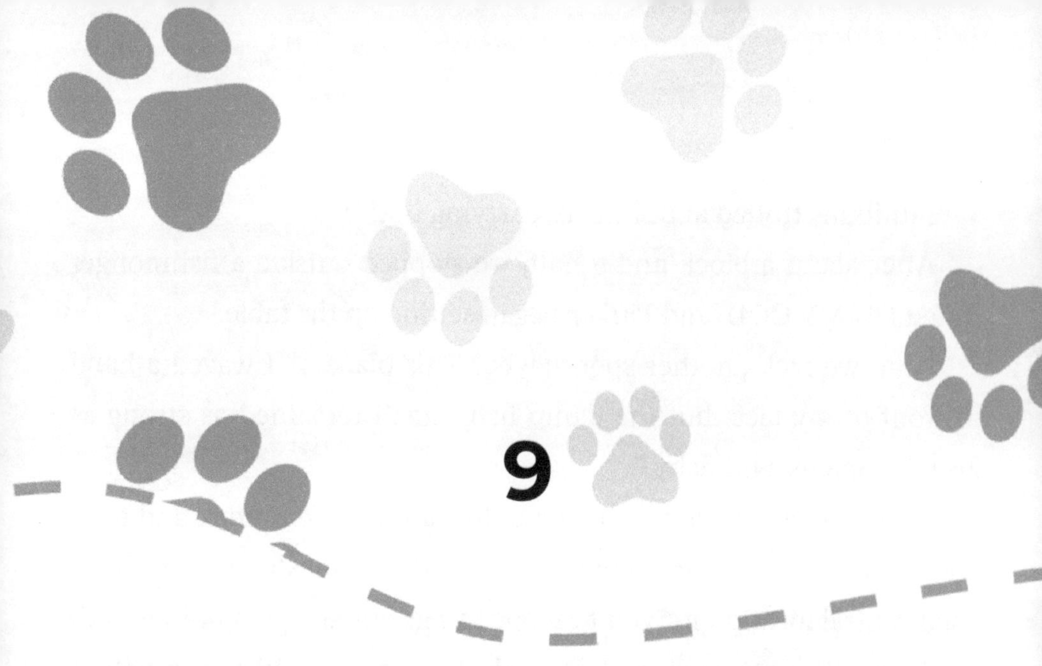

9

Downtown Beech Grove, Georgia, was but a stone's throw from my cottage... At least it would have been if we had skipped the large detour to the Paranormal Temp Agency HQ first. The quaint commercial district was a big part of why I'd chosen to move here in the first place. The old-fashioned storefronts were both odd and charming. Despite its status as an incredibly small town, Beech Grove attracted a fair number of retirees due to the fact it had perfect weather almost the entire year round.

Now that I knew more about the hidden paranormal operatives, I suspected magic had more than a little bit to do with that. I'd have to remember to ask about that later, provided Fluffikins didn't try to wipe my memory again after today's spy mission.

Parker grabbed a duffel bag from the truck bed and handed it to me, then pulled out a folding card table and a pair of chairs and slammed the access door shut.

Fluffikins trotted at our heels, carrying nothing.

After about a block and a half, we stopped outside a fishmonger called OH MY COD, and Parker began setting up the table.

"Can we pick another spot maybe? This place…" I waved a hand in front of my face, but the damp fishy smell remained as strong as ever. "…Smells a bit fishy."

"The field agents love to come to this alleyway on break and feast on the leftovers the fishmonger puts in the dumpster for us. It's a good central location for you to scope things out and get familiar with the team," the cat explained after checking no one else was within earshot.

Parker motioned for me to hand him the bag, and I did. Then he set it on the table and began pulling things out.

"What's all this?" I asked, studying the colorful assortment of cards, crystals, and what have you. I jumped back in fright when he pulled a human skull from inside.

Parker pushed it toward me and chuckled. "This is just Fred Head. Don't fear Fred Head."

"Is it alive?" A shudder racked through me. Of course, I knew a disembodied skull couldn't hurt me, but it still freaked me out.

"He was once a long time ago. Now we just use him as a communication device. Go on," Parker said, pushing that creepy Fred Head even closer. "Say hello."

"Um, hi," I squeaked, wiggling my fingers in a wave.

The skull's jaw open and closed in speech, but it was Mr. Fluffikins's voice that came forth. "Stop playing around, and get to work!"

"Whoa," I said stupidly. Even with all the magic I'd seen the past several days, Fred Head still stopped me dead in my tracks.

"Now you and I will be able to converse freely. The normies will just assume it's a gag," Fluffikins explained via Fred.

Parker set the skull back down on the edge of the table. "If you need to call the boss cat, pat Fred twice on the head and then say what you need to say."

I wrapped my arms around myself in a hug. "I suppose a cell phone would have been too obvious?"

"Bah, boring," Fluffikins growled as he jumped up onto the table beside the macabre comm device. "Besides, we developed Fred technology centuries before that Bell guy came a long and brought a taste of our awesomeness to the general population."

"Uh-huh. And what does that do?" I asked, pointing toward the glass ball Parker had extracted and was now carefully arranging on a gold stand right before one of the two chairs.

"This is your beacon," Parker explained. "If there's a problem, it will flash a color that corresponds to the warning we want to give."

This time I actually rolled my eyes. It seemed they made things needlessly difficult just so they could add a bit of stylistic flair. "Again… You guys do realize cell phones are a thing, right?"

"Stop questioning everything and just listen," Fluffikins spat.

"Right." Parker nodded. "It flashes three colors: red, yellow, and green."

Mr. Fluffikins picks up the explanation from there. "Yellow means a potential danger is coming and green—"

"Means everything is good to go?" I guessed.

Fluffikins reared up and hissed. "Heavens, no. Green means be on high alert. Danger is imminent. And don't interrupt."

"Um, shouldn't that be red? You know, red alert?" This system made no sense, and if its senselessness got me killed, I'd be so angry.

"Red means the problem has been dispersed and you can go back to normal," Parker said placing his hand over the orb and tapping his fingers.

"Oh, I guess that kind of makes sense," I conceded, even though it would require completely recoding what those colors meant in my brain from years of (mostly) observing traffic laws.

Parker grinned. "Yup."

"It's also kind of confusing, though," I added.

His grin widened. "Yup."

Great. Well, as long as we were all on the same page here.

"If you took things at face value, this would be much easier for all of us," the creepy skull told me. And even though I knew Mr. Fluffikins was the one speaking through him, I couldn't help but address Fred Head directly with my response.

"That pretty much goes against the whole hidden paranormal world thing you have going here. Doesn't it?"

Fluffikins hissed.

Parker hung his head and laughed.

I just stood there confused. Maybe this new assignment wouldn't be easier than the last one, after all.

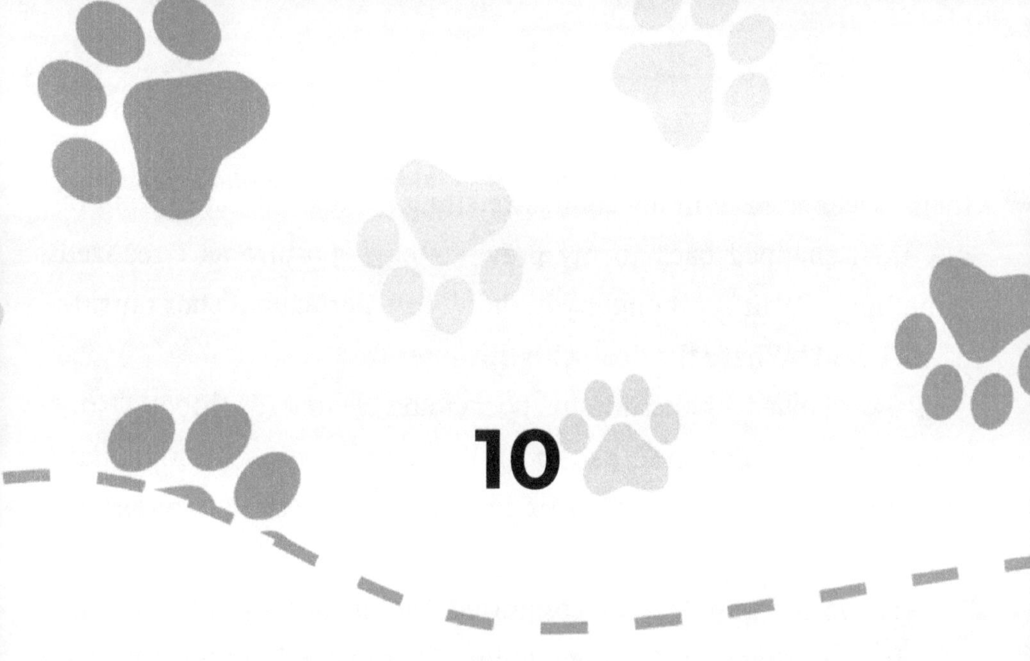

10

“What’s the second chair for?” I asked, after I finally took a deep breath and settled into mine.

Parker and Fluffikins exchanged funny glances.

“Go on. Tell her,” Parker urged from where he stood at my side. “You’ve kept this from her long enough. She’ll find out any minute anyway.”

The cat groaned, then sat down in front of me on the table. He jerked his head to the side, widened his eyes, and then looked over to Parker.

I twisted to glance in the direction he’d been looking and noticed an elderly couple walking hand in hand, approaching us quite slowly.

“Right, I guess it falls to me then.” Parker cleared his throat. “Long story short, the PTA has a new intern, and she’ll be assisting on this assignment.”

“Oh, good. It won’t be quite as boring sitting out here all day then." I leaned back in my chair, stretching my legs out far in front of me, then snapped back to my previous erect posture as I realized something. "Wait... I thought you didn't hire permanent staff outside of the board? What's the deal with this intern?"

Parker jabbed a hand into his pocket and cleared his throat. "Normally, uh... No. But she'd like to fill the open position for force liaison, and we'd prefer to trial her first before making such an important decision."

His words would have comforted me if not for the strange mannerisms that accompanied them. They were intentionally not telling me something, and I didn't like that one bit.

I nodded slowly. "That makes sense, but then why do you need me at all? It seems someone qualified enough to be considered should be fine on her own. Am I wrong?"

Parker glanced toward the elderly couple and smiled. They were still several paces away. He kept his eyes focused just above my head as he spoke. "We need someone to keep a close eye on her, and seeing as you're already acquainted..."

"What? I hardly know anyone here!" I argued. At the same time a heavy weight of dread dropped into my stomach.

Parker suddenly became very interested in the sidewalk. His lips moved and he mumbled something, but I couldn't make it out.

So I got out of my chair and came to stand right beside him. "What did you say?"

He briefly met my eyes. "Um, it's... Uh... Melony Haberdash."

"What?" I exploded. "But she tried to kill me!"

"She didn't, though," Parker pointed out with a hesitant grin and impossibly slow shrug of his shoulders.

"And somehow that qualifies her to work for you guys now?"

When he didn't answer, I threw my hands up in the air. "If she's in, I'm out." Home wasn't far. I could rush back and barricade the door. Or I could find somewhere to hide. Or hire a ride share and leave town without bothering to pack up my things first. None of these were great options, but they all beat dying at the hands of a snarly teenager.

Unfortunately, before I could stomp off, Fred Head spoke. "Keep your friends close, and your enemies closer," urged Fluffikins's sibilant voice.

"That's right," Parker said, apparently finding strength now that his superior had weighed in, too. "Like it or not, Melony's tied to this town because of her family's lineage. She can't be Town Witch, obviously, since I now fill that role and I definitely don't plan on getting murdered any time soon. Still, she's a powerful young magick. We have to give her the chance to redeem herself."

"No, you don't," I said coldly. I still couldn't believe he believed this crappy logic. Melony and her grandfather had tried to kill him, too. They'd tried to kill all of us! And I was all for forgiving grudges—dirty, cheating ex-husbands aside—but it had only been a few days!

I seethed where I stood, still deciding my best course of action. I doubted I could actually run or hide from the Paranormal Temp Agency. One way or another, they'd get me and drag me back into duty.

As I weighed my non-options, the elderly couple passed me and entered OH MY COD, one after the other. The sickening scent of the fresh-ish catch of the day made my stomach turn again.

"Think about it," Parker said gently. "She could be especially useful if her grandfather continues to cause problems. And this is the quickest possible way to fill our vacant position. Otherwise, it could be years. These things take so much time, and all the while, our position in the region will be vulnerable."

They were telling me to think about it, but they really meant that I should just accept their logic and do as told. That was not okay with me. "I don't—" I began.

But I was cut off with the door to the fishmonger swung open to reveal Greta, the angel who served as liaison to schools and who had saved my life last time around. I ran forward to hug her, still so grateful for all she'd done. I didn't even care that moving closer only strengthened the smell of whatever fish was on sale for the day.

But instead of returning my gesture of affection, Greta flinched. It was only then I looked past her to see a second person standing in the doorway.

Melony.

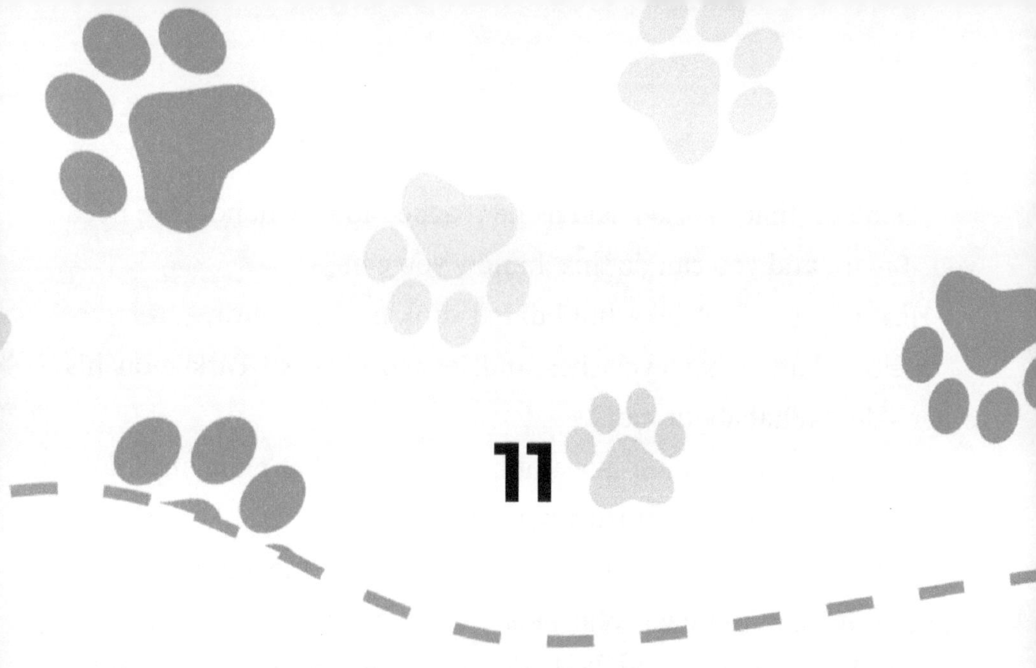

11

Melony spotted me about the same time I spotted her. Immediately, she narrowed her eyes and raised her hand as if about to cast a spell on me… again.

"You've gotta be kidding me. This is my babysitter," she spat to the others without taking her eyes off me.

Well, at least my ill feelings were mutual.

"I don't like it, either," I said, crossing my arms over my chest and averting my gaze. Hopefully I didn't just mess up some alpha power play by being the first to break eye contact.

"And I don't care what either of you like," Fluffikins intervened via Fred Head. "You'll be on your best behavior, or you'll both be excommunicated."

I smirked at the little contract loop he'd just revealed. "Oh, so if I just throw one good punch right now, then you'll stop forcing all these random temp jobs on me?"

"Don't do that," Parker said as he reached for my hand. "We need you, Tawny, and you can do this. I know you can."

Heat rose to my cheeks, but I didn't yank my hand away.

Melony batted her eyelashes and leaned close to Parker on his other side. "What about me?"

He glanced toward her questioningly, and in that moment, I definitely saw he didn't like or trust her, either.

While she had his attention, Melony winked at me, then stuck her tongue out. Ugh. Eighteen-year-olds.

Fluffikins jumped into Parker's arms, and both Melony and I drew back. "Let's be on our way, Barnes. They should have it from here."

Parker nodded. "Sure thing." Then turning back toward me for a brief moment, he said, "Tawny, remember the tools that are here for you. If you need anything, don't hesitate to use them. I'll be by to check on you later."

"Yup, the talking skull and colorful orb. Got it." I flashed him a thumbs up and a forced grin.

Parker smiled, then took off down the street with the cat boss in tow. I kept my eyes trained on them until they reached the truck and climbed inside.

"Guess it's just us," I murmured to my new companion as the engine rumbled to life and the guys drove away. We both stood on the sidewalk outside the fishmonger, a couple steps back from our table. It couldn't have been much later than nine o'clock in the morning, and while foot traffic had begun to pick up nearby, it still seemed too early for anyone to be going to market for fish.

That gave us an uncomfortable amount of privacy.

I glanced at Melony through my peripheral vision. Today she wore the same beat-up combat boots as she had the last time we'd met, AKA when she and her grandfather had tied me up and taken me prisoner with the intent to kill me. She also wore a long flowy dress that was mostly navy blue with small black roses pattered on the wispy fabric. She'd added a black pashmina wrapped around her shoulders but, unlike me, wore not a single piece of jewelry.

"Don't talk to me." Melony thrust back one of the folding chairs and fell heavily into it.

I met her eyes, which were rimmed in heavy black kohl. She also wore a dark blue shade of lipstick that was probably meant to complement her dress but instead gave her a corpse-like appearance.

"Yeah, I guess that makes sense," I said to her. "Seeing as last time we talked, I kind of outsmarted you and totally ruined your evil plans. I'm guessing your grandpa wasn't too happy about that. Huh?"

"Shut up," she said, kicking a boot at the ground like a toddler on the verge of a tantrum.

I knew I probably shouldn't bait her, but I was still pretty angry about the whole thing where she tried to kill me a few days earlier. "Why do you even want to work for Mr. Fluffikins? Is it because cheating your way into power failed, and this is your backup plan?"

"I don't have to tell you anything," she fumed. I hadn't seen any of this attitude with the others. Did she hate me more because of my non-magical status? I couldn't tell if it was some kind of new prejudice to which I was previously unaccustomed, or if she disliked me for personal reasons. I supposed neither option was great, seeing as I was stuck with her for the time being.

"You know, all your non-answers aren't helping me to trust you any better," I pointed out with a shrug as if it didn't matter, though it actually mattered very much.

She rolled her eyes and grabbed her phone from her pocket. "I don't need you to trust me. I just need you to stop talking and focus on finishing this assignment so we never have to see each other again."

"What happened to your grandpa, by the way?" I asked, wishing I'd been awake enough that morning to remember my phone. It definitely would have given me something to focus on other than the animosity between us.

Melony sighed heavily. "I don't know."

"So too afraid to be on your own?" I raised an eyebrow in question, but she didn't glance away from the tiny screen in her hands. "Better to switch sides than be without a boss telling you what to do?"

"I don't owe you any explanations," she repeated, then pushed a pair of earbuds in.

Now I sighed. "I can see this is going to be a long day."

She glanced at me briefly and removed one bud. "It'll go by faster if you—"

"Stop talking. Yeah, I got it."

Yup, I'd definitely be moving away from Beech Grove as soon as possible to avoid future neighborly get-togethers like this one. I just needed to survive today, then I could start packing my bags.

And hopefully forget magic ever existed.

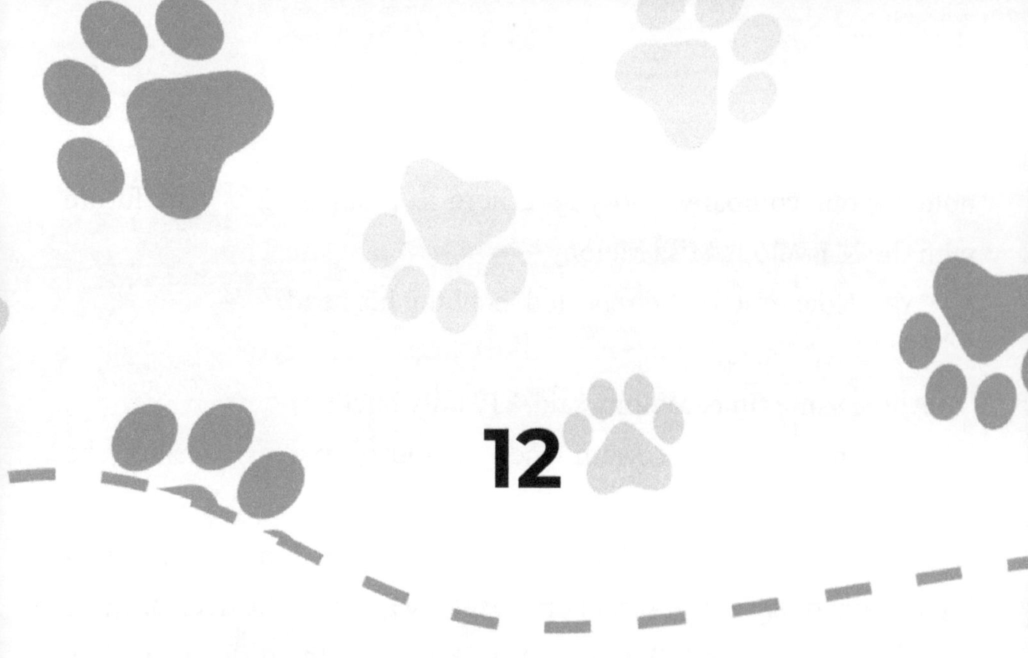

12

At first, I glanced around in search of anything suspicious happening downtown. After a couple hours passed with no activity, though, I reasoned that Fluffikins would probably just pick up whatever he needed via my brooch cam and switched to staring off into space and seeing how long I could wait before I surreptitiously stole a peek at Melony's phone to check how much time had passed since last I checked.

Around eleven, people at last started to drift toward the fishmonger in hopes of an early lunch. And fifteen minutes later, we had the first taker for our services.

"How much to get my fortune told?" asked a man wearing dingy khakis and an army green flannel over a sports T-shirt.

"Oh, hello there." I elbowed Melony in the side to get her attention.

"What did I say about—" She put on a huge phony grin upon

noticing our company. “So you’re here to glimpse into your future with the Marvelous Miss Melony?”

“Yes. How much?” he repeated, bobbing his head.

“It’s free,” I said.

At the same time, Melony said, “Twenty bucks.”

The man looked toward me, obviously having decided he preferred my pricing.

“Don’t listen to her. She’s just the assistant. I’m the one with highly honed psychic powers here.” Melony grabbed the deck of cards and began to shuffle. “Tell you what. We’ll split the difference. Only ten dollars, and believe me, you’re getting one heck of a deal here.”

He nodded and pulled out his wallet to pay Melony.

She grabbed the money and stuffed it into her phone case. “Now. Pick a card.” She stopped shuffling and fanned the cards out on the table before him.

Our customer did as instructed, choosing from the center of the pile and pointing.

And my companion psychic nodded and picked up the card, keeping it hidden from both the man and me. “Now, what’s your name?”

“Tom,” he said with a smile that revealed crooked teeth. “Nice to meet you. I’m hoping you can tell me whether my wife would—”

Melony flipped the card face up on the table, interrupting him mid-speech. “*Death.* I think that’s self-explanatory. Enjoy your day. You don’t have too many of those left now.”

“Melony!” I shouted, shoving the cards at her so that several flew off the table.

The morose man had already begun to skitter away from our table with slumped shoulders and a shuffling gait. Poor guy.

"Wait, Tom," I stood and called after him. "Don't listen to her. That's just a bit of comic relief before you get your real fortune. Come, let's have a look in my crystal ball."

His pinched expression practically broke my heart as he turned back our way and approached my side of the table.

I pulled the orb in front of me. It sat clear and unassuming. Meanwhile, Melony was already back on her phone, which meant it fell to me to improve his mood.

Say general things and observe the target for clues as to what they might like to hear. That's what Parker had suggested, and that's what I would do now.

Before Melony had interrupted with her cruel prediction, Tom had begun to ask a question about his wife. I also noted that he wore a simple gold band on his left ring finger. His appearance was a bit disheveled, and I guessed he worked a low-paying job in manual labor. He'd also approached us wanting to have his fortune told, which meant he was after an answer of some sort.

I waved both hands over the crystal orb, keeping my expression serious. "Yes, yes. It's all becoming clear now, Tom."

"Really? What do you see?" he asked, a small smile playing at the edges of his mouth.

I reached in and let my inner romance author out to play. "Despite recent hardships, your wife still loves you very much. For your next anniversary, skip the usual gifts and offer her a romantic getaway. Spending that quality time just the two of you away from the normal hustle and bustle of everyday life will make your marriage stronger than ever and revitalize you both."

Tom's smile faltered. "But what about the death card your friend pulled?"

Ick. I tried not to flinch at his casual referral to Melony as my friend, seeing as we were anything but. I also knew very little about Tarot, but I tended to be pretty good at talking my way out of trouble, so I decided to give it a shot rather than once again reminding him that Melony had only been trying to get his goat with her phony prediction.

Not that mine was any more authentic, but still...

"The death card, yes." I brought a finger to each temple and rubbed as if deep in thought. "It's a very powerful card, but it does not predict literal death. Rather the end of an era. Your troubles will soon be over. Keep on your current path, and soon you'll see."

If possible, he looked even sadder now than when Melony had told him he'd soon be dead. "You mean I am going to lose my job? I was afraid of that."

"No, no, no," I cried. "It's a positive change. Not a bad one."

"But you said—"

"You're taking it too literally," I sputtered. "Go home and meditate on what I've said, and soon all will become clear."

"Okay, thanks. I guess." Tom hung his head and ambled away.

I watched him go, wondering what I could have done differently and hoping that Melony and I hadn't ruined his day too much.

That was when a blurry flash of black caught my eye.

It was moving fast and coming straight at us...

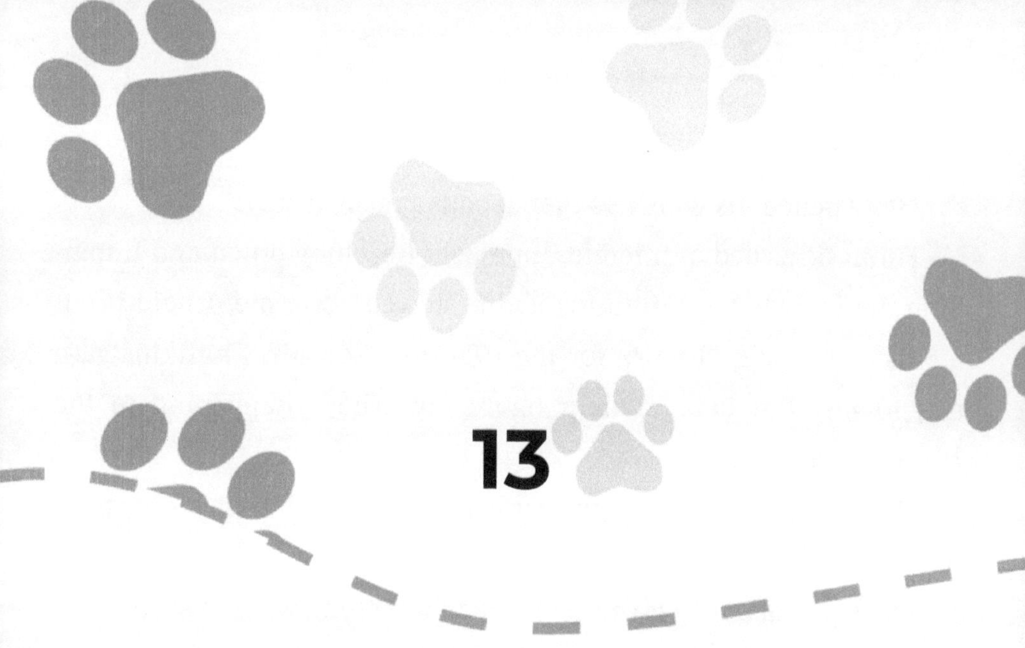

13

As the blur grew closer, two things happened. I realized I probably needed to see an eye doctor… and also the dark shape finally began to come into focus.

It was a lanky long-haired cat, mostly dark gray with black tabby stripes. He took a sharp turn into the nearby alley, and I immediately got up to follow.

If Melony noticed my abrupt departure, she didn't say anything about it—or make any effort to follow. Definitely better that way.

"Hey, you!" I bellowed as I tore into the alley.

Sure enough, the shaggy Maine Coon stood at the edge of the dumpster, ready to dive in. Noticing me, he straightened himself and waited.

"Can you talk?" I asked.

His tail quivered, but he said nothing.

"You're a field agent, right?" I tried again.

He twitched his whiskers then let out a raspy meow.

Hmm. I needed a different approach. Reaching down and unpinning the brooch Mr. Fluffikins had bestowed upon me, I held it out for the cat to see. "I work for the PTA, too. See, Mr. Fluffikins gave this to me. I'm here to help figure out what's happening to the missing field agents."

He regarded me stonily, not budging in his unwillingness to speak with me.

I was just about to give up on the whole thing when a second cat jumped out of the dumpster and landed on its edge with a clumsy thump. The chubby calico took a moment to struggle for purchase before addressing me.

"Why would the boss send you?" she asked in a high-pitched voice that hurt my ears.

"Stop it, Mungo," the previously silent Maine Coon hissed. "She was just about to go away and leave us to our vittles."

"Hey, hey. I come in peace." I put both my hands out in front of me and approached slowly. "I just want to find out what's happening here, so no more field agents go missing and so that I can go home and get back to my life."

The fur on Mungo's back raised. "Wait, Lester. What about the ones who have already gone missing? Doesn't she want to get them back?" her shrill voice dug deep into my brain, giving me an instant headache.

It took me a moment to regather myself. "Yes, yes, of course. I want to do that, too."

“Then why didn’t you say that?” the silver Maine Coon asked, pushing his nose into the air.

“I guess I got put off by the whole not talking thing—You know what? No. It doesn’t matter. I want what you guys want. Don’t you want to stay safe while you’re on the job?”

“There is no guarantee of a field agent’s safety. We knew that when we signed up,” Lester informed me dispassionately.

Mungo’s ears perked up and she crept along the lip of the dumpster to come closer to her companion. “But, Les, what about that time you—”

“Enough!” he yowled in warning.

“Remember, you were patrolling with Percy when he got taken, and—Ahhhh!” Mungo’s words were replaced by a giant scream when Lester took a swipe at her and knocked her back into the dumpster.

Wouldn’t you know it? I was just about to give up on this pair when they revealed this back-alley conversation might not be such a waste of time, anyway. Clearly, Lester didn’t want to talk to me, but if I kept trying, the other cat might just tell me in his stead.

“What was she saying about Percy? Was he abducted? Did you see anything that might lead us to who took him?” I asked, keeping my voice calm, as if I weren’t dying to know the answer so I could complete this case and go home to my poor neglected shower stall.

Lester flattened his ears back against his head. “We’re done here.”

But then Mungo pulled herself back onto the dumpster with an oof. “But, Les, what if this human can help us? I don’t want to get catnapped like Percy.”

“No one’s going to take you. No one would want to,” he spat.

"Oh, like a day with you is such a walk in the park!" Mungo reared up and attempted to take a swipe at Lester but lost her balance and fell into the dumpster again.

"Really," I pleaded. "I just want to help."

Lester's voice grew deeper, his tone more threatening. "Then go away and leave cats' business to cats."

"But Mr. Fluffikins sent her," Mungo called from inside the dumpster. "Won't he be angry if we don't tell her what we know?"

Her argument made, the fat calico hopped out of the dumpster, bypassing the rim and landing beside me on the asphalt.

The silver Maine Coon groaned. "If a broken clock can be right two times per day, I guess you can be, too, Mungo."

"Yup!" The other cat now sat straight and proud, thrusting her nose into the air as she danced happily on her front paws. "Now tell her about Percy."

"Not so fast." Lester jumped down to join us. A new mischief lit in his eyes, telling me it would require much more work to get a straight answer out of these two.

Sure enough, he flopped over onto his side and whined, "If you want me to talk about these awful, painful memories, it will cost you, and it will cost you good."

14

Lester rolled back onto his feet, raised a paw, and let his claws out with an unnerving schlink. "You help us, and we'll think about helping you."

"But you already said we would help," Mungo pointed out, eliciting a low rumble of warning from her comrade.

"Hey now!" I shouted, beginning to panic. Sure, I could probably take a couple of stray cats if things came to blows, but I really didn't want to beat up on the poor little kitty cats—no matter how nefarious. "Like I said, I want what you guys want."

"I'd like old man McCaverty to toss the day's expired lot so we can get to our lunch," Mungo purred with a thoughtful flick of her patchy tail.

"That's not what I was going to ask for," Lester raged, showing off his fangs.

"Now don't get snippy with me, Les," Mungo warned, her tail now puffy and full like a raccoon's. "If you knew what you wanted to ask for, you'd have asked already."

I was beginning to see how Mr. Fluffikins was the cat to have gotten promoted out of the field. For all his faults, he could intellect circles around these two. "You don't have to eat spoiled leftovers. I can buy you fresh fish, if you want," I offered, hoping it would be enough to stop the coming fight. I had a feeling these two had more than just this score to settle.

Mungo deflated, returning to her normal size, then cocked her head to the side as she considered my words.

"Ohhhhh," she purred. "Did you hear that, Lester? She'll buy us some fresh. We haven't had a treat like that in ages."

"This is supposed to be a quick break, and then back to work," Lester growled, but even he seemed to be coming around now.

I saw my opportunity and decided to go for it. "Tell you what. You stay here and think about my offer. I'll go inside and buy some fish. You know, just in case. When I get back, the two of you can tell me what to do with it."

"Deal!" Mungo squeaked enthusiastically.

Lester rolled his eyes but made no verbal argument.

"Okay, just wait there. I'll be back. Right back." I walked backward until my heel snagged a stray box and caused me to trip, then I turned around and jogged back to our pop-up psychic shop.

"Give me that ten dollars we got from Tom," I said, nudging Melony's shoulder and holding a hand out.

"Hey, this is mine. You didn't want to charge him anything at all.

Remember?" She turned away from me, hunching her shoulders and disappearing into her phone.

I stomped my foot. "Just give it to me."

"No," she mumbled.

I didn't want to tell her anything, but giving her a trace bit of info was better than having to physically pry the money away from her. "But I have a lead on our case," I said.

She turned to me, eyes wide. "What kind of lead?"

"There are a couple field agents hanging back in the alley. I think they'll talk to me if I bring them some fish." That was enough. She didn't need anything more. She just needed to give me the money.

She shrugged and went back to her phone. "So bring them fish." We were now to the point where even if she hadn't tried to kill me previously, I still wouldn't like her very much. Was this a teenager thing, or a foiled villain thing? Suddenly, I was quite glad I'd never had any kids.

I clamped a hand down onto her shoulder. "I don't have any money on me, and I am not robbing a fishmonger when you have a perfectly good ten-dollar bill sitting in your wallet."

"Fine. Whatever. Just go away, please." She sighed and slipped the bill from her wallet, then balled it up and threw it at my chest.

Of course, I fumbled the crumpled currency, causing Melony to snicker and heat to rise to my cheeks. It's not like I wanted to impress her, but I didn't appreciate her making fun of me, either.

Once I had the tenner in hand, I hurried into OH MY COD and hoped the cats would at least be a bit patient when the promise of a fresh lunch was involved. Of course a line several customers deep had already formed before me with only a single old man to serve everyone.

“C’mon, c’mon,” I muttered under my breath.

With my luck, both Mungo and Lester would be gone by the time I returned to the alley.

15

After completing my purchase of a laughably small tilapia filet, I returned to the streets ready to wow my witnesses. Um, provided they were still there.

When I hurried out of the shop, the first thing I noticed was that the orb had begun to flash a powerful yellow that rivaled the brightness of the sun. The next was that Melony had gone missing.

Well, actually, I knew exactly where she'd gone—to commandeer my witnesses and steal all the glory for herself, no doubt.

Well, not on my watch, kiddo.

I picked up my pace and turned sharply into the alley. What I saw made me drop my newly procured bribe to the pavement.

"Melony!" I whisper-yelled, doing my best not to attract attention to the unseemly sight. "Stop that right now!"

She just laughed as Mungo, Lester, and one other cat I hadn't yet met hung in the air a couple feet above the dumpster, unable to move anything but their wide, terrified eyes. She'd pulled this same trick on me and Greta when we first met, but that was in a private residence. Right now anyone could walk by and see her obvious display of magic.

"Let them go," I repeated, shoving her hard from behind. "They haven't done anything wrong."

"Then why were you questioning them?" she said without breaking focus. Her spell held strong.

I briefly contemplated rushing forward and tearing the frozen cats from the air. But besides having magic when I had done, I was willing to bet Melony moved much faster, too. The only way I could get out of this one was by either distracting her or outsmarting her. I'd managed to do both during our last encounter. I could best her again, especially seeing as that was my only option in the moment.

"I was questioning to see what I can learn about the missing field agents," I explained numbly. "That's all. Not because they're suspects."

"Yeah, I think I'll do things my way. Thanks." Melony let out a low rumbly laugh, and for the second time that day I swear I'd never wanted to punch someone so bad in all my life. If she fought back, though, I'd be toast. *Thanks a lot for not giving me any magic to protect myself, Mr. Fluffikins,* I thought bitterly.

Fluffikins! That was it.

I ran out of the alley and stopped just short of crashing into our table. I tapped the Fred Head twice as Parker had instructed. "Melony's gone rogue!" I screamed at the talking skull.

A couple came out of one of the shops across the street, and I smiled awkwardly at them. "Just rehearsing for an upcoming performance of Hamlet," I explained, grabbing Fred Head and bringing him close to my face. "To be or not to be, haha."

They shook their heads and continued on their way.

"Fluffikins," I hissed again.

But he didn't answer, instead the bright yellow orb switched to a piney green full of swirls.

Green. What did that mean? It was either really good or really bad. But which?

"Mr. Fluffikins," I hissed yet again. "Answer me."

He didn't.

I hit Fred Head two more times in frustration. I was starting to think that maybe magic and technology shouldn't mix. Maybe our whole mission was doomed from the start.

"What is it?" the boss cat answered at last via our freaky communicator.

"It's Melony," I rushed to explain before he grew impatient and cut the connection. "She's cornered three agents and immobilized them with her magic. I can't get her to let them go. Anyone can see. She'll blow our cover. All of ours."

My favorite black cat let out a string of explicit kitty curses. "Never send a normie to do a magick's job," he grumbled.

I narrowed my eyes at the skull. "Hey, none of this is my fault. It's all on Melony."

"But clearly you don't know how to stop her, or you would have already," Fred Head told me, and I imagined Fluffikins on the other end of our connection shaking his head in disappointment.

"Well, if you'd given me magic..." My words fell away when I saw the same nosy couple had turned back to watch me from further up the street.

I waved the skull at them. "Did I mention it's a Hamlet Hocus Pocus mashup?" I offered meekly. "Stop that, Thackeray Binx. You're so crazy. Ahhh!"

"I'm on my way," Mr. Fluffikins promised before Fred Head's jaw snapped shut.

I wanted to rush back into the alley and wait for him there, but that busybody couple kept staring at me as if I had sprouted horns or something. It's like they'd never seen a talking skull before!

Growing increasingly agitated, I started to rattle off random soliloquies that I'd memorized a long time ago for my theater elective in college. When they still didn't budge, I shouted, "Come back next weekend for the proper show. This is just the dress rehearsal."

They turned and looked at each other and then graced me with a polite round of open-palmed claps. Still, they didn't leave.

"That's it for now. I'm taking an hour's intermission!"

And finally—finally!—they left. When I was sure they wouldn't turn back a second time, I got up and calmly walked toward the alley, even though I wanted nothing more than to sprint.

Hopefully I wasn't too late to make a difference.

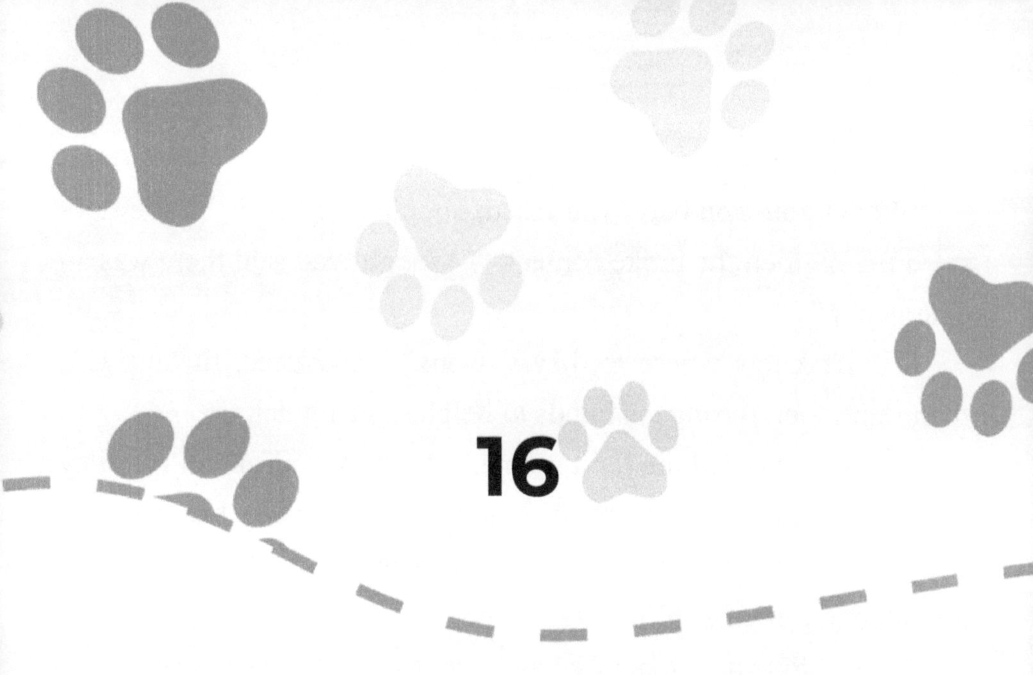

16

As it turned out I *was* too late to make a difference.

Where Melony once stood levitating her three feline puppets, the alley now lay empty and lifeless.

"Melony?" I called hesitantly as I tiptoed toward the dumpster, afraid of what I might find. "Mungo? Lester? Anybody?"

There was nothing in the oversized bin beyond the expected mix of trash and things that probably would have been better off in recycles.

"Hello?" I tried again warily.

Yes, I still wanted to go home, but how could I, given that whatever had happened here happened on my watch? I was turning out to be a reluctant hero, but this was still my story—and I couldn't bear to leave it unfinished.

Something zipped overhead, and I spun around just in time to catch sight of Fluffikins falling from the sky on a puff of pink magic.

"What's going on here?" he asked, hopping off his cloud. It evaporated the moment he broke contact. "I thought you said there was an emergency."

"I don't know where th-they w-went," I sputtered, turning left, then right, then raising my hands in helpless surrender.

Fluffikins studied me for a moment, then took off down the alley toward the street. He stopped suddenly and turned back to me, golden eyes flashing with irritation. Apparently, in all my shock, I'd forgotten to trail after him.

"Why didn't you tell me we have a code green?" he shouted.

"What?"

He ran back to join me partway down the alley. "The orb. It's green!"

Oh, yeah. I'd forgotten about that in my desperation to get through to Fluffikins and then to get that gawking couple to stop watching me. "Green means go, right?" I asked with a nervous squeak.

"No, green means we've got a huge problem on our paws!"

"I-I know," I stammered, twisting my hands in front of me. "Melony took three field agents and disappeared."

Fluffikins shook his head and took a deep, steadying breath before explaining, "No. It's much worse than that. Whoever took the field agents also took Melony."

I stared at him, shaking my head, still unsure of what he wanted me to do. "She was threatening them. She'd frozen them with her magic, and—"

"Made both them and herself an easy target," the black cat

finished for me. Not what I'd intended to say, but I guess he'd know better than me.

"Oh" was all I could manage upon learning this revised interpretation of events.

"Follow me," he said in a low growl, leading me into a tight space to the side of the dumpster. "Crouch low."

I did as told, recoiling from the stench. "What's going on?" I raised a hand to cover my mouth and nose and murmured through them.

Mr. Fluffikins curled his tail around his feet and dropped his ears low. "I didn't think our abductor would strike with the two of you sitting out there flaunting your presence."

"Wait, I thought we were undercover." I instantly regretted uncovering my mouth to speak.

My companion waited for me to stop hacking before he went on. "Mmm, actually, you were but a diversion to buy the real investigative task force some time. The fact that they struck while you were right there and absconded with an intern as well as more field agents sends a very clear message."

I didn't know whether to be more offended by his ruse or upset that it hadn't worked, so I chose to focus on finding out whatever facts I could. "What message?" I mumbled.

He puffed out his chest, drawing my eyes to the stark white patch. He held his breath for a moment, then let it go so he could answer my question. "That they're not going to stop until they get what they want."

"What do they want?" I wondered aloud.

Fluffikins simply shrugged. “I don’t know. They haven’t told us.”

“Oh.” I felt increasingly useless as this conversation went on. I had no great insights to contribute, and Fluffikins had begged for my help simply so he could use me as a distraction. As much as I hadn’t wanted this job, it hurt that he didn’t think I could do it.

“There is one thing we can do,” he said after several beats of silence. “When Melony applied to join us, I naturally fitted her with a magical tracker.”

I gasped. “So you expected her to betray you?”

“What’s that old sign you humans have? Plan for the worst, hope for the best? Besides, she didn’t do this.” He seemed so calm in his assessment, but now I had yet another reason to be angry with him—he’d intentionally stuck me with a loose cannon. If I’d have died on this farce of an assignment, would he even care? Just one more normie who mistakenly got herself mixed up in magical affairs…

“So what now? You go track her and I go home?” I asked hesitantly. Despite my hurt at how he’d chosen to handle our relationship thus far, I still wanted to help. What if by turning my back on him now, cats died? What if Melony died? Yeah, I hated her, but not enough to wish her dead. I did have some morals, after all.

“Nope. We’re both going,” he said decisively.

“But I was just a diversion.”

“Yes, and I may need a diversion again.” He winked at me, then tilted his chin up and said, “Take us to Melony Haberdash.”

Pink sparkling magic shot down from the sky and enveloped us. It felt warm and soothing like a nice bath, and I allowed myself to relax into it.

Magic. It should be mine always. Not just in times of crisis. This felt right… Like it was meant to be…

17

The fog of pink magic dispersed mere seconds later, and despite its brief presence, I felt almost naked without it.

The first thing that struck me, of course, was a gnawing absence followed by the intense cold. The temperature must have dropped at least thirty degrees. The smell of fish and rotting trash had also vanished, leaving behind the crisp, cool taste of clean sky.

I sucked in the fresh air and glanced around at the unfamiliar scenery, trying to make sense of what I saw. We appeared to be in some kind of park with wide open expanses of green and a cluster of brightly colored ramps, tunnels, and runways off to one side.

A border collie tore through the obstacle course, then jumped into his owner's arms with a long leap. Along the far fence line, a pair of smaller dogs walked circles around each other, both wagging tails and sniffing butts.

Fluffikins staggered forward a few steps, then looked back over his shoulder at me. "Where are we?"

"What? Why are you asking me? You're the one who brought us here," I reminded him.

"It was the world magic, and you know that," he hissed. Apparently, he'd become so wrapped up in the division between magicks and normies that he'd forgotten about the equally perilous divide between cats and dogs.

I lifted a finger to my lips to warn him that he should keep quiet, then whispered, "Yeah, well, I don't see Melony or any of the others, anywhere. I thought it was supposed to deliver us to her location."

"There must be some kind of magical wall keeping us from going any further."

"So now what? Do we go back to Beech Grove?"

He growled and flicked his tail. "What's with you and wanting to give up and go home non-stop?"

"You don't even need me," I ground out, still very much hurt by his previous revelation. "Why should I possibly risk my life when I add nothing?"

The black cat's eyes bore into me and his whiskers twitched as if he was in deep contemplation.

"What aren't you telling me?" I asked, reaching toward him with outstretched fingers. He'd let me pet him once as a way of showing me a vision from the past. If he wouldn't tell me why he'd involved me in this, then maybe he'd be willing to show me. Or maybe I could sneak a quick jump into his memories and find out for myself.

He leaped back, fur twitching spasmodically. "Do not touch me without first receiving an invitation," he growled.

Across the field, a beagle's ears perked up. He became rigid and pointed toward us, then took off in a run.

I was just about to grab Fluffikins for safe keeping when he spun a quick circle near my feet. The dog yipped and ran to its owner.

I shook my head to rid it of the distraction and carried on with the earlier topic. "You're keeping something from me. How can I be safe if I don't know—?"

"I'm not telling you in order to keep you safe, so stop prying!"

"Shouldn't I be able to decide things that involve me and my safety?"

Fluffikins's jaw dropped, his tail twitched, and I could have sworn he was about to say something.

But somebody else spoke first. "Lovely day for it, eh?"

I rose up and smiled at a man approaching with a leashed dog at his side. Judging from the giant head, short legs, and derpy expression, it was a corgi. Spotting my feline companion, he gave a joyous bark and began to strain against the leash.

I had to raise my voice to be heard over the dog. "Very nice."

The owner nodded and continued on his way.

"Wait," I called after him. "We're from out of town. Just stopping by for a quick stretch, and then we'll be on our way. Would you mind telling us where we are right now?"

His mouth hung slightly slack as he regarded me. "Where we are? Didn't you notice where you were going when you got on the ferry?"

I slapped a palm to my forehead. "Silly me, I've already forgotten."

"You're on Caraway Island. It's not really a place where one just stops on by. The ferry's the only way here from the mainland," he informed me, complete with furrowed brow.

"Oh." I crossed my eyes in confusion. I knew I appeared to be an idiot, but I still needed more information. "And what's the mainland?"

"Maine," he answered matter-of-factly.

Ugh. Why was it so hard to get such simple information? "Yeah, what's the mainland, please?" I repeated.

"Maine. Maine. The state of Maine. Look, are you okay? Should I take you to a hospital to get your head checked maybe?"

I laughed and waved off his concern. "Oh, I'll be fine. The fresh air is already clearing my head."

"I don't think it needing cleared was the problem," the man muttered, then power-walked away with his corgi protesting in his wake.

"Real smooth, Tawny," the boss cat spat with a little chuckle that sounded like he was about to cough up a hairball.

I shrugged. "Hey, I didn't see you getting any answers."

"Okay, so if you have all the answers, then what do we do now, Mrs. Smart Normie?" He blinked up into the sun with a self-righteous expression I wanted to wipe clean off his face.

"Ew, don't call me Mrs. anything," I grumbled as I dragged my eyes around the park in search of… something.

Luckily, something is just what I found.

"We go talk to your twin," I said with a triumphant grin, pointing toward the black cat hanging out beneath a bench at the far end of the park. Could this be one of our abducted field agents?

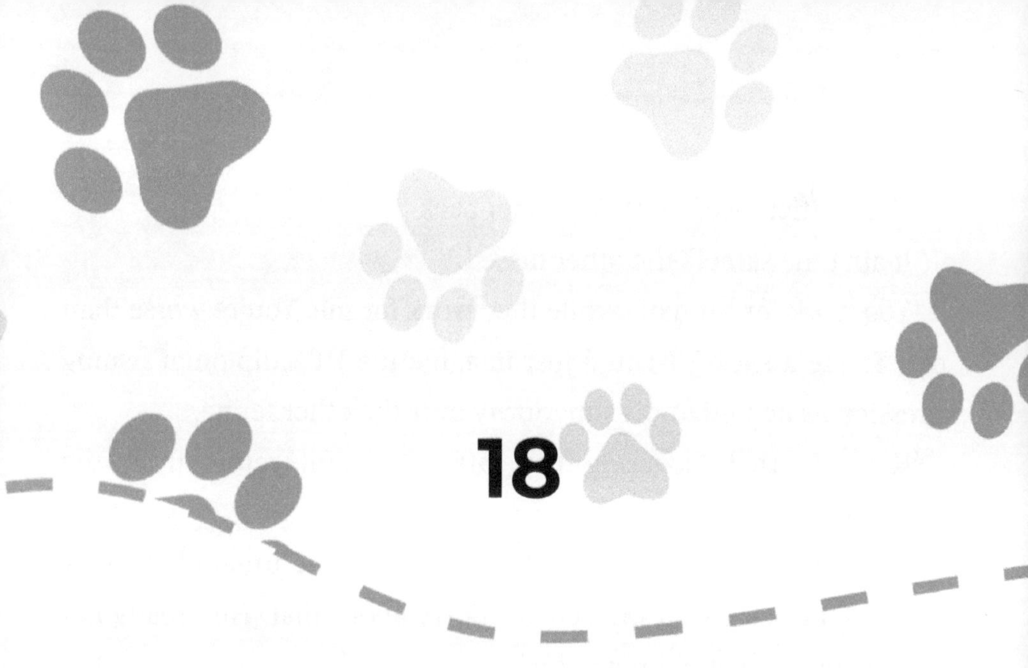

18

Fluffikins jogged ahead and joined the other black cat under the bench while I causally strode over. After all, we definitely didn't need the man with the corgi growing even more suspicious and calling someone. Whatever magic my cat companion had worked on the beagle seemed to translate to the other dogs in the park. Even the corgi quickly lost interest and left us to ourselves.

When at last I reached the bench, I took a seat and raised a hand to my ear, pretending I'd hidden a Bluetooth device there.

"One of your field agents, Mr. F?" I asked, shortening his obviously cat-like name in case any of the other park-goers overheard.

"He's a pet," Fluffikins rumbled from beneath me.

"I'm a familiar," the other voice corrected in irritation. Apparently our new friend was male. He also had a thick Boston accent, making him seem just as out of place here in Maine as me and Fluffikins.

"Same difference," Fluffikins shot back.

"It ain't the same!" the other hissed.

"You work for humans while they work for me. You're worse than a pet. You're a slave." I could just imagine the PTA diplomat's smug expression as he lorded his superiority over the other feline.

"Hey," I cried, covering the rather colorful retort from the offended cat.

I glanced down and made eye contact with the unfamiliar black cat through the slats on my bench. "Sorry about that. He's really not so bad when you get to know him."

He narrowed his eyes at me. "Yeah, I got no intention of that. Now get outta here. You're compromising my stakeout."

"Stakeout? You sound like a cop," I mused with a sight chuckle.

"I *am* a cop."

"I thought you were a familiar," Fluffikins corrected him, referring to some part of the conversation I'd missed.

"I can't be both?" He crouched closer to the ground, breaking eye contact with me. "Now get out of here before Scavo catches wise, and the whole gig's up."

Fluffikins sucked in a startled breath. "Scavo?"

"Yeah, Scavo. What about it?" All I saw was a blurry black body to one side of me and another blurry black body to the other. Yes, I'd definitely be needing that eye exam.

Mr. Fluffikins took on that same pedantic tone he took whenever describing anything magical to me. "The PTA's been tracking him for decades. He's that normie mobster who found out about magic and started using it for personal gains. Created a whole black market."

"That ain't even the half of it. So go back to your litter box and 'please try again,' or whatever your PTA thing is."

"Your disrespect has been noted and will be thusly punished," Fluffikins promised in a low rasp. "I am a diplomat for the Paranormal Temp Agency, so I can do that, you know."

"So go be diplomatic somewhere else and leave this one to the Blueberry Bay Paranormal Division," our new acquaintance countered.

"Is this like a national versus local thing?" I suggested.

Both cats hissed at me, and I returned to being a silent observer as their conversation continued.

Mr. Fluffikins spoke next. "Scavo died a couple years back, so unless he's walking around as a reanimated corpse, your mission is pointless."

"Wait. Are zombies real, too?" I squeaked. A chilly gust of air swept past, making me shiver and wrap my arms around my torso.

Both cats ignored my question.

"Shows what you know," the cop cat spat. "He's back and up to his old tricks, too."

"Not possible," Fluffikins maintained.

"Yeah, I bet you also don't think a guy fifty years in the grave can wind up as a magical talking cat, and yet here I am."

"Fine. If Scavo's back, then where is he? Because if you haven't noticed we're a long way from Boston."

"If I knew where he was, I wouldn't be on this stakeout, ya chowderhead. He's close, though."

"Yup, this one's a straight nutter," Mr. Fluffikins told me, hopping onto the bench at my side. I couldn't say I disagreed, exactly, but still, a crummy lead was better than no lead.

"Stop bullying him. He may be able to help," I said gently, then got down on my hands and knees to address the other cat head-on. Now that I saw him a bit more closely, I noticed that he wasn't an exact replica of Mr. Fluffikins. For one thing, he didn't have a white patch on his chest. And for another, he wore a thick buckle collar with an odd star symbol on it.

"Again, I'm sorry about him," I said with a polite smile. "I'm Tawny. What's your name?"

"It's Blackjack now," he revealed with a bemused smirk.

"We're a long way from home on an investigation of our own. Cats have been disappearing from the streets in our hometown of Beech Grove, Georgia, and we have reason to believe they've ended up here on Caraway Island. Any ideas how we might find them?"

He balked at me. "This whole thing is about cats? I thought you were tracking Scavo?"

"That's right. We're trying to find several missing field agents. One human girl is missing, too, I guess." I couldn't even tell him how many cats had disappeared, seeing as Mr. Fluffikins had given me the bare minimum in our debriefing.

Blackjack tilted his head to the side, then nodded. "Well, why didn't you start with that? Come with me, kid. I know someone who might be able to point you in the right direction."

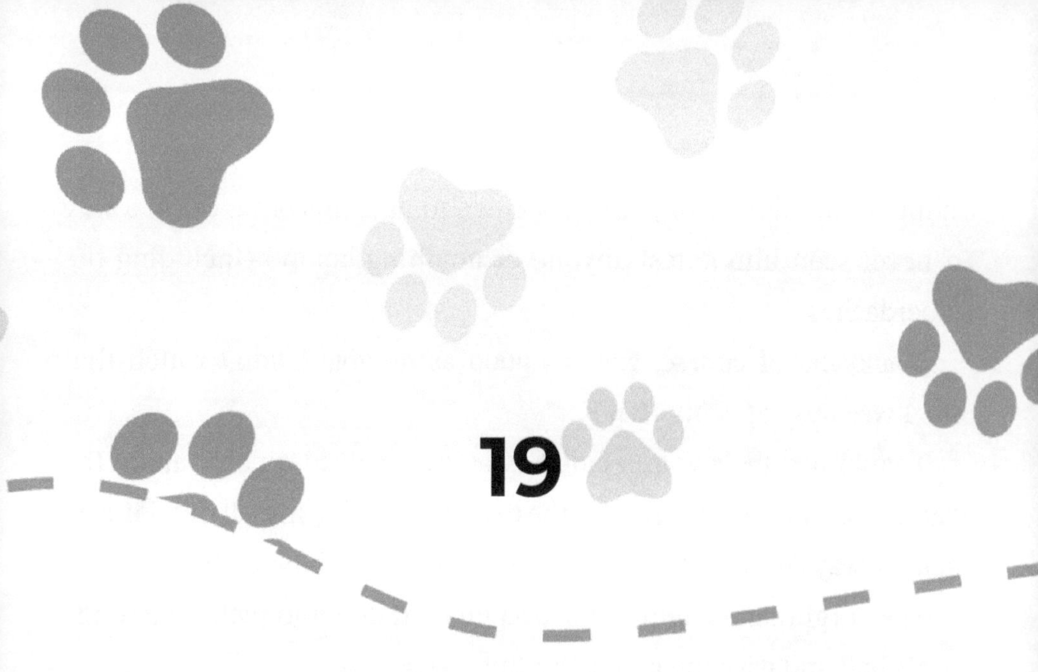

19

I got up and followed Blackjack toward a hole in the fence. He squeezed right through, then turned back to wait for me.

"Um." I shifted my weight from foot to foot. I couldn't fit through that hole, and climbing over the fence when there were already two perfectly fine exits would definitely raise the suspicions of other humans in the park.

"I'll go around and meet you on the other side," I offered.

"Suit yourself," Blackjack said with a sneer. "We'll be in the west parking lot."

"Cover me," Fluffikins said, then blinked out of view and flashed back on the side of the fence.

"Neat trick," Blackjack said with a twitch of a tail. "You pick that up in diplomat school?"

"Yeah, it was right after we removed the *R*s from Sesame Street for Boston public access." Who was this new Fluffikins? He normally had a superior air about him, but he seemed to hate this other cat in a way I'd never seen him detest anyone or anything before—including the Haberdashes.

Blackjack, of course, gave as good as he got. "Didn't watch that one. I was busy at ya mother's..."

Thankfully, their voices faded away as I walked quickly along the edge of the fence until I reached the exit. After letting myself out, I traced back the way I'd come. I found the hole in the fence, but not the cats.

The corgi man caught my eye as he bent down to pick up a dingy tennis ball and gave me a questioning glance.

I waved briefly, then turned and pushed through the uncut grasses on the wild side of the fence, searching for either parking lot or feline, whichever I could find first.

I wished for two things at this point—a warm jacket and my cell phone. Yeah, I may have been smart when it came to words, but I'd never been able to discern east from west without the aid of tech. Glancing toward the sun only hurt my eyes. It didn't tell me the direction from which it had risen.

Darn cats! Why couldn't they have just gone through the normal exit with me?

A woman with bright teal hair wearing ripped jeans and a leather biker jacket approached from the side. "Tawny?" she called.

I nervously tucked a strand of pink hair behind my ear and swallowed. "Yes, hi."

She smiled kindly. "I'm Val. Your familiar said you'd probably be lost."

"Oh, I'm not... Um." I turned back but could no longer see the corgi man or any of the people from the park, thanks to a slight incline behind me.

"You are a witch, right?" Val said as she studied me and my gothy garb. And honestly, who even knew anymore? I didn't have magic, but I doubted I was just a "normie," anymore, either.

I struggled with how to respond to Val. "No. Yes. I mean, I was, but I'm not now."

She tilted her head to the side, and a sympathetic smile flickered across her face. "Feeling all right there?"

Great. Now both normies and magicks thought I needed to get my head examined. Maybe I did. I could add that to my list for when I was safe and sound back home. First the eye doctor and then the shrink.

"I'm fine," I managed at last. "Fluffikins and I are here to investigate a string of abductions."

"So he says. C'mon, walk with me." A shiny badge that matched the star pendant on Blackjack's collar glinted from Val's belt, showing the world they belonged together. But me and Fluffikins? If there was anything actually tying us to each other, he'd chosen to keep it a secret.

"Tell me about these abductions," she pressed in a way that told me she was a far more experienced interrogator than I'd ever be.

She didn't even have to offer me a bribe to get me to sing like a canary. Unfortunately for her, I knew almost nothing.

"I don't know much," I said to establish how little I'd be able to help right from the get-go. "Several cats were taken, and one young witch named Melony Haberdash."

Val halted suddenly and turned back to face me. "Did you say Haberdash?"

I nodded emphatically. "Yeah. Silly name, right?"

Val bit her lip. "It's probably just a coincidence, but... Yeah, I'll definitely need to think on that for a bit." Her words trailed away, she shook her head, and then she kept walking.

A mostly empty parking lot came into view several paces away, but I still couldn't see either Fluffikins or Blackjack. I had no idea what business it serviced as it seemed too far a jaunt from the pet park and I could see no other businesses nearby.

"Val, wait. What is it?" I called as I jogged to catch up with her. For all I knew, she was leading me to my doom. I needed to stop trusting people so easily. After all, that's what had gotten me into this whole magical mess in the first place.

Val's steps came much faster now, and I longed for my running shoes rather than the useless black clogs Connie had forced upon me.

Was this chick really running away from me?

So much for the kindness of strangers.

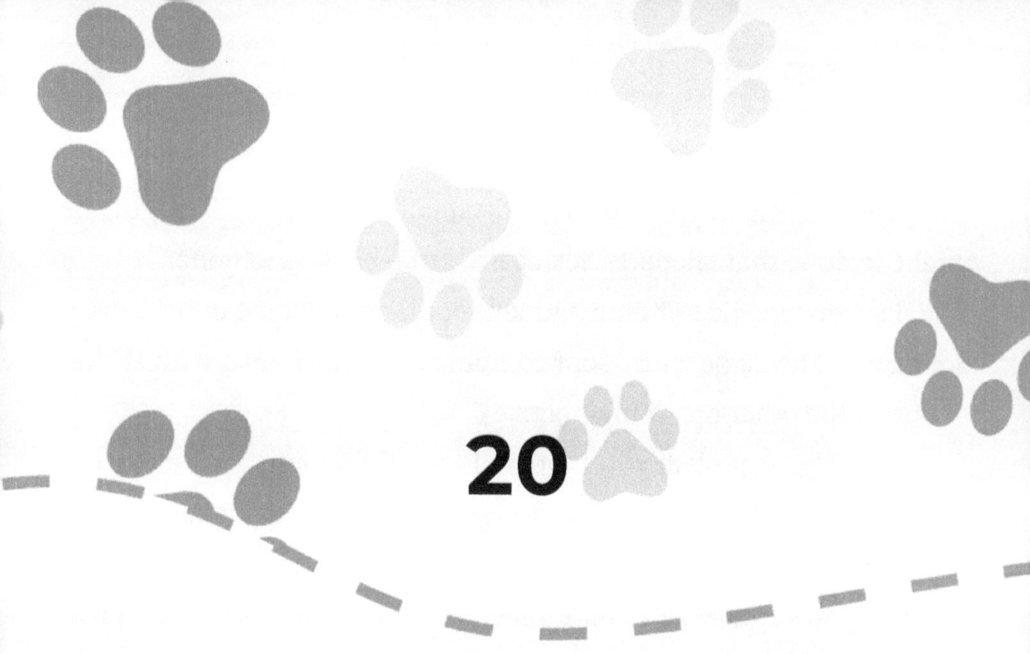

20

Blackjack trotted over to join us at the spot where the overgrowth gave way to pavement. "He's gone!" he somehow managed to mewl with a Boston accent.

Val appeared white as a freshly painted wall. I should know—I lived with several of them in my undecorated cottage. "What do you mean he's gone? Who's gone?" she demanded of her partner.

Blackjack held his tail high. Only the very end twitched. "The what's-his-name schoolboy. Fluffy? He just up and vanished."

"Weren't you with him?" I demanded, placing a hand on each hip and trying to appear scary, sassy, something. If they decided to turn on me, I'd be toast. Fluffikins and I had been much better off before connecting with this troublesome duo.

"Yeah. The whole time. I blinked, and he was gone, quicker than a nun in the Combat Zone." Blackjack raised a paw and stared at his toe beans as if they'd gravely disappointed him. "Thought he might've done that teleport trick again, but—*poof*—just gone."

Okay, my one tie to home had left, but that didn't mean he'd abandoned me. Maybe he'd just popped home for a quick chat with Parker or one of the other board members.

Yes, that was probably it. I mean, I thought Melony had left of her own volition, but Fluffikins had been certain she'd been taken.

Wait...

"Did you see a swirl of pink magic?" I asked the Boston cat, practically begging him to say yes. Seriously, even if it wasn't true, I could really use some good news just then.

"Nothing," he informed me, eyes wide as if he worried blinking again would steal me away, too.

Suddenly I felt as if I were underwater—not in that soothing, peaceful way that happened when immersed in the pink world magic, but in that horrible, terrifying way of being trapped in an undertow with no hope of escaping to break the surface.

"Guys," I managed despite the throes of panic taken hold. "He didn't leave. He was taken. Whoever took the agents took Mr. Fluffikins, too." Giving the voice to the words made me realize just how true they were. He wouldn't intentionally leave me stranded without money, identification, or any way of reaching the PTA back home. He was a pain in the butt, but he wasn't evil. Well, at least not pure evil.

"What should I do?" I squeaked in desperation.

Val placed a gentle hand on my shoulder, but it did little to quell my panic. "We'll keep working our side of this case and see what we turn up. Maybe we'll luck out and find your familiar in the process. But we can't drop our investigation to go looking for him."

"But I have no phone, no money, no one to help. How am I supposed to get him back?" I argued. The panic grew thicker around me, and I struggled to catch a breath.

"I wish we could do more, but here..." Val reached into her pocket, then pressed a roll of bills into my hand. "After you leave the parking lot, head right down Main Street. Around the corner of Main and Yarrow there's a scuzzy-looking motel called The All-Nighter. It looks bad, but it's actually really clean, and the owner is one of us. Crash there for tonight, and in the morning hop the ferry to Glendale. The first one runs at seven thirty."

I nodded along, glad Val seemed to have a plan because I was still totally lost. "Okay, okay. And then what?"

"There's a woman there who can talk to animals. Her name is Angie Russo. Not a magic bone in her body, but Jack bumped into her when we first got here. We checked into her and she seems legit. Fancies herself a bit of a private investigator, so just play that angle and she'll help you find your familiar."

"Thank you," I said, rather than correcting her about the true nature of my relationship with Mr. Fluffikins. "I will."

Nobody said anything, so I took the opportunity to ask a question. "How can I get in touch with you if I need something?"

"You don't. Maybe we'll meet again one day, but for your sake, I hope not," Val said grimly.

"Now go. We can't waste any more time standing here chitchatting when we've got a crook to catch." Blackjack motioned me away with his paw.

I took a deep breath and walked to the end of the parking lot. When I turned back, both Val and her cat familiar had vanished.

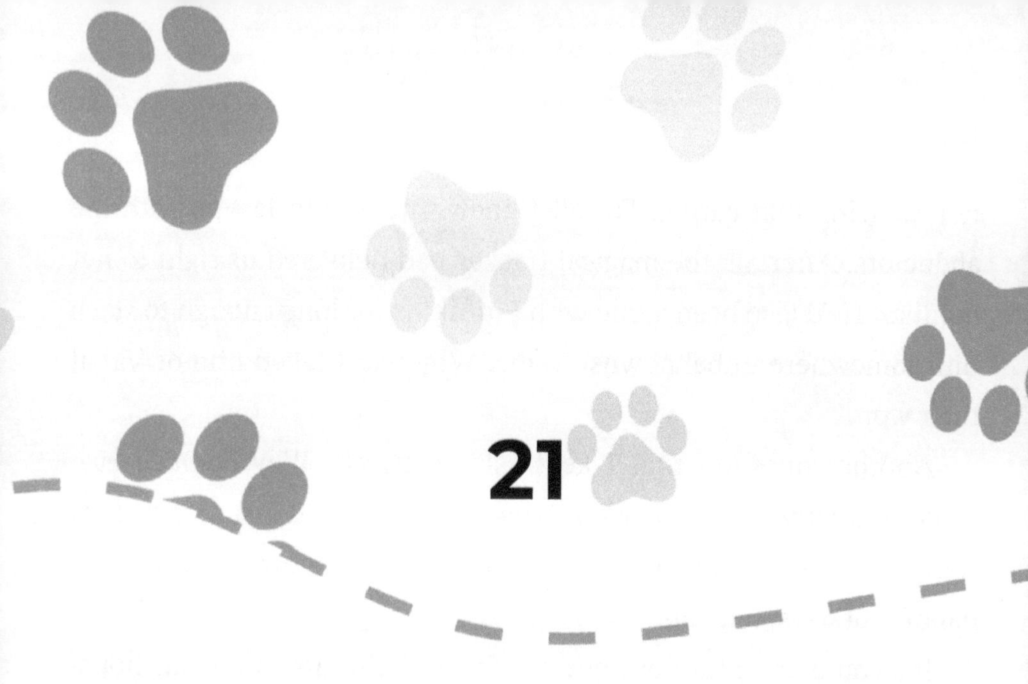

21

As promised, the All-Nighter looked terrible from the outside but was mostly okay from the inside. I resisted the urge to turn away from the cracked brick exterior that was largely in need of a power wash, knowing that I could either sleep here or on the streets.

My room smelled like a heady blend of Clorox and Pinesol, which I took to be a good sign. The first thing I did after examining my room for either hidden corpses, used contraceptives, or little baggies of powdered drugs—none of which I found, thank goodness—was to take a long, hot shower. As the water sluiced over me, I fought the temptation to relax into it and instead combed my mind for solutions to that day's outlandish string of problems.

While I was grateful to Val for offering me money and a lead, it seemed she'd taken advantage of Fluffikins's disappearance to avoid telling me what she knew about the Haberdashes. I chided myself for not realizing that earlier. For all I knew, she was in league with the abductors. After all, the magical tracker had delivered us right to her familiar. He'd also been alone with Fluffikins for long enough to stash him somewhere unbeknownst to me. Why had I taken him or Val at their word?

Another question that I kept asking myself: *Why hadn't I ever exchanged phone numbers with Parker?* True, I could just take a short walk to visit him and vice versa. We'd also only known each other a handful of days, but still.

If I could call him now, he'd be able to help. Instead, I was hopelessly alone in a far-off place and with only half the money left from the wad Val had entrusted to me. I needed to find my way out of this one and fast, because I doubted I'd be able to afford a second night in this place.

Grasping at straws, I picked up the hotel phone and dialed information. "OH MY COD in Beech Grove, Georgia, please," I said when the operator picked up.

She patched me through at once, but the line just rang and rang. Either the proprietor was too busy to answer or he'd already closed for the day. Just my luck.

I called information back and gave her the names of a few other businesses from the downtown area. This time she gave me a list of numbers, which I jotted down on the motel's stationery. I called every single one, asking whoever picked up if they knew Parker Barnes, but no one did.

Strange. How could he have lived in Beech Grove his entire life and not made a mark on any of the locals? It was like the man was a ghost.

This, of course, left me worse than I'd started, because now I was beginning to lose that last thin thread of hope I'd managed to cling to.

I tore off the sheet of paper with the numbers written on it and tossed that into the trash, then sat with a fresh piece before me and began to write a new list. This one was for any clues and inconsistencies I'd noted until this point.

First I listed the names of those who had gone missing. I still didn't know how many cats had disappeared, but I remembered Mungo and Lester talking about Percy in the alley. I jotted down their names, then added Melony and Fluffikins. That made for five missing people—er, creatures.

Next I wrote down places. So far all I had was OH MY COD and the Caraway Island Pet Park. Yes, I'd be headed to the mainland in the morning, but I didn't know yet whether that was actually relevant.

Suspects included Melony—I wasn't letting her off the hook just because she'd been taken, too—Val and Blackjack, that Scavo guy they'd talked about, and maybe even Melony's grandfather. Val certainly had a strong reaction to the mention of the Haberdash surname.

That was everything. All I knew could be condensed to a single narrow sheet of paper. *Sigh.*

I stared at it for a good long while, willing the words to rearrange themselves into some kind of revelation that would explain everything. But that didn't happen.

Frustrated, I folded my list up and stuck it in my pocket

Not knowing what else to do now, I walked to a fast-food restaurant I'd passed on my way to the motel and ate until my stomach hurt. I took a few cheeseburgers back to the motel for later, then went to bed early so that I'd be bursting with energy and ready to go the next morning.

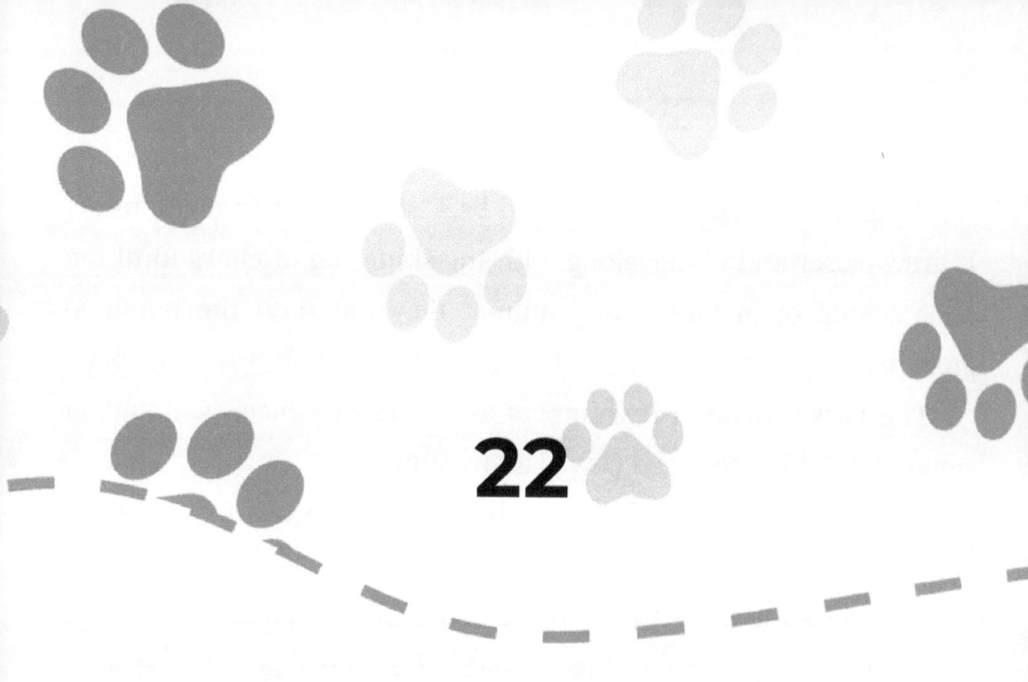

22

Apparently my Angie Russo was a bit of a local institution around this quaint seaside area called Blueberry Bay. I had no trouble at all finding someone on the ferry who could give me directions to her house in Glendale—and here I thought Beech Grove was a small town!

Most people thought the so-called "Pet Whisperer P.I." was a bit touched in the head, but they liked her all the same.

"She and her grandmother had this huge charity benefit to help the shelter. Just last night, as a matter of fact," a woman about ten years my senior revealed when she overheard me asking after Ms. Russo.

A few minutes later, one of my new friends from the ferry said she was heading in the same direction and would drop me off. And that's how I arrived on the porch of a massive Eastern Seaboard manor house just a little after eight o'clock in the morning.

When I knocked, a high-pitched bark sounded from deep inside. It grew closer and closer along with the skittering of claws until the door swung open and a tiny animal flew out onto the porch to greet me.

The barks turned to whimpers as the mostly black Chihuahua stood on her hind legs and pawed at my shin.

"She wants you to pick her up, dear," a woman's voice said from the other side of the doorway.

I grabbed the squirming canine and then straightened back up. "Are you Angie?" I asked the woman who I now saw was at least seventy years old and wearing a close-fitting hot pink velour sweat suit.

She burst out laughing as if I'd just told the world's greatest joke. "Oh, heavens no! I'm Nan, and that sweet girl in your arms is my Paisley. Angie is still sleeping off last night. We had quite the *fete.* Perhaps you'd like to come back in the afternoon?"

I mindlessly stroked the little dog's head as she shook and shivered in my arms. "Well, it's just that I have a big problem, and the longer I wait, the bigger it will get," I tried to explain. What would I do if she turned me away? Where would I go next?

Nan pressed her lips in a thin line. "I see."

I decided to get straight to the matter at heart, hoping it would endear Nan to me rather than cause her to get angry and send me away. "Is it true she can talk to animals?"

The old woman began to nod, but then paused. Her face fell. "Um, I'm not really supposed to talk about that anymore."

She chewed on her lip as we stood facing each other in silence.

The Chihuahua continued to shake with excitement.

"Would you like to come in for a nice cup of tea while you wait?" Nan offered at last.

I nodded and followed her into the living room, where a rather large brown tabby sat on the sofa watching me with what appeared to be skepticism. Could he talk like the other cats I'd met over the past week? Was he also some kind of cop, spy, or diplomat? It was hard to think of him as anything much more than a house cat, given the lazy demeanor and poorly hidden paunch.

When she noticed me staring at the tabby cat, Nan chuckled and said, "Oh, don't mind our Octo-Cat. He was born angry, I'm afraid. Come with me into the kitchen. Are you hungry? I have a batch of vanilla bean scones finishing in the oven."

My stomach rumbled at the promise of fresh baked goods, and I nodded enthusiastically.

Nan sidestepped a pop-up card table covered in balled-up napkins and other trash. "You'll have to excuse the mess. We had a big charity gala last night and are still playing catch-up on the cleaning part. We'd planned to finish, but then the dead body showed up, and—"

"Dead body?" I squeaked, taking a step back to put some distance between us. I clutched the little dog to my chest like a shield. This crazy old lady wouldn't hurt me as long as I was holding her pet, right?

Nan just tutted. "Oh, don't look at me like that. It wasn't me who killed him."

"Maybe this was a bad idea," I whimpered, ready to leave this place and try hitchhiking back to Georgia, or maybe I could stop by my publisher in New York and ask for them to send me the rest of the way.

Footsteps sounded behind me, and I turned to see a tall woman with sandy brown hair who was wearing a matching set of polka-dotted pajamas. "Good morning," she told me with a friendly smile. "Who's this, Nan?"

"She hasn't given me a name yet, but she's here for you, dear," the old woman said with a shrug.

"Why does she look like she's seen a ghost? *Nan.*" Her voice held a note of warning.

Nan shrugged again. "I was just catching her up on the events of last night is all."

"How many times do I have to remind you, murder is never a good ice-breaker?"

Nan chuckled as she put the kettle on.

"Are you Angie?" I asked, feeling at least a little safer now that I wasn't alone with Nan. "I heard you might be able to help me. My name's Tawny, and I'm not from around here."

She gave me a huge smile and swept her arm to the side in invitation. "Yes, that's me. Let's go get cozy in the living room and you can tell me all about it."

23

Angie settled onto the couch next to her cat, leaving me to take up my place on an adjacent wingback chair. The furniture was stiff, yet somehow also inviting.

I set the wiggly Chihuahua on the floor, but she immediately hopped back into the chair with me and snuggled beside my thigh.

"Do you have a case for me?" Angie asked, leaning forward slightly to convey her interest.

I nodded, wondering how much I could rightly share. "I do. It's about a missing cat. Well, several, actually."

"I can find a missing cat," Angie boasted, her eyes wide with excitement. "I've found a missing dog before—the mayor's dog, actually—and once my own cat went missing, but as you can see, he's back now."

She set a hand on the tabby's back, and he flinched. She ripped her hand away as if she'd been burned, then fixed her gaze back on me.

Maybe I was just imagining it, but Angie seemed almost too eager to assist.

"Val referred me to you. Said you could talk to animals," I mentioned, watching this new acquaintance for any signs that the rumors could be true.

And she didn't make me work very hard for it. Angie laughed so hard her face turned red. "What a kidder, that Val is. In fact, I don't even know a Val." She shrugged and rolled her eyes, overselling it so much, I had no question that what Val had told me was, in fact, quite true.

"It's okay. I'm not going to tell your secret," I promised, wishing we could just get on with it. After all, I didn't have all day to sit around trying to convince her to help me. "It's just I'm really desperate to find one lost cat in particular. His name is Mr. Fluffikins."

Angie's head snapped to the side and she glared at me with a new intensity that set me on edge. "That's not a very common name."

I shook my head. "No, I guess it's not. So can you help me?"

Nan entered with a tray of the aforementioned vanilla bean scones and three mugs of what appeared to be English Breakfast tea.

The snuggly little Chihuahua immediately left me to join her.

"What did I miss?" she asked, taking a seat beside her granddaughter. "Anything good?"

Angie appeared to have calmed down a bit now that Nan had

joined the conversation. "Tawny here is trying to locate her missing cat, Mr. Fluffikins," she explained.

Nan's eyes widened at this news. "Isn't that the cat from last night who told you—"

"Nan, you know that whole thing about me talking to animals is just a well-circulated rumor," Angie interrupted with a goofy smile and another big eye roll. She held Nan's gaze for several moments until at last the old woman looked away and took a long slurp of her tea.

"We hosted an event last night called the Black Cat Benefit," Angie continued. "Our goal was to find homes for black cats from the local shelter and to raise funds. There was a cat named Mr. Fluffikins who came in with the adoptable felines."

"But how?" I asked, wrapping my hands around my mug of tea and squeezing tight. "He was only just taken yesterday afternoon. And from Caraway Island at that."

Angie appeared unbothered by this. "Well, we're all kind of one big small town around the bay. It's totally possible that Glendale's shelter brought a few black cats from other area rescues."

I stood. "Does that mean he's back at the shelter? Should I go there now?"

Angie sighed heavily and motioned for me to sit back down. "No, he was adopted."

"Adopted!" I exploded. "No, no, no. That's not possible. He's my cat, and I really need him back!"

"It's going to be okay. If he's yours, I'm sure the new owners will give him back. We can just refund his adoption fee." Angie picked up a warm scone and took a big, luxuriating bite.

"No harm, no foul," Nan agreed.

"But where are these new owners?" I demanded. Weren't shelters at least supposed to try to find the owners before giving a cat away? It seemed they'd have at least taken the time to give him health and temperament checks. Something definitely wasn't right here.

"Let me shoot off a quick text to see if the shelter can send that over. I'm sure, given the circumstances..." Angie pulled out her phone and began typing far faster than I'd ever manage. A few moments later, she looked up at me with a satisfied grin. "There. We should hear back from them any minute."

"Please do enjoy your tea," Nan said, pointing to the mug that remained clutched firmly between my hands.

I took one tentative sip, then another. It didn't take long for me to drain the entire cup.

"Oh, here we go!" Angie said, waving her phone overhead. "The shelter just texted back."

I set my empty mug back on the tray and watched as Angie's face fell.

"Oh," she said plainly.

"What is it, dear?" Nan pressed, saving me the trouble of doing so myself.

"Mr. Fluffikins has been placed in a home on Caraway Island," she said with a strange expression.

Of course he was.

And now it looked like my strange magical journey had jumped straight into fantasy, mainly JRR Tolkien's *Hobbit: There and Back Again.*

24

Angie drove me back to the ferry and parked to wait with me. "It's not true what they say, you know."

"Hmmm?" I asked, staring off into the horizon mindlessly.

"About me talking to animals, I mean. That's crazy, right?" Angie's eyes bore into me. I could feel her intense gaze without even needing to turn and meet it.

"Yeah, totally," I agreed, offering her a placating grin.

"I just understand their body language really well. Apparently that makes me a pet whisperer." She laughed uncomfortably, and I joined in to be polite. This was going to be a long wait. I had no idea how frequently the ferry came in, and with my luck we'd be waiting around all day. Not for the first time that day, I longed for Fluffikins and his ability to fly us from place to place at record-breaking speeds.

"So what's your story, Tawny?" Angie asked next. "The pink hair and black clothes, they make quite an impression. What are you trying to tell the world?"

Oh, like she was one to judge. Before we let her house, she changed out of her polka-dotted pajama set and into what appeared to be leg warmers and an off the shoulder sweater. I was no great fashionista, but at least I knew what decade we all lived in.

"My dress is deep purple, more like a blackberry than true black," I corrected, keeping the rest of my thoughts to myself.

"But still, why so much jewelry? It's almost like you're in a costume." She offered me a goofy smile to soften the blow.

Well, she was right about one thing. I'd debated long and hard about whether to leave the heaps of jewelry in the motel that morning. I'd ultimately decided to keep it on me to avoid eliciting unnecessary anger from Connie. Even though she claimed to feed on money instead of blood, I just wasn't ready to take any chances when it came to the cranky vamp.

Then again, if Angie was sticking to her poorly constructed cover story, I could give her mine. I'd spoken too freely with Blackjack and Val, but I didn't have to make the same mistake twice.

"I'm a psychic," I said simply with a toothy smile of my own.

Angie seemed a bit surprised. "That's cool. So you can tell the future and what not?"

I shook my head. "Not really. I'm just good at reading people's body language and then telling them what they want to hear."

"Oh, so we're kind of the same?" she said with another girlish laugh.

"Yup." Both frauds with shoddy cover stories.

"I knew you didn't mean for real," she said after a moment.

I nodded but kept quiet.

The ferry arrived a short while later, freeing me from Angie's clumsy attempts to engage me in small talk.

Relief washed over me, until something awful and unexpected happened…

"I'm coming with you," Angie informed me just as I had begun to reach my hand toward the door.

Before I could argue, she pulled her car into the boarding queue. Well, I guess my investigation would be quicker with a wheeled escort. And it's not like Angie could make things even more awkward than she already had… Right?

"So you like solving mysteries, right?" I asked, at last choosing to trust her despite my hesitations. Such was my desperation.

She gave me her biggest smile yet. "Oh, yes. It's my job. Did you want to officially hire me to work your case?"

"I don't really have much money at the moment. I could get you some after we solve this, but…" I shrugged. "I can't expect you to work for free."

"Oh, yes, yes, you can. I work for free all the time. My cat's trust fund pays all our bills and then some. Plus I need the experience to keep my skills from getting rusty."

Well, that was weird.

"So you want to help?" I asked, raising both eyebrows in surprise.

Angie bobbed her head. "If you'll let me."

"Then here." I reached into my pocket and handed her the list I had made the night before. “This is all the information I have right now.”

Angie scrutinized the list; her brows pushed together in deep thought. “So many people have gone missing and you lead with your cat?”

“Oh, no. Just one person. Melony.” I pointed to her name emphasize my point. “The others are cats.”

“And what’s the rest of this?” she asked, her eyes creeping down the paper.

“Suspects and key places.”

“OH MY COD?” she asked with a giggle.

“That’s a fishmonger back home. In Georgia.”

“Georgia?” Angie burst out, shoving the list back at me. “What are you doing all the way over here? Do you really think someone kidnapped your cats and drove twenty hours to get here?”

I stared at her in awe. Maybe she wasn’t as clueless as she first appeared. “How did you estimate the length of the drive so quick? I don’t even know it.”

“My cousin lives in Georgia,” she revealed with a far-off smile. “In the Peach Plains area. Do you know it?”

“Uh, yeah, that’s where I live.”

Something new lit in her eyes. “Larkhaven?”

“No, Beech Grove.”

And that light almost instantly distinguished. “Oh,” she whispered.

“Oh,” I whispered back.

Angie didn't talk to me again for the rest of the ferry ride, proving that—yes—she could be more awkward still.

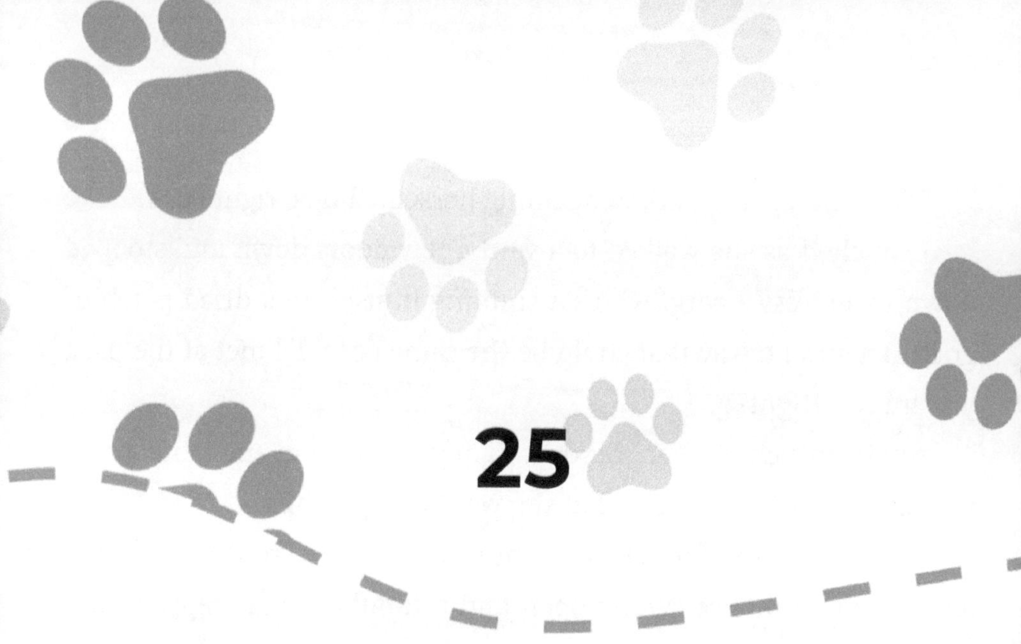

25

Once the ferry docked, Angie drove us straight to the address listed on the adoption paperwork the shelter had emailed over.

Or rather, she tried.

"Hmm, somehow I passed it. Keep your eyes peeled for house number 748," she muttered, driving slowly along the residential street.

We both watched closely, but the numbers skipped from 743 straight to 752. Definitely not a good sign.

"Did someone really give a fake address? Who does that?" Angie fumed and slapped the steering wheel.

"Someone who doesn't want to be found," I pointed out. Angie pulled the car to the side of the street and groaned in frustration.

Something was happening here. Something big. Would me and my half-mad new sidekick be enough to put an end to it?

"Wait there," she said, unbuckling herself. "I'll be right back."

I watched as she walked to a yard a few doors down and stooped down to address a corgi who sat sunning himself in a dried patch of grass. There's no way that could be the same corgi I'd met at the park yesterday… Right?

Angie crouched near the dog, facing away from me. And yet it was still incredibly obvious that she was talking to him.

They conversed for several minutes before the front door to the accompanying house swung open and a familiar man stepped onto the porch. It was the man from the pet park who thought I needed psychiatric help.

I bolted out of Angie's car and raced to help explain away our misdeeds.

"You again," the corgi owner said, his eyes locking onto mine.

"Hi, yes. Remember the cat I had with me the other day? He's gone missing, and my friend here is trying to help me find him."

He crossed his arms over his chest and stared down the bridge of his nose at us. "By trespassing in my yard?"

"N-no," I sputtered and took a step back. "Sorry. She just loves animals. She saw your cute dog here and just wanted to say hello."

Angie finally caught wise and jumped in to help. She also jumped up to her feet. "I just love corgis and their little heart butts. I've been thinking of adopting one for myself, but still want to do more research. Say, would you recommend one to a friend?"

"I'd recommend you get out of my yard," the man grumbled, staring daggers Angie's way. "C'mon, Baron. Let's get inside!"

The dog ran surprisingly fast, considering how tiny his little legs were. He slipped inside, and then the man slammed the door.

"Rude," Angie pouted as we both walked back to the car.

"What did Baron tell you?" I asked when we were both safely inside. "With his body language, I mean."

"Oh, right." Angie lay her head back and closed her eyes. For a moment, I thought she wasn't going to answer me, but then she did. "He's seen a lot of strange passers-by around here lately. First there was a tall man, then a cat, and then us."

Fluffikins! Maybe the incorrect address had just been a blunder. The boss cat might still be nearby.

"Was it a black cat with a white patch?" I asked eagerly, sitting up straighter in my seat.

"No, I think he said it was a tortoise shell. Um... At least that's how I interpreted it." No wonder so many rumors swirled about this girl. She did an absolutely horrible job keeping her secret.

But that was her problem. I had much bigger, more urgent matters to worry about. And, oh boy, was I worried.

"Can we just drive around a bit?" I asked, my spirits falling faster than, well, something that falls famously fast.

"Oh, sure." Angie put the car in drive and did slow laps around the neighborhood, taking care to avoid the mean corgi man's house.

Neither of us spoke as she began to snake out into the surrounding streets. I'd just about lost all hope when...

"Angie, stop the car!" I shouted at the top of my lungs.

We jerked to a sudden stop, and my seatbelt hugged me tightly, digging right into my chest.

“What’s going on?” Angie cried as she scanned the area in search of answers.

But I was already out the door and running down the street.

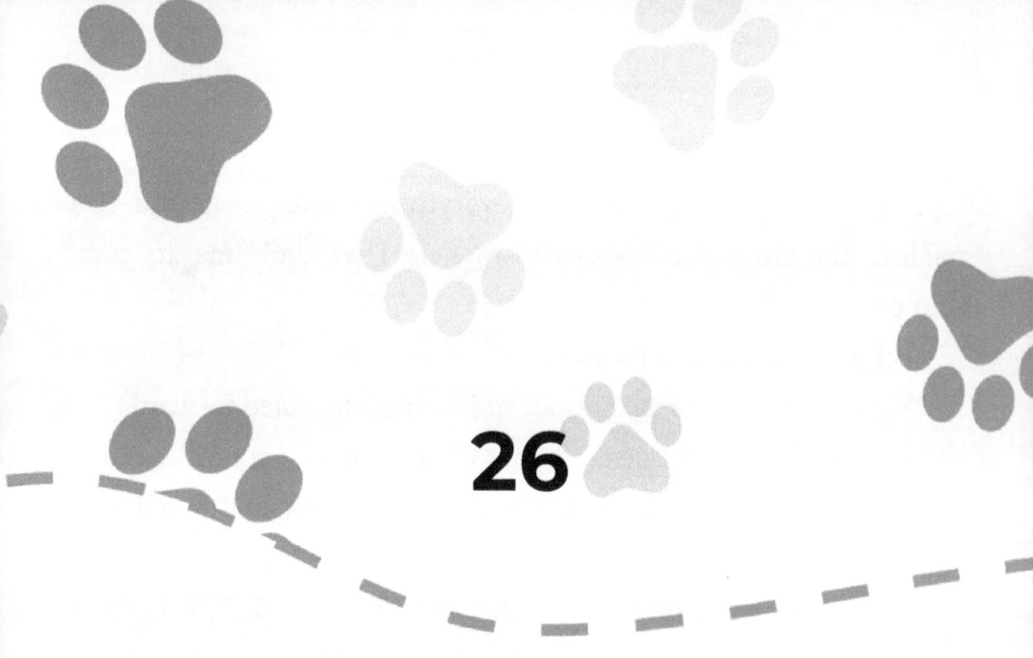

26

I jumped straight into Parker's arms, and we both staggered backward from the high-speed collision.

"You found me!" I cried—actually cried—from being so fantastically relieved.

"You're a tough woman to find, Tawny Bigford," he murmured, reaching for my cheek to swipe away an errant tear. "I'm so glad you're safe."

"How did you know I'd be here?" I asked, staring into his gorgeous gray eyes and wondering if now might be a good time for the first kiss we both knew was coming.

"When you, Melony, and Mr. Fluffikins went missing, I panicked. I didn't know until I swung by later that afternoon to check on you. When I couldn't find you or Melony, I tried reaching out to Mr. Fluffikins, but he was gone, too. No one knew anything, so I started combing through all of Fluffikins's paperwork—that guy records everything—and I found the magical signature for Melony's tracker. That took me to some kind of—"

"Pet park," I finished for him.

"Yeah." Parker gave me a weak smile, then stumbled forward.

I reached forward to steady him. "Whoa. What's wrong?"

He yawned and listed slightly to the side. "I feel so drained. Like I've been up for days without any sleep. It's strange."

"Are you hurt?" I immediately began to inspect him for injuries. Perhaps teleporting was more dangerous than Fluffikins had let on before whisking the both of us away.

"I think..." He paused and took a deep breath. "I think now that I'm a town witch, I have a hard time being away from my town. My magic..."

He raised a hand and flicked his wrist. A small spark flew from his fingertips and fizzled in the air. "I think that was the last of it," Parker told me and then slumped at my side.

"We have to get you back!" I looped one of his arms over my shoulders and turned back toward the car.

Angie stood just outside of it, staring wide-eyed at us both.

"We have to help him," I yelled to her and tried to guide Parker toward the car.

But he resisted. "I can't go without Fluffikins. Without the Diplomat, there is no PTA."

Angie's features pinched and she shook her head. "What's he talking about, Tawny? What was that trick he did with the burst of light?"

"A friend of yours?" Parker wheezed, turning his head toward me in a jerky moment that almost looked painful.

"Sort of," I whispered so only he could hear. "She's helping me search for Fluffikins."

"Why were you guys talking about magic?" Angie called as she laughed uncomfortably. "I mean, magic's not real."

Parker and I exchanged a worried glance.

"Is it?" Angie squeaked, bringing a hand to her chest like she wanted to check that her heart was still beating beneath it.

"We have to wipe her memory," Parker rasped, then pulled his arm off my shoulders and raised both hands high and grunted.

Angie took a step back. "Look, guys. I don't know what this is, but it's not very funny."

"It didn't work," Parker moaned as his knees buckled from the exertion. "I've got nothing left in the tank."

"We'll find Mr. Fluffikins, and he'll take care of everything," I decided aloud as I helped him back to his feet.

Angie pulled the driver's side door open. "Well, I should be going. Don't worry about that payment. Okay, byeeee!"

I saw a chance then, so I took it. I let Parker go, hoping he could keep himself upright, then bolted for the passenger side door and threw myself inside. "Nonsense, we'll have your payment soon. Just bear with us a little longer."

Parker staggered toward the car like some kind of ripe and rosy zombie, and I left the door open so Angie would be less inclined to drive away without him.

She sighed heavily and pressed her forehead against the top of the steering wheel. “I deal with murderers, embezzlers, and other types of crooks all the time, but I don’t think I’ve ever been quite as scared as I am now. Please just let me go home and pretend I never heard or saw what just happened out there. I won’t tell anyone, I swear.”

“Please help us,” I begged, knowing full well just how much I was asking of her. “You have a cat, too. Wouldn’t you do anything to get him back?”

She lifted her head and regarded me warily. Unshed tears glistened in her eyes, and I felt deeply sorry for involving her in this. After all, I’d been in the exact same position only a few days back. We needed her, though. Parker and I wouldn’t be able to make it a block without her assistance, and I couldn’t abandon him when he’d come all this way to find me.

“I promise we’ll keep you safe,” I said, desperate for her to believe me. “Everything will be okay, and you’ll get a big fat paycheck at the end of the day for your troubles.”

She sighed, and just when I thought she’d tell me to get the heck out of her car and pretend I’d never met her, she smiled, wrapped both hands around the steering wheel, and turned to me. “Okay. Let’s do this.”

27

Once Parker had clambered his way into the back seat, we began driving through the various neighborhoods and side streets of Caraway Island once more. As much as I hated being so far away from home, at least we were dealing with a confined search area here on this little island.

While Angie drove, I handed Parker the list I made from the hotel to help get him caught up on what we knew, which admittedly wasn't much.

"I can add a few things," he said after studying it for a moment. "Without magic or much physical energy, I know I'm mostly a liability for this mission, but my brain still works decently enough. For starters, I have no idea who this Val and Blackjack duo is, but they're right about Scavo being back."

I shook my head in disbelief as the suburban scenery slowly

rolled past. "But Mr. Fluffikins said he died a couple years ago," I reminded him.

"His body died, yes, but Scavo dealt deep and dark enough in magic that he'd already managed to arrange for his return before he..." Parker raised his hands to make half-hearted air quotes. "... died peacefully in his sleep."

Angie toed the break and we lurched to a stop. "S-s-sorry," she sputtered. "Go on."

"So he's back but looks different?" I asked to bring us back on topic.

"That's the working theory. We believe he's adopted a new name but held onto some of his old contacts."

Hmm. Like Angie, I was also creeped out by this new revelation as to what magic could accomplish.

"Why didn't he just become a vampire?" I questioned, recalling what Tawny had told me.

"For one thing, he himself was not a magick, and no Diplomat in their right mind would lend him that kind of power. Seems you and Connie had a nice chat during your makeover montage, huh?" Parker laughed weakly. Was he getting worse the longer he stayed away from his town? Gosh, I hoped not.

I had to keep him talking, just in case this magical withdrawal worked kind of like a concussion. I couldn't risk him falling asleep on me and possibly never awakening again. "Okay, so Scavo's back and possibly involved in all this. But how come you know about his return and Fluffikins doesn't?"

When he didn't answer right away, I turned and found him leaning back with his eyes closed. "Parker!" I shouted and nudged his knee.

His eyes blinked open and he tried to sit taller on the car's rear bench seat. "Right. Fluffikins doesn't know because it's a recent development. We found out right before I stepped out of the role of Liaison to the Force and into the role of Town Witch."

I turned back to face front and found Parker's eyes in the rearview mirror. "But shouldn't Fluffikins have known? As your boss?" I prompted. This Scavo definitely felt like a good lead, but none of us knew what he looked like these days, and I also had no way of getting in touch with Val or Blackjack to request further assistance.

"I did submit a report, but I doubt he's gotten to it yet. There's always so much paperwork to sift through. Bureaucracy at work." Parker's smile was barely discernible, but at least it was still there. "I didn't know he was working out of Blueberry Bay instead of Boston now, but it makes sense."

"What else can you tell me?" The new information was beginning to click into place, but still nothing resolved this mystery. With Parker ill and Angie frightened, we were now in far worse shape than we'd started.

"Parker?" I prompted when he didn't answer immediately.

"I'm thinking," he said. "Making sure I get things right."

"Okay," I said, then waited several moments while he composed his thoughts. The whole time I watched him through the rearview mirror to make sure he didn't nod off again.

When Parker spoke again, his words slurred together. "Five field agents were abducted before this latest batch, one of which was Percy as you've noted. The others were called Cricket, Harry, Darjeeling, and Bill."

Angie surprised us both by speaking up next. "Did any of them have tortoise shell coats?" she wanted to know.

"Yes," Parker answered at once. "Percy did. Why?"

Angie slowed the car to a stop and turned to face Parker in the back. "We met a corgi earlier who told me about a bunch of strangers walking by today. I assume you're the man he mentioned, but in addition to you, he also saw a tortoise shell cat. Like the one we just passed."

"You can talk to animals?" Parker asked, raising an eyebrow with great effort.

"With all your free talk of magical crime rings and conspiracies, my secret doesn't seem quite so weird anymore," she said slowly as if it had to be pulled out of her.

"He's coming this way," I said, spying the little tortoise shell cat approaching our car. "Get down, Parker."

Parker fell to the side, seeming relieved to not have to keep himself upright anymore.

I waited for the cat to advance several paces past the car, studiously avoiding his gaze so as not to draw suspicion.

"Now look," I whispered to Parker. "Is that Percy?"

Parker struggled to pull himself up, but eventually did by grabbing onto the back of my seat and using whatever strength was left in his arms to aid in the motion. “Yup, sure is,” he said after a quick glance out the window.

Bingo! Now we had a real clue to go on.

“Follow that cat!” I told Angie, excitement bubbling up inside me. We weren’t too late to fix this, and if my suspicions were right, then Percy would lead us straight to our missing persons... um, cats and person.

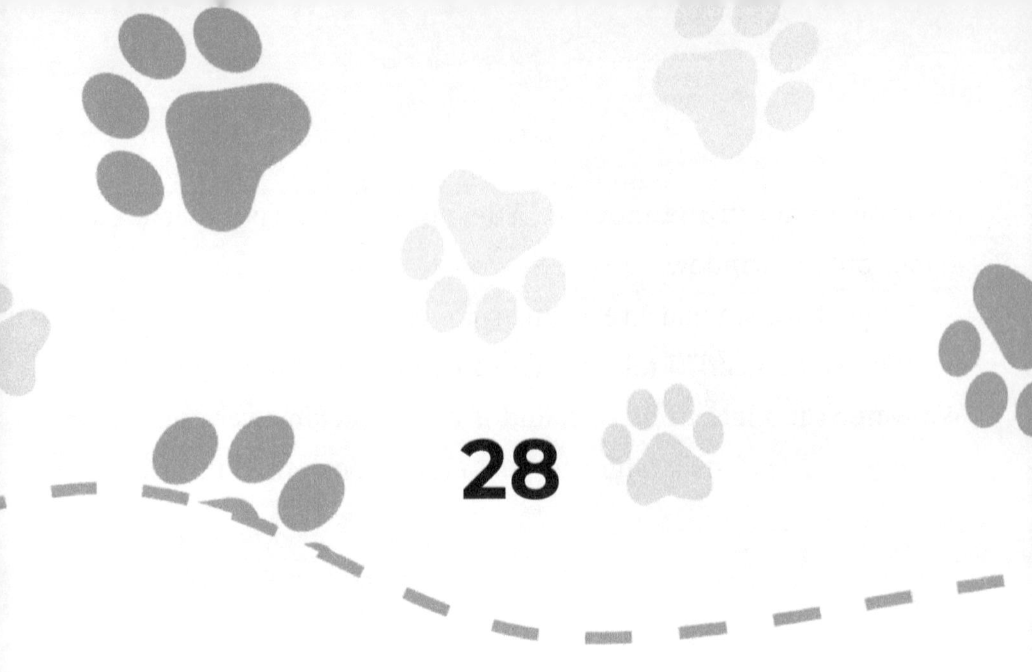

28

Percy led us to a brick colonial with a foreclosure sign in the front yard. How he didn't notice us trailing him, I have no clue. Maybe he was too focused on the road ahead to worry about looking back.

Once he was out of eyesight, Angie parked at the curb and the three of us quietly exited. I marched straight for the front door, then looked back to see I was on my own.

"Guys," I hissed, powerwalking back to them at the edge of the yard. "What are you doing? We need to see what's inside!"

"We can't enter. It's warded against magic," Parker explained as if this was a normal everyday occurrence. Perhaps for him, it was.

"But I'm not magic, and I can't cross, either," Angie argued, trying to push through the invisible wall and failing.

"You can talk to animals. How is that not magic?" Parker pointed out, lowering himself to the ground.

Her face fell. “Oh.”

“Looks like you’re on your own for this one,” Parker told me, offering a half-hearted thumbs up from his seat on the pavement. “Are you going to be okay?”

“I have to be,” I said, trying to summon my courage. “I’m our last hope.”

“You can do it,” Angie said with a little whoop. “You’ve come all the way from Georgia. You can’t lose now.”

I nodded, then returned to the door, which I was surprised to find unlocked. The main floor had been completely cleared of furniture and stripped of all its appliances. Nothing looked unusual to my eye, but the wards outside were proof enough that I’d find something as long as I kept looking.

After exploring the living room, kitchen, and a powder room, I found a pair of staircases, one going up and one going down. I chose to visit the second floor before braving the basement. Slowly I crept up the steps, praying my approach would go unnoticed.

When I finished my ascent, a short hall greeted me with two doors on each side. The first led to a bathroom. Unlike the lower floor, the upper level still appeared fully livable. The shower even had a curtain, complete with a bright yellow smiley face print.

The next door revealed a small home library. After that I found an empty bedroom. The last door also opened up to a bedroom, but this one was not empty. There in this small room with pink walls and a princess bed set, a girl with black hair and heavy makeup slept fitfully. Recognizing her the exact moment I spotted her, I rushed to the girl’s side and tried to shake her awake.

"Melony! Melony!" I whisper-yelled.

She rubbed at her eyes sleepily, then noticing me at last, shot up in bed as if afraid. "What are you doing here?"

"What are you doing here?" I countered, pulling at the covers and trying to force her out of the bed.

"I'm being held as a ransom, duh."

"So you didn't kidnap the cats?" Even though Fluffikins had assured me she didn't, I still hadn't fully believed her innocence until this very moment.

She scoffed, appearing truly offended. "Why would I?"

"You said you're being held ransom. Why?"

"My grandpa. When we failed to take the board, his boss got super angry. He took me to make sure Grandpa didn't fail this time."

"Fail at what?" I asked as fresh fear coiled at the base of my spine.

"He wants Fluffikins for some kind of ritual. He took the other cats to lure him here. Apparently capturing me as well was just some kind of lucky break and not part of the original plan."

I didn't know how Melony had all these answers, but I was glad she did. "Why does he want Fluffikins so bad?"

She stared at me as if the answer to my question should have been obvious. "He's one of the most powerful Diplomats in the world."

"How do you know all this?" I asked at last.

She shrugged. "You know how bad guys love to reveal their dastardly plans before trying to kill everyone? I'm guessing it's that."

I pulled at the covers again, but Melony yanked them away from me. "We've got to get you out of here."

"I can't leave this floor. It's warded," she informed me in a bored monotone. Had she really given up so soon after being captured?

"Okay, so how do I break the ward?"

Melony groaned in irritation. "You don't. You have no magic, remember?"

"Yeah, that's why I could get in and the others couldn't."

"Interesting. Well, if you feel like going on a suicide mission, Fluffikins is being held in the basement until the preparations for the ritual are complete."

"What ritual? Actually, wait. I don't want to know. Just tell me, where are the other cats?" I could stand here talking to her all day, or I could take action. I'd already wasted enough time traveling from one end of Blueberry Bay to the other.

"Most of them were placed in local shelters once they weren't needed anymore. Some idiot henchman accidentally gave Fluffikins to a shelter, too, not realizing who he was. Far as I know that guy's now been vaporized." She chuckled bitterly.

"What about Percy? We just saw him outside," I said.

Her expression grew cold and jagged. "He was the inside man. Betrayed us all."

"Us? Does that mean you're one of the good guys now?"

Melony smiled devilishly. "Yeah, I guess I am. I still don't like you, though. Even if we are on the same side now."

"I don't like you, either," I told her with a grin.

"Aww, so many warm fuzzies." Melony rolled her eyes. "Now stop wasting my time and head to the basement. You'll either save everyone or get yourself killed. My money’s on the latter. Good luck, though!”

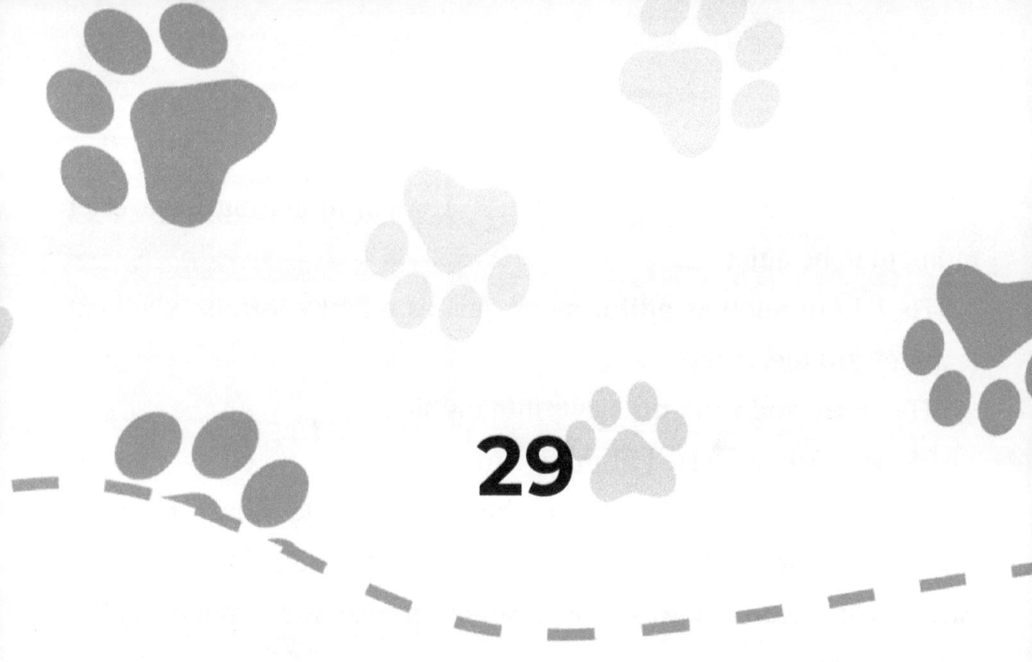

29

Here's what I knew...

Melony was trapped inside, and supposedly so was Fluffikins; meanwhile, Parker and Angie were trapped outside. Only I could enter and exit the house, and I had my normie status to thank. Ha, I'd like to see them condescend to me after this!

With growing confidence, I crept down the stairs to the basement, which was dingy, unfinished, and filled to bursting with boxes. I didn't see anyone, and I couldn't see much by the light of the tiny glass block windows.

"Hello?" I chanced calling into the darkness.

An agonized meow rose up to greet me. I rushed toward the sound and found a tiny black crate surrounded by boxes stacked above and to both sides.

I blinked hard to make sure I was really seeing what—or rather who—sat before me. “Mr. Fluffikins!” I cried, forgetting for a brief moment to be quiet.

He let out another pitiful meow just as a lanky tortoise shell cat leapt toward me. *Percy!*

He hissed and sunk his claws into my side.

“Meow! Meow!” cried Fluffikins in a panic.

Percy reared up and took another swipe at me. Sharp pain cut through my torso. What was I supposed to do? Could I really fight a cat? I mean, clearly he was an evil cat, but he was still a much smaller creature, and—

OUCH!

As I was puzzling over the ethical considerations of battling him, Percy had landed yet another blow—and he was rearing up to go at me again. He’d claw me to death if I didn’t do something and fast.

“Meow! Meow!” Fluffikins called, and when I looked over at him, he moved his glowing golden eyes upward toward the boxes atop his crate.

Yes! Okay!

I grabbed one and shook out the contents. This time when Percy came at me, I pushed down the box and trapped him between it and the cold concrete floor.

He hissed and spat and struggled against the cardboard prison, but still he failed to break free. Careful to keep consistent pressure on Percy’s box, I slid him next to a tall stack of packages and began to pile them on top of him. Hopefully the big bad would be by to free him before he ran out of oxygen under there... but also not before I managed to free both of my captured team members. Who'd have ever thought that I'd be working to save Melony's life a mere four days after she'd tried to end mine?

I swear, sometimes life really was stranger than fiction—especially when it included magic.

After watching for a moment to make sure Percy was secure within his trap, I returned to Mr. Fluffikins and unlocked his cage. "C'mon. We have to hurry."

He meowed and shook his head.

"Stop messing around," I hissed.

Fluffikins growled and pressed himself against the entrance, demonstrating the presence of another magical barrier. Well, no wonder he hadn't escaped before now—he couldn't use magic in the cage nor could he get out. That also explained why he wasn't talking to me.

This whole set-up had been erected to keep magicks away, but being a non-magical person, I had slipped through the barrier just fine. What if…?

Taking a chance, I reached into the cage and grabbed Fluffikins. He came straight out into my arms. *Yes!*

When we'd flown yesterday, holding him had transferred his magic to me briefly. And by holding him now, I was able to transfer my non-magic. Interesting how the absence of a thing was also a thing. I'd have to give that one a good think later.

I clutched Mr. Fluffikins tightly to my chest as I ran up the stairs and out into the yard.

When she saw me emerge from the threshold, Angie clapped excitedly and hopped up and down.

"You did it! Tawny, you did it!" Parker said, still too weak to offer much more than his words and a smile.

I set Fluffikins on the street, and he began to groom himself obsessively, washing off my touch.

Parker nudged the black cat with his foot.

"I can't believe I had to be rescued by a temp," the boss cat spat.

Parker stared daggers at him, but Fluffikins either didn't notice or didn't much care.

"It's fine!" I said with a chuckle, taking a quick moment to catch my breath. This next part wouldn't be easy. "I'm going back in for Melony."

I raced back inside and found Melony waiting at the top of the stairs.

"So you didn't die, I see," she said rather drolly.

"Nope, now let's get you out of here." I moved behind her and wrapped my hands around her waist.

"Eww, what are you doing?" she shouted, slapping at my hands and arms.

"Rescuing you. I need to transfer my non-magic through touch, then you'll be able to walk through the barrier," I explained breathlessly.

"No, thanks. I'd rather remain a prisoner."

"Would you just shut up and come with me already?" I yelled right into her ear.

She sighed and shuddered but didn't fight me when I wrapped my arms around her a second time.

And thus we began our awkward descent, stumbling more than once as we worked to move our feet in tandem.

"I hate you," Melony reminded me.

"No, you don't," I said, and she didn't bother arguing.

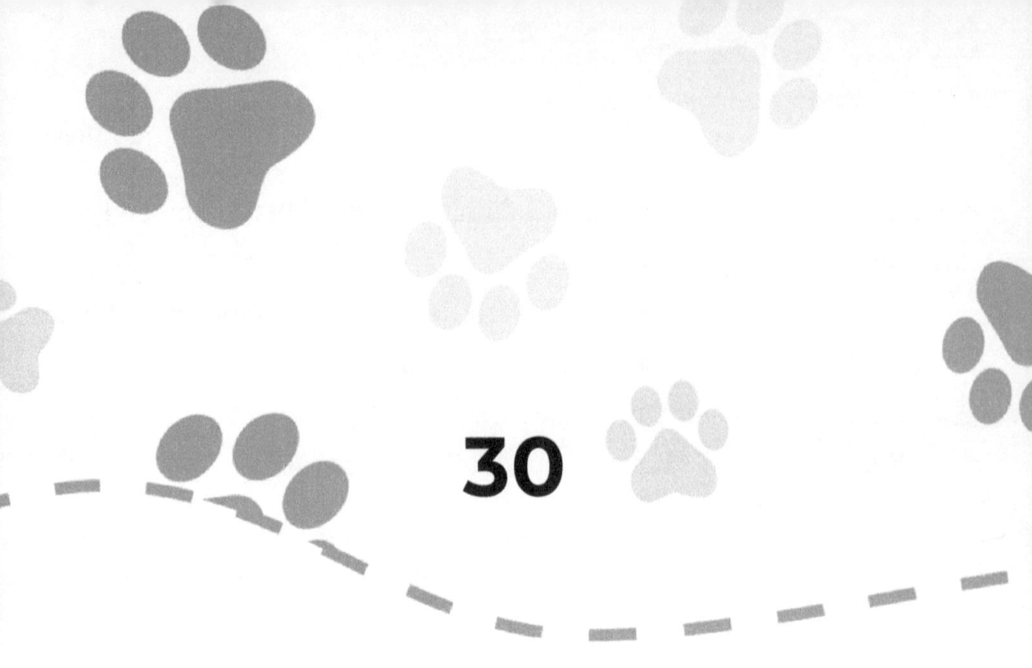

30

When Melony and I burst out of the house, Fluffikins still sat in the middle of the street grooming himself.

"We should probably get out of here before Percy gets loose or one of the other bad guys comes back to base," I suggested irritably.

"Percy gets out?" Parker asked with raised eyebrows.

"Yeah, I trapped him in a cardboard box. He beat me up pretty good first, though." I winced as I lifted the side of my shirt to show off the angry red scratches. They stung even worse when exposed to the cool outside air.

"Mr. Fluffikins, get Greta," Parker ordered, his voice sounding stronger than it had since his arrival.

"I'm not done cleansing myself," the boss cat growled.

But Parker didn't capitulate. Not this time. "I don't care. Tawny is hurt and needs Greta."

"Um, could you bring Connie, too?" I asked, drawing the cat's ire.

Fluffikins growled mightily but then sighed and flashed away in a cloud of glittery pink.

"Whoa," Angie said, blinking hard as she stared at the spot where Mr. Fluffikins had just been.

And she was still blinking and staring slack-jawed when Fluffikins returned with both the angel and vampire in tow.

"Who's this?" Fluffikins asked, apparently noticing Angie for the first time. "You know what, it doesn't matter."

He spun in a circle and pointed a paw her way. "Memory wipe. Boom!"

Angie teetered woozily as if she'd had one too many drinks. I guess that was the non-magical way to wipe someone's memory, now that I thought about it.

"Connie, give me some money," I ordered, taking a chance that she'd have some on her given that it was how she fed.

"I don't want to," the vampire said flatly.

The angel's eyes blazed with fire at Connie's easy dismissal. "But you will," Greta compelled her.

Luckily, Angie still appeared too dazed to notice much of anything. She'd have to sleep it off, like I had.

"Fine," Connie grumbled, then pulled a wad of bills from her purse and handed them to me.

I didn't even bother counting them before handing the whole stack over to Angie. "Thank you so much for your help finding my lost cat. Here are your fees as promised."

She took the money and gasped. “But there’s over a thousand dollars here.”

“You did a great job,” I assured her, patting her gently on the back. “Now that we have Mr. Fluffikins back, we can all go home.”

“Oh, okay. Happy I could be of service.” She shook my hand, glanced at the others, then headed back to her car.

We all stood waving until she finally pulled out of view.

“Please do something to make sure she gets home safe,” I mumbled through clenched teeth as I continued to smile and wave.

“Already done,” Greta said with a wink. Of course it would be the angel to act as our human accomplice’s protector, even though she’d only just arrived on the scene.

“Tawny’s hurt,” Parker blurted out.

Greta frowned as I pulled up my shirt for her to examine my fresh wounds. “Oh, heavens,” she muttered, then placed a warm hand over the scratches.

I grew warmer and warmer as she pressed her palm into me. The glowing light from her angel armor crept from her heart, down her arm, and into my side. She held it there for a moment, then pulled the light back and removed her hand.

The scratches were gone, replaced by smooth, clean skin.

“What do we do about Scavo?” I asked. “We can’t just let him get away.”

“Who’s Scavo?” Melony wanted to know.

I balked at this. “Wasn’t he the guy who held you captive?”

She shrugged. “Dunno. I never got his name.”

"Well, I guess if it is Scavo, Val and Blackjack will take care of him sooner than later," I told everyone.

"And if it wasn't?" Melony countered.

"Then we'll be back," Mr. Fluffikins declared, pacing the curb. "This isn't over yet."

Melony nodded. "My grandpa is still out there somewhere. He's not going to give up this easily."

I shivered as a gust of cold wind swept by.

"Let's go home," Parker said, extending his hand toward me.

I grabbed it in mine, then Greta took my other hand, and Connie took hers.

"Back to HQ," Fluffikins commanded, and the sparkly pink fog descended.

I closed my eyes and luxuriated in the magic wafting over me. When I opened them again, we'd returned to the boardroom.

Fluffikins stood at the head of the table in his usual place of power. "And that solves the case of the missing field agents. Tawny, you are dismissed."

"Wait, but I…"

"Dismissed!" he repeated, louder this time.

Wow, not even a quick thanks.

I shook my head and stumbled out of the office, feeling more disrespected than ever before.

"Tawny, wait!" Parker called after me.

I turned and waited for him to catch up to me. When he did, he wrapped strong arms around my waist. Now that we'd returned to Beech Grove, he was back to his usual self.

“Mr. Fluffikins is bad with thank-yous, but I’m not,” he said before covering my mouth with his. And that’s when I realized that this moment with him was also a special kind of magic. A warm buzzing sensation shot through me and all at once I became dizzy.

I giggled against his lips. “If that was from Fluffikins, then you can take it back.”

“Okay, I will,” he said, then kissed me again. And again.

“Pheromones!” Fluffikins cried from somewhere in the distance, but neither of us paid any attention as we basked in our hard-won moment.

I still didn’t know what to think of all that had happened over the course of the last several days, but I liked the person I was becoming.

Maybe being a temp really wasn’t the worst job in the whole entire world…

And maybe I wanted—needed—more.

VAMPIRE FOR HIRE

Something's up with the Paranormal Temp Agency, and I'm going to find out what that is. For my last two assignments, the cat boss Mr. Fluffikins had to drag me in kicking and screaming. This time around, I'm all too willing to play their little game. It's high time I learned why they plucked me from my ordinary everyday life and thrust me into this crazy new world filled with danger and magic.

But it's not going to be easy. Especially when the PTA orders me to help resident vampire Connie investigate a new coven that's just popped up in our sleepy little town of Beech Grove. For this mission, they grant me temporary vampire status—and all the perks and the punishments that come with it.

The real kicker? If we don't solve this one soon, I could be stuck as an immortal monster forever…

But that's just how it goes when you're a part-time vampire.

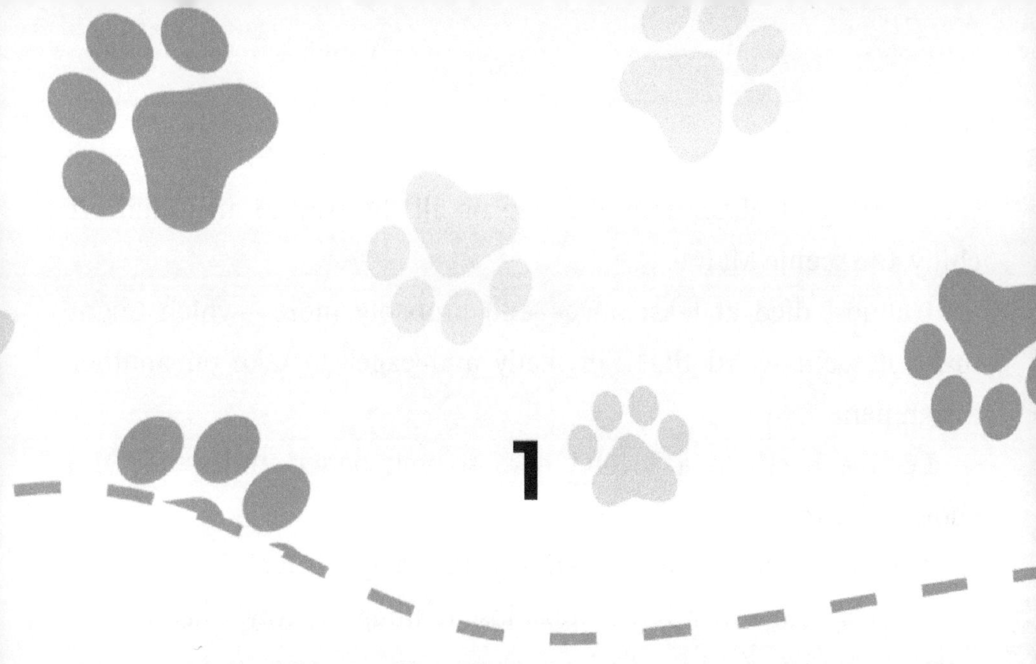

1

My name's Tawny Bigford. I used to think the most interesting thing about me was that I write romance novels part-time to make my meager living... But then I met a little black cat who changed everything.

His name? Mr. Fluffikins.

His role? Diplomat in charge of the local PTA. That's Paranormal Temp Agency, by the way—not the other organization that goes by the same unfortunate acronym. Just trust me when I say I have a fairly sordid history with those other guys.

Cough, cough. Cheating ex-husband.

Anyway...

Even though Fluffikins and I just met and I never asked for a job, he hired me as a temp and forced me to work two cases over the past week. The first was the murder of my former landlady. The second was a string of abductions that led us all the way to an island off chilly and scenic Maine.

I almost died at least once—and probably more—which might make it seem weird that I'm ready and eager to take on another assignment.

Let me back up a second here so you better understand the choices I've made.

The first thing you need to know is that magic is real. Seriously!

We're all born with it, but most lose it along the way. I had a brief taste of that special brand of power on my first case, and I've been craving more ever since.

But even though I know about magic, I'm not part of the community. I'm an outsider, what the others derisively call a "normie." Real magical folk are referred to simply as magicks. And the aforementioned PTA is a special governing body that protects their interests in our fair Peach Plains region of Georgia. They are but one of many such boards set up all across the globe.

There are seven permanent members of the board. Anyone else they need to work joins briefly as a temp.

Like me.

Usually temps get their minds wiped once they've served their purpose, but for better or worse, I remember everything.

The big boss is the bureaucratic black cat, Fluffikins. He is joined by the Town Witch, a role currently filled by my smoking hot neighbor Parker Barnes. I think we may be dating now, but we haven't kissed again since that first time almost a week ago, so who really knows...

Anyway, after Parker and Fluffikins, we have the five board liaisons. Greta is an honest-to-goodness angel who oversees the Schools. Connie is the cranky vampire in charge of Commerce. Then there's Buckley in Agriculture and some old dude in a suit for the Cemeteries. I know almost nothing about either of them.

We're supposed to have a liaison for the police force, too, but that position was recently vacated due to an unfortunate string of events that would take way too long to explain here...

So instead we have an intern who is applying to be the provisional liaison, if only she can prove herself worthy of the job. I don't have high hopes, considering she tried to kill me—and almost succeeded.

Yeah, I'm really not a fan, and that feeling is definitely mutual.

If you had asked me a week ago, I'd have told you I hate the PTA and want nothing to do with them. But our last big case made me spin a one-eighty.

There's something the others are hiding from me, something important, something about me. And I won't rest until I get some answers.

Last time, they dragged me to the local Paranormal HQ against my will. This time I'm going to show up at their door and demand their attention.

Our first two adventures also taught me something far more mundane. Namely, that it's hard to survive in this world without a car. So much for shrinking my carbon footprint, because I used my last royalty check to purchase a ten-year-old sedan to help get me from point A to point B.

The last two times I visited PTA HQ, Mr. Fluffikins had flown me there with his magic, but I liked being in charge of my own transportation this time.

And I arrived almost as soon as I'd pulled out of my driveway, given the old office complex that houses the PTA sat just a couple miles past downtown Beech Grove.

The windows hung dark, but I knew that was just a ruse to keep outsiders away. And magic or not, I was part of this now. At least that's what I kept telling myself as I gathered my carefully prepared package into my arms and marched up to the front door.

It was locked, so I knocked.

When no one answered, I grabbed a rock and smashed it though the glass door. Tiny shards flew everywhere, but I didn't care. I needed a way in, and it's not like they couldn't fix my little oopsie with a bit of well-placed magic.

What I had to say was just too important to wait. Hopefully I could find someone who was willing to not only listen, but also to speak.

I'd been their pawn up until this point, but now I was ready to be a stronger player in the game…

Just call me "Bishop Tawny."

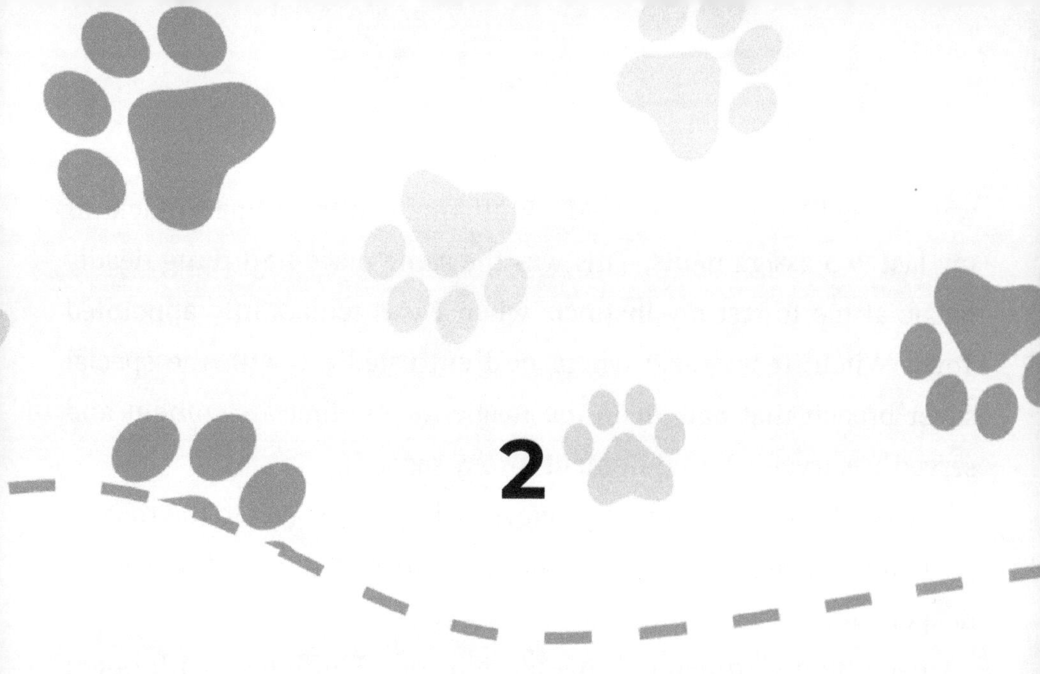

2

No one came running to investigate my violent break-in. Even though I waited by the door for a few long, uncomfortable moments, no one came at all.

Huh. Didn't expect that.

I shook my head, took a deep breath, and continued deeper into the dark building. First I checked the glass-enclosed conference room where the various members of the board got together to discuss important matters. No one was there, so I left the basket I'd prepared for my visit at the edge of the table and continued on to explore the rest of the building.

When I walked by Connie's office door, I couldn't suppress the shiver that ran down my spine. Even if she was there, I didn't want to disturb the vampire head of Commerce. Sure, she'd claimed she had no plans to eat me, but I felt better off not taking any chances.

I hurried down the long hall until at last I came to the vacant warehouse-like space where Mr. Fluffikins had taken me to kick off my last two assignments. This was the same place he'd flung deadly magic at me to test my instincts when I was temporarily appointed Town Witch. It was also where he'd entrusted me with the special silver brooch that had given me magic for my first assignment and served as surveillance equipment for my second.

"Hello?" I called hesitantly before inching my way into the room.

Only a weak echo of my own voice answered, so I dared to go deeper still.

Each time we'd entered this place before, Fluffikins had brought me to the center of the room and then jumped into the ceiling to retrieve that brooch. Might there be other magical goodies up there?

I decided to find out.

Now before you get all angry with me for snooping around uninvited, I'd like to remind you that this was the same agency that had already played fast and loose with my safety twice before. For whatever reason, they'd brought me on to help with their supernatural kerfuffle, and now I wanted to find out why.

Sure, the first time they brought me in, it was because I'd stumbled right into the middle of a crime scene. It made sense they'd keep me close by until things got sorted out.

But the second time they forced a job upon me? There was no obvious reason they needed me specifically. Not at first. But then Mr. Fluffikins accidentally dropped a few stray hints that there might be something special about me, something he and the others had yet to share.

For one thing, the boss cat couldn't undo the one spell I'd accidentally cast during my stint as Town Witch. He'd tried to turn my bubblegum pink hair back to its natural color but couldn't. Then after we transported to middle-of-nowhere Maine, he'd been about to tell me something before the investigation came crashing into us head-first.

I'd taken that all in stride and focused on the assignment, believing someone would surely explain everything once we saved the day and brought everyone home safely.

No such luck, however.

Not even a full three days passed between my first assignment and the second.

But now almost a week had passed since job number two, and nobody had bothered to get in touch. Not even Parker who lived mere feet away from me and used to drop by to visit unannounced.

So what was everyone hiding? And perhaps even more importantly, why were they hiding it?

I scanned the warehouse for an object that would be strong enough to support me but light enough for me to move on my own. *Nothing.*

Not one to be deterred, I headed back to the boardroom and grabbed a chair. This solution wouldn't allow me to look into the ceiling space with my own eyes, but if I stretched my arms high above and swept the area with my phone's camera and flashlight, I'd still be able to catch a glimpse.

Satisfied with this plan, I placed the wheeled executive chair beneath the missing ceiling panel in the center of the warehouse and climbed onto it slowly so as not to set it rolling. I probably would have been able to peek into the space myself if I stood on my tiptoes, but I did not trust my coordination enough to attempt that particular feat —especially with no one around to help if I fell and gave myself a concussion.

So I reached one arm up, phone in hand and already recording, and held the other out to my side to help with balance.

As carefully as I could, I slowly rotated my wrist to make sure I scanned as much of the area as possible without having to turn the chair and myself around to face the other way, and then brought it back down to study the footage.

About ten seconds in, the glint of silver caught my eye. *My brooch!*

Before I could finish watching the full video, something heavy dropped from above, knocking me off the chair and onto the cold hard cement.

Ouch...

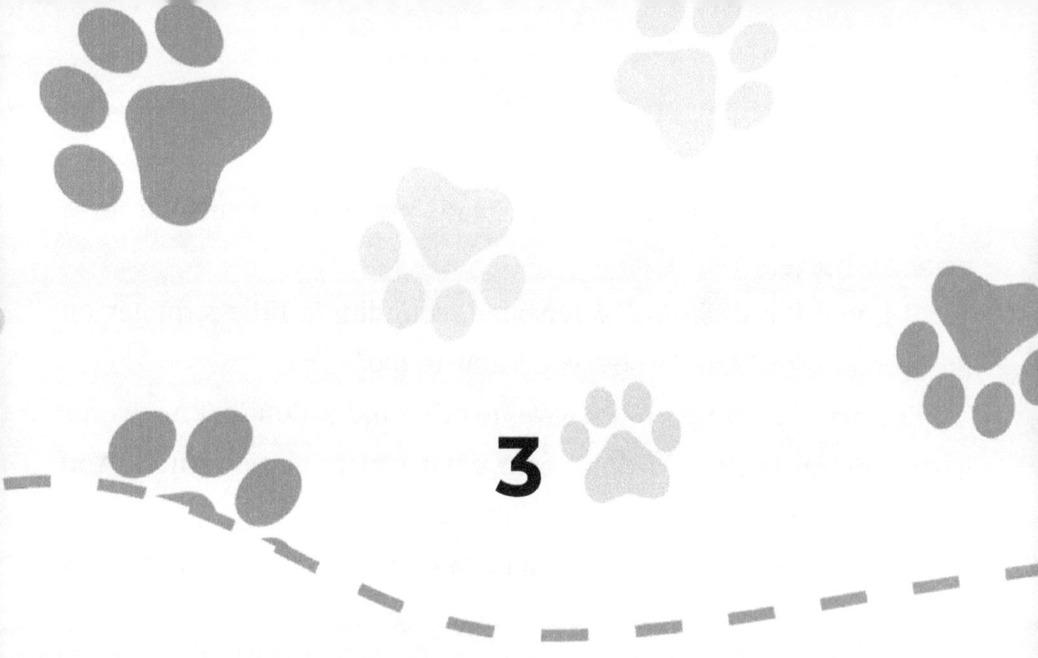

3

"Intruder!" Fluffikins hissed, staring down at me from the chair with judgment burning bright in his golden eyes.

"I'm sorry," I moaned as I tried to shift into a sitting position. Everything hurt so bad that I just stayed on the ground with my arms and legs akimbo. "No one had followed up about my next assignment this past week. And then no one was answering the door, so I—"

The cat shifted in the chair with a low growl. "So you thought you'd burgle us?"

"N-n-no," I sputtered. "I was just trying to find some answers, I swear!"

Mr. Fluffikins turned his nose up and let out an indignant huff. "You were just a temp, Tawny. *Were*. Now it's time to let this go."

"I know I'm different." I wanted to sound serious, knowledgeable, and even a little intimidating. Instead, my words came out in a pained wheeze.

"I know I'm different," I repeated, sounding a little stronger on the second take. "And I know you know it, too."

The black cat flinched but gave no other indication that my words had made an impact. "I don't care what you think you know. You were not invited, and you shouldn't be here."

"Oh, I get it," I said, finally managing to roll onto my side with a grunt. "You only want me around when it benefits you."

Fluffikins chuckled dryly. "You really don't know much about how business works. Do you? Or cats for that matter."

"Whatever," I bit back. "You put my life on the line twice and didn't even pay me for it. The least you can do is tell me the truth about who I am."

The cat's tail flicked back and forth in irritation. "If you think you can goad me into saying something I don't want to say, then you're wrong."

Clearly, I couldn't appeal to the bureau-cat's compassion, so I'd have to bring out the final trick I had at my disposal. "I brought steak," I revealed with a scheming smile.

Fluffikins sniffed at the air. "What's that you say? Steak?"

"Yup, and it's no rump roast, either. I brought the good stuff." I paused to heighten the anticipation. "How do you feel about filet mignon?"

The black cat spun in an excited circle before hopping down to the ground and coming to my side. "Where is this steak, and why is it not in my belly yet?"

Leave it to a well-placed bribe to do what kindness would not. Inwardly, I breathed a giant sigh of relief. Outwardly, though, I kept my game face on.

"I'll get it for you," I offered, "if you agree to tell me what I want to know."

"Or I could beat you up and take it for myself." Fluffikins sneered me as he weighed his options. "Come to think of it, you're already down and out. I just need to find that sweet, sweet steak myself." He sniffed at the air again, whiskers twitching as he trotted toward the edge of the room.

"Wait," I called before he could fully leave me behind. "It won't taste as good if it's ill-gotten gains."

The cat's mouth dropped open. "Is this true?"

I raised an eyebrow. "Do you really want to risk it?"

Mr. Fluffikins let out a massive sigh, then waved his paw at me. Instantly the pain from my fall disappeared just as fully as if it had never been there in the first place.

I pressed my palms into the floor, then pushed myself to my feet and waved for the boss cat to follow me back to the conference room where I'd left my carefully prepared parcel. Inside were seven Tupperware containers filled with freshly seared filet mignon. Yes, I'd gone all out, just in case I came across the full board in session and needed to bribe them all. Of course, I had no idea what Connie ate, given that she was a vampire. I also hadn't worried myself over bribing Melony since she was little better than a temp herself.

Having only Fluffikins to appease made this a very expensive bribe per capita, but I hadn't wanted to take any chances with what could very well be life-or-death information. Otherwise, why would he be working so hard to keep it a secret?

"First answers, then steak," I told the cat who was practically drooling as he sat across from me on top of the conference table.

"Steak, then answers," he countered, his voice slurring even more than usual as he focused on the prize with wide eyes.

Well, I guess beggars couldn't be choosers. And in this case, I was definitely the beggar. I sighed. "Do you promise?"

"Yes, yes, and my promise is magically bound. Now make with the good stuff."

I nodded, opened the first container of steak, and slid it over to him. Luckily I'd already pre-chopped the piece, otherwise it would have taken much longer to sit there and watch him devour this medium rare cut into my last paycheck.

When Mr. Fluffikins finished, he licked his chops and lowered his eyelids with contentment.

"Well?" I said, when he made no move to keep up his end of the bargain. "Now it's your turn to make good on our deal. Tell me how I'm different."

"Ah yes. That," the cat said with a wink. "I promised to give you answers after steak, but I didn't say how soon I'd provide them. You'll just have to wait." He hopped off the table and trotted off down the hall, openly laughing at me the whole way.

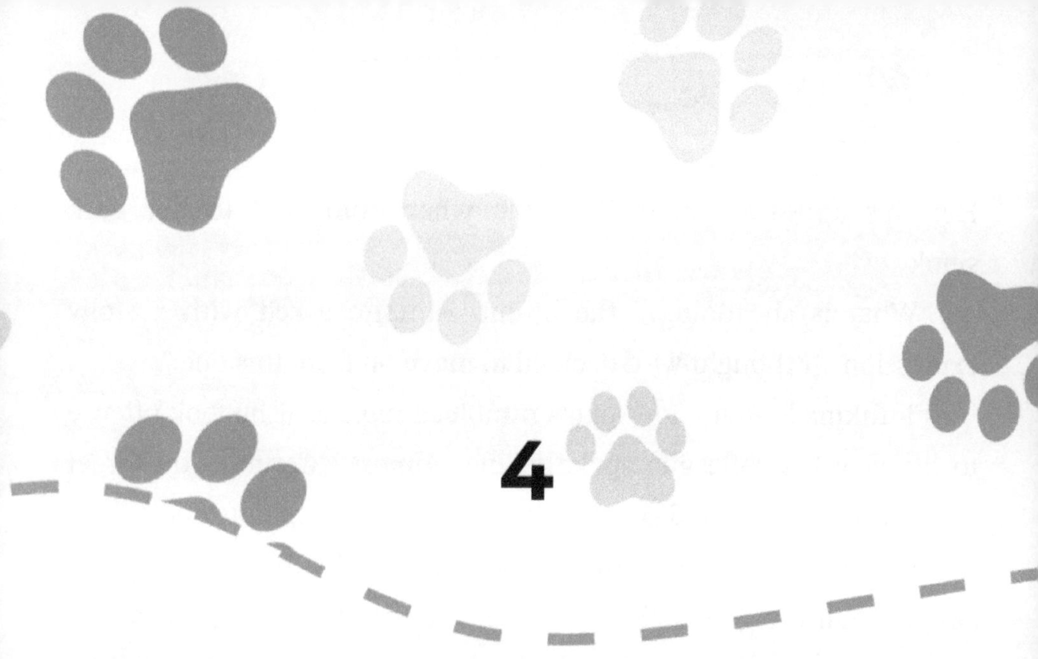

4

I charged down the hall in pursuit of that no-good trickster cat. Once I caught him, I'd hold him down and force him to sign a contract. If I had to, I'd use the rest of the steak I'd prepared as leverage. I hoped it would work, because this was the only move I had left.

Now that I knew there was something special about me, how could I go the rest of my life without finding out what it was?

I caught up to Fluffikins in the building's abandoned front lobby. He stopped running and paused before the broken glass door. I had assumed he planned to yell at me about the destruction of PTA property, but he simply waved his paw and wedged the glass back together as if it had never been broken.

A moment later, the door opened and in walked Connie—the single board member I feared most. Today she wore a red crushed velvet shirt with an expensive-looking pencil skirt and designer heels.

Her lips appeared impossibly pale when compared to her dark smoky eye.

"What is she doing?" the plump vampire asked with a stony expression. "I thought we'd decided to move on from this one."

Fluffikins let out a low angry rumble, almost as if he took offense to the way his colleague spoke of me. *Almost.* "Connie, you forget your oath. There is no discussing board business with outsiders."

"I have not forgotten mine," she answered with a sneer. "I am simply reminding you of yours. We've already broken protocol by including her in two separate jobs. So, why is she here yet again? Why hasn't her memory of us been erased?"

The two supernatural entities stared each other down, but neither budged in their position.

Maybe if I restated my case, Connie might be more willing to help than her boss had been. "I know I'm different. Not just a normie, I mean. And I want to know why. The cat and I made a deal, but it doesn't seem like he's going to hold up his end of it."

Connie's eyes narrowed, and she shot a dirty look toward Mr. Fluffikins. "You made a deal with her?"

He shrugged his little kitty shoulders. "It had open-ended terms."

"Still, you made a deal with a normie. You know that's binding."

"She's not—" He stopped himself by hissing and unleashing a string of kitty curses.

"I want to know what you know," I said, standing firm in my resolve. I even thrust one hand on my hip in case that made me look tougher or more serious. Somehow.

"If you don't wipe her mind right now, I'll do it," Connie said with her jaw clenched. She looked so close to snapping, and I didn't want to be around when that happened. Still…

"But he promised me!" I cried, taking a giant step back as if it would do any good.

"You're lucky I have no desire to head the board, or you'd be out of a job," the vampire growled, curling her upper lip to show off those unsettling fangs of hers.

"Tell me and tell me right now," I demanded with a stomp of my foot.

"Let's make a provision to our agreement," Fluffikins shouted, his paw apparently having finally been forced—or so I assumed. "Steak for answers. Like you said."

"Now?" I had a hard time trusting him, given that last ruse of his.

The cat shook his head. "After one more job. With Connie." He turned toward the vampire head of Commerce. "I received your request for a temp to investigate the new coven downtown. Tawny will assist you in whatever way you need."

"Unacceptable." Connie's gaze turned even icier as she regarded us both.

"Actually," Mr. Fluffikins corrected. "It's perfectly acceptable, seeing as I'm in charge here. You need a temp, and this one's ready to take the job. Aren't you, Tawny?"

"If I do this, you'll tell me everything?" I asked, raising a suspicious eyebrow and crossing my arms over my chest like a shield.

He nodded, watching Connie instead of me. "After you've completed the job to the board's satisfaction, I will tell you what you want to know."

There was no way I was getting tricked by another of his loopholes. "Define, *to the board's satisfaction.*"

The cat narrowed his eyes at me. "Until the coven either submits to Connie's leadership or leaves town," he answered with a small shake of his head.

"Deal," I said with a slight nod to show my agreement.

Connie cried and threw her hands up in the air. "This is not what I wanted when I filed that request, and you know that. I understand your desire to punish the normie, but why me? I've been nothing but—"

Fluffikins pushed off the ground with his back feet, then floated up to meet Connie's line of sight. He hovered in mid-air in a pink glittery swirl and said, "I don't care what you want. I make the decisions here, and this is what you got. As you know, I can't go back on a deal with a normie once made. You'll accept Tawny's help, or you'll forfeit your seat at the table. Do I make myself clear?"

Even though the boss cat wasn't speaking to me, I bobbed my head vigorously. Connie terrified me, but I could survive anything temporarily—and that's all this job would be. My last two assignments had been over in a couple days each. And I had to believe that this one would be no different. Otherwise I might run away screaming long before I got any of the answers I craved.

Be brave, Tawny. Be brave.

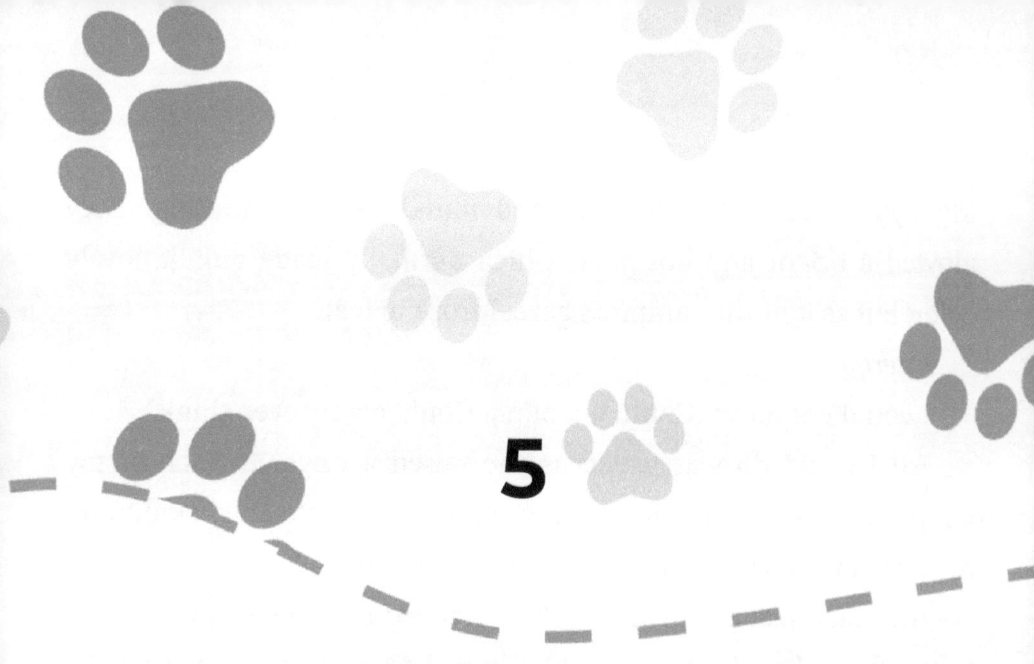

5

"Not so fast, Fluffikins," Connie hissed. "I know you think your word is law, but I refuse to work with someone I don't like simply because you used your stomach to make a decision instead of your brain."

"I have already made our promise. It is done," he said before floating back to the floor and landing with a soft thud.

"I have made no such promises to this mortal, so I will be the one to wipe her mind and free us all from the burden of her company." Connie grabbed my head and pulled it toward her. The rest of me followed.

"Please don't," I wheezed. I couldn't even struggle to get away. Connie's super-human strength controlled my muscles even better than I could.

"Look at me," she snarled.

And as much as I didn't want to, I couldn't resist the invitation.

My eyes lifted from the floor and found Connie's waiting. They glowed a bright and hot pink, which normally made quite a lovely color, but as it lit the vampire's gaze, I froze in fear.

Literally.

I could not move. Could not blink. Could barely even think.

All I could do was watch as she raised a finger to each of my temples, pressed her manicured nails hard into my skin, and mumbled words in a language I couldn't understand.

And then just as quickly as she'd grabbed me, she let go and I fell to the floor. Thank goodness, Fluffikins had already cleaned up the broken glass or I'd be done for.

"Please," I mumbled, weak, tired, angry. "I only want to know the truth about who I am."

Connie gasped and looked as if she herself were about to faint. "She remembers? How is that possible?"

Fluffikins jumped up onto an empty desk. "I cleared her mind once before. Barnes restored it after."

"But my magic is stronger than his!" Connie shouted and stamped her foot. "What is happening? Why isn't it working on her?"

"That's what I want to know," I added as I slowly rose to my feet. "This is the third time something like this has happened, and I just want to know why."

It was Fluffikins who spoke up next. "Our contract has been made. First tend to the new coven, then I will tell you both what I have discovered about our dear Tawny."

Connie folded her arms over her chest and turned her face away from both of us. "I will place a call for your removal," she promised the little black cat.

"And it will fail. Just as it has failed before," he responded without an ounce of emotion.

Connie huffed and pulled at her hair in distress, which seemed to please the boss cat. "I'll be in my office while she undergoes orientation," she said before storming off down the hall.

"Well, Tawny…" Fluffikins looked up at me with glowing golden eyes. "Are you ready to become a vampire?"

My breath caught in my throat. "Um, what? That wasn't part of the deal."

Fluffikins merely chuckled. "Actually it was. For your job with Connie, you will be provided with vampire magic."

"Fangs and all?" I recoiled at the thought. Even if Connie didn't suck blood, she was still cold, cruel, and downright villainous. I could probably survive working with her, but to become like her?

"Yes, you'll receive all the makings of the vampire. The power, the prestige…" He flicked his tail for several beats even though he clearly hadn't finished speaking yet. "The curse."

"The curse!" I exploded. "Nobody said anything about a curse."

"Come now. We should get you started. You'll have exactly forty-eight hours to complete your job, and there's no time to waste."

"What if I don't complete it in time?" I asked, chasing after him as he headed toward the warehouse.

Fluffikins turned to glance over at his shoulder, his eyes twinkling with delight. "Then the change will be permanent."

That's when it hit me.

If I turned into a vampire for good, then he wouldn't have to tell me why I was different. Because the answer would be obvious: *You're a vampire, Tawny.*

This was his last-ditch effort to keep his secret. He knew Connie wouldn't make my job easy. Heck, he was counting on it.

But I was counting on getting my answers. I'd survived two PTA assignments to date, and I'd survive this one as well.

My mortality depended on it.

I could've killed the sneaky bureau-cat. Instead I followed him back to the training room—ready to put everything on the line just so I could learn something about myself that I should have already known long ago.

If he wanted a vampire, then a vampire I would become.

I'd be the best vampire he ever saw, but only for forty-eight hours, tops. Then I'd be me again, and I'd finally know what all that entailed.

Game on, Mr. Fluffikins.

6

The warehouse was exactly as Fluffikins and I had left it only a short while ago. I pulled the chair I'd dragged in a couple feet away from the opening in the ceiling and took a seat. My body ached from my latest fall, thanks to Connie, but I doubted Fluffikins would have the good grace to heal me twice.

In fact, right now he was eyeing me with what appeared to be disappointment. "You look exhausted."

"I am exhausted," I snapped back. "And that's not a very nice thing to say to a woman… or to anyone for that matter."

A smile stretched between his whiskers. I wished he'd just get on with it already.

"You should be happy," he said dryly. "After all, you're getting exactly what you want. You came to steal the artifact, and now here I am about to offer it to you for your next assignment."

I slumped back farther in the chair and crossed my arms over my chest. "We both know this isn't what I wanted."

The cat's smile widened. I thought he might be planning to say something particularly mean-spirited, but he simply jumped into his ceiling hold, leaving me beneath him.

I expected him to return quickly as he had both of the other times he'd gone up there for me, but instead I found myself sitting alone for what felt like ages.

At one point, Connie even peeked her head in to check on our progress. She left, muttering something under her breath about "that no-good feline menace."

When Fluffikins finally returned, he held the magical brooch in his mouth, then turned and guided a second, larger object down from above with a sparkly swirl of pink magic.

"What's that?" I nodded toward the unexpected additional piece of equipment.

He gently lowered the brooch to the ground, then looked back up at me. "It's your vampire armor," he answered matter-of-factly.

I cocked my head to the side. "Vampire armor? Like Greta's angel armor?"

"Not exactly. This will keep you from getting staked in the heart." Fluffikins sat and curled his tail in front of his feet.

My chest clenched at the fact that such a thing was even a possibility. "But I've never seen Connie wear anything like this," I pointed out, eyeing the ornate chest plate and the leather straps that presumably held it in place.

The cat scoffed. "Connie doesn't need to wear hers unless she's knowingly heading into a dangerous situation. She's a much more experienced vampire than you."

A shiver ran through me. "I'm not a vampire."

"Not yet, but you will be in about two minutes here."

"Okay, so do I need to wear this thing the entire time I'm on this assignment?" I took a deep breath in an attempt to ready myself. The thought of wielding vampire magic was far more terrifying than anything I'd experienced at the hands of the Paranormal Temp Agency so far. I mean, witches could be both good and bad, but weren't vampires always bad, horrible monsters? If Connie was any indication for how the rest of her species operated, then yes.

Fluffikins seemed to enjoy my discomfort and even took efforts to make it more pronounced. "I added the straps for you," he said with a small flick of his tail, "since you have a penchant for exposing the flesh on your chest, and we needed some way to secure it."

"You make it sound like I'm running around with my boobs hanging out. I only show a little bit of cleavage, and only sometimes. It's tasteful. Not wanton." Still, I pulled my top up higher and wondered if I should invest in some new turtlenecks for my wardrobe.

He looked me up and down and sighed. "Yes, well... The straps remain essential, nonetheless. We can't risk you dying mid-job."

"Aww, Fluffikins. I had no idea you cared." My voice came out syrupy and sweet. I hated that.

"Losing a temp mid-assignment creates too much paperwork," he deadpanned.

I groaned and rolled my eyes at the snarky cat.

He motioned with his paw to catch my attention. “Go ahead and put it on. I can use my magic to adjust the fit if it’s not right.”

I stood and hesitantly grabbed the floating vampire armor. It had a thick leather collar that buckled at the back of my neck along with straps that went under my arms and around my back to keep the chest plate from slipping. The metal piece was covered with intricately carved scroll work—an absolute stunner. Still, that didn’t stop me from feeling as if I were wearing an oversized pet collar and that the boss cat may be trying to get one over on me rather than actually protecting me from getting staked in the heart.

The fit, however, was perfect.

I banged on my chest plate to show that it remained perfectly in place.

Fluffikins nodded. “Excellent. Now this.” He nudged the brooch toward me with his paw. I wasn’t sure where exactly I could put it, since the magical artifact was meant to stay close to my heart, and my heart was already covered with the breast plate. I ended up clipping it on my bra and hoping the metal wouldn’t dig into the sensitive flesh below.

As soon as this artifact was in place, a glow lit me up from inside. At least that’s how it felt. I don’t think I was actually glowing.

What I do know is I felt very different.

We humans have become accustomed to a certain level of pain in our day-to-day lives, especially those of us nearing forty like myself. We have so many little aches and discomforts that become part of our norm—a rickety joint, an itchy patch of skin, that kind of thing.

The vampire magic took all of it away.

I no longer felt the pain from my earlier fall. I no longer felt anything. Not physically spent or in need of a second cup of coffee. Nothing.

I even held my breath for a moment and found that my lungs didn't yearn for oxygen.

Wow. It was as if I'd lost the sensation of living altogether.

"Well, how do you feel?" the cat asked, circling me now.

I didn't know how I felt about this change. On the one hand it was freeing, but on the other, it felt so at odds with my normal state that I no longer felt human. In that way, I guess I wasn't. I was a vampire. Did that mean I was technically the undead now? Yeah, it probably did. At least for a little while.

I ran my hands over my body and shook my head. "I feel... nothing."

"Oh, just you wait," Mr. Fluffikins added with a smirk.

"Huh?"

"Come with me. Now it's time for the real test of your magic."

I gulped hard, but it did nothing to quell my growing anxiety as I followed the boss-cat to whatever he had planned next.

Let's just hope it wasn't to my doom.

7

I easily matched pace with Fluffikins as he ran full tilt through the office building's long halls. This was so weird. At least when I'd had the town witch magic, I'd still felt like me.

Now, as a temporary vampire, I felt both elated and terrified. I could operate with extreme ease. Feeling no pain was a definite game changer.

But it made me wonder just how Fluffikins and Connie intended for me to put these new powers to use. Whatever the particulars of this assignment, I assumed they must be quite dangerous.

Instead of returning us to the conference room, Fluffikins took me to a small office in the back corner of the complex. "Wait here," he instructed, leaving me on my own.

I tiptoed inside and found what looked like an old-fashioned drawing room. The absence of windows and the presence of a busy floral-patterned wallpaper made the room feel much smaller than it otherwise should have. Hand-knitted doilies covered every surface, and a honey-wood curio cabinet proudly displayed a mismatched collection of dainty tea cups and saucers.

Unclear of how long my wait might be, I settled into a tall wing-back chair, trying not to upset the doilies that rested over its thick arms.

The door swung open a moment later.

"Tawny? Hi." Parker offered a shy smile from the doorway. "What are you doing in my office?"

"Your office?" I crossed my legs, settling deeper into the chair. Still I felt no comfort from the plush, overstuffed seat. I felt nothing at all. "I had no idea this was your style."

Parker chuckled. "I haven't had a chance to redecorate since taking over the Town Witch post for Lilah. And part of me doesn't want to do it at all. It's nice, remembering her."

"You've been avoiding me," I told him. I'd tried so hard to get his attention this past week, but he'd definitely been avoiding me since our impromptu kiss at the end of my last assignment. I should have been overjoyed to see him now, to get the chance to talk. More than anything, though, I was curious about his sudden change of heart.

He sighed and leaned back against the closed door. "Since our kiss, I know. I'm sorry."

"Why?" I wanted to know. My foot twitched with impatience as if counting down the seconds to his answer.

Parker closed his eyes and tilted his head toward the ceiling. "I really like you, Tawny, but it's a lot to ask of someone, to accept all this PTA stuff. Plus, as you've seen firsthand, it's dangerous."

"I already know all that," I said, unwilling to let him off the hook.

"You know a little, but there's so much more, things that you shouldn't ever have to worry about. It's all my fault for dragging you in even this deep. I was selfish to bring back your memories. To kiss you." He winced as if the words caused him physical pain.

"Shouldn't I have a say in this, too?" I wondered aloud. I also wondered why he was being so dramatic. We'd kissed. Sure, it had felt momentous and earth-shattering at the time, but now? I didn't know how I felt. Mostly tired of having him run away from me, curious about why he had.

"We can't have a future," Parker revealed, concern reflecting in his gray eyes. "Magicks and normies, we don't mix for a reason."

There was only one logical conclusion here. We had to put this to the test. "Kiss me again," I said. "If you feel nothing for me, I'll let it go. But if there really is something special between us, shouldn't we at least see it through?"

Parker nodded and licked his lips as I rose from my chair and sauntered over to him. I placed a hand on his arm and brought my face to his—something I'd been longing to do all week.

And now that our big moment had arrived, I felt...

Nothing.

In fact, I'd felt nothing more than an amused curiosity from the moment he stepped into the office. Yes, we'd talked back and forth, and I'd made my argument for why we should be together. But that's all it was, a logical discussion. No pounding heart or shortness of breath as we drew close. No shivers of excitement from his kiss.

I'd crushed on him hard ever since we first met, but now he

seemed little more than a stranger to me—one of billions on this planet. He could have been anyone.

Yes, I knew him, and I knew our history together. But that wasn't enough.

Parker pulled back and smiled at me, but when he caught the expression on my face, his brow furrowed with worry. "Tawny? What's wrong?"

I glanced down toward my new breast plate and shook my head.

"What's that? What are you wearing?" He raised a hand and brought it to rest on my armor.

"Mr. Fluffikins just gave me a new job," I whispered. "With Connie."

Parker's eyes lit with rage. He pushed me to the side and bolted out of the office without so much as a word of explanation.

I didn't try to stop him, but I did follow—curious more than invested in the outcome.

"You gave her vampire magic?" he shouted after storming into the conference room and finding the sleek black cat sitting across from Connie at the long table.

"Yes. Connie had a job," he answered with a shrug.

"But you know how dangerous it is! How sometimes the change isn't temporary!"

"And what's your point? We needed a temp, and she wanted another assignment. Remember, it's you who returned her memory after the first one. We could have all moved on with our lives by now if you hadn't interfered."

Connie smirked as she studied her freshly painted nails. I could still smell the sick chemical tang in the air.

"Are you ready to give us the rundown on the job?" I asked, stepping deeper into the room and moving toward Connie and Fluffikins to take my seat with them.

"Tawny..." Parker's voice cracked. I could see his anguish but felt none of it myself.

"Parker," I addressed him coolly, ready to move this along. "I have a job to do now, but we can talk more later. Okay?"

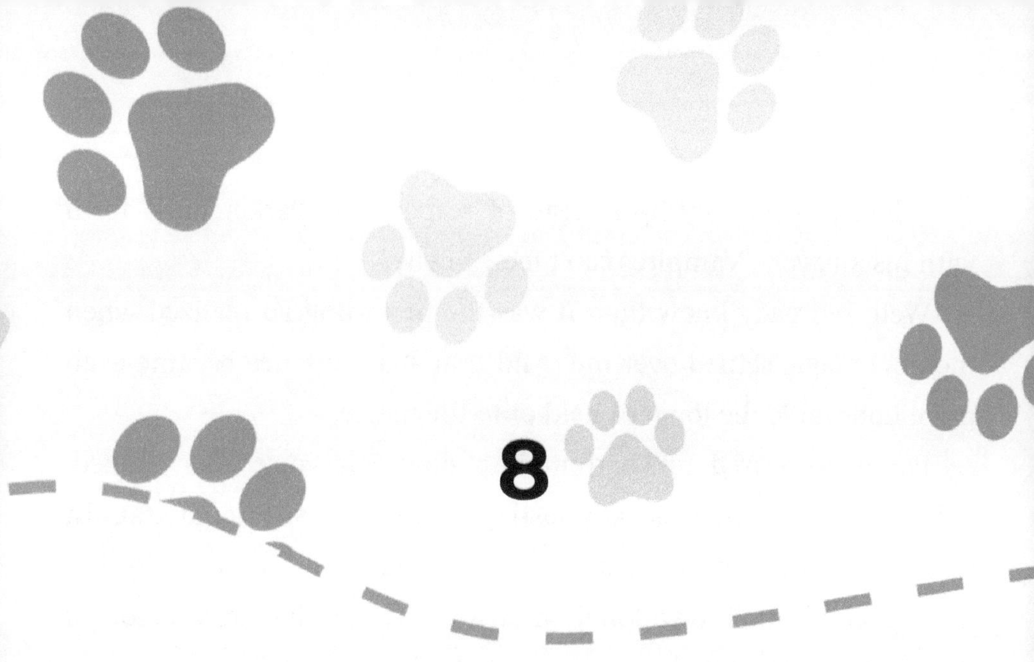

8

Despite my request for him to leave and let us get down to business, Parker remained rooted to the spot. I had forty-eight hours, tops, to do this job, and here he was stubbornly delaying the start. If I failed this task, I'd remain a vampire forever—and he'd be at least partially to blame. How could he not see that?

"Have you told her about the curse?" he asked Mr. Fluffikins in a booming voice. I'd never seen him so riled up.

"I have temporary vampire magic," I informed Parker, pulling out a chair beside Connie and taking a seat. "That means everything that comes with it. And, yes, I know there's a curse."

"But do you know what it is?" he pushed even harder. Why couldn't he just come out and say what he meant rather than asking all these senseless questions?

When I curled my lip instead of responding, Parker burst forth with his answer. “Vampires can’t feel, Tawny.”

Well, I already knew that. It was the first thing I’d realized when the new magic settled over me. And that stark absence became even more noticeable the longer I held onto the magic.

Parker appeared to be trembling now. His voice also quaked. “They can’t love or keep any lasting relationships. Friends, family, romance. None of it. If you stay this way, you’ll have immortality, but at what cost? You’ll be a lonely monster forced to live by yourself in the shadows forever.”

“Stop being so melodramatic,” Connie spat. “I have the curse, and I get along just fine. Besides, she’s not staying a vampire. I intend to finish this job and be rid of her as fast as I possibly can.”

“So that’s why you hate everyone,” I quipped with a quick glance toward Connie.

She straightened in her seat and held her chin in the air. “No, the curse is why I don’t like anyone. Hating them is a choice.”

Fluffikins spoke next. “Barnes, your work here is done. Thank you for helping me make sure Tawny’s full magic is in effect before sending her out into the field.”

“I want to help. Surely, whatever this assignment is, it will be done more satisfactorily with three people rather than just two.”

“No, this is a vampire-only job. At least for now. See yourself out, witch,” Connie commanded.

Parker looked as if he desperately wanted to say something to me, but instead he stalked off, slamming the door behind him.

“I thought he’d never leave,” I said, which drew a laugh from

Connie. I didn't want him to be upset, because it was such an unpleasant thing to witness. I needed everyone to keep their emotions in check so we could get down to business.

"Ha! I no longer hate you quite as much as the others," Connie mumbled. "I still can't wait to be rid of you, though."

That made sense. I nodded. "Mr. Fluffikins, are we ready to begin the debriefing?"

The cat rose to all fours and began to pace up and down the table in his classic war general stride. "The long vacant storefront at the corner of Main and Grand downtown has recently been purchased by one Vanessa Vane. A vampire."

"Just one vampire? That doesn't seem like much of a problem to me." I couldn't believe that all of this fuss was about a single vampire moving to town.

"Where one settles, there will be more," Connie said with a snarl, apparently having already made her mind up about this new resident.

Fluffikins strode back toward us, blinking slowly. "Before now, Connie was the only vampire in Beech Grove. Due to their long lives and extreme wealth, vampires are quite territorial. It's possible that Ms. Vane purchased property in town without realizing this area has already been claimed by Connie, but it's also possible she wishes to start a dispute. And if that's the case, the rest of her coven will be arriving soon."

"Okay, so what do you need us to do?" I asked, not quite understanding.

"As a lone vampire, Connie looks weak, but with your help, she'll appear more official. It means the newcomers will be less likely to make a play for the area."

"So what? We pay this new vampire a visit and nicely ask for her to leave?" This seemed far too simple, but both of my companions nodded emphatically in response.

"Exactly," they said.

I tapped my fingers on the table, growing impatient with them both. "And if that doesn't work?"

"Then you'll really get to see what those new powers of yours can do," Connie remarked with a sinister smile.

My curiosity sparked to life once more. I'd heard the expression about curiosity killing the cat many times before, but it seemed the saying was much more apt when it came to vampires. Rather than blood, I thirsted for knowledge, understanding. And presumably wealth, though I hadn't yet felt the avarice come to life within me.

Fluffikins purred with delight. "So are we all clear on the mission here?"

Yeah, about as clear as mud.

I bit my lip to keep from speaking. More out of self-preservation than any obligation to respect the boss cat. It looked like this job could go one of two ways. It could be the easiest one yet, or it could throw me straight into the middle of a violent vampire war...

And I honestly couldn't say which I preferred.

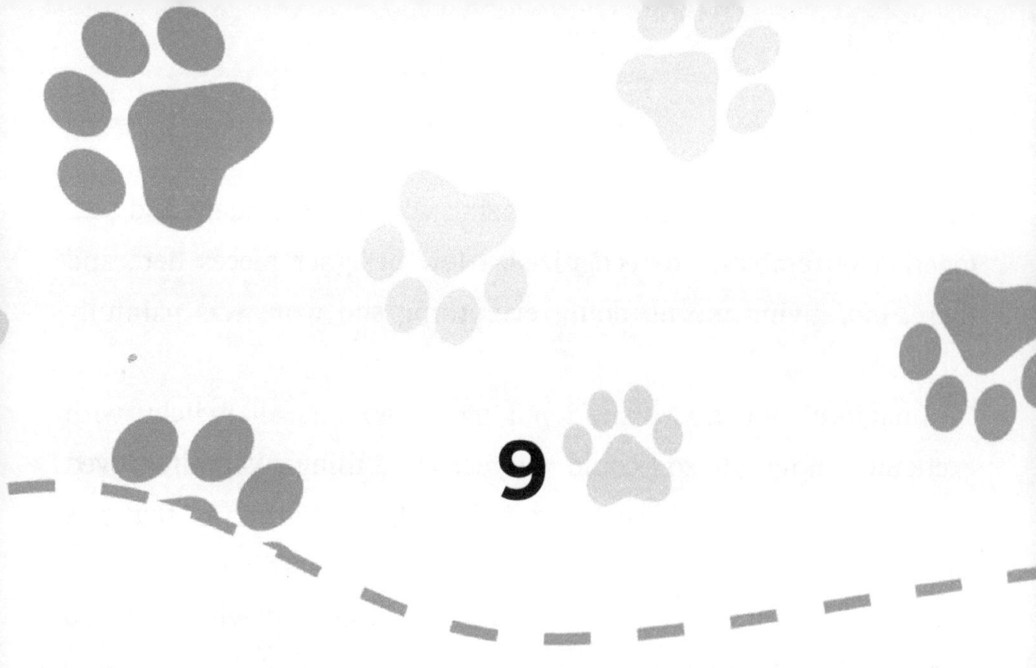

9

Fluffikins dismissed us from the board room, which meant it was time for Connie and me to find and confront this new vampire named Vanessa Vane.

"You look ridiculous," Connie informed me as we walked side-by-side down the hall. "Like you need to be attached to a leash and led around on all fours."

I brought a hand to my breast plate and ran my fingers over the scrolling metalwork. "Too much?" I asked.

"It's a fine accessory, I suppose, but it doesn't fit the outfit. A quick trip to my closet should have you looking like more of a respectable vampire, though."

I remembered Connie dressing me up as a phony psychic for my last assignment. That walk-in closet of hers went so far back, I couldn't see the end of it. Then again, Connie always looked like she'd stepped right out of a fashion magazine with her confident and put-together ensembles. I'd recognized a few designer pieces here and there, too, giving me no doubt everything she wore was painfully expensive.

Imagining the finery she'd put me in got me all twitchy with excitement now. Oh, so I could still feel some things. Vampires loved power and wealth, and according to Connie and Fluffikins, that was also how they now fed. Parker's kiss had meant nothing to me even though I knew it should have, but the prospect of playing dress-up had me all kinds of giddy.

What a strange new world I found myself in.

I tried to remind myself that this change was temporary. That I didn't have to guilt myself about not caring about Parker while I was equipped with vampire magic. But honestly, I much preferred focusing on the makeover ahead. How expensive an outfit would Connie put me in? I bet it would be more valuable than my entire wardrobe back home combined. I'd be so fancy, so deserving of admiration and respect. I could hardly wait!

Connie wasted no time in selecting a crushed red velvet blouse with bell sleeves and a pair of black pin-stripe pants from her closet and handing both to me. "If you're going to wear that ridiculous armor, we might as well make it work with your ensemble." She wrinkled her nose in distaste at my current attire.

"It's my vampire armor, to protect me from getting staked in the heart," I explained. Shouldn't she know this already?

She let out a sarcastic laugh. "Is that what Fluffikins told you?"

"Um, yeah. Are you saying he was lying? What does it—?"

"No time for questions. Get dressed, and let's go." She returned to the walk-in to give me some privacy and returned a few minutes later with a black leather corset in hand.

I eyed it—and her—skeptically.

"It completes the look," she said, helping me into it.

As Connie's hands wrapped around my waist to place the corset, I realized that we now wore the same crushed red velvet fabric. "Is there a reason we match?"

"No, not match," she corrected with a disgusted growl. "We coordinate."

"Fine." Working with her would be mentally exhausting. In fact, it already was. "Is there a reason we coordinate?"

She rolled her eyes. "Coven colors. Makes this little farce appear more official. Now, no more questions. With any luck, this Vanessa Vane will be a clueless coward and go running with her tail between her legs the moment we show up."

"Do you really think it will be that easy?" I asked as she yanked the straps on my corset as tight as they would go.

"No," she said, startling with me the abruptness of her response. "You've had two assignments with us now. Was either of them easy?"

"Fair point. Um, so how are we getting downtown?" I asked as she locked her office behind us.

"Well, we'll change into our bat forms and fly there, of course."

"Really?" I squeaked.

"No. Now stop asking stupid questions, and let's go." She moved quickly down the halls, but I had no trouble keeping up. We left the PTA headquarters, but instead of heading to the parking lot, we moved toward the woods.

As soon as we passed the tree line, Connie shifted into high gear. Together we moved through the forest so fast, it was as if we were flying. My new vampire magic removed all limits from what my body could do, it seemed. Not even wind resistance was an issue as we cut through the air and across the land.

In hardly any time at all, we reached the other side of the vast forest, and Connie slowed herself to an appropriate pace.

"That was amazing!" I cried, jumping into the air and pumping my fist.

"We move without restriction only when human eyes aren't near," she informed me, and for the first time I realized it took incredible effort to walk at this comparative snail's pace now that I knew how fast my magical body could move.

"What else can we do?" I asked, falling into step at her side.

"There is no we, and you'll do well to remember that."

"Vampires, I mean."

"You are not a vampire. You merely have one's magic."

I growled in frustration. "You know what I'm getting at. Just tell me."

Connie stopped walking and turned to face me with a stony expression. "I owe you nothing. If you have questions, find the answers for yourself. We're almost to Vanessa Vane's building. When we get there, I don't want to hear a peep out of you. In fact, it would be great not to hear any more peeps out of you before then. Just shut up, look tough, and let me handle everything."

Oh, was that all?

I was starting to think Connie would be an even worse boss than Mr. Fluffikins.

Less than forty-eight hours to go. I'd be counting down each one now...

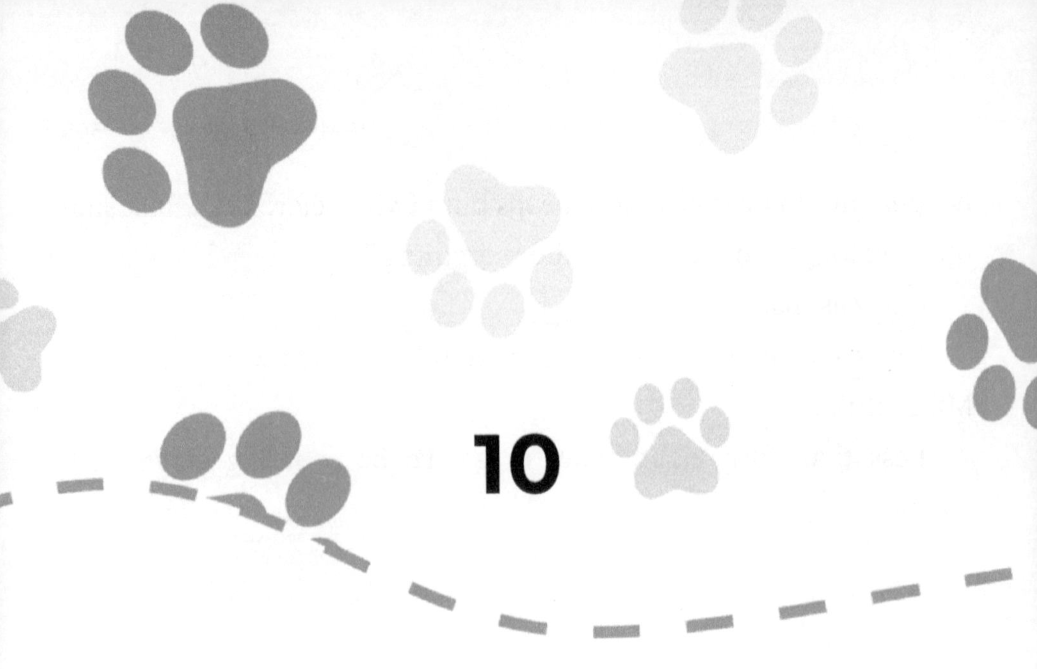

10

I kept quiet to avoid any further arguments with Connie, counting down the minutes until this assignment would be over. Not only would I avoid staying a vampire forever, but I'd also find out the big secret Fluffikins wanted so desperately to hide from me. And I'd get another chance with Parker, which—logically—was something I knew I wanted, even though I couldn't bring myself to care in my current state.

What strange creatures vampires were. No wonder people feared them. If they only knew...

"We're here," Connie said, reaching out to clasp my wrist with her freshly manicured hand. We stood outside a storefront that had been bare ever since I arrived in town and likely a long time before that. When I saw it a week ago, it had been covered with cobwebs and layers of filth. Now the interior was decked out in bright, rich reds, yellows, and purples. Fantastic beaded mini chandeliers hung over each table, and a polished metal serving station stood at the back of the space.

"Is this a restaurant?" I asked in disbelief. "I thought vam—"

Connie shot me a look of warning.

"I mean, I thought people like you didn't have to eat." I glanced away from Connie and spotted the sleek sign that now hung above the shopfront: *BOLLYWEIRD.*

Connie saw it, too, and snorted. "We don't have to eat, but we can. Normally our heightened sense of taste makes the task more tedious than pleasurable. I suspect this get-up is for normie customers, though. Terrible name for a restaurant."

"I guess they're planning on serving Indian food. Not that it matters, if we're here to send them packing."

Connie tightened her hold on my wrist and waited for me to look her in the eyes. "Let's go. Don't forget your place."

Yes, I was the backup. There for no other purpose than to add to Connie's numbers.

I nodded, and she let go of my wrist. When I pulled the door open, she stepped in ahead of me.

A young woman stepped into the main dining area while drying her hands with a dish towel. She looked like she could hardly be more than twenty, but I knew very well that she could be centuries old, thanks to her vampire immortality.

"Can I help you?" she asked with a business-like smile. Her eyes narrowed when she caught sight of Connie, however.

Connie nodded in the direction from which the other woman had just come and quirked an eyebrow.

"Yes, we're alone," she said, crossing her arms and letting the dish towel dangle. "Now what do you want?"

This was obviously our good friend Vanessa Vane, and she also clearly knew who Connie was and why we'd come.

"As you can see, this town already has a coven in residence, so we'd like to ask you to leave and find another place to set up shop." Connie spoke in a chilling monotone, taking no efforts to hide her contempt.

"One vampire does not a coven make," Vanessa answered with an impatient cluck of her tongue.

"I'm a vampire, too!" I squeaked.

Both women shot daggers at me, and I nervously took a step back.

"What? Did you turn this one on your way over?" Vanessa asked with a cruel laugh. "Doesn't even have fangs yet."

"I've been in this town for a long time," Connie continued without answering Vanessa's question. "It's not big enough for the both of us, and you know that."

Suddenly, it felt very much like we were in an old western. I imagined the two vampires squaring off with cowboy hats and pistols. Never mind that we were currently standing in Bollyweird. This moment was all spaghetti western.

"I won't bother you, if you don't bother me," Vanessa supplied with a challenging glare. "Grand opening is tonight, and I refuse to miss my own event."

"We both know that's not true. It's not the way of our kind."

Vanessa sighed. "*Hmm.* Then maybe it should be."

I couldn't say I disagreed with her. Both Fluffikins and Connie had pressed the importance of getting Vanessa to leave town, but neither had told me why. What if Vanessa simply wanted to share her passion for south Asian cuisine with the rest of the world? Wasn't that a possibility? And if it was, did that mean we were the bad guys here?

I hung my head, wishing I'd asked more questions or at least been given more answers before marching in here to threaten a stranger.

"This is your last chance," Connie warned the other vampire through gritted teeth. "Leave."

Vanessa smirked. "Or what? You gonna make me?"

They continued to stare each other down, neither budging. Tension rippled through the room, growing thicker and thicker as the two vampires sized each other up.

I hung back, wondering what would happen next. Would we fight now, or...?

Connie let out an animalistic roar and spun toward the door. If this was the first battle, then we'd just lost. And that did not bode well for whatever happened next.

Connie swept back toward the door, grabbing my arm in the process. "C'mon, Tawny. We have a war to prepare for!"

Vanessa's amused laughter followed us to the streets. She wasn't afraid. In fact, she clearly wanted this confrontation to escalate.

Which meant she was far better prepared than either me or Connie.

Which meant we had a pretty good chance of losing.

Crud.

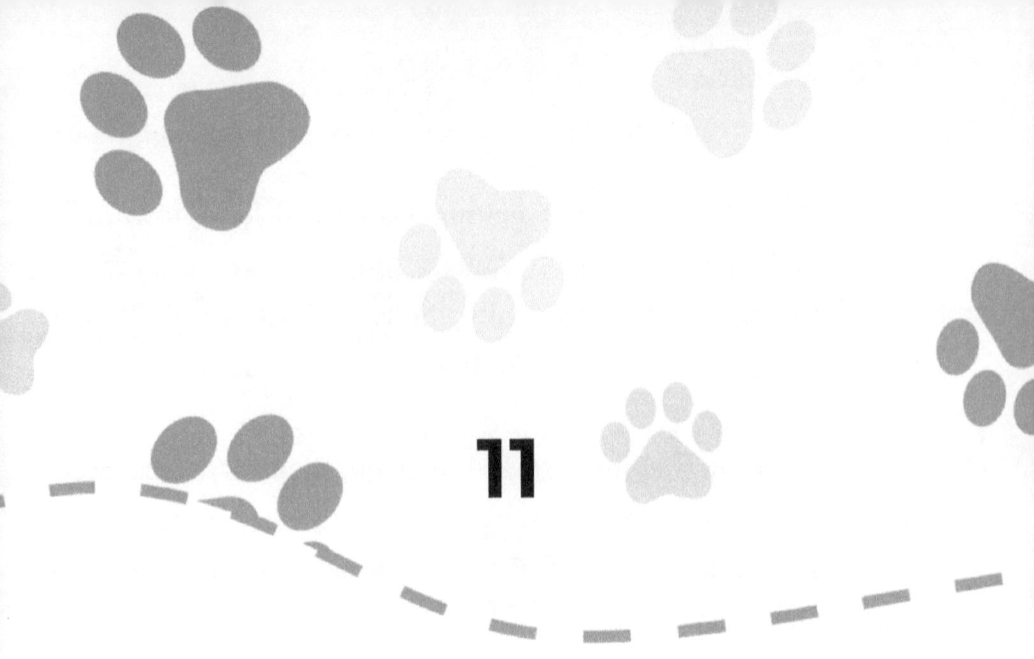

11

I chased Connie through the streets of downtown. We both power-walked quickly enough to draw concerned glances from some of the other pedestrians, but I knew better than to mention it to Connie.

I waited until we were safely ensconced in the forest to unleash my long list of questions. "Why can't both you and Vanessa live here? Why is she refusing to go? Do we really need to declare a war?"

"Such pointless questions!" Connie hissed without slowing to discuss things with me.

"Tell me," I demanded. These were perfectly reasonable questions to ask in light of the situation and how very quickly it had escalated. "Why did—?"

Connie spun on me suddenly, and I nearly crashed into her. Luckily, I managed to catch myself just in time to avoid an embarrassing collision.

"When we first met..." the vampire said with a clenched jaw. Her muscles twitched as if she were trying very hard to hold herself back. "You were afraid of me. Why?"

Honestly, I was still afraid of her, but that was beside the point. "I thought you'd suck my blood," I answered meekly.

Connie eased up a little, straightening to her full height and looking down at me over her nose. "And what did I tell you?"

"That vampires don't do that anymore. They feed on wealth now." That was easy. Normally my memory wasn't the best, but when it came to the paranormal world, I now made sure that nothing I learned was forgotten. Even the smallest little factoid could mean the difference between seeing a job to completion or messing up so badly I lost my life in the process. I'd learned that the hard way when I'd forgotten what the various colors meant on the flashing crystal ball Fluffikins had saddled me with for my last assignment.

Connie's brows scrunched together as she regarded me. "That's not strictly true."

I gasped and stumbled back a step. "You still drink blood?" As a newly christened vampire, did that mean I, too, would soon be drinking blood? I shuddered at the thought.

Connie hung her head and eyed the leaves scattered across the forest floor as she spoke. "I don't, but I would if I have no other choice."

I chanced a step closer. "What would take away that choice?"

Her eyes snapped up to meet mine. "When too many vampires live within a confined area, and especially within more than one coven, there isn't enough wealth to go around. This leaves us to seek out other, baser ways of sating our hunger."

"Blood," I said, almost tasting the word as it left my mouth.

She bared her teeth, putting her fangs on full display. "We still have the equipment."

I ran my tongue along my upper teeth. They still felt the same as they had before Fluffikins provided me with my new vampire magic.

"You don't have them yet," Connie said, watching me closely. "But if the change remains permanent, you will. They only take a few months to grow in. It gives new recruits the chance to learn our new way of feeding and helps curb what would otherwise be a frenzy."

"Wow," I said and sucked a deep breath in, even though I know my lungs didn't need it. "So we really do need to get Vanessa to leave Beech Grove."

"Yes, and seeing my peaceful attempts at negotiation failed, we now must prepare for war." Connie's words came out dispassionate as she sighed and shook her head. She seemed tired, battle-weary before the war had even truly begun. Did she mean she was afraid? And if she was afraid, what did that mean for the rest of us?

"Have you been in a vampire war before?" I asked gently, hoping she may actually open up to me. "It sounds really scary."

She laughed dryly. "Vampire strength mixed with human weakness, what a joke."

"Have you?" I insisted. I'd seen that flash of despair, regret, fear, something—and I needed to know why.

"Many times. Where there is hunger, there is also greed. Some vampires aren't content with their current resources and seek to claim other towns. They must be stopped, swiftly and permanently."

"You mean…?" I took a deep breath and held it inside me.

The elder vampire reached down and grabbed a short branch from the forest floor, pointing it at my chest plate. "Stake to the heart. It's the only way to kill us, after all."

"You said *us.*" My heart would have warmed if it had still been beating.

"I didn't mean *you.* I'm talking about the real vampires," she corrected with a growl. Oh, good. I'd offended her. That would make it easier for us to work nicely together.

"Then why did Fluffikins give me this armor to protect my heart?" I challenged, raising a hand to my chest.

She chuffed. "I don't know why he gave you that ridiculous collar, but it's not for the reasons he said."

"You think he lied to me?"

"I know he lied to you."

"But why? What's he hiding?" *And what aren't you telling me about your own past?*

"I don't know. I haven't been paying enough attention to catch on to the big secret you and he have been going on about. I also don't care enough to go digging."

Well, that made sense with everything I knew about Connie so far. She'd never liked me, and she never would. She couldn't. That was her curse, and for a short while, it was also mine.

She hurled the stick so hard I couldn't see where it eventually landed. Once the projectile flew out of sight, she looked over her shoulder at me and said, “Now can we please go back to base and start preparing for our battle? I’m going to need a lot more than you as backup.”

Connie didn’t wait for me to answer. Instead, she fled deeper into the woods, leaving me no choice but to run after her.

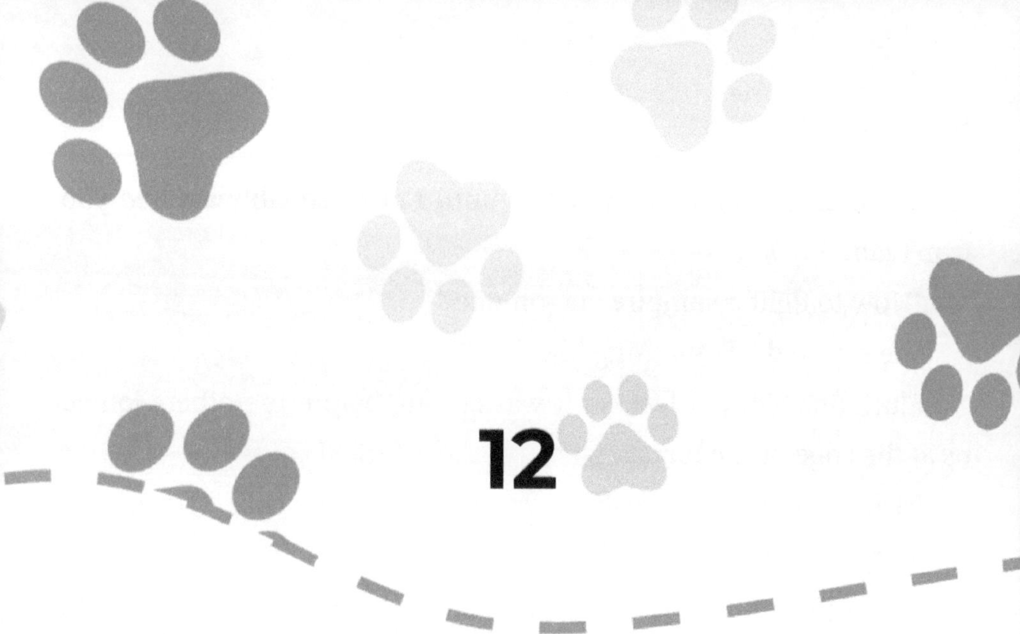

12

Mr. Fluffikins sat waiting for us at the edge of the forest. "Well, what's the report?" he asked as soon as we stepped out onto the lawn behind HQ.

"Time for phase two," Connie answered before setting her mouth in a firm line.

Fluffikins rose to his feet at once. "I'll gather the team."

"Leave the angel out of it," Connie snarled, her expression growing dark in an instant. "She's never liked my methods, and she doesn't hesitate to say so, either. If we're going to create a strong team, we need no dissidents."

The cat nodded. "Very well."

"What now?" I asked Connie as Mr. Fluffikins trotted back toward HQ.

She stared after him rather than shifting her gaze to meet mine.

"Now we form a plan and practice until I'm reasonably assured you won't fail."

"How to fight a vampire one-oh-one?"

She smirked. "Something like that."

Fluffikins worked fast, so it wasn't long before the others joined us at the edge of the forest.

Parker immediately rushed over to stand at my side. "Tawny, are you okay? What's going on?"

I shrugged and shook my head. I didn't fully know the answer to either of his questions.

"All eyes on me, please," Connie shouted at us. "You're here to learn how to dispatch an unwanted coven in the area. I'll formulate a plan and then teach each of you how to execute it."

The old guy in the suit lowered himself to the forest floor, struggling for breath. If his waist-length white beard hadn't given away his age, then his complete lack of physical fitness would have sold him out. I still didn't know his name, and at this point, it felt rude to ask. I did know that he was the head of Cemeteries, which was the most cringey job of the bunch. Seriously, though, what good would such a feeble old man be when it came to violent hand-to-hand combat?

Connie cleared her throat to draw everyone's attention back to her and continued. "Clearly, we are at a disadvantage here with our hodgepodge group of supernaturals, a normie with magic she doesn't know how to use, and a teenager."

"Hey!" Melony and I cried in unison.

"I'd know how to use my magic if you'd just teach me," I shouted at Connie.

"And I'm eighteen. That makes me an adult!" Melony protested.

"If you say so," I muttered loud enough for her to hear.

"At least I come from a line of powerful magicks!" she shot back.

"At least I save lives instead of trying to take them!"

"Well, at least I—"

"Enough!" Connie yelled so loudly her reprimand shook the trees.

Melony and I immediately stopped our bickering and crossed our arms over our chests. Again in perfect unison.

If you thought that my saving her life last week would have turned her to my side, then you'd be wrong. She was still bent out of shape about our first encounter a few days before that—the one where she and her grandpa tried to kill me, but I survived and managed to help foil their evil plans. It didn't matter that I'd gone all the way to Maine to free her from some weird magical hostage situation. She still hated my guts. The brat.

"Vampires are stronger, faster, and smarter than all of you put together. They're also much harder to kill," Connie continued.

"Wait, why isn't Greta here?" Buckley, our head of Agriculture, asked.

"You know how I feel about the angel," Connie answered stonily.

Tension rolled off Connie in thick, angry waves, and we all averted our eyes to keep from upsetting her further.

"So as I was saying, under normal circumstances, none of you stand a chance against a vampire. That's why we have to make sure the circumstances aren't normal." She paused to let that sink in.

"The temp and I went downtown to meet Vanessa Vane this morning, and she mentioned her restaurant would be opening tonight. If there are more in her coven, I have no doubt they'll turn up for the event. What we don't know is how many outsider vampires we're actually dealing with. We can't know, which makes it that much more important to be prepared for anything."

Mr. Fluffikins, who had been uncharacteristically quiet up until the point, hopped onto a low tree branch to address the group. "For this assignment, Connie is lead. I expect you to give her the full measure of respect you'd normally give me."

I began to snicker under my breath but quickly covered it with a cough. "Sorry," I mumbled, bringing a hand in front of my mouth to hide the smile that lingered.

"We'll go in tonight during the opening." Connie kept her threatening gaze on me while she addressed the full group. "I'll need half of you inside and half on the streets."

Parker raised his hand. "Tawny and I can go inside. Make it look like a date."

"Perfect," Connie agreed, a slow smile curling on her lips. "Melony, you can team up with Buckley to do the same."

"But he's like the same age as my dad!" the eighteen-year-old witch protested.

Buckley tossed her a wink, which drew laughs from me, Parker, and the old dude in the suit.

"I promise to be the perfect gentleman," Buckley said, rolling up the sleeves on his ubiquitous plaid shirt as if he were ready to get down to business right now. "Although I'll probably need to change into something more suitable."

"Exactly what I was thinking," Connie said.

“Will I need to wear something fancy, too?” I asked, unsure whether my vampire get-up fit the bill for a small-town restaurant opening.

“She’s not talking about clothes.” Buckley gave me a bright smile, and then with a poof, he disappeared right before my eyes.

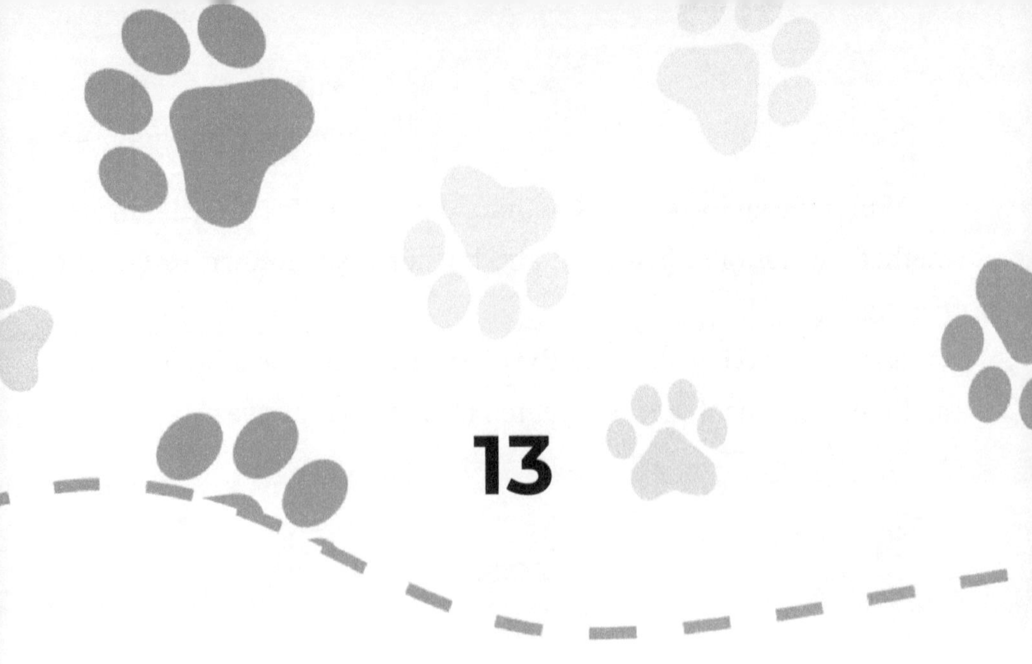

13

A little sparrow appeared as if out of thin air and flew over to perch next to Mr. Fluffikins on his tree branch.

"Whoa, what just happened? Where's Buckley?" I cried, spinning around to search for him.

"Relax, I'm right here," the little bird chirped. "Didn't you know that I'm a shifter?"

"That's why he oversees Agriculture," Parker explained from beside me. "It's easy for him to get a lay of the land because he can turn himself into any animal he wants, so long as its native to this area."

I stared at the sparrow, my jaw hanging open in astonishment. "Why the restriction? Can't magic do anything?"

"Magic isn't meant to be flamboyant and attention-catching. It can only exist if safely hidden," Parker explained.

"Enough," the vampire in charge bellowed. "This isn't meant to be a lesson on shifters for our one normie. This is about vampires and making a plan to stop them. Buckley, go scope out the building. It's that new Indian restaurant at the corner of Main and Grand. Try to get a sense of how many vampires we're dealing with here. Don't return until you have gained information we can use."

The bird nodded its cute little head and then flitted away. I soon lost sight of it amidst the tall dark trees.

"You're a vampire, Connie," Parker said with a playful grin. "So, then tell us, how do we kill you?"

Connie bared her fangs and fixed a predatory gaze on Parker.

"Rules for the undead are different," the old guy in the suit said. "Otherwise, I'd give 'em a whoosh and a whoop." He mimed swinging something—maybe a baseball bat—then whooped again.

Parker nudged me in the arm with an explanation for that, too. "He's our reaper."

A reaper, oh!

I stood on tiptoe to whisper into Parker's ear. "What's his name?"

Parker shrugged. "That's the thing. No one knows. I don't even think he does."

"How could he not know his own name?" I asked, perhaps a little too loudly.

"Call me R," the old guy shot in. "And thank you for asking... even if you didn't ask me."

"How do you not—?"

"All side conversations must cease!" Connie bellowed, sending another vibration through the forest.

The next thing I knew she stood behind me with an arm drawn

across my neck in a tight hold. "Vampires are fast," she said, then nipped at the air beside my ear. "They can kill you just as soon as look at you."

Connie let me go and popped up behind Melony, putting her in the same chokehold. "So what do you do?"

Melony writhed and struggled in Connie's arms but failed to break free.

Connie laughed. "Vampires are strong, too. Think you can spar with one and come out the victor? Think again, princess."

She released Melony, and the young witch fell to the ground in a heap.

Next Connie came for Parker, but instead of taking him in her hold, she wound up face down on the forest floor. It all happened so fast, I had no idea how he'd bested her.

"Very good," Connie said, popping back to her feet and dusting herself off. "Now tell the others how you did that."

"Never lose sight of the target."

Connie nodded. "Good. What else?"

"Use their speed against them. Fast movements can lead to powerful falls."

Connie zoomed up behind R. He took a step to the side, and Connie flew past him, moving too fast to change course at the last fraction of a second.

"Evasive tactics work," Connie announced with a tight smile. "Until they don't."

She flew at R again, but he sidestepped her once more. She kept doubling back and hurling herself at him until she at last managed to tackle him.

"See," she said with a huff. "Evasion is a stall tactic, not a winning one."

"Oh, I could have gone all day," R revealed with a wink. "But I figured the sooner you made your point, the sooner we could all get on with our day." The old guy could certainly move fast when he wanted to. I was beginning to think our reaper in residence was much more than he seemed at first glance.

Connie growled in frustration, then launched herself at me. She moved fast, but now so did I. I threw my arm back, making a fist.

It connected with my target.

"Ouch!" Connie shouted, even though I knew she couldn't feel the pain. Maybe she was so used to having to pass as human, it had become an automatic reaction. Or maybe her pride had been wounded so badly, she couldn't help crying out.

She turned around and came rushing back. This time, she managed to overtake me.

"The moment you become overconfident is the moment you lose," she warned with a haughty look of satisfaction.

She let me go but continued to throw herself at us, one at a time.

Again and again.

And again.

I'd never been an exercise person, but this training activity was fairly easy now that I knew what to do. The vampire magic came with perfect physical fitness. I couldn't grow tired, get injured, or slow down.

But neither could Connie.

Nor could our enemies.

While helpful, I doubted this afternoon of training would actually be enough to prepare us for victory.

Oh, how I hoped I was wrong about that.

14

Connie's training went on for so long that the non-vampires among us showed notable signs of fatigue. Their success rate for besting Connie had already spiked and was now on a clear and rapid decline. Which made me wonder if, by this point, it was even helping at all.

"Um, maybe we should all take some time to recharge before tonight's operation," I suggested as Connie clutched Melony against her chest.

"Vampires don't need rest!" Connie spat back.

"But people and witches do," Parker pointed out.

I glanced toward R with burning curiosity.

He just smiled and shrugged. "Reapers aren't like vampires or humans, or really anything or anyone else. Don't worry about me. I'll manage."

"I'm worried about all of you," Connie grumbled. "Our chances aren't good, especially if we're dealing with a full coven."

A rustling of leaves sounded from deeper in the forest. Connie and I both turned toward the sound, but the others didn't seem to hear anything until the rustling drew closer.

A tall, tan buck with a massive rack of antlers ran straight for us, his hooves beating hard against the earth as he approached.

"Buckley, report," Fluffikins called from the spot where he'd been napping in his tree for much of the day. I hadn't realized that he'd woken up until he spoke.

When I shifted my eyes from the cat back to the deer, I found the buck had gone and left Buckley standing in his place.

Oh, now I got it.

Buck. Buckley. Ha.

Thankfully, his shifting magic returned him in a fully dressed state. I don't think I could have handled getting so intimately acquainted with him—or anyone else—in the midst of all of this.

In addition to his flannel shirt and jeans, however, Buckley also wore a frown. And that concerned me.

"Speak," Connie prompted when Buckley hesitated for too long.

"It's n-not good," he sputtered at last. "I counted at least four more vampires joining the first."

"Will there be more?" Connie demanded. "Did you hear anything of their plans?"

"That all remains unclear. Regardless, we should act fast to minimize risk."

Fluffikins jumped down from the tree branch and paced our way.

"Agreed," he said, walking past our group and heading for the edge of the woods.

"What time do they open tonight?" Connie asked.

"Seven," Buckley answered, eager to show he had at least brought some answers back with him.

"Then we'll plan to be there at seven thirty. Our four inside men are dismissed. R, join me and Fluffikins at HQ, so we can plan our movements on the outside."

Melony crossed her arms and kicked at the ground. "Um, men? It's the twenty-first century, lady vampire. Perhaps you could try being a bit more gender inclusive?"

"Oh, did I hurt your little mortal feelings?" Connie mocked, her eyebrows arching high. "Try living for several centuries, then tell me how important current social niceties seem to you. Now like I said, dismissed. Don't make me tell you a third time."

"Or what?" Melony challenged, flinging a defiant hand on her hip.

"Okay, that's enough. C'mon, Melony." I wrapped an arm over her shoulders and forced her to exit the forest with me.

"Let go of me!" she roared, but she was unable to escape my strong grasp, thanks to my vampire magic. I was just as strong and fast as Connie, although still unpracticed.

I would be okay tonight, but what about Melony? Parker? The others?

The witches seemed so vulnerable. Even Buckley would be at a disadvantage as a shifter. So far I'd only seen him transform into a sparrow and a deer. Parker had said he could only turn himself into local animals, and I doubted he'd get far as a wolf or a gator in the middle of a packed restaurant or busy street.

I still didn't fully understand what Fluffikins could do, even though I knew he was a powerful magic user. Good offense didn't necessarily translate to a superior defense, though. For all I knew, he could be the most at risk of us all.

Which meant it was that much more important that Connie and I take lead on this.

The two of us against at least five vampires who presumably already knew how to work well together and had had much more time to come up with a plan. Those weren't good odds.

But if the PTA didn't succeed, everyone in town would be at risk. I didn't know how often vampires needed to feed, but I doubted anyone in Beech Grove would want to lose their lives to a late-night predator.

If they took even one person, it would be too much.

We had to win.

Or die trying.

It felt as if an eternity had passed since I'd turned up at HQ hoping to trade a basket full of steaks for one single answer. Now I had more questions than ever, and I might not live long enough to find a single one.

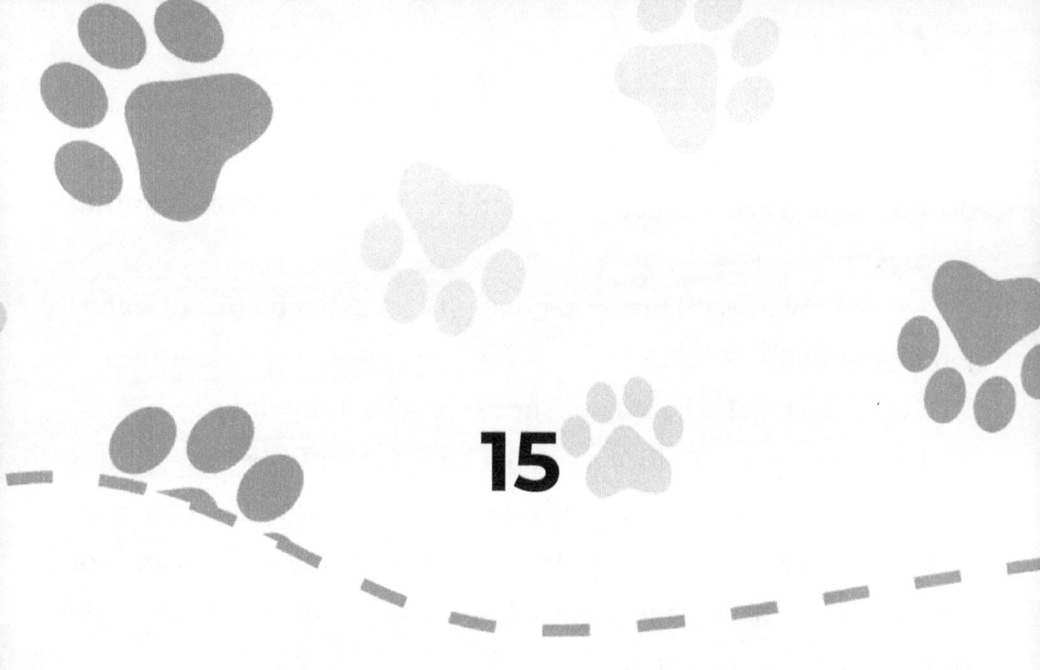

15

Parker turned up outside my door at seven on the nose.

"Ready for our big date?" he asked, hope reflecting in his pale eyes. He looked handsome in his navy-blue suit and loafers, but I wished more than anything he'd have stayed home and let me and Connie handle this dispute by ourselves.

He, Melony, and the others would all be liabilities in this fight. While my vampire curse kept me from wanting to protect him because of some misguided emotional attachment, I still didn't want the added obstacle. If he got in the way or messed something up, then I'd be more likely to die myself.

And as Connie was quick to point out, I was a young and inexperienced vampire—not really a vampire at all. We already had the odds stacked against us.

"Well, I'm ready enough for the both of us," Parker said with a dreamy sigh when I failed to respond myself. "You look beautiful, Tawny."

I rolled my eyes. "This isn't a date. It's an assignment. An important one at that."

"Why can't it also be a date?" he asked with a shy smile.

I opened my mouth to answer, but he cut me off.

"I know, I know. You're a big, mean vampire now. But that won't last forever, Tawny. Hopefully, we can end this thing tonight, and you can go back to being you. Then I'll take you out on a real date. One you'll actually want to go on."

"We need to focus on what needs to be done," I reminded him as I sat and yanked a red pump onto each foot. They were the only pair of nice heels I had. I'd paired them with a black high-necked maxi dress, taking care to hide my chest piece beneath. Fluffikins said it would protect me. Connie said the cat was making things up. In the end, it cost me nothing to wear the thing since I couldn't feel pain or discomfort while under the influence of vampire magic. Because of this, I decided to hedge my bets and keep it on until Fluffikins asked for me to return it to him.

I hoped Vanessa wouldn't recognize me out of context, but I also knew that my bubble-gum pink hair had a way of standing out in the crowd. It wouldn't be the worst thing, being recognized. In fact, if the other vampire fixated on me, then it would be easier for Connie to sneak in and take her by surprise.

So either way, I was good to go.

"Mind if I drive?" Parker asked when I grabbed my handbag and stepped out onto the porch.

I motioned for him to have at it. "You might as well."

I could see him going toward the passenger side and used my swift feet to beat him to it. "I've got my own door, thanks."

He just chuckled.

"What's so funny?" I asked when he sank down into the driver's seat and closed the door.

Parker studied me for a moment, then shook his head. "Don't worry about it."

He reached up to jab the key in the ignition, but I clutched his wrist and forced him to look at me. "Tell me."

He sighed and ran a hand through his hair, messing up the gel job he'd done before picking me up. "It's just you're you, but not. It's like I both have Tawny with me, and I don't."

I quirked an eyebrow and tried not to grin. "So what you're saying is I'm Schrodinger's vampire?"

Parker let out a loud peal of laughter. "Something like that."

"It wasn't a joke," I said, releasing his wrist and then folding my arms over my chest.

"I know," Parker responded as he twisted the key in the ignition and brought the vehicle to life. "I guess it serves me right, huh? I avoided you for days, thinking I was doing the right thing. All I wanted was to keep you safe, but now here you are, Schrodinger's vampire marching to war in high-heeled shoes."

"I make my own choices," I mumbled.

"Now that we're clear on that point, I'll give you many more opportunities to do so," he promised. "Which means you'll be seeing lots more of me."

I shifted toward the window, blocking him out. "No, thanks."

"That's just the vampire talking," he said. "The real Tawny wants that date I offered. There's something special between us. It's been there from the start. And she knows it."

"Yeah, well, I guess that something special between us died when I did," I muttered. It's something I'd been wondering about since Fluffikins gave me this new magic. Was I dead? Undead? Something else entirely?

Parker answered it for me. "You're not dead, Tawny. You're not even undead."

I turned back to face him, but he kept his eyes on the road. "Isn't that what being a vampire means, though?"

"You're not a full vampire," he said firmly. Perhaps for me, and perhaps to remind himself, too. "Just playing dress-up as one for a little while."

"Only if we succeed," I pointed out. "The odds are stacked against us, you know."

"That may be true, but there is no if here. We will succeed."

I cocked my head to the side, considering. "What makes you so sure?"

He glanced toward me with a big, toothy smile and winked. "Because it's the only way you'll agree to that date. Which means I will make sure we win this thing. You can count on me, Tawny. Count on what we have."

Yeah, I guess we'd see about that...

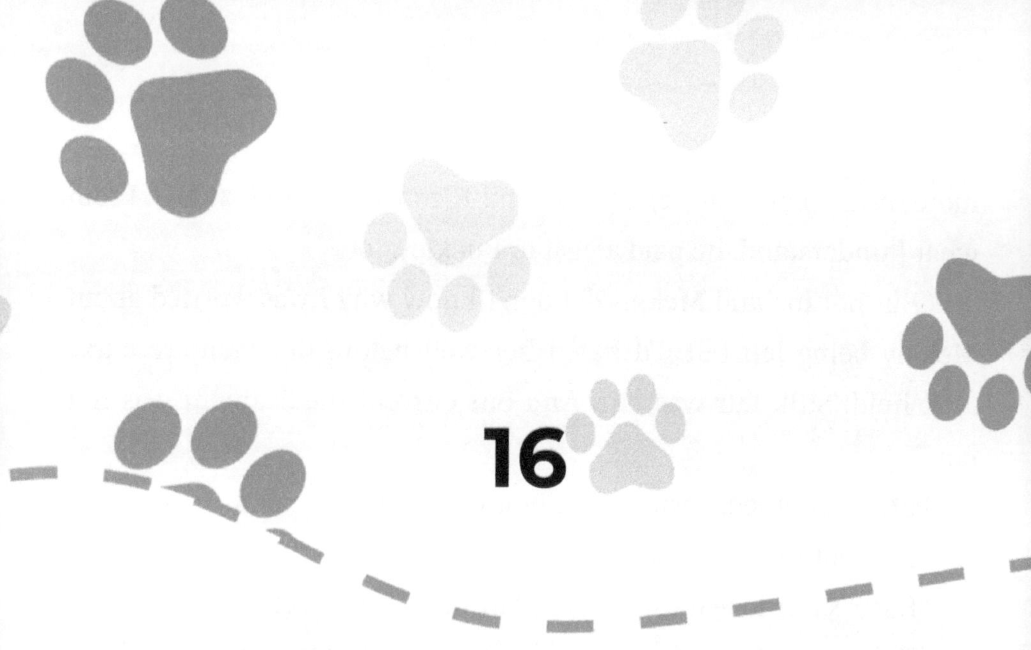

16

Our drive wasn't even three minutes long. One of the reasons I'd decided to rent my cottage was because of its proximity to downtown. I guess Parker wanted to have a getaway car at the ready, which is why he decided to drive us there. He now guided the car into the lot a couple blocks away from Vanessa's restaurant, and the two of us sat waiting in place until Fluffikins appeared in the lot and motioned for us to proceed. I hadn't known we were waiting for his cue, but Parker clearly had.

"Did you get a more detailed rundown of the mission than I did?" I asked, feeling frustrated as we picked our way across the gravel parking lot.

Parker strolled leisurely toward our destination, and I had a hard time forcing myself to keep pace.

"Yes. Fluffikins came by to talk with me this afternoon and share more of the plan that he, Connie, and R concocted back at HQ. From what I understand, he paid a visit to Buckley, too."

"But not me and Melony?" I don't know why I was worried about Melony being left out. I'd hated her well before this vampire curse took hold. Still, fair was fair. And our current predicament was not fair.

Parker frowned. "You and Melony are still very new. It wouldn't be fair to put too much on you."

"But it's fair to leave us out of planning?" I bit back.

"This isn't about what's fair," he whispered as we approached the restaurant and began to mix with other pedestrians on the street. "It's about what gets the job done. Now hold my hand and look like you're happy to be with me."

I laced my fingers through his, despite not appreciating him telling me what to do. He then pulled open the door and held it as I led the way in.

A smiling hostess greeted us. No fangs, which meant she either wasn't a vampire yet or was still too young to have grown into her full powers.

"Welcome to the grand opening of Bollyweird. We offer a bold new take on traditional Indian flavors. Table for two?"

"Please," Parker answered with a matching grin.

The hostess grabbed two menus and led us to a table in the back near the silver buffet I'd spotted during my earlier visit with Connie.

"Looks busy," Parker said, then pulled a chair out for me.

I took a seat, unfolded a cloth napkin, and placed it over my lap.

"This place basically appeared overnight. I wonder how they managed to get the word out so fast," I observed as I took in the full house.

"Well, va—I mean, let's say, vegetarians," Parker said with a half-cocked grin. "Vegetarians can be very charming when they want to be. It's easy for them to pull others near."

A chill ran through me. Could I do that, too? And if not now, would I be able to soon? Would I lose myself to this newfound power? I shook my head and whispered, "I'm starting to think there's not much that vegetarians can't do."

"Yes, that's why they're a problem."

"To be honest, I don't see how anyone except me or Connie stands a chance against them."

Parker scoffed at this. "You've been a v... vegetarian for all of ten hours and already you think you're better than me?"

I picked up the laminated menu and opened it before me. "It's not an emotional thing. I'm simply stating facts here."

"Maybe, but you don't have enough information to reach an accurate conclusion."

The waitress appeared then, notepad in hand. Also not a vampire, I realized. She seemed to have a difficult time navigating the pathways between tables while wearing her deep purple sari with gold trim.

"The lady and I will have the buffet," Parker announced before I'd even had a chance to finish looking over the appetizers. "Provided you have suitable options for vegetarians?"

I kicked Parker under the table while smiling up at the waitress. We had to keep our cover, and he knew that, which is why he was teasing me. *Ugh.*

"Oh, yes. We actually specialize in vegetarian cuisine," the waitress answered in a sing-song voice. "I'll be back around with your waters. Go ahead and help yourselves to the buffet. Enjoy!"

"After you," Parker offered with a smug look of satisfaction.

I rose from the table, working hard not to show how irritated I was with my "date." He followed behind me, even trying to grab my hand, but I refused to let him take it.

We each picked up a plate from the warmer and began to make our way down the serving line. I'd enjoyed feasting on Indian food whenever I found myself in New York or another big city to meet with my editor or host a book signing. Rural Georgia felt like a strange place for a restaurant like this, but who was I to judge? I knew next to nothing about the food business.

I passed over the butter chicken with a sigh. Normally, that was my favorite, but Parker had gone and told the waitress I was a vegetarian, and I would hate to draw suspicion to us over such a small and unimportant detail. So instead, I loaded up on chickpea curry, various paneer dishes, and a massive stack of naan.

Did I actually feel hungry? No.

Was I going to miss an opportunity to stuff my face with such delicious looking food? Not a chance.

As soon as we sat, I tore off a piece of naan and added a spoonful of curry before popping the giant morsel in my mouth.

But the moment the food hit my tongue, I grabbed the napkin from my lap and spit out my entire mouthful.

“Don’t eat anything,” I whispered to Parker in warning. “Something’s wrong with the food.”

17

"What's wrong?" Parker asked, thankfully setting his spoon down without drawing the compromised food to his mouth.

"Don't overreact..." I leaned over the table to whisper to him. "But I'm pretty sure the food is poisoned."

"How would you know that?" he asked at full volume.

"It tastes..." I rolled my hand at the wrist, searching for the right word.

"Weird?" Parker supplied with one eyebrow raised. "It's in the name, remember? Bolly*WEIRD*."

I shook my head and fell back into my chair. "No, something's off. I don't know what exactly, but something. I can taste it."

"You haven't eaten yet since becoming a, uh, vegetarian, though, right? Maybe you're just overwhelmed by all the flavors and how they're hitting your enhanced senses," Parker pointed out. I understood his reasoning, but it still irked me that he couldn't just take my word on this. We were losing precious time here.

Remembering what Parker had said about vampires being able to draw people to them, I chose my next words carefully. Could I use my magic to stop all arguments?

"There's something that shouldn't be there. *Trust me.*" I gave that last command extra emphasis, tasting each syllable as it rolled over my tongue.

Parker reached across the table and put his hand over mine. "I believe you," he acquiesced at last. Had I changed his mind with my magic? Part of me didn't want to know. Being able to compel anyone to my will felt like too much power. Perhaps that's why neither Connie nor Fluffikins had mentioned it to me.

I pushed my seat back and stood. "I'm going to the bathroom," I announced, putting on a pleasant smile for anyone who was watching. "See if you can get through to the others," I whispered to Parker before heading off.

He pulled out his phone and immediately began texting. I eyed Buckley seated on the other side of the restaurant with Melony as I made my way toward the bathrooms. He had his phone out and was already studying the screen with a furrowed brow.

With a quick glance back to make sure Parker's attention was otherwise occupied, I slipped past the restrooms and into the kitchen.

The swinging doors announced my arrival with a sudden flourish of movement that drew the eyes of the full kitchen staff.

Well, I'd just found where Vanessa was hiding all the vegetarians —erm, vampires. The four others Buckley had counted all busied themselves at various stations, stirring, braising, baking, and plating. Vanessa stood before a stainless-steel counter chopping an onion at lightning speed.

"I should have turned you away at the door," she muttered, then abruptly stopped dicing and hurled the chef's knife at me. It flew end over end, embedding in the door less than an inch from my ear.

Whoa, I had not been prepared for that. As fast as I could now move, Vanessa was faster—and she seemed to have zero hang-ups about getting violent.

"That was your warning," the vampire chef hissed. "The next one won't miss."

I took a step back but bumped into the door. Okay, now I was afraid. There was still so much I didn't know about vampires. Would a knife kill me, or did it have to be a wooden stake? And vampire or not, did I even have it in me to chop off someone's head? I was guessing the old garlic trick didn't work, given how much of the spice I'd detected in the food and now saw around the kitchen. So where did that leave me in this fight?

Now that I'd revealed myself, I couldn't back down.

But could I somehow manage to win?

I lowered my gaze and narrowed my eyes at Vanessa, hoping the stance made me appear more menacing than terrified. "What are you putting in the food here? Why are you poisoning the normies?" I demanded, my voice strong and mostly not shaking.

"Who says we're doing anything out of sorts here?" Vanessa answered with a shrug, approaching me with a gentle swing to her hips. She stopped mere inches before me and raised her hand to grasp the knife beside my head. She didn't pull it out, though. Instead, she leaned in closer. I could smell her stale breath over the other, more pungent aromas in the kitchen.

"What we do to normies is our business. As is this restaurant. It's OUR business, and you're not welcome here. Go. Now." She bit out each of these last words with her glistening fangs on full display.

I could have pushed back through the door, leaving this whole confrontation behind me. Whatever Vanessa hoped to accomplish with her poisoned food, she probably didn't want to create a scene in the middle of the restaurant where all her customers could see. I could have run to Parker or Melony and Buckley, but hadn't I already decided they would only slow me down?

"Connie already asked you nicely," I growled, leaning in even closer. "You know you can't stay in Beech Grove. It's already claimed."

"And I already asked you nicely. It seems both of us have a hard time listening. Huh. Guess that means talking isn't going to get us anywhere."

With that, Vanessa grabbed the chef's knife from the door. I caught the movement and followed it with my eyes, ready to block the attack, but while I was focused on this threat, my opponent withdrew a wooden stake from her apron and shoved it straight into my chest.

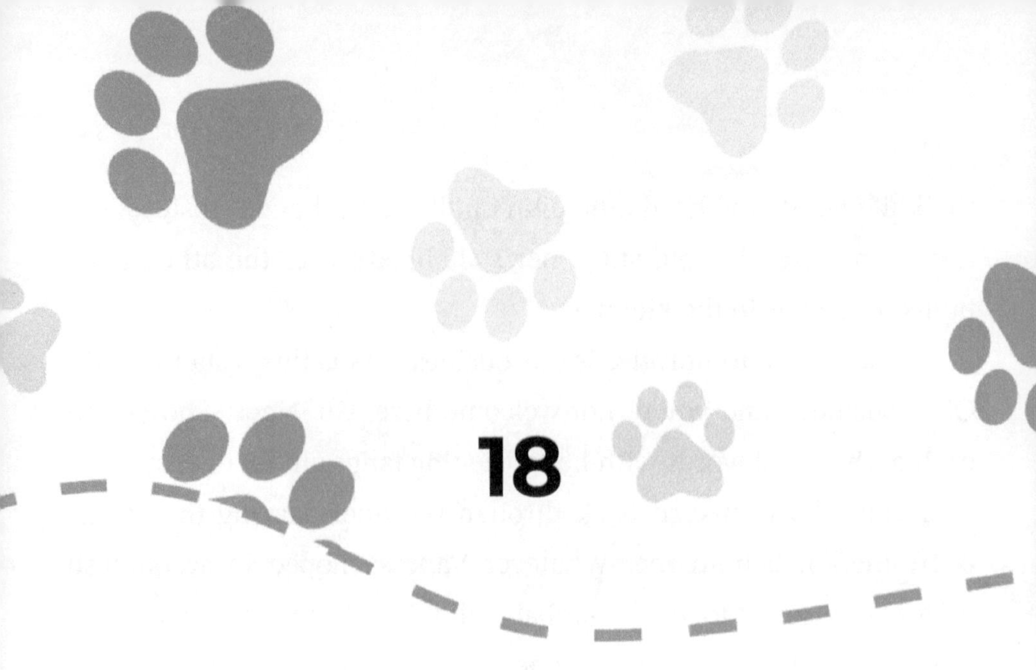

18

I gasped in surprise but felt no pain. A stake to the heart should have killed me, right?

My eyes and Vanessa's both shot down to where she held the stake against my chest. The wood had splintered straight up to where Vanessa gripped the weapon in her fist.

It hadn't entered my heart.

The breastplate!

That silly little accessory had held and very likely saved my life in the process.

Our eyes locked and Vanessa swung with her other arm, the one that held the knife. I darted out of the way, unwilling to lose my head or any other appendage. I'd need those when I became human again.

I forgot to adjust for my new strength, however, and hurled myself with too much force, knocking into an industrial stainless-steel dishwasher spewing steam.

No, no, no, no!

I needed to get back to my feet before Vanessa threw herself at me again. I found myself at a distinct disadvantage now. These Bollyweird vampires had the experience, the numbers, and the higher ground.

I was toast.

Or I would have been if the door hadn't boomed open, sending a powerful magical fog swirling through the kitchen. A tall man wearing a dark blue suit and loafers stormed in behind.

Parker!

I wanted to go to him, to clutch his hand, to apologize for thinking of him as a liability, and thank him for saving my life. No, I still didn't love him or anything even close to that. I was, however, incredibly grateful to still have my head attached, to live another day in this crazy world.

One problem, though; I couldn't move. I struggled and strained but couldn't even bat an eyelash.

"Tawny! Tawny!" Parker called as he maneuvered past the vampire chefs, each stuck in perfect stasis.

Much as I wanted to, I couldn't call out in response. Luckily, it didn't take Parker long to find me on the sticky tile floor by the dishwasher.

"Tawny!" he exclaimed, placing a hand to my chest and freeing me from the spell he'd cast.

I let him help me into an upright position even though I didn't need any assistance now that the magical fog no longer trapped me.

He searched me for wounds, his breath panicked, heart wild.

"When you didn't come back, I realized you'd probably gone off and tried to take on the coven by yourself. And look, I was right." He smiled at me gently even though his brow remained furrowed with concern.

"How'd you know that?" I asked. I thought I'd had him fooled. That I'd made the perfect plan to give our team the best chance at victory.

"Because I know you. The real you." He raised my hand in his and kissed it.

"Does that mean I'm no longer Schrodinger's vampire?" I asked with a slow grin.

"I don't know what you are exactly. Just that you're pretty spectacular."

"And brave?" I offered.

"I think foolish might be the better word," he retorted. "Seriously, though. Are you all right?"

"I'm fine," I answered, then pounded on my chest plate. "Good as new, thanks to this baby."

He frowned and placed his hand to my chest once again. "Is that what you were wearing earlier today? That collar? What's it for?"

"To keep me from getting staked in the heart, and obviously it worked. Connie should really consider wearing hers more often." I'd been wrong about something important, but so had Connie. Even though vampires were smart and strong, they weren't always right, and they weren't the only ones who had skills of value.

Parker seemed confused. "May I see it?" he asked, sitting back on his heels to give me some space.

"I mean it's kind of under my dress right now, so…"

He flashed a cocky grin, then used his magic to unclasp the armor from behind my neck and untie it from around my waist. A moment later, the armor phased through my dress and floated into Parker's grasp.

"Seems like you have some experience with that," I quipped with an unbecoming snort.

But Parker didn't say anything back. Not even to make a joke.

"Fluffikins gave this to you?" he asked, running his hands over the metal.

I nodded, studying him as he studied the armor. "To protect me."

"No, that's not why." Parker shook his head. "I didn't realize it, earlier in my office. I was too swept away by my feelings to think clearly."

I ignored the feelings part, preferring to focus on the facts—or at least the facts as Parker now saw them. "Realize what? What's wrong?"

"This isn't armor to protect you," he whispered. "It's actually meant to dampen your magic."

I snorted again. "Well, that's ridiculous. I can use my magic just fine."

"Your vampire magic," Parker corrected. "The alloy here isn't meant to drown that out. It's for your witch magic."

Now he had me really confused. "No, I don't have that anymore. Remember? Fluffikins took it back."

Parker helped me to my feet and set the breastplate aside on one of the kitchen counters. “Did he, though? When’s the last time you tried to use it?”

“I haven’t tried, because I knew I didn’t have it anymore.” I glanced around the kitchen, eyeing Vanessa and the four other members of her coven with hesitation. They may have been frozen in place, but they were still very much alive and angrier than ever.

“Try to use it now,” Parker urged, focusing only on me.

I glared down at my hands. Could they still cast magic? Spells?

He raced across the kitchen, eyes still on me. “Here, we can stuff the chefs in this cooler and magically seal it until we’re ready to take them in to HQ.”

“You want me to do all that?” I balked.

“No, just open the door. One little thing. Now that you’re not wearing the dampener you can do it. Tawny, look at me.”

He waited until my eyes met his.

“I believe in you,” he said, and that was all I needed to hear to believe that his ridiculous assertion might actually be true. That somehow I was a witch and a vampire and me all at the same time.

I took a deep breath and raised my arms…

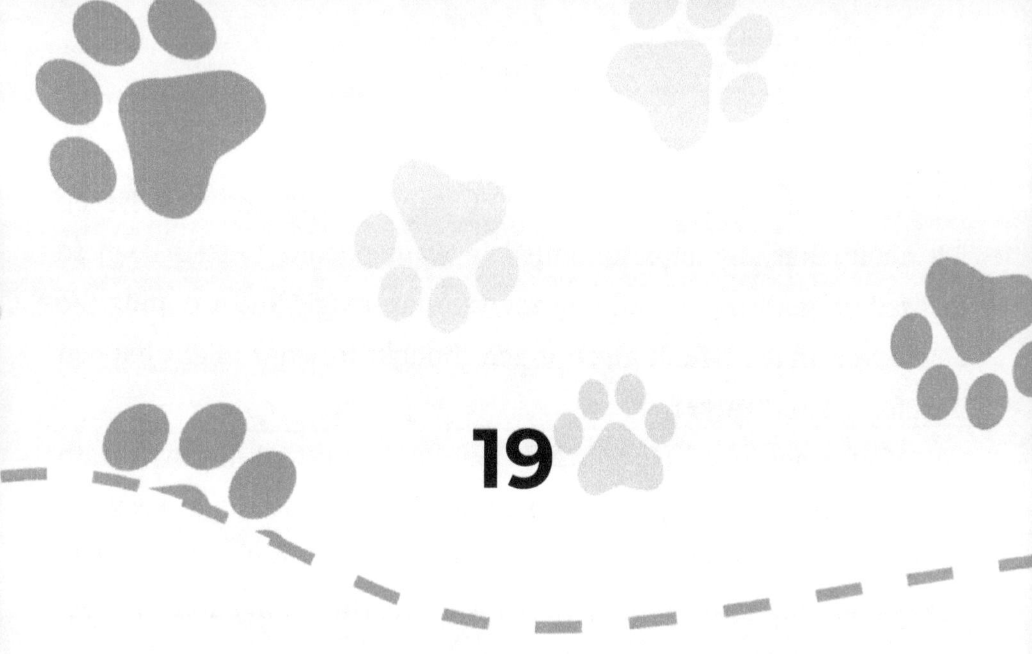

19

The door swung open with unexpected force, banging hard against the wall. I stared into the walk-in cooler with complete amazement. *I did that?*

"Told you," Parker said, running toward me and then taking me in his arms. "You're not a normie, Tawny."

"Then what am I?" I choked out, still unable to believe that I'd kept my temporary witch magic this whole time without knowing it.

"I don't know," Parker murmured into my hair.

"But Fluffikins does." Every muscle in my body tensed. Fluffikins knew what I was and had chosen to keep it from me. Even if not knowing got me killed. He would have to answer for that. I'd make sure of it.

"If he kept it from you, he had his reasons," Parker said, rubbing his hands up and down my arms. "Whatever you are, you're not a full vampire. Which means the curse doesn't affect you in the same way."

"Which means I can still love?" I asked, not certain how I even felt about that anymore. I wanted to want people, but I'd been so focused on getting a handle on my vampire magic and stopping the new coven that I hadn't given much thought to what might happen next for me and Parker.

"Maybe not love." He squeezed my hand and took a slow breath before continuing. "If you kept the witch magic, you might keep the vampire's, too. I don't know what that means, how they'll react to each other long-term. What I do know is, the rules don't apply to you. You're different."

"Yeah, you keep saying that." I bit my lip, wishing so badly I could feel pain in my current form. But no. At least not yet. "So what now?" I asked, afraid of all the answers he might give.

"We take the Bollyweird vampires captive. Figure out why they targeted us. Complete your job. Make Fluffikins tell you the truth." His words trailed off.

"And then?" My voice hitched.

"I don't know," he answered with a small shake of his head.

We embraced for a few moments longer. It didn't light me up from the inside as it once had, but I found comfort there as I readied myself for what I knew must happen next.

Whether we chose to kill all the members of the outsider coven, hold them captive forever, or simply wipe their memories, a reckoning was coming. Somehow I just knew it deep within my bones.

First the deadly battle for town witch. Then the field agents, Fluffikins, and Melony being kidnapped by a magical mafia in

Maine. And now this? Too much was happening too quickly in too small of a rural Georgia town for these events to be isolated coincidences.

Fluffikins knew I was different. Might others, too?

Or were they after something else, and I simply had the dumb luck to get caught up in it all?

I wished I knew...

"Help me round these guys up and jam them in there," Parker said, letting me go with a beleaguered sigh.

I watched as he wrapped a magical tendril around the first vampire chef and lifted him into the cooler. He then grabbed for another, picking his way through the crew.

I walked over to Vanessa, not far from where I'd left her. She stood with that same chef's knife raised in her hand, head twisted to the side. If Parker had been even a few seconds later, that knife would have found its target. *Me.*

"Why are you here?" I asked her immobile form. "Did you come for me?"

I watched for any sign of recognition, but she was nothing more than a statue while Parker's magic held on to her. He continued to round up the others, I raised my fingers to Vanessa's mouth and let my magic pour from their tips into her lips.

"Why are you here?" I asked our captured foe again.

Vanessa's lips flexed, but her mouth remained closed.

I waved my hand in a circle over her face and neck. Could I use my vampire and witch magic at the same time? There was only one way to find out.

"Tell me," I demanded, attempting my compulsion trick from earlier.

"Why should I tell you anything?" she snarled, then spat at me.

"I can take your life, or I can save it. The choice is yours."

"There are more of us than you can possibly imagine. Killing me will change nothing."

"Do you really value your cause above your own life?"

"What life?" she growled. "You think we enjoy this waifish existence, stuck between life and death? There is nothing for us. No love. No purpose. Nothing but the cause. It gives us purpose. A reason to continue to exist. Anything I tell you could lead you to destroying it. My life is but a small price to pay to protect what so many of us have worked so long for."

"I don't understand," I said with a frown. "None of what you're saying makes sense."

"I don't owe you anything." She laughed viciously. "Silly girl. You don't even know who you are. Do you?"

"Tell me. I need to know," I begged. I didn't care if it made me look weak. In the moment, I was weak. I didn't even know the truth about who I was.

Vanessa opened her mouth to say something but then let out a guttural groan. I watched in horror as a wooden stake emerged from her chest.

"Well, that's one less thing to worry about," Connie remarked before pulling the stake back out of Vanessa and twirling it in her hand. "Let's get the others back to HQ so we can interrogate them."

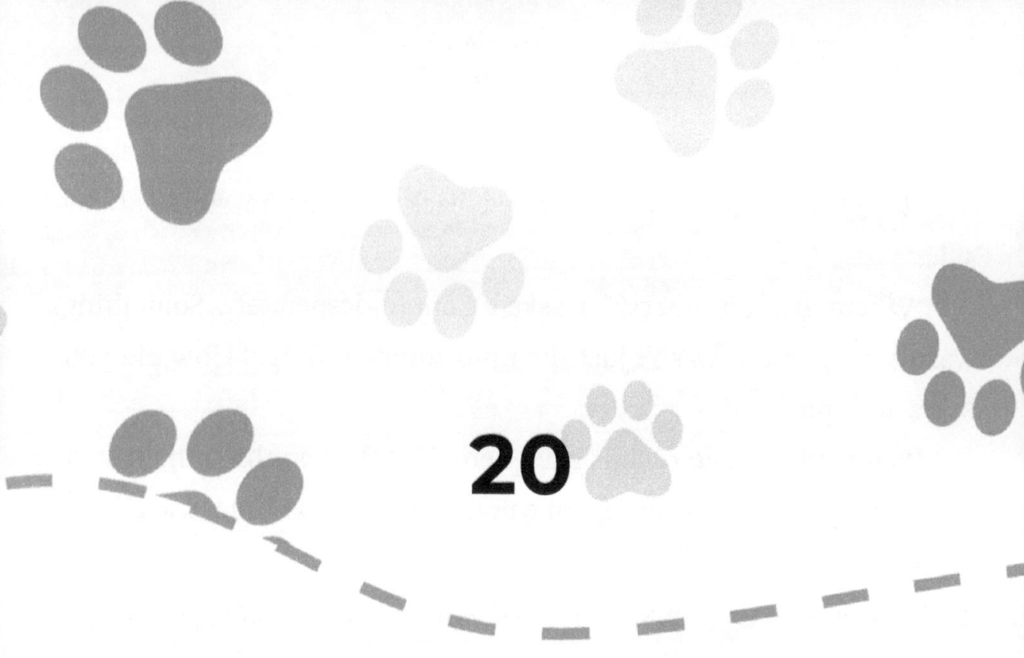

20

"Connie!" I roared in frustration. "I had her right where I wanted her!"

"And now I have her right where I want her. Dead at my feet."

"What was she going to tell me?" I demanded, cursing the poor timing.

"Like I know or care," the vampire responded, shoving her stake into an ankle holster, then popping back up to her full height. "How did you immobilize them all?" she asked me instead.

"P-Parker," I sputtered, searching the kitchen for him.

He let himself out of the cooler, then turned and sealed the door with a bright line of glowing magic. When he finished creating the seal, he blew on his finger and pretended to tuck it into his waistband.

"Good work, witch," Connie said with an almost-smile.

"Thanks, vampire," he answered back, coming to stand at my side.

"Where are the others?" I asked Connie desperately. Something wasn't right, and it wasn't just the unfortunate timing. "How did you know to come?"

"You made a huge ruckus back here. It took everything the rest of us had to keep the normies from catching wise. Next time, use a little more discretion, huh?"

"The food," I shouted, just now remembering. "They tampered with it somehow."

"Yes, Buckley passed that little bit of news on, too. Next time you need to report directly to your superior."

"You're not my superior," I said, surprising even myself.

Connie's eyes widened so far I thought they might pop out of her head. "What did you just say to me?"

I flicked my wrist and used my witch magic to levitate the dampening armor Fluffikins had bestowed upon me. When it reached me, I grabbed it from the air and handed it over to Connie.

The elder vampire's eyes widened even more. Her mouth dropped open, too.

"How?" she demanded. "You were supposed to have vampire magic."

I darted around her in quick circles, creating a wind that blew her coiffed hair out of place. "I still do."

"But you can't have both at the same time. That would be impossible, unless you were a—" She clamped her mouth shut, refusing to say more.

"Unless I were a what? Tell me!" I yelled.

"It's not my place," she said, turning away from me.

I sent Parker a pleading glance.

"I don't know," he mumbled. "I mean, I'm mortal like you. I haven't lived long enough to amass all the knowledge she has."

"And Fluffikins?" I suddenly needed to know. Who was he really? How had he figured out my true nature before anyone else, and why did he think he had the right to keep it from me?

"He definitely knows," Parker answered.

"But he's not immortal, either. Is he?"

"He's on his seventh life, which makes him well over one hundred. Plus he's privy to more information than I am as a diplomat."

I considered this for a moment. "Will he tell me?"

"We've defeated the encroaching coven," Connie spoke up. "I believe that means it's time for him to fulfill his end of the deal."

I needed to know, but somehow I dreaded to find out. "What if finding this big secret out changes everything?"

"Everything's already changed," Parker pointed out, wrapping an arm around my waist. I leaned into him, willing to take the comfort wherever it came from. Now that my witch magic was no longer suppressed, I enjoyed his touch again.

"What about the people who ate the poisoned food?" I asked, realizing that almost nothing had been resolved even though we had somehow managed to emerge victorious.

Something was holding me back. I didn't want to leave this place, even though I had no reason to stay.

Connie seemed unconcerned as she sauntered over to the cooler and scowled at the prisoners trapped inside. "We have IDs on all the diners who came in and out tonight. As our head of Agriculture, I'm sure Buckley can figure out what the poison was meant to do and find a way to counteract it."

"I'll get the others in here," Parker said, pulling his phone out of his pocket and beginning to text even as he spoke. "They can help us escort our guys in the cooler to HQ."

"What about the customers who are still in the restaurant?" No, we couldn't leave yet. I didn't know why, only that it was important.

"Easy," Melony said as she pushed through the swinging doors. She must have been standing right there, waiting to be called in.

Rather than explaining herself, she sent a plume of fire into the air. Everyone watched as it hovered near the ceiling.

And then the sprinklers went off, and shocked cries rose up from the dining room.

"That should send everyone outside," Melony said with a huge grin. She clearly loved causing mischief.

"Let's move fast," Connie said, "before the front-of-house staff comes back in and starts searching for the owner."

"Melony, help me guide the hostages out of here," Parker called over to the only person who had less seniority than me. "They're already magically bound. We just need to make sure no normies see until we can stuff them into our cars and out of sight."

Melony nodded and moved toward the cooler to join him.

Those two set to work while Connie hoisted Vanessa's prone body into her arms. "I'll dispose of this one."

"And I'll grab some food to go so I can reverse engineer the poison and create the antidote," Buckley added. I hadn't even noticed him come in, yet there he was.

That left me as the only one without a job. I stood in place and watched as the others got to work.

I didn't want to leave, even though I had no reason to stay.

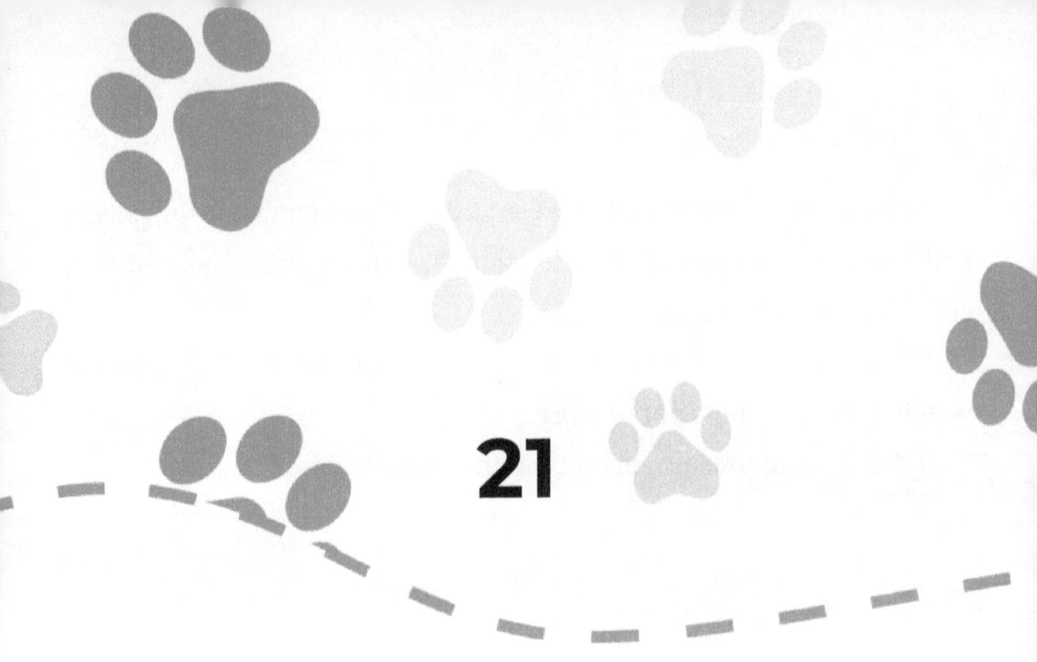

21

I paced the empty kitchen, wondering why I couldn't bring myself to leave. My thorough investigation of every cabinet, cupboard, and drawer came up empty. Nothing appeared out of sorts. But it sure felt that way.

Before Connie had killed her, Vanessa promised we hadn't seen the last of our enemies, of those who adhered to some unnamed cause.

And I believed her.

I just wished I knew more. That I could have compelled her to say more in her final moments.

A flash of black caught my eye as Fluffikins slipped in through the swinging doors.

"Come, Tawny," he urged. "There's nothing more to be done here."

"Something's going to happen," I told him without any hesitation.

I felt so sure we weren't done here yet even though I had no obvious reason to feel that way. Still, my intuition gnawed at me.

Fluffikins turned toward the door and motioned for me to follow. "Barnes just delivered them to HQ for questioning. They're safely secured. It's over."

I shook my head, refusing to budge. "I don't think it is."

"If there is to be a round two, we'll be ready," he promised while waiting for me at the door. "But for now we rest."

I shook my head and took a step back. Why was I so resistant?

The black cat sighed. "Don't you want to know why you're different? You've completed your end of our bargain. It's time for me to finish mine. Come. There is much we need to discuss."

I glanced toward the cooler where Parker had temporarily kept the captured coven members. Already I knew they wouldn't talk, no matter what tactics the PTA tried to use against them. Like Vanessa, they would gladly die for their cause without revealing a single hint as to its purpose.

"This job is over, but you're still my temp." The boss's patience had worn very thin, and his words came out rough. "Come with me. That's a direct order," the cat said with a flick of his tail.

At last I gave in to his wishes. Whatever business I still had in this place, it hadn't revealed itself to me yet. Maybe I was just being silly.

"Pick me up," the boss cat ordered when I joined him at the door.

I did, and a moment later, a sparkling pink fog wrapped around our bodies and teleported us back to the conference room at HQ. After delivering us to our seats, the swirling magic began to recede toward the ceiling.

“Stay,” Fluffikins commanded, and the magic rearranged itself into a tight sphere, hovering above the table as if it, too, had a seat in this meeting.

I knew very little of the special magic that tied our region to the others in the world. Only that they all drew from the same source and helped maintain balance, keeping any one region or person from growing too powerful.

“Will the others be coming?” I asked, wishing I had Parker at my side for whatever came next. He had my best wishes at heart, but I still didn’t know whether the black cat or any of the others did.

“This is a private matter. The fewer who know what I am about to tell you, the safer we will all be.” Fluffikins’s eyes appeared dull, whereas usually they shone bright and inquisitive. Whatever he had to tell me, he clearly didn’t look forward to saying it.

“What’s wrong?” I asked, sucking in a nervous breath and holding it inside.

“You, Tawny. You’re what’s wrong.”

I scoffed at this. Hadn’t he agreed to play it straight now that I’d finished my latest assignment? He’d seemed so eager to get me here, and now this.

“That’s a terrible thing to say,” I grumbled, exhaustion finally sinking in. “I’ve done everything you’ve asked of me.” Was he only going to speak in riddles and half-truths rather than directly revealing what I needed to know?

“You misunderstand me. What I’m saying is you shouldn’t exist.”

I swallowed hard as my heart sped up in my chest. When had it even started beating again? So much had happened since Parker removed my dampening armor. I hadn't paid attention to these physical sensations, just assuming they were still absent. But now I felt my heart thrumming, the swell of oxygen in my lungs, the pain of Mr. Fluffikins's words.

"Are you going to kill me?" I asked him point-blank.

Rather than pacing as he normally did, the cat lay down and tucked his front paws under himself. "No, Tawny, I'm not going to kill you. But others will likely try if they ever find out what you are. We can't let them. Do you understand?"

I thought back to my final confrontation with Vanessa. "They already know," I said with a quiver in my voice. "The head vampire told me. Said I don't even know what I am. That others would come."

Fluffikins moaned long and loud. "Then it's exactly as I feared."

"I don't understand. I didn't even know magic existed until a little over a week ago. Why is everyone so concerned about me now?"

"You're not a normie," the cat said, staring at me with large, unblinking eyes.

"Yeah, I've kind of gathered that I'm a magick by now." I let out a chuckle to ease the tension in the room. My attempt at levity, however, only increased the cat's anxiety.

He licked his paw several times—a nervous tic—before speaking again. "No, Tawny. You aren't a magick, either. You're something else altogether."

22

"Enough with the big, sweeping statements. Just tell me what I am and why it seems to matter so much," I demanded, growing tired of the cat's circumlocution.

"You're a Terran," he answered in an eerie monotone.

"A Terran?" I let out a dry laugh and slapped the table. "Isn't that what humans are called in science fiction novels? Please just be honest with me. I've waited long enough to—"

"I am being honest with you!" he bit out. "Terrans are extinct, or at least everyone thought they were, until..." He raised his chin and widened his eyes.

I lifted a hand to my chest. "Until me?"

"Yes. They were spoken of often in old stories. When they went extinct centuries ago, normies no longer had any frame of reference to understand the Terran kind. They saw their frequent mentions in connection to the world and assumed they couldn't find any

Terrans, because all on Earth were of this species. But they got it wrong."

"What am I?" I asked hardly above a whisper.

"You are a class to your own. As you continue to interact with the magical world, your powers will only grow."

"But in Caraway Island, I was able to rescue you and Melony because I was a normie. No magick could break through the barriers, but I could," I reminded him, thinking back to that strange adventure. How in the end, I'd been the only one capable of mounting the rescue.

"You're not a magick, and you're not a normie. Since Terrans were thought to be extinct, they didn't account for them when erecting their defenses."

"So I'm magic, but not magick?" I asked. Wow, I really was Schrodinger's something.

He nodded and licked his paw again. "Think of it this way. Most magic users channel their powers through their hearts. That's why vampires can only be killed by destroying the source of their magic—the heart."

"You gave me the chest piece to cover my heart and block my witch magic," I realized, understanding his ruse better and better as more was revealed.

The cat nodded again. "I had my suspicions about what you were, but I also knew you were too unpracticed to have full command of your abilities. When you wouldn't stay away, I thought I might instead keep you hidden in plain sight. Tawny, a Terran doesn't just store magic in her heart. Your entire body is a vessel. You can hold so much power inside you. Hundreds of times what most magicks can. But your real strength is in the ability to wield the world magic."

My eyes snapped to the glowing pink ball coiled beside us.

"Yes," the cat said with reverence. "When the last known Terran died, we erected regional boards to oversee the world magic. We figured that in the absence of its true keeper, the world magic would best be served by a board of supernaturals from multiple classes. Together, we hoped we could approximate the abilities of a single Terran. But it's been an imperfect solution, and both normies and magicks fight more than they were ever meant to. The world isn't balanced, but maybe it can be again, now that we've found you." He paused to let the weight of his words sink in.

Not only was I magical. I was the most powerful being to live for centuries. Being just a little bit special I could handle, but being so above and beyond everyone else? It terrified me.

"Not everyone wants peace," I muttered, thinking of the mainstream politicians and fringe terrorist factions who both pushed war, violence, and discontent with seemingly every breath.

"Not those who seek power, no." Fluffikins's tail now beat against the table as if keeping time. As hard as this conversation was on me, I could tell it hit him just as deeply. He knew much better than me what my existence and discovery could mean for the world at large.

"Does that mean they'll try to kill me?" I squeaked.

The cat nodded glumly. "Yes, or capture you for use as a weapon."

No, I refused to be changed, to be turned into something I was never meant to become. "What can I do to stop either of those things from happening?"

"I do not know. We are in uncharted territory here. No one thought it was possible, but if you're here, then there could be others, too."

"Does that mean we need to go find them? Bring them to our side?" Surely, we had to do something. But what? If Fluffikins didn't have the answer, there was almost no chance I'd be able to find it myself.

The cat sucked in a deep breath before continuing. "I intend to train you in each branch of magic and hope you'll have a way of finding other Terrans, yes. But it won't be easy. We got lucky in finding you before anyone with ill intentions could. It's truly a one in one trillion coincidence, unless there are others out there, just waiting to be discovered."

"I want to help find them," I said with a jolt of enthusiasm. It was too much pressure, being the only one of my kind, especially since the way Mr. Fluffikins explained it, the Terrans wielded a great deal of power and influence. I'd only ever really been responsible for myself. I'd never even had a pet for goodness' sake.

Fluffikins seemed to sense the fear that lay beneath my determination. "The board and I will teach you everything we know, but your training will be imperfect. We can only teach what we know, which is so little compared to what you will need to learn."

A part of me wished I could go back, could choose a town other than Beech Grove. But if the world needed a hero, I guess I'd have to do.

23

"This is a lot to take in," I said when it seemed Mr. Fluffikins had run out of warnings to give.

He stood and stretched. "I know. I wouldn't wish it on anyone. Because of what you are, every single choice you make could change the entire course of history."

"You're not making it any easier on me," I told him with a tired smile. He hadn't been keeping the secret to irritate me. He really had hoped to protect me. Now that I understood, I felt grateful for his efforts.

"I had hoped you would fail and be forced to remain a vampire," he admitted now.

"I will remain a vampire. Well, at least in part," I said thoughtfully. I still didn't know how this all worked, but I was beginning to see patterns emerge. "The witch magic you gave me hasn't left. The vampire magic won't, either. I absorb it all and keep it inside."

The black cat chuffed. “Like a sponge.”

I nodded. “Yeah, and I have no idea how to get rid of it.”

“I think I might,” Fluffikins revealed, slowly rising to his feet. “The vampire curse was my last-ditch attempt to save you from what you are. I didn’t know if it would work, if the curse could erase your Terran heritage, but I had to try.”

“I understand that now. Thank you.” I didn’t always appreciate his methods or attitude, but at least now I saw where he was coming from. At the end of the day, Mr. Fluffikins was just a simple cat who suddenly found himself with far more power than he’d ever expected to wield. We were the same in that way.

He paced to the far corner of the table, then turned back toward me. “It’s time we stop denying what you were born to be. We need to unite you with your purpose.”

The glittering pink orb of world magic floated across the table, drawing close to me.

“Reach out and take it,” the cat commanded from a few strides away.

I raised my hand and extended my index finger. I didn’t take any time to think or consider the implications of accepting such a huge responsibility. In my bones, I knew this was right. Necessary.

The orb began to pulse as it moved forward and gently lapped into my skin. I watched in amazement as its rosy glow spread over me, not just settling in my heart like the other magics that had come before but filling my whole body.

Fluffikins gasped. “In all my lives, I never thought I’d see such a sight. You’re… incandescent.”

When the vampire magic had been dominant in my system, I felt a constant absence, emptiness. Holding the world magic inside me now, I felt the exact opposite—whole, complete, able to feel every sensation that competed for my attention.

And it was wonderful.

"How do you feel?" Mr. Fluffikins asked, examining me with awe.

"Right," I murmured in awe. "Like this is the way it should have always been."

An enormous smile stretched between his whiskers. The first I'd seen from him in quite some time. "Do you remember how we tested the curse earlier today?"

"Parker," I said with a wistful grin. Remembering the feelings I'd developed for him over the past couple weeks, I now yearned for him with renewed intensity. Was I making up for lost time? Or did everything burn more brightly now that I had stepped away from the vampire curse and back into the light?

"I can bring him to you, see if the curse is removed to your satisfaction. However, you can't tell him what you are. You can't tell anyone." He plopped his rear on the table, daring me to argue with his decree.

And what he asked was huge. How could Parker and I grow our relationship if this huge part of me had to remain a secret between us? "Won't he be in danger protecting me? Won't all of you be in danger?"

"Unfortunately, yes, but they'll be far safer if they don't know the exact nature of what you are." Fluffikins titled his head to the side and mewed. I'd never seen him look so much like an actual cat before. Was this his way of communicating regret or pity? Or had he simply grown weary of me, of this conversation, of what we both knew would come next?

"Connie knows," I said, bringing this strange moment between us to an end. "She figured it out at the restaurant."

He sighed and hung his head. "You are the strongest of us all. You can wipe her memory if you choose. You could even clear mine."

"No," I said and then realized something strange and startling. "I trust her. But I agree not to tell the others."

"Very well then, but if you change your mind, you know what to do."

I nodded, feeling the weight of this new responsibility deep down. I'd never been anyone special. I'd always just done enough to get by. But now?

Now I was the most important person on the entire planet.

I kind of wished I could tell my ex-husband and his new wife, just to rub it in their faces, but I had far more important things to worry about now.

"I'll send Barnes in," Fluffikins said. "But first you need to control your glow. This is supposed to be a secret, remember?"

A secret. Yes.

Keeping it would not be easy.

Though it would be vital.

24

Parker appeared a few minutes after Mr. Fluffikins left the conference room. Thankfully, I'd quickly managed to tame the powerful new force within me. The added pressure of a deadline seemed to help. I wondered if that would be important later. I'd have time to figure it all out when the moment was right. Not much time, but it would have to be enough.

"Is everything okay?" Parker asked as he pulled out a chair beside me. "The boss cat sent me in. Did he tell you what's going on?"

I nodded, afraid to meet his eyes in light of the lies that would be coming. That was another thing Fluffikins had left to me, coming up with an explanation that would minimize any further questions. "My witch magic didn't go away because it's my natural magic," I explained, preferring not to hide my magical nature completely. "Joining the PTA awakened what was already in me."

Waves of joy undulated from his chest and crashed into me. I could not only feel my emotions now, but his, too. And I didn't even have to look to know he wore a giant smile on his face. How many new abilities would I discover? Did I even have any limitations left at all?

"Tawny, that's fantastic! You're like me. Our magics match."

I let out a soft laugh. "Yeah."

"Did Fluffikins already take back your vampire magic, then?"

I nodded. "He also wants to keep me around for a while longer to help me get a hold on my new abilities." Well, at least that part wasn't a lie.

The soft gray eyes that had initially sparked my attraction to Parker now shone with happiness. "Seriously, this is perfect," he continued, not realizing that my mood didn't match his own. "I don't have to try to protect you, and I don't have to worry about your safety anymore. You're not a helpless normie stuck in a world of magic. Now you can take care of yourself."

Now this, this I didn't like. "I could always take care of myself. And I was never helpless."

"Sorry, sorry, you're right. I apologize for my misguided chivalry, but I promise that's the last you'll see of it. Oh, Tawny. I'm so happy. I wanted to date you, anyway, but now that our magics match, so many things will be so much easier." He pulled me to my feet and wrapped his arms around me.

"That is good news," I said, forcing a smile. He had no idea that our situation had gotten so much worse. But if I told him, I'd be putting him in the direct line of fire.

He raised his hand to caress my cheek, and I leaned into it. "May I try to kiss you again? Since last time didn't... Well, you know."

Yes, I wanted this. I wanted him. Even though now I would be the one keeping myself at a distance to protect the other.

I tilted my head up and closed my eyes, and a moment later his lips found mine—soft, gentle, and searching for answers.

Yes, I wanted him. Needed him. Even in a crazy new world that seemed so wrong, I knew Parker was right for me. We were just getting started, but already he elicited feelings in me that I had never felt with my ex-husband.

Joy. Trust... Hope.

Hope that Fluffikins's grim predictions for the future would not come to pass, that one day this man and I could live out our happily ever after.

But our story was just getting started, and we still had many monsters to slay.

I pulled back and placed a hand on Parker's chest.

"Did you feel anything?" he asked, studying me carefully.

"I felt many things," I teased. "And they were all right."

He let out a quick sigh of relief and then kissed me again.

"Your curse. It's gone! I don't know what I would have done if you stayed a vampire, Tawny."

"Well, now you don't need to worry about that anymore," I said, holding back the fact that what I actually was might be even worse. I'd just been entrusted with this secret, and already I wanted to share it with him. Wanted to but couldn't.

Ugh. I needed to change the topic.

"Did you finish questioning the vampire chefs?" I asked casually before realizing that this was, in fact, a very good question to ask. With the world magic coiled inside me, I might be able to get them to talk, to tell me things they hadn't told the others.

Sure enough, Parker pressed his lips into a firm line and took a deep, doleful breath. "Not a peep out of them. I'm not sure what we're going to do. Connie wants to stake them all, but what if they didn't know what Vanessa had planned? What if they're innocent in all of this?"

"Can I talk to them?"

He shook his head. "It won't do any good. They're pretty firm in their decision not to talk to us."

I placed a gentle hand on his arm. "It will do me good. Even if they don't say anything, I'll feel better knowing I've tried."

Parker leaned in and placed a kiss on my cheek. "I love your determination. You've really taken all this magic stuff in stride."

I laughed at that. Seriously, he had no idea.

25

Parker held my hand as he guided me toward the warehouse-like room where Fluffikins kept his stash of magical artifacts hidden in a special ceiling hold.

We walked right up to the opening in the ceiling, but instead of looking up, Parker looked down. He tapped his foot four times, then moved a couple paces to the side and tapped it twice more. He moved and tapped again, then one last time with a single stomp.

And a section of the hard floors disappeared, revealing a long, dark staircase.

"Has this been here the whole time?" I asked in disbelief.

He flashed me a grin and then motioned for me to go down ahead of him. The steps lit up beneath me with a magical glow to guide our descent.

We walked for a long time, at least forty steps deep, until finally we came upon a hidden room that appeared to be carved from one giant slab of stone. A magical sheen separated the far corner, cutting diagonally to create a small, triangular cell where four prisoners sat.

"Are you sure about this?" Parker asked one more time. "You'll be safer if I go in with you."

"Hey now," I said, giving him a playful jab. "You said you were done with the misguided chivalry."

He at least had the good grace to look abashed. "Sorry. Old habits and all that. I'll leave you to it." He squeezed my hand before rising back up the stairs and locking the trapdoor behind him. I waited until I heard the clunk of the floor phasing back together above, then passed through the shimmering barrier and into the prison cell.

The four vampire chefs sat side by side on a long bench, each with their hands folded in their laps and wrists bound by magical cuffs that glowed neon.

"Look, as we've already told your colleagues, we don't know anything," the vampire on the far left muttered, fixing his cold eyes on me.

I'd never interrogated anyone before, but now that I was the most powerful being in existence, I couldn't pass up the opportunity to gain information from this quartet. "Where did you come from? Before you arrived in Beech Grove?"

"Why should we tell you?" It seemed that this vampire had been elected as their collective voice.

I paced the small prison hold until I was standing directly in front of him. Then I closed my eyes and focused on what I wanted to happen. I imagined the vampire readily and truthfully answering my questions, then held that image in my brain as I asked again. “Where did you come from?”

“Blueberry Bay. In Maine,” he offered at once.

Whoa, that was almost too easy.

“I’ve been there,” I said. This time I focused on the undulating magic inside me, how it comforted and calmed, then pushed that feeling out toward the vampire seated before me.

He visibly relaxed, loosening his posture and slowing his breaths. “We know. That’s how we first learned of you. That’s why we came.”

“The four of you and Vanessa?”

“No, our boss.”

“Who’s your boss?”

“We don’t know.”

“Did Vanessa know?”

“No. We only know the people at our level and directly above. Leadership remains a secret to protect the cause.”

“What is the cause?”

He hesitated, turning his face away from mine.

“What is the cause?” I repeated, imagining him giving me the answer and then immediately following up with my calming magical touch.

The captive vampire’s face contorted in a quickly flashing array of emotions—rage, temptation, sorrow, remorse. Still he didn’t speak.

But the vampire beside him did. “To unite the world under one magic. One power.”

“A global dictatorship?”

"To his power," all four vampires chimed as one.

"Whose?"

"We don't know," the first answered again.

I sighed. "Ah, yes, the layers of leadership." Whoever was in charge had clearly prepared for this scenario. Our prisoners couldn't talk if they didn't even know anything.

"Why do you want to unite the world? What's in it for you if you won't even be the one in charge?"

"We will—" the second began.

"Silence!" the first vampire cut him off with a growled warning. "We've already said too much."

"I can't resist," the other moaned. He began to shake violently as if having a seizure.

"Then you know what we must do. What we all must do."

I watched in horror as all the vampire captives began to scream and shake until one by one they slumped over.

"What's happening in here?" Connie cried as she, Parker, and Fluffikins wrenched the trapdoor open and charged down the long flight of stairs.

"I… I don't know."

Fluffikins jumped up onto the first vampire's lap and pawed at his chest. "My word. I've heard of this, but I've never seen it."

"What happened?" Parker asked, moving to my side.

"I was asking them questions, and then all of a sudden, they screamed and shook and passed out."

"They're dead." Fluffikins confirmed what I'd already guessed.

"But how? I thought a stake was the only way to…"

"The heart," the cat mumbled. "Destroy the heart, destroy the magic."

"They used their superior strength to crush their own hearts. You must have been very close to getting answers," Connie said, regarding me warily.

"Barnes, come with me," Fluffikins shouted, jumping off the dead vampire's lap and scurrying toward the stairs. I sent him a silent note of thanks. If Parker had asked me too many questions about what happened here, I doubted I'd be able to answer them while maintaining my Terran secret.

Parker dutifully followed the cat boss, leaving me and Connie alone in the basement prison.

"Has the cat told you what you are?" she asked, looking me up and down.

I summoned the pink, sparkly world magic to my fingertips, and it unfurled, taking the shape of a balloon.

"Ah, there it is," she said dryly. "What were you able to find out before they took their own lives?"

"They came here for me," I whispered, wishing the answer had been different.

Connie frowned. "Yes, that much is obvious."

"You were all in danger, because of me. I can't—" I shook my head when my voice cracked. Was I really something so terrible that these vampire henchmen would rather die than have a discussion?

Connie grabbed me by the shoulders and shook. Hard. "Whatever stupid thing you're thinking right now, remember this. We'll be in much more danger if the bad guys get ahold of you. Right now the best thing we can do is keep you safe and out of their reach. Well, actually, I suggested we kill you and save ourselves a world of problems, but Fluffikins won't allow it."

Then I owed the little black cat my life, it seemed. That is, if I could even die. That would definitely be an important question to ask the next time he and I had a heart-to-heart.

26

"Did you really want to kill me?" I asked, not sure if I was surprised.

Connie's face lit with a cruel smile. "Yup, and I'd have done it myself, too. I still might if you become too much of a handful."

I'd seen Connie stake Vanessa without a moment's hesitation or regret. Still, I'd like to think it would mean something to kill someone she'd known and worked with.

"You hate me that much?" I asked pointedly.

"How many times have we been over this?" the vampire snarled and pointed emphatically toward herself. "Cursed. Remember?"

I leaned against the wall with a heavy sigh. "You're the only person I can be my real self with. It would be nice to get to know you."

"Fluffikins—"

"Is a cat," I interrupted with a scowl. "And our boss."

"If you think this shared secret will suddenly make us best friends, you're wrong."

"I know all about the vampire curse, but I also know I can overcome it."

Connie's eyes shot to my face and she opened her mouth without speaking, then shook her head and chuckled. "No. I'll believe that when I see it."

"Then come here, and let me show you."

Connie stepped out of the shadows and toward the well-lit staircase.

I followed. "Are you sure about this?" I asked, flexing my fingers in preparation.

She thought about it for such a long while, I wondered if I'd lost her. Finally, she tilted her head thoughtfully and regarded me with cold, black eyes. "I don't want to be a normie again, but it would be nice to feel, to love."

"Do you remember what it's like? Any of those things?" I'd already started to forget during the short time I carried the curse. I couldn't imagine what it was like for Connie to shoulder that burden for so many endless years with no promise of reprieve.

"It's been so long." She closed her eyes and sucked in a deep breath through her nostrils, one we both knew she didn't need.

I shrugged. "You don't have to tell me, if you don't want."

"Yes, but you'll keep asking. I might as well save myself the annoyance."

I waited in silence until she spoke again.

When she did, her voice came out at a strange cadence. "When I was mortal, I fell in love with an angel named Symont. Supernaturals didn't have to hide in those days. The Terrans reigned and kept all species living in easy harmony. Symont and I enjoyed many blissful years together. Unfortunately, I aged normally while he hardly grew any older at all. I developed crow's feet and smile lines, but he remained the perfect picture of youth. Forty might not seem old these days, but many centuries ago it was quite the advanced age. My love couldn't stand to lose me, so he sought for a way to give me immortality so we could always be together."

"So he turned you into a vampire," I murmured.

She straightened to her full height, several inches taller than me. "I chose to become a vampire. It's not like there's any way to turn a mortal into an angel, so I agreed to it as the only possible solution. Once I was transformed, though, Symont hated the monster I had become. Vampires and angels are natural enemies, and what we were proved stronger than what was in our hearts."

"He left you." Even though I knew Connie couldn't feel the sting of this pain from long ago, my heart ached for her.

She fixed her eyes on a spot in the far corner of the room. "Yes. He had no choice. We thought our love could overcome the curse, but we were fools."

"Do you miss him? Are you hoping you might be able to reunite?"

She shrugged and shook her head. "I can't remember. I remember what happened, but I'm completely removed from it. Like it happened to someone else instead of me. As for hope..." She sighed.

"How could I ever think that anyone would lift the curse if we couldn't?"

"Fluffikins tells me I am the most powerful person living. And when the world magic entered me, everything came back to me. Maybe I can help you get it back, too. Will you let me try?" I asked, raising my hands and showing off the pink glow surging within.

Connie nodded slowly. "I can't remember how it felt to love, but logically I know it must have been amazing for me to voluntarily turn myself into this... this thing for the chance to preserve it." She reached her hands forward and wedged her fingers between mine.

I still didn't know exactly how my magic worked, but it was something I'd have to learn by myself. Nobody else could tell me exactly what to do. The only way to find out whether I could even lift Connie's curse was to give it a try.

I took several deep breaths and closed my eyes, pushing magic out through my fingers into hers.

The vampire squeezed my hands tight but didn't back away.

I kept moving forward, infusing my magic with love, compassion, humanity—even though neither of us was truly human. And apparently I had never been.

Connie sucked in a sharp breath. "I feel..." she said, but then her words broke off as she sucked in a deep, shaky breath.

I held steady, keeping the connection between us open but not pushing anything else through to her.

When Connie didn't speak again, I blinked my eyes open just in time to see her collapse lifeless to the ground.

27

I dropped to my knees and placed my head to Connie's chest. No heartbeat, but she also hadn't had one before.

"Connie!" I cried out, shaking her shoulders. I was too afraid to use any more of my magic until I learned what had gone wrong here.

When she didn't rouse, I shot the world magic from my fingertips like powerful bolts of lightning, allowing it to form in the air before me.

"Find Fluffikins," I pleaded. "Bring him here."

The sparkling pink swirls united in a long tendril and snaked through the ceiling.

I continued my efforts to revive Connie, but nothing I tried had any effect. *No, no, no!*

I wasn't a killer, and yet five vampires had dropped dead at my feet in less than fifteen minutes.

"What did you do?" Fluffikins roared, zooming down the steps after taking care to seal the trapdoor behind him.

My magic returned and crashed into me from behind. I drew in a sharp breath from the shock. The suddenness of it hurt. My system had been given no time to adjust to the intense change, and I definitely wasn't adept at controlling my Terran magic yet. Just look at what I'd done to Connie!

At the same time I could tell the magic had craved my touch for a long time. Centuries maybe. Fluffikins had explained that this world magic was as old as the earth itself. It didn't belong to me nor did I belong to it, but we belonged together.

Symbiotic.

My moment of pain was nothing compared to the long years it had been forced to endure without me or others like me. We would figure this thing out.

But first we had to save Connie.

"I tried to lift the curse for her. The same way I did for myself," I told the frantic cat at my side.

"You flooded her with the world magic?" he asked, aghast.

"No, I very slowly fed it into her. I was careful. I—"

"Didn't listen! You didn't listen!" he shouted in my face. "It's too much. Her heart couldn't hold it all. You killed her."

"No!" I shouted. "That's not possible! She's a vampire. She shouldn't have—"

Fluffikins spun and scratched at the ground, sending wave after wave of magic into Connie. Nothing happened.

"I didn't m-mean to," I sputtered as tears splashed across my cheeks.

"You need to learn to control your magic before you use it again," the cat hissed.

"That's enough for today. Return to me," he commanded the magic inside me.

Again nothing happened.

"Return!" the boss cat shouted, spittle flying.

My skin flashed pink, then returned to its normal peach.

"You refuse?" he hissed in rage.

"Not me," I said, trying to summon and expel the magic.

I glowed pink again, but the magic remained where it was.

The magic inside me, it was sentient. It had its own mind, and now it shared my body.

As I realized this, my hand raised of its own volition and came to rest on Connie's chest. I watched my fingers light up as they sunk into the deceased vampire's chest. I felt it, cold and squishy in my hand, Connie's heart.

I cried as my hand clamped around the lifeless organ.

"What are you doing?" Fluffikins demanded in horror.

"I'm not," I said, beginning to hyperventilate, such was my fear.

"Then stop."

"I can't," I cried, even as I tried—and failed—to yank my hand free from Connie's chest.

But then her heart began to beat within my hand. Faint and slow at first, but then faster, stronger.

The magic released me, and I pulled my hand free, gasping and crying when Connie opened her eyes and rose to a sitting position.

"What happened?" she croaked, bringing a hand up to rub at her chest. "Where am I?"

"No, it's not possible." Fluffikins walked back until he bumped into the wall. His wide eyes glowed with what I took to be equal parts fright and respect. Somehow I just knew how others felt now. At least some of the time.

"Are you okay?" I asked Connie breathlessly as my frazzled nerves began to relax again.

"I feel..." she began, echoing the same words she'd spoken just before she'd crumpled in a heap on the ground.

"Alive," she said at last, her eyes blinking rapidly as she studied her arms and chest. "How?"

I opened my mouth to answer, but there was no explanation.

Connie twisted with a grunt and grabbed the wooden stake from the holster at her ankle and dragged it across the soft flesh of her forearm.

"Ahhh!" she cried as deep scarlet blood poured from the wound.

"Alive!" Fluffikins wailed. "Alive! But no one can raise the dead!"

"Tawny did," the vampire said with that familiar smirk of hers, and then she flung her arms around me and sobbed into my hair.

I hesitated. "Are you...?"

"Human again, yes!" She kissed both of my cheeks in such effusive delight that I could scarcely recognize her.

"It's not possible," the boss cat muttered again.

"The curse is gone?" I asked hopefully, hesitantly.

Connie rose to her feet and then laughed when she stumbled back a step. "I'm clumsy. And I can feel. And hurt. And, and... Thank you, Tawny. Thank you so much for freeing me from that life!"

"This is not good," Fluffikins hissed as he ran for the stairs.

Had I done something wrong? The boss cat seemed to think so, but how could saving a life ever be a bad thing?

I let Connie wrap me in her arms and sob into my hair with wave after wave of joy and told myself I'd done something good—even if I hadn't exactly been the one to do it.

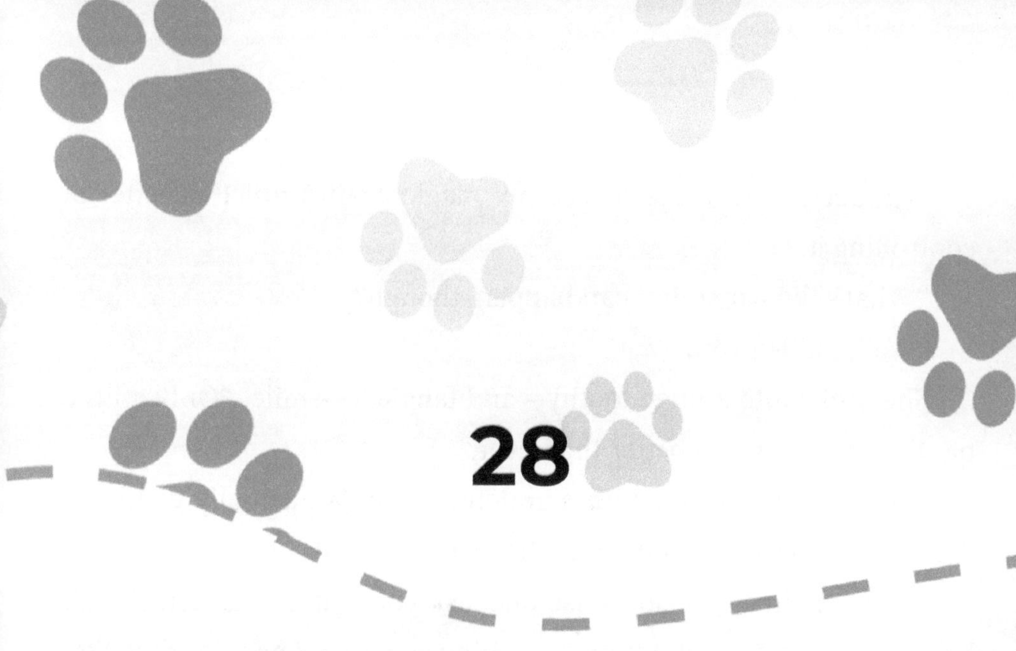

28

"Connie," I cried as a sudden revelation hit me. "If I raised you, I can—"

I turned to the four vampire captives hunched over in the jail cell, and Connie followed my line of sight.

"Raise the others, yes!" she squealed.

"They told me some things before..." I broke off, not wanting to describe the horrific scene I'd witnessed.

"This one." I stopped before the second captive on the bench. "He was going to tell me more before the other stopped him, and then they... you know."

"Can you stop them from doing it again?"

"I don't know. Maybe, but Fluffikins said—"

"Who cares what Fluffikins said. We've got a great chance here. You have to take it."

"He doesn't want me to use my magic again until I'm better at controlling it."

"What's the worst that can happen, though?"

"Well, I killed you."

She broke into a huge toothy—and fangless—smile. "Only a little bit. I'm back now and better than ever."

"Yes, you are," I said with a grateful laugh. We actually would be friends, Connie and I, and—oh—how I'd needed it.

"They're already dead. Raise one, ask your questions. They're all bound and imprisoned. Literally nothing can go wrong with this. You have to do it."

I nodded and flexed my fingers, drawing the magic forward. "It's gross," I warned.

Connie rolled her eyes and blew a raspberry. Wow, it was going to take me some time to get used to the new version of her. "Um, I drank human blood for more than a century until the gilded age came and changed our ways."

"You're not a vampire anymore," I reminded her as a smile quirked at my lips.

"Oh, right!" She smacked a palm into her forehead then let out an oof of pain. "Wow, that's going to take some getting used to."

That's what I had just thought. Well, at least we were on the same page now. I probably would have laughed had I not been dreading what I had to do next.

I sunk to my knees before my subject, closed my eyes, and took three slow breaths in and out before plunging my hand into his chest and grabbing hold of his heart.

When the vampire's heart began to beat within my fist, I kept my hold to prevent him from being able to crush his own heart again. I was reasonably certain that he was now human like Connie, but I didn't want to take any chances.

"What's going on?" the prisoner asked, blinking his eyes open slowly. "What did you do to me? I don't feel right."

"Never mind about that. We were having a nice chat before, and you were just about to tell me your plans for uniting the world under one power."

"Not my plans, his."

"Who is he, this one with the plans?"

"I don't know."

"Then why are you helping him?"

"We will no longer have to live in the shadows. Magicks will openly rule."

"What about the humans?"

"They can submit of their own free will or be forced to do so. He will be good to those who accept his leadership."

"What about the ones who don't?"

"Will be destroyed, naturally."

"And you want this?"

"It doesn't matter what I want. It's about all of us."

"It matters to me. Why are you going along with all this?"

"I'm tired of being made to feel like I shouldn't exist. That my very survival is a sin."

"But isn't that what you want to do to people without magic?"

"No, they will be put out of their misery. Meanwhile I am trapped in mine."

I let go and pulled my hand from his chest. "Thank you."

"What will happen to me now?"

Connie put a hand on my shoulder. "Tawny, go. Let me tie up this last loose end."

"But..." I wanted to argue, to defend this vampire's life, especially now that he may be mortal again.

"He already made his choice," Connie reminded me. "I'm just setting him back to the way he was. I promise to do so gently."

I shook my head, not wanting to answer either way.

The magic decided for me, carrying me up the steps before I could decide what action I wanted to take.

29

Melony stood waiting for me in the warehouse. "C'mon," she said once I emerged from the hidden dungeon. "Everyone's gathering in the conference room. Boss cat told me to get you, so consider yourself got."

I nodded and followed her through the office building and into the glass conference room where the board gathered to discuss its most important business. As soon as I stepped inside, the world magic unspooled from inside me and rose to the ceiling in a thick fog.

"Oh, so now you want to behave," Fluffikins groaned.

"I'm sorry," I murmured, quickly grabbing a chair.

"I wasn't talking to you," the cat snapped, which I took as my cue to sit quietly and wait for whatever news the board had to share.

Connie was the last to join us, not five minutes later. When she took her seat beside me, Fluffikins assumed his war general march up and down the table.

"The rival coven has been dispatched," he revealed, although by now, I assume everyone already knew. "Buckley was able to identify the potion they laced in the food at Bollyweird."

"What was it?" Melony asked, drawing a look of ire from the cat.

"*Verstärker,*" Buckley answered after rising to stand awkwardly before the rest of us. "It's a magical amplifier."

"Why would they feed a bunch of normies a magical amplifier?" Parker wondered aloud.

I'd wondered the same thing silently and found the answer quickly.

Connie squeezed my hand under the table. She and I both knew what the coven had been up to. They'd been trying to draw out other Terrans.

"We can't know," Fluffikins lied to the others without so much as a glance my way. "The good news is that it won't hurt them and doesn't need to be reversed."

"Still, we should follow up," the angel Greta said, offering me a matronly smile.

"I agree," Mr. Fluffikins said with a quick nod. "Which is why I'll be sending Tawny door to door to follow up with all those who dined at Bollyweird before we shut it down."

"Are you sure the normie is the right choice for this assignment? I could have it done faster and better," Melony argued, crossing her arms and slumping back in her chair.

"Yes," the cat said. "Tawny is the right choice, especially considering my next announcement."

All eyes zoomed to me.

Connie kept tight hold of my hand and leaned to whisper in my ear. "They can't know I've changed. Keep my secret if you want to keep yours."

Fluffikins strode over and plopped down in front of me on the table. "During this mission we discovered the most magnificent thing."

"Oh?" Greta offered me a bright, encouraging smile. It seemed so long ago that she offered me her angel armor and ultimately saved my life. I hoped she'd be proud of what I was becoming, even though I was under strict orders never to reveal the truth to her or anyone else.

"Go ahead, Tawny," Parker urged, pointing an equally gigantic grin my way. "Tell them what you told me."

Oh, right.

"I'm not a normie. I'm a witch. Surprise!"

Gasps rose from those who hadn't heard the news yet—either the fake news or the actual discovery Fluffikins had made about me.

"You promised me liaison to the force first!" Melony protested.

"Relax, Haberdash," the cat growled, the fur on his back pricking up. "Your job is safe, even though Tawny will no longer be a temp."

"Is her work with the PTA done?" Greta asked with a pinched brow. She'd rooted for me from day one, and unlike Parker, she'd never doubted that I could make it in this strange new world of magic.

"No, but mine will be soon," the cat announced solemnly.

More gasps.

"As you all know, I'm on my seventh life. I'd like to be able to retire some time during my eighth and enjoy my ninth pursuing the various luxuries available to a cat of my stature. As such, I will be training Tawny as my replacement."

"A diplomat!" R balked, twisting his long beard around his hand pensively. "That's a pretty big promotion."

"Yes, it is," Fluffikins said, keeping his eyes fixed on mine. "But I have full faith that Tawny can handle whatever comes next."

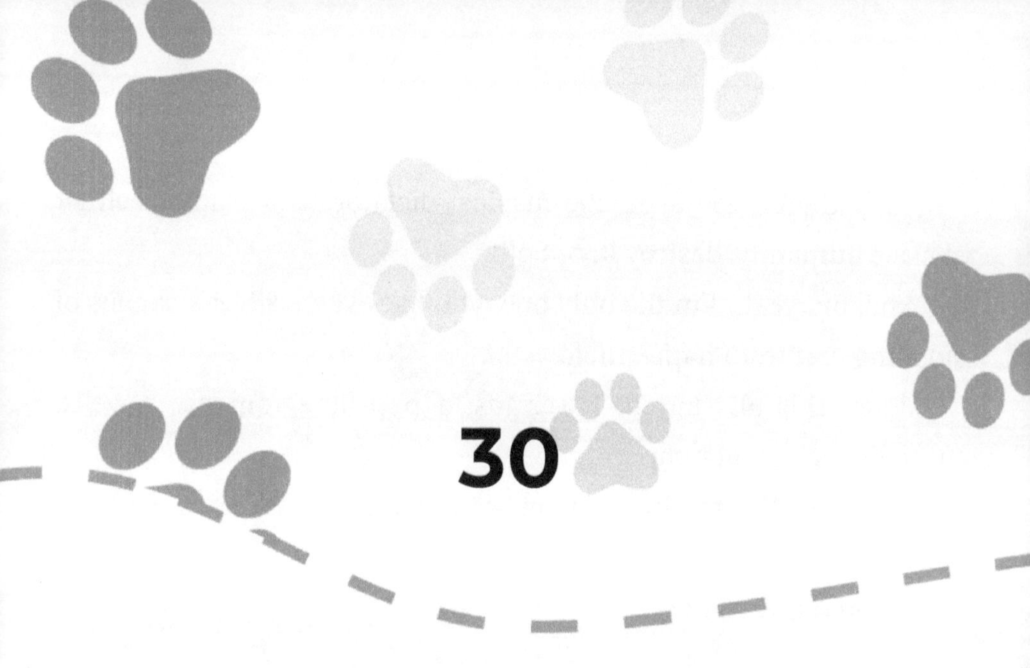

30

So there you have it...

In the span of not even twenty-four hours, I found out that I was the last known member of the most powerful species to ever exist.

I absorbed a strong magical current and found out it was able to control me just as much as I could control it.

I raised the dead, not just once but twice.

The irritating cat boss was revealed to be my biggest supporter all along.

An ornery vampire became my best friend.

I got a fake promotion.

And was directed to keep my true nature a secret from everyone, including Parker.

The two of us officially became an item, of course.

Then there's the wannabe magical dictator who plans to either enslave humanity, destroy it, or both.

And, oh, yeah. I'm the only one who has even a sliver's chance of stopping that from happening...

When this all started, I was just a part-time romance novelist turned paranormal temp.

And now I'm the one person who can either save the world or end it.

No pressure, right?

WHAT TO READ NEXT!

Merlin is just your ordinary, everyday Maine Coon. Except he's a witch. With a human familiar.

In the sleepy Georgian town of Elderberry Heights, danger lurks around every counter but the laughs are never far behind. Join Merlin and his sidekick Gracie as they fight off evil ex-girlfriends, vicious ghosts, and even a horde of zombie squirrels.

If you love quirky humor and madcap magical adventures, then you do not want to miss this hot new series from a USA Today bestselling author. Here it is! This is your chance to binge read the full trilogy—Merlin Takes a Familiar, Merlin Fights a Ghost, and Merlin Kills a Zombie—in this special boxed collection… Enjoy!

The *Merlin's Magical Mysteries: Complete Trilogy Edition* is now available.

Get your copy so that you can start reading this series today!

SNEAK PEEK

MERLIN TAKES A FAMILIAR

I returned home physically exhausted and emotionally wrung out. Everything happened so fast after Harold collapsed. The severity of Officer Dash's implication didn't fully sink in until I finally escaped the coffeehouse and began my quiet drive home. Now that I had a moment to think, a few very important questions crowded into my mind. Why was she so sure that he had been murdered? And even more puzzling, why did she believe I'd done it?

True, lots of people disliked Harold, but nobody had a reason to kill him—least of all me. I mean, why would I when I could have just quit my job and never seen him another day in my life?

The whole thing made me sick… and terrified. All I wanted to do was wake up from this horrible nightmare and go back to my normal, if a tad unexciting, life.

So I changed into my favorite matching flannel pajama set even though it was still the afternoon and the outside temperature was well over eighty degrees. Sometimes I missed my hometown in Northern Michigan where it was chilly more often than not, and my jammies—along with the added help of an overworked tabletop fan —helped allay the occasional bout of homesickness.

Right now, I wanted my mama. It didn't matter that I was an independent twenty-something. I'd been hurt, and I was scared. And just because I'd grown up didn't mean I couldn't turn to my mother in times of great need...

The fact that she didn't answer the phone when I called, however, meant precisely that. I hung up instead of leaving a voicemail, then fired off a quick text asking her to call me back whenever she got the chance.

Fluffy meowed and jumped up on the couch beside me. His whiskers twitched as he tried to discern whether I had anything worth eating. When he didn't find any food, he sunk his teeth into the edge of my sleeve and growled softly.

"Good idea," I said. "Today definitely calls for some ice cream."

I scooped up some of our favorite flavor—plain vanilla bean—into one of my lesser used breakfast bowls, grabbed a spoon and the remainder of the gallon, and settled myself back on the couch. The bowl was for Fluffy. I needed the entire container.

As we ate together, I began to share the events of my day with my feline companion. "That cop was so mean," I whined. "I mean, why would she just automatically assume I killed my boss? It was terrible. Just awful. To see the life leave his eyes. I don't think I'll ever forget it."

Fluffy sat up straight and cocked his head to the side. Sometimes, in moments like this, it felt like he could actually understand me.

"Mew?" my Maine Coon asked.

"Oh, yeah. I guess I should start at the beginning, huh? Well, my boss at the coffee shop, Harold. He died today."

"Harold is an awful name," Fluffy rasped.

"I know. I never thought anyone in the—" I stopped suddenly and closed my mouth up tight, then just stared at Fluffy for a long moment. Was I really so worked up that I was now hearing things?

I laughed at myself. "Silly me," I said with a deep breath out. "Thinking you're talking to me, Fluffy."

"My name's not Fluffy," the cat said, then hopped off the coffee table and onto the sofa beside me. "So don't call me that anymore."

"Wh-wh-what?" I sputtered, rubbing my eyes until I saw stars. "I'm seeing things. This isn't real."

Fluffy clucked his little sandpaper tongue. "You meant to say you're hearing things, and no, you're not. I'm talking to you, Gracie."

I jumped off the couch and spun wildly around the living room. "Come out, come out wherever you are!" I shouted with a mad laugh, not really sure who I was confronting here. "The joke's up. Haha, you actually had me convinced Fluffy was talking. Yup, I'm crazy! You win! Now come out and fess up!"

Fluffy let out an enormous yawn, then settled down with his paws tucked into himself. "You are most definitely acting crazy. Also I already told you my name's not Fluffy, so will you please stop calling me that?"

I gasped, then sunk to the floor before I could pass out and crash down onto it. "This is not real. This is not real," I murmured, acting quite similarly to how Kelley had when she was balled up and rocking in that club chair back at the coffee shop.

"What's not real?" Fluffy asked, jumping off the sofa and striding over to me.

"You can't talk."

"I can talk, but it seems you're not very good at listening."

"Are you going to hurt me?"

"Of course I'm not going to hurt you. I need you to feed me, don't I? Silly human."

"What do you want from me?"

"The aforementioned food and also for you to stop calling me Fluffy. I much prefer the name given to me by my ancestors, thank you."

"Um... Okay. What should I call you?"

"The name's Merlin, and I come from a long and noble lineage of wizards dating all the way back to King Arthur."

"You're magic?" I asked with a quick breath in.

"Duh," my cat spat, and then I officially passed out.

***Merlin Takes a Familiar* is available as part of the *Merlin's Magical Mysteries: Complete Trilogy Edition*.**

Get your copy so that you can start reading this series today!

ABOUT MOLLY FITZ

While *USA Today bestselling* author Molly Fitz can't technically talk to animals, she and her three feline writing assistants have deep and very animated conversations as they navigate their days.

She lives with her child and their own private zoo somewhere in the wilds of Alaska. Molly will occasionally venture out for good food, great coffee, or to meet new animal friends.

Learn more about Molly and her books, and be sure to sign up for her newsletter at **www.MollyMysteries.com**.

ALSO BY MOLLY FITZ

Learn more about Molly's collected works, so that you can decide which book you'd like to read next...

PET WHISPERER P.I.

Angie Russo just partnered up with Blueberry Bay's first ever talking cat detective. Along with his ragtag gang of human and animal helpers, Octo-Cat is determined to save the day... so long as it doesn't interfere with his schedule.

Start with book 1, ***Kitty Confidential***.

MERLIN'S MAGICAL MYSTERIES

Gracie Springs is not a witch... but her cat is. Now she must help to keep his secret or risk spending the rest of her life in some magical prison. Too bad trouble seems to find them at every turn!

Start with book 1, ***Merlin Takes a Familiar***.

PARANORMAL TEMP AGENCY

Tawny Bigford's simple life takes a turn for the magical when she stumbles upon her landlady's murder and is recruited by a talking black cat named Fluffikins to take over the deceased's role as the official Town Witch for Beech Grove, Georgia.

Start with book 1, ***Witch for Hire***.

THE MYSTERIES OF MOONLIGHT MANOR (WITH TRIXIE SILVERTALE)

Sydney Coleman has it all—until she doesn't. No sooner does she launch her bed and breakfast, than a trio of ghosts turn up oppose her at every turn. They insist she solve the murder of their mistress, but Sydney is desperate for cash. If she can't book some guests fast, her haunted mansion is utterly doomed.

Start with book 1, ***Moonlight & Mischief***.

CONNECT WITH MOLLY

Sign up for my newsletter and get a special digital prize pack for joining, including an exclusive story, *Meowy Christmas Mayhem*, fun quiz, and lots of cat pictures!

Sign up: **MollyMysteries.com/subscribe**

Now, if you ever wished you could converse with cats, here's your opportunity! This is me officially inviting you into my whacky inner world as part of my Cozy Kitty Book Club.

For those who just can't get enough of my zany cat characters and their hapless humans, this book club will provide new content to devour and the chance to get to know my best author friends.

From exclusive stories, behind-the-scenes trivia to never-before-released bonus content, and monthly giveaways, there's a lot to love about the Cozy Kitty Book Club. Join today to find out what we're reading next!

Join: **MollyMysteries.com/club**

www.ingramcontent.com/pod-product-compliance
Lightning Source LLC
Chambersburg PA
CBHW030628310726
48979CB00003B/926

* 9 7 8 1 6 4 4 5 1 5 8 3 9 *